THE EVENTS UNFOLDING ON THESE PAGES are about the lives of three extraordinary women. They are not related, but, there is a thread that binds them. They are strong; planted by rivers of water.

SARAH lives in the past. She is like one of the pioneering and enterprising slaves we've sometimes read about. Yet, her life reflects, to some extent, what it was like to be a slave in the South between 1830 and 1860. Sarah cannot accept the lifestyle her family and loved ones have settled into. Unlike most slaves, she is fortunate to learn to read and write. Once she opened a book, she couldn't stop dreaming. Her grandmother taught her that it was good to dream. One day she sets out to make her dreams come true. Her love for her family strengthens her resolve to risk *everything* for them. Although Sarah lives decades before Celia and Raini, there is a connection.

CELIA lives closer to the present times. She and her family left Cleveland, Ohio several years ago when her husband accepted a promising job offer as a CPA in Nashville. They decided that Nashville would be a good place to raise their three children. It was a smaller city, with cultural and educational opportunities. Then, an early morning phone call disrupts their organized, well-structured lives. They are forced to return to Cleveland to confront and deal with a tragedy that happened a decade ago. Their lives would never be the same.

RAINI's life takes us into the future. She grows up in Alexandria, Virginia. Her parents are college professors. Raini enjoys a privileged lifestyle. Senators and other prominent individuals are frequent guests at her parent's northern Virginia home. She is educated at some of the top schools in the country. She decides early to pursue a career in political science. This path enables her to meet and establish relationships with powerful political figures. However, her mother's sudden illness exposes a painful revelation.

 As Soft As Cotton

A Novel
by

J. Carter-Ball

PUBLISHED BY WESTVIEW, INC., NASHVILLE, TENNESSEE

First Edition, November 2008

Printed in the United States of America on acid-free paper.

ISBN 9780981932576

PUBLISHED BY WESTVIEW, INC.
P.O. Box 210183
Nashville, Tennessee 37221

www.publishedbywestview.com

Dedicated with Love

To the special women in my life:

❀ Mamie Carter, my mother

❀ Ashley and Jamie Ball, my daughters

❀ Sharon Boone, my sister

Acknowledgements

I am thankful for, and sincerely appreciate:

 **Meta McMillan,** my editor. Meta's suggestions, ideas and attention to detail are priceless.

 **Gloria McKissack**, my friend and fellow church member. Gloria helped me better understand what life could possibly have been like for a young slave girl on a plantation in Holly Springs, Mississippi.

 **Professor Reavis Mitchell**, an asset to Fisk University. Professor Mitchell helped me create a picture of African-Americans living in the North in the 1800s.

 **Henrietta Sweeney**, a dear friend for many years. I can pour my heart out to Henrietta at any time, about anything. She's always there for me.

 **Almond Gatewood,** a busy mother and entrepreneur. Almond always has time to listen as I bounce ideas and thoughts around.

 **James H. Ball, Jr.,** my husband and best friend. James' love, support and encouragement throughout the years have helped me reach each of my goals.

 My **Heavenly Father** has blessed me in so many ways, including the desire and ability to write.

Author's Note

Dear Reader:

For years I wanted to study law, but didn't get the opportunity to go to law school until we moved to Memphis. My husband was offered a job there that he couldn't say "no" to. I was accepted at the University of Mississippi School of Law shortly after the move. Our daughters were 8 and 4 years old at that time.

After getting the girls ready for school, I enthusiastically left home each morning for my commute from Memphis to Oxford, Mississippi, eager to learn and earn a law degree. That first year I had all 8:00 classes, therefore I had to leave home very early. I enjoyed a 90-minute drive, with plenty of time to think about everything – my class assignments, the next school trip with my daughters, the next PTA meeting, and, of course, what to prepare for dinner.

In the fall, as I drove during the early morning hours, I observed large fields of cotton along highway 78. These fields sometimes appeared to be covered with a blanket of snow. The sight was captivating. So were the stately antebellum homes in nearby Holly Springs, Mississippi.

I began to wonder about the daily lives of slaves, old and young, male and female. I thought about how fortunate I was to have the opportunity to quit a job and go to law school; and, on the other hand, how unfortunate my ancestors had been to live as slaves.

I thought about the early hours the slaves had to start their chores, in the fields and in the "big house." I especially thought about the females who wanted more out of life. Surely each of them wanted their freedom, and perhaps the opportunity to be educated, or to leave the plantation from time to time.

I thought about this daily, as I traveled, sat in class, or interacted with my family at home. I wanted to talk to these special people from the past. I wanted to tell them that I was sorry about all the pain and suffering they had to endure.

Writing this novel helped me bring some of these special people to life. Surely they must have had dreams and desires, just like me. They loved their children, and wanted their children's lives to be better than theirs, just like me.

Writing this novel has allowed me to give these special people a voice; the opportunity to tell us about what life may have been like on a plantation in Holly Springs. Also, it shows us that African-American women who lived in the 1800s aren't so very different from their sisters who live today, and on into the future, like Celia and Raini. You will laugh and cry with each of them.

Table of Contents

1. Sarah

M Y NAME IS SARAH. I was once a slave. My story is quite unique. That's why I want to tell it. Most slaves did not have surnames. However, my family was given the surname of my mother's master, Austin Johnson. I was very fortunate to secretly learn to read and write. Gradually, I managed to scribble words, trying to make sentences. As the years passed, my reading and writing skills improved, with the help of very special people. Finally, I was able to translate those scribbled words into "English." Here is my story.

I became inquisitive about my life around 1841. We lived in Holly Springs, Mississippi. Holly Springs is in Marshall County, in the western part of the state. The county was organized in 1836. It is approximately 40 miles southeast of Memphis. I can still remember those dry summers with sweltering heat. Cotton was the main agricultural product. My family and I were slaves. We were owned by Frank and Charlotte Wilmington by this time. My Pappy, Joshua Johnson, worked in the cotton and corn fields. He was now a driver. A driver is a slave chosen to assist the slave foreman or overseer. Pappy had a white overseer. My Mammy, Bertha Johnson, and I worked in the "big house," as we called the Wilmington house.

I can remember Mammy and Pappy telling stories about our African ancestors. They often told stories about our homeland, although they were born in Mississippi. This was their way of trying to hold on to the African culture that was slowly slipping away from our people. Mammy always said it was important to know who you are. I loved sitting on Pappy's lap as a young girl in our little cabin, listening to him and Mammy talk about my grandparents. My grandparents were born in Kenya, in the eastern part of the continent. I can remember asking Mammy why so many of our people had chosen to leave their native land and customs, and journey to a country so far away. When I was around 8, Mammy explained to me that my grandparents had been forced to come to this new land against their will, to serve white people and work in their fields. She said they had to do whatever was necessary to help white people prosper. I listened to these stories, but did not fully understand what Mammy was saying.

As a young girl, I remember Mammy telling me that darker-skinned people worked for white people. Some worked in the fields, cooked meals, sewed clothes or cared for white people's children. I thought this was what we were created to do, since Mammy and Pappy did not believe in complaining about anything.

One day, around 1836, my big brother, Tom, who was about 10, just disappeared. I must have been 5 at that time. Tom used to help Pappy in the cotton fields. Pappy had said he was a really good worker. When I asked Mammy what happened to my brother, she had only said, "Some white people need him to work for dem. God willin, som day I go see my boy agin." I remember hearing Mammy cry at night after Tom disappeared. But, the next morning she would simply say, "Ise fine, chile, now we gotta do our chores." I missed my big brother dearly. Mammy and Pappy seemed so sad after he left, but they always said everything would somehow work out. I believed them. They did not know it, but they taught me how to believe and have faith and hope.

I also remember crying when Mammy combed my long thick hair each morning. She would tell me that my eyes were too big and pretty to have tears in them, then she would kiss me. She helped me get dressed, then we were off to the big house so that Mammy could prepare breakfast for the Wilmington family, Frank and Charlotte Wilmington and their two daughters, Kate and Melissa.

This house was so much bigger than the little wooden cabin we lived in. The Wilmington house was brick with six large columns in the front, three on each side of the porch. The porch had chairs and plants on it that seemed to say "welcome" when you approached the door. There were huge oak trees that provided lots of shade, and, when the wind blew, the limbs appeared to be dancing. The flowers in the yard were always varied and colorful. I got into trouble one day for picking two stems to bring to Mammy. I liked going to the big house each morning with Mammy because it made me feel special just to be there, although Mammy and I always had lots of work to do.

The big house had two floors. The three bedrooms were located on the second floor. There were vivid paintings on the walls on the first floor. The wood floors were always polished and shiny. There were times when I pretended that I lived there. I often wondered if somehow my family would one day live like the Wilmingtons. But then I would think it was a foolish thought.

The slaves on the Wilmington plantation lived in small, one-room cabins made of logs, with dirt floors. The five cabins were behind the big house, in a single row. This was known as the slave quarters. Housing for slaves was poorly constructed. Windows and floors were rare. There were practically no furnishings in these cabins. We did not have beds. We slept on old, thick blankets that covered the cool, damp, dirt floors. Mammy, Pappy and I shared a cabin. Our beds were collections of old blankets and straw. We had a table and three chairs that Pappy had built. There was also a fireplace where our meals were cooked. We also had a small window, for ventilation. Mammy and Pappy worked hard to make this little cabin a home for us.

Pappy spent a lot of time stuffing cracks in the logs of the cabin with old clothes or wood during the winter months, trying to keep us warm. After working in the fields all day, he was never too tired to ask Mammy and me what he could do to make us comfortable. There were over a hundred acres of land on the Wilmington plantation. After Mammy finished her work in the big house each day, she spent her "free" time in the cabin washing or mending our clothes, and cooking pork, beans, cornbread and sweet potatoes. Some days Mammy brought back food from the big house.

Whenever Missus Wilmington gave her scraps of material, Mammy used these scraps to make clothes for us, or braided rugs or quilts. Mammy's quilts had symbols that carried messages she sewed in them about our family history, such as our love for nature. Her quilts lifted my spirit. Compared to the Wilmingtons, we had few material comforts, but, I always knew I was loved.

Unfortunately, most slave families on plantations in Holly Springs had to share their small cabins with other slave families. Sometimes two or three families huddled into a single cabin. They slept on dirt floors under the worst of conditions, with flimsy covering for instance, and were expected to rise early the next morning to put in a full day of work in the fields, or do whatever they were told to do. I thought it was heartless and merciless of the mastahs to allow this. Mastah Wilmington owned 20 slaves, 13 adults and seven children. Living conditions for his slaves were poor, just as they were on most plantations in the area.

Pappy did not join us in the big house, but headed to the fields each morning. As the driver, he had to make sure the field slaves worked hard so Mastah Wilmington always had a good crop. For a long time I did not understand why Pappy could not join Mammy and me in the big house, where it was cool and comfortable. He always had to work in the hot, dirty fields. Pappy said he had to help the mastah, and that good people did not go around complaining. I spent most of the day helping Mammy prepare meals, clean up and fold clothes that Mammy washed for the Wilmington family.

One bright morning in June 1844, I remember Missus Wilmington telling Mammy that she had to work especially hard that day for a special occasion. Missus Wilmington was a refined white lady. She was attractive. She was not thin by any means, but she was not fat either. Her eyes were brown. So was her long hair, which she kept pulled back in a bun. Her features were not very keen, but quite expressive. One could almost guess what Missus Wilmington was thinking just by looking at her. She was always dressed well. She spoke in a soft, but firm voice. She loved having parties and inviting friends over to enjoy her lovely home. I do not ever recall her being cruel to me or my family. I guess that was one of the reasons my parents did not like to complain about the Wilmingtons.

Mammy and Missus Wilmington had a somewhat special relationship because they grew up together. Missus Wilmington's parents, Austin and Victoria Johnson, owned Mammy's family. They were bought at an auction, fresh off a slave ship from the homeland. Pappy was purchased by Missus Wilmington's family at some point, when Mammy was around 18. Pappy was a very handsome, dark-skinned man. He had a big dimple in his left cheek, and compassionate, brown eyes. His expression was always pleasant, no matter how tired he was. Mammy loved him dearly, and he loved her.

Mammy was beautiful. She had the biggest smile. Her light-brown skin was always smooth, even though she worked hard all of her life. She and Pappy were thin. Most importantly, they were kind, thoughtful people. There could not have been a more perfectly matched couple.

Missus Wilmington grew up in the big house, where she now lives with her family. Missus Wilmington's family was educated and wealthy. Having been with this family all of her life, Mammy learned to speak well, but not perfect English. She learned much of the language by listening to the educated, refined white people around her every day of her life. However, when in the presence of the Wilmingtons and their friends, Mammy intentionally used "slave diction." She knew they might be threatened by her intelligence and ability to speak well.

Most white people in the South did not think slaves had the ability, or right, to be educated. Besides, it was against the law. Missus Wilmington's parents had often read Bible stories to their two daughters, Charlotte and Elizabeth. Mammy was allowed to listen. She also had to go to church with her mastah's family. The slaves sat in the crow's nest, the upper section of the church. The slaves would only attend church, they did not get baptized, and were not members of the mastah's church. Mammy listened carefully as the preacher read and explained the Bible each Sunday. Whenever she had the opportunity, Mammy opened the Bible the mistus had given my grandmother, and tried to read the verses the preacher had explained in church. Mammy especially enjoyed listening to the book of Proverbs. It was a source of strength for her.

Slaves on the Wilmington plantation had to attend church services with the Wilmington family in a large cabin on the plantation. Mammy and Pappy had told me that Mastah Wilmington did not want his slaves having their own church services because he was afraid we would wind up plotting against him. The preacher was white. Using the Bible, he preached about slaves being obedient to their mastahs.

Sometimes, but not often, the slaves managed to gather secretly on Sundays to have church services in one of the cabins in the slave quarters. We would pray and sing. We held hands, and tried to comfort and encourage each other to be strong.

Through patience and perseverance over the years, Mammy taught herself to read and write. She was highly intelligent. Unfortunately, she had to conceal that intelligence. She would have been severely punished for her knowledge. Mammy did not talk about her ability to read. I certainly understood why. However, I watched her as she read through the words in the book of Proverbs each night before going to bed.

Kate and Melissa Wilmington attended the nearby Holly Springs Female Institute, a finishing school for the white girls in the community. Melissa was my age, 13, and Kate was two years older. They laid their books around the big house, as if they did not care whether or not I looked through them. I did just that when I was not in the presence of the Wilmingtons. I listened to Kate and Melissa talk about the new words they had learned, and how to spell the words. Like Mammy, I was blessed with the ability to learn quickly. After years of listening to educated white people speak, and looking through their books when possible, like Mammy, I slowly learned to read. The letters began to make words, the words began to make sentences, and the sentences began to make sense to me.

Mammy was too wise to teach me to read. She would never have done anything that would have harmed my brother or me. I learned at an early age that it was dangerous for a slave to even talk about reading or writing. I once heard Pappy say that he wished he could read the Bible to help him get through the long days in the field. But, he never mentioned that again. As a child, I did not understand the problems and pressures that Pappy had endured as a male who had spent all of his life as a slave. I often heard Pappy tell Mammy that he was too tired to think straight after working in the cotton and corn fields all day. Mammy never grew tired of loving and caring for her family.

Mammy and Missus Wilmington were around the same age, somewhere in their late 30s, I guess. Missus Wilmington's only sister had died when she was very young from pneumonia. When Mammy worked in the big house as a child, Missus Wilmington often turned to Mammy for comfort after the death of her sister. Mammy was a slave and Missus Wilmington was the mastah's daughter, but, they had a unique relationship.

Mastah Wilmington was a very tall, muscular man. His hair was grayish-white. He rarely smiled. The deep tone of his voice frightened me. Although I had never heard Mammy or Pappy speak ill of Missus

Wilmington, I had heard them say that Mastah Wilmington was a cruel man. Pappy had seen him whip some of his slaves. I had overheard Pappy telling Mammy about a young slave Mastah Wilmington had whipped until his legs bled because he overslept, so was late getting to the cotton fields one morning. Pappy had said that business and money were more important to Mastah Wilmington than human life. However, I do not recall Pappy ever saying that he had been whipped. Even if he had been, he would never have told me.

Missus Wilmington was excited about her upcoming dinner party. She told Mammy everything she had to do to prepare for the party. I can still hear her instructions.

"We're having 20 guests for dinner on Friday and everything has to be just perfect. Bertha, wash my very best china, crystal and silverware, and make sure the linen tablecloth is clean. Also, this house needs to be spotless for the party. You must do a great job cleaning." Mammy and I had overheard Missus Wilmington telling her friend earlier in the week that the party was for very influential guests. Mastah Wilmington was running for state senator. The guests were his supporters.

I immediately grabbed a towel and began polishing the silver that was stored in the pantry in the dining room. Mammy gathered the good crystal and china. She wanted this party to be as wonderful as Missus Wilmington had planned it to be.

On the day of the party, Mammy and I left our cabin earlier than usual to go to the big house.

"I don't see any spots," Missus Wilmington said, as she carefully inspected each dish and glass. "These are very clean, just as I expected them to be. You and Sarah must help with the serving tonight. It's going to be a long day, but it'll all be worth it."

Mammy was excited about the dinner party as well. I still remember how clean the house looked and smelled for this special event. It was scheduled to start early that Friday night in June 1844. Fresh flowers had been brought in from the yard for the party. The house was filled with their scent. The guests arrived. I will never forget the dainty dresses the ladies were wearing. Some were decorated with flowers, some with ruffles, colorful ribbons and lace trims. All of the dresses were worn over crinoline petticoats. Several of the ladies wore bonnets that matched their dresses. I imagined Mammy in one of those fancy dresses.

I helped Mammy set the large dining room table and serve the food that smelled so good. Mammy had done all of the cooking. She had prepared cured ham, other smoked meats, corn bread, fresh vegetables, cakes and pies. After dinner, several of the men went into the library, while the women sat on the porch and talked about their dresses, hairdos and the next big social event of the season. Mammy sent me to the library to gather the empty glasses. I heard the men talking about completely different subjects: the cotton crop and how to keep niggers in their places.

That night, when we were finally dismissed and back in our cabin, Mammy came in to kiss me goodnight.

"Mammy, whut do it mean to keep niggers in dere places?" Mammy stared at me with a strange expression, one that I had never seen before. She embraced me tightly. With tears in her eyes, she said, "It ain't nuttin fer you to worry bout, honey. Sometime white men talk bout unplesent thangs. You need to git some sleep." She kissed me good night. Still, I could not forget the men's conversation in the library. They sounded so cruel when they talked about us, as if they were talking about animals or the like. My presence did not seem to distract them. They were drinking, and at times raised their voices. As I lay in bed, I began to cry softly. Pappy worked in the cotton fields. I wondered if he "stayed in his place." What would happen to him if he did not?

Mammy and I arose early to get to the Wilmington house to begin our chores the next morning. Mastah and Missus Wilmington came into the dining room to eat their breakfast of eggs and ham. Missus Wilmington was delighted over what she considered a successful evening. Mastah Wilmington talked about nothing other than becoming a prominent political figure in Mississippi, and bringing more business to the rural towns of the state. He wanted larger cotton fields, more slaves and to have banks here in Holly Springs. I often heard him tell Missus Wilmington that Holly Springs should have banks, like those in Memphis and other cities. I learned a lot about Mastah Wilmington's business sense from working in the big house, and listening to him talk to his wife and friends.

"Sarah, I need you in here," Mammy called. She was in the sewing room, a small room next to the dining room, making dresses for Kate and Melissa. When I entered the room, I could only gasp and stare at the delicate fabric Mammy had cut and begun sewing. The colors were bright blue and white. I imagined how lovely I would look wearing a dress made from that fabric.

"Mammy, kin you make me a dress dat purdy?" I was curious and asked questions. In my young, naïve mind, I did not understand why I could not have dresses as pretty as those Kate and Melissa wore.

I held up one of the silk dresses and put it next to my small, brown body. It was blue and white with a wide neckline and dropped-shoulder line. The skirt of the dress was full and trimmed with white lace. A large white sash covered the waist line. The short, puffed sleeves were also trimmed in white lace. I stared at the mirror. Sometimes I wondered why Kate and Melissa got to wear such pretty dresses, but I could not.

The dresses I wore were very simple, made of calico. However, they were still special because Mammy made them. There were no wide, full crinolines, ruffles or lace, although I wore petticoats under them. They were inexpensive to make. They were not tight-fitting, but comfortable. They usually had white collars. The bodice buttoned down the front, with long sleeves. Mammy and I wore aprons the same length as our dresses.

Slave women could not dress to look pretty because there was too much work to be done. Most of them worked in the fields. A few, like Mammy and me, worked in the big house. We washed clothes, sewed, ironed, cooked and cleaned. When Kate and Melissa were younger, Mammy cared for them, in addition to doing her house chores. Because Melissa was my age, Mammy had even wet-nursed her. Mammy loved Kate and Melissa Wilmington.

"Sarah," Mammy called again, "put dose dresses down an brin me de scissors."

"Mammy, I wanna purdy dress. Kin you make me one lak dis? I would feel so specia in a dress lak dis." Mammy just stared at me, then lowered her head. I brought her the scissors and put the dress down.

"I know you an Pappy luv me. Someday I go wear purdy dresses lak dis." I began gathering unused scraps of material. Mammy would use these for quilts and rugs.

As Mammy put the dresses together, piece by piece, for the Wilmington girls, I carefully watched her. Soon I began cutting scraps of fabric to wrap my dolls in. My two cloth dolls were hand-me-downs from the Wilmington girls. However, I had no time to play during the day. There was too much work to do at the big house. Sometimes I talked to my dolls before falling asleep at night on my straw bed. I even shared some of my dreams with them.

Later that afternoon, I heard Missus Wilmington tell Mammy to pack for Mastah Wilmington, who was about to leave for a few days to raise money for his campaign. I helped Mammy with the packing. As we gathered Mastah Wilmington's clothes and folded them, I wondered what it would be like to leave Holly Springs and see other places. As I secretly looked through books that were lying around the Wilmington house, I became more curious about life outside of Holly Springs.

Did all places look and smell like Holly Springs, Mississippi? Did all dark-skinned people live like we did here on the plantation? Did all white people live in big houses? Did all white girls and women wear dainty dresses? Did any dark-skinned children go to finishing school like Kate and Melissa Wilmington? And, I wondered about my brother, Tom. Where was he; why had he gone away? Mammy and Pappy did not like to talk about him. I had so many questions. Perhaps one day I would get the answers. But, now, it was time to go home to our little cabin for suppa.

2. Raini

UNTIL NOW, I HADN'T REALIZED I had spent all of my life preparing for this moment. I am sitting on a cushioned lounge in a television studio, getting last minute instructions on how to answer some of the tougher questions, while someone touches up my hair and makeup. The black suit I'm wearing feels loose in the waist. I've lost 10 pounds over the past six weeks, so my size six clothes don't quite fit perfectly anymore.

I'm average height, so can't afford to lose another pound. My hair has been cut to just below my ears, so I won't look too thin. My appearance is critical these days. I am advised on everything, from the color of lipstick to the color of pantyhose I should wear.

So much is running through my mind as I wait for the network television crew to set up in the studio, then call when they are ready for me. It is critical that I present myself as an intelligent, competent and caring human being. This morning I must persuade viewers that I know what I'm talking about, even if I don't. The studio lights are too bright for me, in my opinion. It's tough to stay calm and cool, as I've been instructed to do. This certainly isn't my first television appearance, but perhaps my most important.

I have 30 minutes to get millions of people acquainted with Raini Hamilton-Carrington. My life has been a whirlwind of events over the past several weeks. Some mornings I wake up wondering if it has all been a dream. But, it hasn't. It's all real. This is how it all began.

For three years, I was an Associate Professor of Political Science at Brown University in Providence. I stood before a classroom of bright-eyed, curious and carefree college students. Now I'm speaking to millions of viewers I can't see, who will be inspecting me from head to toe. I'm sure my students inspected me each day as I stood before them in the classroom, but it's not the same as the audience I have to face on this chilly, autumn morning in New York City. I felt a certain connection with my students that I can't possibly feel with millions of unseen television viewers.

To be able to speak well in public is a gift. As a child, I remember speaking gracefully in front of my classmates, with absolutely no fear, while my friends practically curled up with fear and anxiety. I learned early that this gift could take me places, so I worked diligently to improve upon it. As a member of the debate team in junior high and high school, in Alexandria, Virginia, I participated in several debates, and won most of them.

I recall standing in the pulpit in church reciting poems. I remember raising my hand in school to answer questions when others tried to dodge them. Mother taught me at an early age that the ability to communicate clearly to others is powerful, that it would affect every phase of my personal and professional life.

My parents are both professors at the same small college in northern Virginia. By the time I was a teenager, I was attending one social event after another with them. We also had guests in our home almost every weekend, and my parents always invited me to join them. Alexandria is a great place to live. I enjoyed growing up there because it is only a short distance from the nation's capital.

After high school, in the fall of 1994, I entered Georgetown University in Washington, D.C., where I majored in political science. I decided to study journalism as a minor. I attended political rallies and discussed controversial issues with my fellow students and professors whenever I had the opportunity. I didn't hesitate to write my congressman if I thought some matter of importance was being overlooked. With a minor in journalism, I was thrilled to meet print and broadcast journalists, and learned as much as possible from each of them.

I was very fortunate during the summer of my freshman year at Georgetown to be offered an internship in U.S. Senator Ashton Cole's office in the capital. I stuffed envelopes, answered calls and made coffee. This experience helped me realize I enjoyed the excitement, stress and uncertainty of the political arena. I don't ever recall being bored. In fact, I often volunteered to work late and on weekends. It was fascinating to discuss current issues with staff members, and speculate where this country was headed. The phones never stopped ringing, and I never grew tired of answering question after question posed by callers. Sometimes I wondered if I was "different" because my circle of friends had little or no interest in politics. Some of them didn't even vote. I soon realized that I was "different," but that it was okay.

I made calls for the Senator and often spoke with other senators and members of Congress during some of those calls. Senator Cole, of Virginia, invited me to attend some of his speaking engagements. I always took notes, especially when he answered tough questions. This man was able to keep it all together, even in the midst of a heated controversy.

There was a park near his office where I often spent my lunch hour sitting under a tree. I enjoyed feeding birds and reading through pages of notes, while enjoying the summer weather. I tried to absorb Senator Cole's speeches so that I could intelligently defend his take on various issues. I worked with older, sharp staff members, who had high expectations of everyone in the office, including summer interns. My goal was to earn their respect, no matter how hard I had to work. When the internship ended, Senator Cole invited me to return the following summer. I promised him I would.

I returned to Georgetown with a different perspective on life. "When I worked in Senator Cole's office this summer," was usually how I began my response to most questions directed at me in my classes. At the end of my sophomore year, my parents were quite pleased with my GPA. They agreed to let me work part-time in Senator Cole's office as a receptionist during the school year. By the time I turned 19, I had met several prominent politicians.

I was in the top 10 academically in the sophomore class at Georgetown. One day Senator Cole asked me about studying abroad at Oxford University, for the second semester of my junior year. I loved the idea; I was accepted. I approached my parents one morning, during a weekend home from school, to tell them the news. We had had breakfast.

"Mother, I would love to go to England."

"Why, dear, what made you think of England?"

"As you know, Oxford is an excellent school. I think it would be a great experience for me." My parents looked at each other, then at me.

"And what about Georgetown, sweetheart?" Dad asked.

"I'm not asking to leave Georgetown," I said quickly, "only to study at Oxford next spring."

"How do you know they will accept you?" Mother asked. That's when I showed them the letter: "Congratulations, you have been accepted to study at Oxford, spring semester 2001." Mother was speechless. She gave the letter to Dad.

"When did you apply, and why didn't you tell us, or, why didn't you ask?" she asked.

"Because I wasn't sure you would approve. All of my professors think I'm an excellent candidate for the political science program, and Senator Cole sent a letter and…" The words were coming out almost faster than I could say them. My parents were still staring, speechless.

"If you don't want me to go, then just say so." I broke into tears and ran from the kitchen table. Mother followed me. After a long discussion, and lecture about keeping them informed about major decisions in my life, they agreed to let me go. I'm their only child, so Mother has always been overprotective. She would have been less hesitant if Oxford University had been within driving distance for her.

England was fascinating and intriguing. I had been to Europe, but never to England. Oxford was all I had imagined it to be, and, needless to say, quite a challenge. I didn't like the cool, damp weather, but competing with top students from around the world was stimulating. The highlight of my stay was our visit to Parliament.

I left England, determined to teach political science at some university. The semester at Oxford only enhanced my love for politics. I knew I had discovered my purpose in life. I was able to work longer hours in Senator Cole's office during my senior year because my class schedule was pretty light. I read books about the structure of political systems around the world, just for pleasure. At 20, I probably should've been reading romance novels or perhaps self-improvement books. But, that just wasn't where my head was.

Biographies of people who had made significant contributions toward shaping our government were especially interesting. I never got tired of discussing issues with others or researching answers to questions that people called in for the Senator. His entire staff was especially loyal to him. We all went to great lengths to make him look good whenever possible. We even sat around the office at times to try to think of questions he might get hit with by reporters. Our senator had to be well-prepared at all times. He usually was.

My best friend, Larkin Landers, had absolutely no interest in politics. She tried to change the subject whenever it came up, but that didn't deter my interest. Teaching political science was one way to contribute to the prosperity of my country.

Before graduating from Georgetown in May 1998, I was accepted into the political science graduate program at Brown University in Providence, Rhode Island. That is where I met John Carrington.

3. Celia

My husband, Cole, and I are at the airport, trying to get a flight to Cleveland, Ohio. We've had very little to say to each other over the past few hours. We're both lost in our thoughts. I can imagine what he's thinking. I'm sure he knows what I'm thinking, so there isn't much point in talking. Plus, it's probably the best thing to do at this time. I dread taking this flight, because suddenly our lives have changed. At this point we don't know what chain of events transpired to turn our lives upside down.

I'll always remember what I was doing at that moment when the telephone rang. It's like when President Kennedy and Dr. Martin Luther King, Jr. were assassinated. Most people know exactly where they were and what they were doing when they heard the news.

Cole had just left home to take Michaela to school, then head to the office. Matthew was in the front yard waiting to be picked up by his best friend's mother. I was helping McAlister finish his breakfast. Our son, Matthew, is 13; Michaela, our daughter, is 10 and McAlister, our youngest, is 2. Getting him to eat – caring for him in general – is a job in itself. Cole and I decided before we married that I would be a stay-at-home mom, and care for our children as long as I could mentally handle it.

Matthew and Michaela were a breeze to care for. I soon became confident that being a mom was natural for me. We wanted four children, just like Cole and I had talked about when we were dating. Well, McAlister changed all of that. Now there are days I find myself daydreaming about being back at work. I gave up a career as a financial advisor to come home to be the "perfect woman" – raise my children, support my husband, decorate my home and play in the Nashville Symphony.

Sometimes I think McAlister is God's way of letting me know that life, and especially motherhood, isn't suppose to be a "breeze." He wakes up with the birds every morning and wants to play. When he takes a nap, I feel like I've gone to heaven for a few hours. Still, I wouldn't trade any of my babies for the world. I'll stay at home until McAlister is in elementary school, then I plan to work part-time.

Our rush to get to Cleveland began with a telephone call earlier this Thursday morning in July 1988. I didn't recognize the area code of the call on our caller ID, and assumed it was some solicitor being a pest. However, the tone of the woman's voice alerted me that this was more than a sales call.

"Hello, I'm calling to speak with Mrs. Celia Bentley," she said. After I identified myself, she continued, "This is Mary Noland from Willow Memorial Hospital in Cleveland, Ohio. I need to ask you some questions about your daughter, Michaela Bentley."

"Who are you, and what do you know about my daughter?" I snapped.

"Mrs. Bentley, I apologize for having to make this call, but I am the Director of Nursing at Willow Memorial Hospital. Our records show that your daughter was born here on December 10, 1977, is that correct?" Her voice sounded strange, almost as if something bad had happened. If my child had not just left with her father for school, I would probably have been screaming, out of fear that something had happened to her.

"Yes, that is my daughter's birth date. So, why are you questioning me about my child?" I was really irritated now, and wanted to hang up on her, but something told me to stay calm and hear her out. I immediately had a flashback to December 10, 1977, the day our beautiful daughter came into the world. Cole and I couldn't have been happier. Our son, Matthew, was 3 years old then, therefore, giving birth to a daughter made us happier than we ever could have imagined.

Cole and I were living in Cleveland at that time. We had met five years earlier while in graduate school at Case Western Reserve University. Ironically, we didn't date when we were students, but hooked up after graduation. A mutual friend, David Compton, threw a big party at his home in June 1973 that we both attended. We ended up walking near the lake by David's home that evening. We talked endlessly about everything, from our families to sharing our individual dreams.

Cole is over six feet tall, with deep, dark brown eyes, and a smile that said he was shy and easy going. I, on the other hand, am of average height, thin, with keen features and shoulder length hair. Well, I soon discovered that he was anything but shy. He was pretty intense about his work, his tennis game and his dog, Brady. He had high expectations of himself and everyone close to him. Sometimes this could be irritating. Still, I liked him a lot, even though I felt like I was playing in a tournament whenever I played tennis and back gammon with him.

We said good night around 12:30 that morning. The following afternoon, my doorbell rang. There stood Cole with a bunch of flowers, a bottle of wine and a basket of food, wanting to know if I could join him in the park near the university. I had a million things to do that afternoon, but didn't have the heart to say "no" to him. He had obviously spent some time preparing this picnic. I quickly changed into a pair of shorts and a sleeveless shirt.

We spent another evening together, eating, talking and thoroughly enjoying each other's company. I'd always thought he was very handsome and polite when we were graduate students. But, we each dated someone else then, so never got to know each other. Now I was thrilled that I'd decided to go to David's party, because I would never have known that Cole and his girlfriend had split. Cole would never have known that Craig and I had decided we just weren't right for each other. By the time we left the park and said good night, I knew this was the beginning of something wonderful.

Still, Cole and I were merely close friends for months. We had a lot in common. We enjoyed playing tennis, training our dogs, biking and working hard to excel at our jobs. I was a financial advisor with a major bank and he was an investment banker. Sometimes we found ourselves throwing around figures and engaging in "money talk" while biking or hitting tennis balls.

Professionally, we were both very ambitious. However, I knew that if I was blessed to have children, I'd put my career on hold in a heartbeat. Cole made it quite clear that he didn't want anyone else raising his children, and if his wife didn't stay home, he would.

I laughed at the thought of that because this man truly loved his work. I couldn't imagine him being at home feeding babies and changing diapers. We were having lunch at a sidewalk café one day when he told me that he cared very deeply about me, and wanted more than a friendship. I was afraid to commit to anything more than just being friends at first, because I didn't want our wonderful relationship to end. Well, he convinced me that people who start out as friends sometimes make great lifetime partners. A year after David's party, we were married. The friendship continued, with the typical bumps and hills couples have. Shortly after our honeymoon, I got pregnant. Although I wasn't ready for babies, Cole was thrilled. I worked as long as I could during my pregnancy, because I really didn't want to leave a career I loved.

Cole began talking about wanting to leave Cleveland after Matthew was born. He wanted to raise our children in a smaller, but progressive city, with professional and cultural opportunities.

Cleveland was an exciting city. Leaving it would be difficult for me. There was Lake Erie, several museums, great places to dine, well-kept yards with colorful spring, summer and fall flowers. I had come here from Charleston, South Carolina after undergraduate school to get a graduate in Business Administration from Case Western Reserve University. I didn't think I would survive the first winter. I will never forget that one. It snowed for days. By the grace of God, I learned to adjust to it, and even like Cleveland. After I met Cole, I had no plans to leave. That changed after we started our family.

Matthew was born April 4, 1975. Surprisingly, after his birth, I had no desire to return to work. He was a calm, adorable baby who slept all night and rarely cried. I thanked God I was able to stay home to care for him. Cole adored his son, and was determined to raise him in a smaller city that offered good opportunities for us.

Two years later, Michaela was born. Needless to say, we were ecstatic to have a daughter. It was a very difficult pregnancy because my blood pressure was quite high. Some days I was too dizzy and nauseous to get out of bed. But Cole and my mother felt confident I was getting the best of care at the prestigious Willow Memorial Hospital.

We referred to our daughter as the "Miracle Baby" because of the health problems I had while carrying her. Although I had second thoughts about having more children, once I recovered, Cole and I decided that two were not enough. We soon began planning for a third child.

Michaela, like Matthew, was a calm and delightful baby. Matthew inherited Cole's dark brown eyes, innocent smile, height, and my keen features and thick hair. Michaela, on the other hand, had her very own look – that of a lovely, hand-sculptured doll. Her sandy-colored hair and light brown eyes were a perfect match for her sunny personality. We believed Matthew would grow to be tall like Cole, and Michaela would probably be of average height like me. Neither Cole nor I had any idea how much joy children could bring to a couple's life. And then there was the move.

When Michaela was 6 months old, Cole was offered a position as an investment banker with a large firm in Nashville. After several visits to the city, we decided it might be a good place to raise our family. Cole had thought about going back to Denver, where he grew up, or to Charleston, where I grew up. But, we ended up in Nashville. It had everything we were looking for, for our growing family. We quickly adjusted to life in the Music City. Eight years later, McAlister was born. Thank God he wasn't born first. If he had been, he would have been an only child. I was 35 then, and he was by far the greatest challenge I had ever faced.

The minute Cole would walk into our home, I would put McAlister into his arms. I wanted to be free to talk with and enjoy Matthew and Michaela. I wanted to know what was going on in their lives at school. Matthew usually has little to say. Michaela, on the other hand, talks endlessly. They are each special and unique.

Our routine changed forever the day of the call. That warm July morning started out like any other. But, suddenly, I was speechless, listening to a nurse from Willow Memorial Hospital tell me that Cole and I had to get up there as soon as possible. Something unfortunate had happened back in December 1977, the year and month Michaela was born, she said. This stranger on the phone continued to talk, but I had tuned her out because all I could think about was whether something was wrong with my child! I only heard and comprehended bits and pieces of what Mary Noland was saying. I focused on images of my daughter. My daughter was a loving, intelligent, wonderful human being. Nothing could possibly be wrong with her!

I forced myself to tell Ms. Noland that my husband and I would be in Cleveland as soon as possible. I immediately called Cole, and tearfully told him that we had to get to Willow Memorial Hospital as soon as possible. I told him something had gone wrong during the time our daughter was born, and we needed to find out what had happened. Cole was speechless, but said he would be home within the hour.

Ms. Noland may actually have told me what the problem was, but I didn't hear her. I knew from the tone of the conversation that it was serious. We needed to get to the hospital as quickly as possible!

4. Sarah

THE LIFE OF A SLAVE GENERALLY DEFIED EXPLANATION in the indignity and inhumane treatment endured. Pappy would talk to Mammy about all that he and other slave men had to endure each day. He had to get up very early each morning. Mammy prepared his breakfast of fried pork and eggs, then he was off to the fields before sunrise. Pappy was always afraid of being late because he knew that he, like the others, would get whipped by the overseer. Pappy was now a driver, someone with special duties, but still a slave.

I do not remember the overseer's name, but Pappy thought he was as cruel as Mastah Wilmington. In addition to working in the cotton fields, depending upon the season, Pappy also worked in the corn fields. One evening during suppa in our cabin, I asked Pappy to tell me what he had to do each day.

"Baby, my day stot erly in de mornin. Befo I kin leave de fields, I gotta make sho all de tools been put way an evrythang is in orda for de nex day. De work neva seem to end." Pappy was exactly right.

The cotton fields had to be tilled and ready for planting by the end of March. Slave men, women and children picked cotton from August to December, and sometimes on through the first of the year. Once they were done with the cotton, it was time to harvest corn. Pappy said there was never any free time. When they were not working in the fields, slaves were busy making repairs around the big house or their cabins, cleaning the plantation grounds, gardening, caring for the horses, maintaining the carriages, killing hogs and preparing the meat, or doing whatever the mastah or mistus told them to do. Mammy and Pappy did not believe in complaining, because it did not accomplish anything. They said it only made you bitter and unpleasant. Mammy and Pappy were kind and pleasant people, in spite of all they had to endure.

It was August 1844. The special election for the state legislature was only two weeks away. I knew very little about politics, but knew that Mastah Wilmington was running for the senate, and was favored to win. Mastah Wilmington was well-known here and around the state. Pappy said he had a good business head. Mastah Wilmington was one of the men responsible for establishing the banking system in Holly Springs. He owned a lot of land here and in other parts of the state.

Mastah Wilmington was born and raised in Memphis. Like Missus Wilmington, his family was also wealthy. His family owned land in Memphis, and were also in the shipping business. The family shipped cotton to other parts of the country. He and Missus Wilmington met at some social gathering in Memphis. After they married, they lived in the big house with her parents. After her parents died, Missus Wilmington inherited everything, since her only sister had died very young.

According to Mammy, Mastah Wilmington had business interests in the North. He dealt with northern bankers and individuals who wanted to invest in southern land and crops. He also did quite a bit of business with Northerners who bought cotton from the Wilmington plantation.

With the prosperity of the cotton crop, and his other businesses, Mastah Wilmington became a very wealthy man. Plus, he inherited his wife's wealth. Since the Wilmingtons often had guests in their home, I heard Mastah Wilmington talk about his businesses as I did my chores. Thank God I was intelligent enough to absorb what I saw and heard around me.

After the election, Missus Wilmington had said she wanted nothing more than to get away to Atlanta, to celebrate and relax with her cousins. She told Mammy that she had to join them and bring me, since I was able to handle many responsibilities. I was thrilled when Mammy kissed me goodnight and told me about the trip. I had heard the Wilmingtons talk about Atlanta, and would finally get the chance to see it!

Election day was sunny and hot. Mammy said lots of people were going to vote for Mastah Wilmington. I wondered what it would be like to vote, and asked Mammy.

"Sarah," Mammy said in her sweet, soft voice, "slaves dont vote, at leas not hure in Misippi."

"Why not?"

"Caus, we neva have an probly neva will."

"But, Mammy, why cain't we vote?"

"Sarah, you ax good quesions, but I ain't got good answers, baby." She continued with her chores.

Mastah Wilmington won the special election handily and the celebrations began. I helped Mammy with all the chores in preparation for the main event at the plantation. Some of the slaves were real happy for Mastah Wilmington.

Lots of people attended the party at the plantation. They all seemed so happy. There was music and dancing. Mammy prepared smoked hams and roasted turkey, corn, sweet potatoes and green vegetables. She also made cakes and pies. Everything was festive at the big house. I especially enjoyed watching the lovely ladies prance around in their elegant dresses. The celebration continued for two days.

On the Sunday following the election, during suppa in the cabin, Mammy, Pappy and I talked about the possibility of slaves voting some day. I still remember what Pappy said to me.

"Sarah, please undastan dat thangs ain't whut dey should be, nor is dey whut dey gonna be. You is smart, Sarah. It go take people lak you who gonna change thangs. You too yung to undastan, but one of dese ol days thangs go change for us slaves."

I had to believe that somehow, someday, I would have a better life than my parents. I would do whatever was necessary to see that my children were happy, like Kate and Melissa Wilmington. Somehow, I would find a way for my children to do more than serve white people. Surely this way of life was not what God intended, or wanted for us. He did not create us to serve white people. As much as I loved my parents, I would rather have died than lived my life the way they had lived theirs. Everything they did was centered around the Wilmingtons. The preacher taught us to pray for our enemies. I wondered why we should pray for those who kept us in bondage.

I tried to picture Atlanta in my mind, but could not, because I had never left Holly Springs. The community had a newspaper, and Mammy sometimes asked Missus Wilmington if she could have the paper when the family was finished with it. She told Missus Wilmington that she needed the papers to help cover cracks in the logs in our cabin, or to plaster the walls. This was the truth. Missus Wilmington usually said "yes" to Mammy when she asked for old papers. I tried to read the papers that were plastered to our walls, but it was too difficult. I did not know enough words at that time. However, I understood the words *Atlanta* and *railroads*. I could not believe Mammy and I were actually going there!

Missus Wilmington often talked to her friends about Atlanta. I learned a lot by listening to them as I worked throughout the big house. It was now September 1844. According to Missus Wilmington, Atlanta was progressing as a center of trade. I imagined that Atlanta would surely be a beautiful place. I just knew I would love it. I had an active imagination, which was good, according to my grandmother. In my mind, I could be whatever I wanted to be.

I had often dreamed about my family going to different places and eating different kinds of foods, like the Wilmingtons did. Sometimes I even talked to my dolls at night and pretended they were people who lived in other places. Most of the slaves here in Holly Springs did not believe they would ever leave this place. But, all I could think about on this cool, September morning was getting my paper bag packed for Atlanta. I wanted to learn more about the world beyond Holly Springs. Nothing and no one could change that about me.

My parents had said many times that I was smart, that people like me would change things. At 13, I really did not know what they meant, but I knew I was somehow different, that I had a purpose in this life.

Mammy was calling for me. I had to stop dreaming and finish ironing clothes. Missus Wilmington had said it would take several days to get to Atlanta. She wanted to leave early the next morning.

Missus Wilmington was a strong-willed person. She said we were leaving at 5:00 and not a minute later. I thought about having to leave Pappy behind, and how much he had talked about Atlanta, and his desire to go there. But, he believed he would never make it. He asked me to pay close attention to everything for him. I cried when I thought about Mammy, Pappy, Tom and me taking a trip together, alone. The Wilmingtons took trips each year to "strengthen family ties" as Missus Wilmington so proudly stated.

I thought about my own family. Slave families had strong bonds and extended family members. We were proud of our heritage, our customs. But many slave families had been torn apart by slaveholders, so did not have the opportunity to form strong bonds. That was one of the saddest things about slavery. Pappy wanted to go to Atlanta, but Mastah Wilmington told him to look after the plantation, to help the overseer with the fall harvesting of crops. Pappy had very little freedom to do anything, other than work in fields and do chores around the big house.

That night, I had a most interesting dream. I was not in Mississippi and my parents were not with me. I was somewhere I had never been before. I was alone, but not afraid. There were lots of people around, but I did not recognize anyone. I was alone, but not lonely. I was walking briskly, as if trying to get somewhere in a hurry. I was wearing a bright-colored dress with a matching, fancy bonnet. The silk dress was pale pink over a wide crinoline, with a shoulder cape attached. It was trimmed with pink and white flowers. A pale pink sash was tied in the back. The silk bonnet was covered with more pink and white flowers. I looked like a special lady. Some people stared as I strolled down the street. I was smiling. I felt strong. I could see a shop some distance away. I appeared to be headed there. But, before I could read the name of the shop, Mammy shook me.

"Sarah, git up. It time to go to Atlanta."

5. Raini

As I sit waiting for the network television crew to set up in the studio, my mind drifts back to the days when I was a young graduate student. I will never forget the day I met John Carrington – nor will I ever forget our first conversation. I was a student at Brown University. My goal was to earn a doctoral degree in political science. I planned to work hard, graduate and possibly go on to law school. At 21, I thought I had life all figured out.

It was September 1998. I walked into the Information Technology Center building, trying to get help with one of the software programs. After several unsuccessful attempts to get into the system, I decided to ask around for help. I found someone.

"Excuse me, I'm Raini Hamilton, and I need help. I've followed the instructions, but still can't get to this screen. Do you have a few minutes to show me where I'm screwing up?"

"Hello, I'm John Carrington. I'll be happy to help you," the stranger I approached said, as he turned around and walked over to examine the screen. My heart must've skipped a few beats. I couldn't even remember which screen I needed. His voice and the expression in his eyes were breathtaking!

"I...I…I'm not sure how to get into this program," was all I could get out. Never before had I been at a loss for words! I was relieved that John Carrington didn't seem to notice my nervousness. In fact, he didn't appear to notice anything about me. He began typing commands into the computer. I quickly glanced at his left hand and noticed he was not wearing a ring. Maybe he was married, but, like some men, didn't wear a ring.

"This should get you in," he said, with a serious look on his face. "Next time try typing in..." He was explaining what I needed to do, but I hadn't heard a word. Although he was speaking to me, he never stopped "playing" with the computer. Perhaps he was a hopeless computer brain who thrived on improving the quality of these things.

"You sure know a lot about computers," I finally managed to say.

"I'd better, because that's what Brown pays me to do."

"Exactly what do you do here?" I asked.

"I'm head of the Computer Science Department for the university, so I spend most of my time experimenting with new programs, and deciding which are best for the institution." He continued to punch keys as he spoke.

"How long have you been here?" I wanted him to look at me, instead of the monitor.

"This is my fifth year at Brown, but only my second as department head." He answered my questions, without looking up.

"I think I can manage now." I thanked him for his help.

"Are you new here?" he asked, as he turned to walk away.

"Yes, I am, and I feel somewhat lost on campus," I said, hoping once again to capture his attention.

"If I can be of any further help, please let me know. I'm usually here late each evening. Nice meeting you, Ms. Hamilton." Then he was gone.

I was crushed. He had hardly noticed me and seemed to have no interest in petty conversation. As an undergraduate student, I got lots of attention, but no one had captured my heart. I spent most of my time studying, working for Senator Cole and being on the debate team. The men I found most interesting were the ones who could carry on an intelligent conversation. They were in short supply. Some of my dates seemed a bit intimidated by me. My grandmother explained that some of my ideas about politics were probably too radical for them.

In the days that followed, I kept busy with my classes, but could not forget John Carrington. I spent most of my time in the Political Science Department. I had no reason to visit the Information Technology Center again, but somehow I had to learn more about this most intriguing man. I decided to approach Professor Robert McWherter, my department head.

"Good morning Professor, how are you? I was just reviewing my schedule and have a few questions."

"Yes, Ms. Hamilton, how can I help you today?"

"Well, professor, I'm not sure if I should take Comparative Politics or Political Philosophy next semester. Also, I've been thinking about topics for my dissertation, although it's early."

"Actually, Ms. Hamilton, you should take American Politics next semester, as well as Comparative Politics," he said, as he studied my schedule. "In American Politics, you will acquire specialized knowledge in American political development and law. In Comparative Politics, you will study the relationship between domestic and international processes. As for your dissertation, no, it is not too early to start thinking about topics, or even research. You want to be very familiar with the subject matter."

"Thank you, Professor. By the way, do you know anything about Mr. Carrington in the Information Technology Center? I'm probably going to need his assistance with some of my research," I quickly added.

"John Carrington is a fine young man. He did some graduate work here at Brown. He is quite competent and knowledgeable about computers. John is much younger than most of the staff here; some of us think of him as a son. He's from Charlottesville, Virginia. He's a long way from home, so we sort of look after him."

"Is his wife also employed here?" I looked away before the professor would see or sense my interest. The words came out before I could stop them. I was embarrassed, and wanted to end the conversation before the professor answered. I headed toward the door, then the professor answered.

"Oh, well, he is married; married to his work and research here at Brown. We're proud of him. He doesn't appear to have much of a social life. You know, Ms. Hamilton, it's ironic that you asked about John. He told me that a young lady had asked for his help with a new soft ware program. Based on his description, Ms. Hamilton, I think you could be that young lady."

"What did he want to know?" I asked, nonchalantly.

"He didn't think he'd spent enough time helping the young lady. He wanted to know how he could get in touch with her."

"Thank you, Professor McWherter." I dashed from his office. "You've been helpful. You've told me everything I need to know, about my schedule, that is." This was just what I needed to hear. John Carrington was a single man! I headed straight for the Information Technology Center.

When we met, John Carrington had just walked away, showing no interest in me, or in our conversation. But, now, I was hoping I was the person he had approached Professor McWherter about. Perhaps he wanted to get to know me better. It was Friday afternoon, around 3:00. I thought perhaps he might be in his office. I entered the Information Technology Center and looked all around, but did not see him. He probably had plans on this chilly fall afternoon.

I looked for his office, and was directed to the third floor of the center. I peeked through the door. There he sat, working diligently. What on earth would I say to him, now that I'd found him? I couldn't ask him about the same program. And what if he didn't want to be bothered this late in the day? The only thing I could think to mention was the fact that we were both from Virginia. I love Virginia and hoped to return some day to teach on a college campus. Alexandria, where I grew up, is in northern Virginia. According to Professor McWherter, John had grown up in Charlottesville, in central Virginia.

Charlottesville is special to me. I remember taking trips there as a child with my parents, and visiting Monticello and nearby Luray Caverns. The Shenandoah Valley was so picturesque. The Blue Ridge Mountains sometimes actually appeared to be blue. I can still feel the peace and calm they generate. I certainly knew enough about Charlottesville to start a conversation with Mr. Carrington.

"Hello, are you very busy?" I asked, awkwardly.

"No, please come in," he said in a professional tone.

"I was told that you're from Virginia. I'm also from Virginia." I felt somewhat uncomfortable trying to make conversation. "Where is your home?" I already knew the answer.

"I'm from Charlottesville. And what about you?"

"I'm from Alexandria. I haven't met anyone even close to my home. How often do you get to go home?" I was hoping he'd show some interest in talking to me.

"Actually, I'm there for the holidays, and whenever my mother insists on seeing me," he said, with a smile, which was warm and sincere. He was obviously attached to his family.

"Are you by chance an only son?"

"Oh no, there are three of us, and I'm the youngest. My brothers are still in Virginia. I'd probably still be there too, but I couldn't turn down this opportunity." I wanted to keep the conversation going between us. He was talking, on a roll, and I didn't want him to stop.

"And, what about you? How often do you get back to Alexandria?"

"Whenever I can. I hope to return to work there someday."

"What do you plan to do there?"

"I'm working on a doctorate in political science, and thinking about going on the law school."

"Do you plan to practice law or teach?"

"I'm not sure, but I think teaching on the graduate level would be great. Do you know anyone else here from Virginia?" The prolonged conversation was exhilarating.

"No, but if I meet anyone, I'll be sure to let you know," he said.

"Thanks, and I'll do the same." I reluctantly began walking away.

"Miss Hamilton, if you ever need help with any of the programs, please feel free to call or come by my office. Let's keep in touch."

"Thank you." He didn't mention that he'd been looking for me. I certainly wasn't going to ask him if I was the young lady he'd been looking for earlier. Maybe I wasn't the one.

A few days later, on a sunny, fall evening, I decided to sit under a tree on campus and enjoy nature. I watched the sun set, then slowly walked back to my nearby apartment. I was enjoying the breeze and thinking about what to prepare for dinner. I had more than enough assignments to keep me busy this weekend.

The master's program was designed to be completed in one year. Students had to complete 10 courses, and earn a GPA of 2.5 or better. Two of these courses involved political science research seminars, which required substantial written work. I was spending most of the time on research papers, which was draining a lot of my energy. As a doctoral candidate, I also was required to take International Politics and Political Theory classes. The work was demanding, but I was honored to be in this selective program.

Soon November was here, and along with it came a lot of cold weather. I was not prepared for the drastic change in temperature. It was especially cold today. I came in from Political Theory class, dropped my books on the kitchen table, fixed a cup of herbal tea and stretched out on my sofa to enjoy a novel and a quiet evening at home. Some of my professors were longwinded. I just wanted to relax this evening.

The hot tea was absolutely delightful. Mother often sent care packages, and the tea had been in this week's package. I loved opening these surprise boxes and going through them, because Mother knew exactly what I liked. However, I think she got a little carried away this time when she sent me six pairs of bikini panties – three with elephants on the front, and three with elephants on the rear. When I called and asked her to explain the meaning, she laughed and said, "Politicians are often confused. Sometimes they don't know if they're running in front or behind."

I was getting used to jokes about politicians, and would soon have to get used to lawyer jokes. As I sipped the tea, I noticed the blinking light on my telephone, which indicated I had a phone message. It was from John Carrington:

"Hello, Miss Hamilton. I've decided to go home for Thanksgiving and wanted to know if you need a ride. I'm leaving early because I have some personal matters to resolve. I got your number from the department secretary. I hope that was okay with you. You can reach me at 401-863-5..."

I was numb! He had invited me to ride home with him! I had several appointments next week, but knew I had to cancel every one. Nothing would stop me from taking what could be the most important trip of my life.

6. Celia

COLE AND I WERE SCHEDULED TO ARRIVE IN CLEVELAND at 5:00 on Thursday evening. We were to meet with Cary Jacobs, the Hospital Administrator for Willow Memorial Hospital, and Mary Noland, Director of Nursing, who had called earlier. Unfortunately, we were delayed at the Nashville airport for an hour because of a mechanical problem with the plane.

Flying commercially has become such a hassle. Cole travels a lot for his job; I don't envy him. We would have driven to Cleveland. But, because of the urgency of this matter, we wanted to get there as quickly as possible to resolve whatever problem existed.

We finally arrived in Cleveland, grabbed our luggage and slid into the back seat of the taxi at the airport. So many thoughts were running through my mind. I thought I'd heard Ms. Noland say something about a very rare illness, but I was so upset during the conversation I didn't get the name of it. All I could think about was that our precious daughter, Michaela, could be terminally ill, and perhaps the symptoms of the illness had not surfaced yet. I kept trying to think about anything different or unusual that I had noticed about my daughter over the past few months.

I remembered her having a cough about two weeks ago, but she had just returned from her swimming class. She always coughed for a short period after swimming. Recently she had broken out in a rash in the lip and throat areas. Cole and I were concerned, so I had taken her to see her pediatrician. But it was nothing serious. The rash disappeared a few days after Michaela began applying the prescribed cream to the affected areas.

Now my heart was racing because I didn't know if the cough and rash were early symptoms of some deadly disease. Perhaps Ms. Noland wanted to sit with my husband and me to break the news to us as gently as possible. Tears were running down my face. I turned to look out the back seat window of the taxi. I didn't want Cole to see me crying. Now that we had arrived in Cleveland, I was even more disturbed. I knew Cole and I would soon find out what was wrong with our daughter.

We had called Ms. Noland from the airport in Nashville to tell her that there would be a delay, and we wouldn't be arriving until sometime after the scheduled 6:30 meeting. Her secretary informed us that Ms. Noland had an appointment at 8:00 and that it would be best for us to meet her in Mr. Jacob's office at 8:30 in the morning. I was hurting emotionally over the anticipated bad news, and angry about the delay at the airport. But, what was that going to accomplish at a time like this? I prayed that everything would be okay. My thinking was disoriented. I knew I had to calm down.

We had only come back to Cleveland three times since we left 10 years ago, and each of those trips had been business related. We actually had no reason to return because neither of us was from here, and the people we had been close to had also moved away.

Driving through the city brought back wonderful memories. I noticed that the flowers and yards in the neighborhoods were just as colorful and well-kept as ever. A warm feeling came over me when we passed the park near the university where Cole and I had spent several evenings, strolling or walking our dogs. Apparently Cole had the same warm feeling, because he tightened his arm around my shoulders. In the midst of my pain, I was able to smile.

Cleveland now has the celebrated Rock and Roll Hall of Fame and Museum, a newly renovated Botanical Garden, a Museum of Natural History, a downtown that is alive with businesses, shoppers and thousands of avid sports fans. And, yes, Case Western Reserve University has grown quite a bit. There are more buildings for classes and more students. Cole and I are proud to be alumni.

My husband and I had not spoken a word to each other since getting into the taxi. I knew he was just as absorbed in his thoughts about our daughter as I was. But riding through the city where we'd met and shared so much together brought some comfort to me, and I'm sure to him. I watched a mother cross the street with her child near the university. I wondered if McAlister was okay. I had asked Mrs. Nola Davenport, a wonderful elderly lady from our church, who has cared for all of our children over the years, to stay with the kids until we returned. I didn't know how long we'd be in Cleveland, and that's what I told her. As usual, she said she would stay as long as we needed her. She was such a blessing. My children thought of her as a third grandma; one who lived close by.

Cole and I checked into a hotel within walking distance of Willow Memorial Hospital. We later decided to go to one of our favorite restaurants in that same area for dinner. We had eaten there frequently when we were dating. The food and atmosphere were just perfect. I ordered my favorite dish, lamb, but only picked at it.

"Lamb is your favorite, Sweetheart, why aren't you eating?" Cole asked. I noticed that he wasn't exactly gulping his food down either. But, I didn't say anything.

"I haven't had an appetite since the phone call. There's so much running through my mind and I just can't seem to process it all. Why, after almost 11 years, would the hospital call to say that it's urgent that we get here, because something unfortunate happened after Michaela's birth? I was sick during the pregnancy, and was on medication, and if you remember, Dr. Caine thought it was possible for me to lose our child at any time. I can't help but wonder if the medication I was on could have some latent affect on Michaela. Or perhaps something is about to show up that we haven't seen, or may not see until some time in the future," I said, without taking a breath.

"Honey, it doesn't make any sense to get yourself all worked up over something that may or may not exist. Why didn't you just ask the nurse what went wrong, and why it was necessary for us to come up?"

"I didn't ask her because, after she made the statement that something unfortunate had happened, something about a disease, I was afraid of what she might say. It was such a shocking phone call that I just couldn't get the words out. You get caught up in your daily routine, so you don't expect anyone to call and tell you that something is, or may be, wrong with your child." There was a long silence. The waiter refilled our water glasses. I had no appetite, but I was very thirsty. It was a hot July evening.

By nature, I was a positive, upbeat person. My spirit was usually high. But, somehow, I knew that whatever had gone wrong at the hospital back in December 1977 was no small matter. Cole slowly ate his baked chicken and steamed vegetables. One of the reasons I loved him so much was because he was so strong. Even if he was worried, he would try hard not to let me know it. He knew I needed his strength.

"What do you think they're going to say to us in the morning?" I knew that was a dumb question.

"I have no idea, Sweetheart, but I think you should try to relax. No matter what happened or went wrong during that time, we have each other, our daughter, and two sons, whom we love dearly, and nothing is going to change that. Whatever it is, we will deal with it together, and get through it." Cole finished his dinner and beckoned the waiter for the check.

We walked back to the hotel, hand-in-hand. Cole started reminiscing about the good times we shared here more than a decade ago. We were young, ambitious and determined to succeed. But, we had fortunately found the time to develop a loving relationship.

My husband is my very best friend in the world. I couldn't imagine life without him. I called Mrs. Davenport from our hotel room to check on the kids. Matthew got on the telephone. He wanted to know why we had to leave so suddenly. I'd always been truthful with my children, so wasn't going to start lying to them now.

"Matthew, I got a call from the hospital, as I told you earlier. The Director of Nursing and Hospital Administrator at Willow Memorial Hospital want to talk with us about something that happened at the hospital during the time your sister was born. I didn't get specific details from her this morning. That's why your dad and I are here to meet with them in the morning." Matthew was quiet for a moment.

"What do you think is wrong, Mom? Is Michaela going to be okay?" I could hear the concern in his voice. He was such a good son. I loved him so much. I'd do anything for my children, and they knew it.

"Yes, son, I think she's going to be just fine." I was trying to stay positive, and remembered what Cole had said at dinner, "No matter what happened or went wrong during that time, we have each other, our daughter, and two sons, whom we love dearly, and nothing is going to change that." I assured my son that everything would be just fine, that we would be home soon.

Mrs. Davenport had already put McAlister to bed. She was cleaning the kitchen, and helping Michaela with a poem she had to turn in next week. Her two sons were married and lived away, so she had "adopted" my three as her neighborhood grandchildren. Mrs. Davenport was a frequent guest at our dinner table, because I could sense that she was lonely. Plus, we all loved her. Her sons weren't able to visit as often as she would have wanted.

Cole wanted to talk to the kids after I finished. He traveled often, but always made a point to talk to his children daily, no matter where he was. Cole had taught Matthew how to play tennis. The two of them could talk endlessly about the sport. I married a family man. This was such a blessing, because we both came from very strong families. I knew he was right when he said whatever the hospital officials had to discuss with us in the morning, we would get through it, together.

I heard Cole tell Matthew to check on some things around the house, then they said goodnight. It was a busy time for Cole at the office these days, so he worked on his laptop while I lay in bed. I tried to put together the brief conversation I'd had with Ms. Noland. I remember her mentioning something about a disease that doctors know more about today than they did 10 years ago. But, there was still a great deal of research to be done.

She had also mentioned symptoms that parents needed to be aware of, and treatment that was now available. However, as she was talking, my mind was racing, trying to think about what I may or may not have noticed about my daughter that could be a sign that she was ill. Every cold, headache, stomachache, cough, rash, scratch and blister that my child had complained about flashed into my mind. That's why I was not able to remember every word Ms. Noland had said.

Suddenly I felt guilty. Here I was a stay-at-home mom, with no career pressures to deal with, and had still somehow overlooked my daughter's illness. There was just no excuse for this! Cole worked very hard to give his family whatever we needed, or wanted. I couldn't even detect that our child was sick. I was crying now, because being a good mother was the most important thing in my life. Somehow I felt I had failed.

I lay in bed, feeling guilty and hurt, when an interesting thought crossed my mind. If Michaela was so sick, why hadn't Ms. Noland asked us to bring her with us today? That thought hadn't even crossed my mind until now. Maybe that was why Cole was so calm. It didn't make any sense for the hospital staff not to want to have her here to run more tests, and take blood samples. Unless, of course, they wanted to break the bad news to us first, to let me fall apart without our daughter being present to see it.

Still, I didn't recall Ms. Noland asking how Michaela was feeling or if I'd noticed certain symptoms. I was quite upset during the conversation, but was pretty sure she never asked about Michaela's health. I jumped out of bed to tell Cole.

"Honey, if Michaela is so sick, why do you think she didn't ask us to bring Michaela with us to check her out and run more tests? I don't even recall this woman asking about her health, or if I'd noticed any symptoms."

"You're the one who has assumed that our daughter has some terminal disease or illness. I didn't speak with Ms. Noland. If I had, I would know exactly why we're here. Try to get some rest tonight. We'll find out in the morning why we're here."

Cole kissed me. I went back to bed and managed to fall asleep. He was right. In the morning, we would find out what had gone wrong at Willow Memorial Hospital on December 10, 1977.

7. Sarah

THE TRIP TO ATLANTA was the most exciting experience of my life. We left in the middle of September 1844. Mammy brought along my favorite quilt, one that she had made for me. She kissed Pappy goodbye, but I found it difficult to remove my arms from around him. He would be left alone for days without his family. Finally, I had to let go. I had to help the Wilmington family pack their luggage.

We left Holly Springs very early that Thursday morning by horse and carriage. It was one of the Wilmington's larger carriages, which had two windows, one on each side. The inside was divided in two. Missus Wilmington, Kate and Melissa sat in the front with Mastah Wilmington. Mammy and I sat in the back.

I was thrilled to see different parts of Holly Springs as we left. Kate and Melissa slept until we reached Alabama, but I was determined not to miss anything. After traveling for several hours, Mastah Wilmington stopped near Birmingham to get food and personal items. While his family enjoyed a hot meal, Mammy and I enjoyed the fried pork she had packed. I loved Mammy so much. It was good to see her resting, instead of working.

When it was time to travel again, I cuddled next to Mammy with my eyes wide open. Through the windows that stretched the length of the carriage, I saw fields of tobacco and sugar cane, and our people working in them. I waved, knowing they could not see me. I thought about Pappy and knew that he was in the fields, too.

My parents had told me that people like me would have to help make things better for us. I had heard other slaves on the plantation talk about free Negroes. They were curious about how they lived. Although no one other than Pappy knew, Mammy and I had managed to teach ourselves to read. This was a blessing from God. Perhaps it would help us have a better life some day. This was my last thought before falling asleep in Mammy's arms.

We traveled until just before dark each day. The first night we stayed with friends of the Wilmingtons, somewhere between Birmingham and Atlanta. The lady of the house, Mrs. Garlett, took Mammy and me to a small cabin in the back of her house for the night. The cabin was cold, and smaller than ours, but we were so tired it did not matter. We left early the next morning and continued on to Atlanta. The second night the Wilmington family stayed at a road house, while Mammy and I slept in the carriage.

Atlanta will be different and wonderful, I thought. Missus Wilmington knew a lot about the city. I listened carefully to the information she shared with her family about the city as we traveled.

"Atlanta's origins are directly related to the growth of the railroads, which began to penetrate the South during the 1830s. Railroads were in demand in the South for two reasons: they are a means of importing western foodstuffs (chiefly wheat, corn, whiskey, bacon, lard and butter), and a means of shipping cotton harvested inland to coastal markets," she said.

According to Missus Wilmington, Atlanta's trade had grown extensively with the completion of the main railroad system, and so had its population. She said railroads brought thousands of bales of cotton to Atlanta each year. Also, Atlanta was a major food distribution center for the lower South. Missus Wilmington had family in Atlanta, so thought it was a wonderful place to live. Then, Mastah Wilmington began talking.

"Atlanta is growing and bustling, unlike some of the older Southern cities. Atlanta is attracting people with carts and wagons, filled with cotton and other crops. People come here every day from everywhere looking for groceries and dry goods. They can purchase them cheaper here than in some other places," he said.

As we entered the city, I saw several horse-drawn wagons along the street. The wagons were loaded with things like cotton and food. Some wagons were drawn by horses wearing bells.

Mastah Wilmington told his family that there were lots of reasons Atlanta was growing and prospering – the railroads, crops, markets and location. He said people were coming here from all parts of the country.

As I listened to the Wilmingtons talk about the city during the trip, I wondered how many slaves lived here. Pappy had told me that there were slaves all over the South. He felt certain that life for our people was as difficult in Atlanta as anywhere.

In Atlanta, we would be staying with Missus Wilmington's cousin, Jane Farmington, and her husband, Joseph. Her husband owned a dry goods shop and was one of the city's most influential men. Missus Wilmington had said that Atlanta was becoming a commercial center of the South. I did not understand everything she was explaining to her family about Atlanta. Still, I enjoyed listening and learning.

Everything about the trip excited me, a slave girl who had only been around cotton and corn fields. Kate and Melissa had seen all of this before. While I was anxious to see everything the Wilmingtons had been talking about, I noticed that Mammy got quiet as we approached the city.

"Mammy, do you lak all dis?" I whispered.

"Yes, Baby, I do," she said, then turned away.

We had finally arrived in Atlanta after a four-day trip. We headed to the Farmington house. Mammy and I hurriedly began unloading the Wilmingtons' luggage. Missus Wilmington's cousin had the largest house I had ever seen, except for Mastah and Missus Wilmington's. It was a two-story brick house with four large white columns along the porch in the front. There were large windows that wrapped around the house. They appeared to be dressed in white lace.

Early fall leaves covered the grass. The front door was a work of art. The glass in the door was thick, with colorful designs. The door handle was made of shiny metal that looked like gold. An arrangement of flowers, which appeared to be fresh, covered the door. There were large pots, made of stone, on either side of the door, filled with yellow and orange flowers. The exterior of the house was as beautiful as the Wilmington house.

Mammy and I helped Missus Wilmington and her daughters get settled in their rooms upstairs. Then, Missus Farmington showed us where we had to sleep. It was a small, almost empty, cabin in the back. The cabin was about the same size as the one we had in Holly Springs. It had the same type of dirt floor and beds made of straw. We were very tired and hungry. I was grateful that there was some pork left that Mammy had packed. We laid on the straw beds after eating, but I was too excited to sleep. Mammy still showed no emotion. Perhaps she missed Pappy and did not like being away from him. I kissed her on the cheek. We both fell asleep.

The next morning I heard voices and ran to the window. From a distance, I could see several young slave men talking as they worked on the Farmington house. They had boxes of tools and were building what appeared to be a porch. Three of them looked to be around 16 or 17 years old, but I was not sure. The others were older men. They were working with their backs to me.

Mammy told me to get dressed because we had to help with household chores. We were introduced to the three slave women who worked inside the house for Missus Farmington. Mattie appeared to be about 16, Esther was around Mammy's age, about 39 or so, and Rachel was maybe in her early 20s. They were not very friendly, and said, with a snicker, that they had never heard of Holly Springs.

I began telling them about Holly Springs and some of the things we did on Sundays, but none of them seemed interested. After ironing clothes in the laundry room, I helped Mammy make a dress for Missus Farmington. She was invited to a gala on Saturday, and had not been able to find a dress she liked. The fabric was a bright yellow silk. The sleeves were long and full. The waist was fitted with a wide skirt. Today was Sunday, so Mammy had several days to finish the dress. I was good at cutting and pinning. This would be a big help to her.

I loved working with different fabrics. Some Sundays, when we did not have to go to the big house, I had even tried to make dresses for my two cloth dolls, with scraps from clothing that Mammy had made. I wished I could wear some of the pretty dresses that Kate and Melissa wore. But, Mammy had made it clear that slave girls could not dress like that. If only I could stop dreaming about those dresses. I never did.

Missus Wilmington was very close to her cousins. She often talked about the Farmingtons. Mammy had heard her say that Joseph and Jane Farmington moved to Atlanta several years ago from a small town just north of the city. He had dreams of owning a large general store and selling almost anything a family would need. His dreams became a reality when he bought a dry goods store three years later. They worked hard to stock it with everything the customers needed or wanted.

Missus Farmington worked in the store and made sure all the shelves were well-stocked. They saved by being careful how they spent their money, and soon became one of the most prominent families in Atlanta. They bought an old house, and, with help from Mastah Farmington's friends, and his business sense, were able to create their larger, beautiful home. Missus Farmington had decided to extend the porch, so Mastah Farmington contacted a friend who owned a large number of slaves on a plantation somewhere outside of Atlanta.

Edward Carnes had several skilled male slaves he "hired out" as carpenters, blacksmiths and bricklayers. Mastah Farmington had asked him to send some of his more skilled carpenters and bricklayers to finish the porch.

Mattie and Rachel were smitten with the young men working outside. They giggled and stared from the front door. I overheard Mattie talking to Rachel.

"Look at de tall, good lookin one. I wonda if he gotta wif. He kin jes bout fix an buil anythang."

"But he dont live hure," Rachel said.

"He from som place nerby," Mattie answered. "Dey come hure evryday wit de massa. He ain't dat far way. I sho woud lak to be his wif."

I cleaned up my sewing area, which was in one of the downstairs bedrooms, and prepared to leave with Mammy. It had been an enjoyable day for me, but I was ready for suppa. Missus Wilmington sent food to us in the cabin that Esther had prepared for the slave quarters of the Farmington family. The food smelled good. We sat down to eat the chicken, beans and cornbread. I began talking about how pretty Missus Farmington's dress was going to be when Mammy finished it.

"Mammy, one day I go have a purdy dress jes lak de one you makin for Missus Farmington. Some day I gonna dress jes lak dey do. Oh, Mammy, I think Mattie is courtin. I heard her tell Rachel she wanna be somebody wife."

"What man is she talkin bout?" Mammy asked.

"Some yung slave men workin on Missus Farmington porch. Dey do not live hure, but somewher close by. Dey come hure evry day to work, den go home. Dey work for some man name Mastah Carnes." Mammy continued to eat her suppa.

"Maybe we kin meet dese men befo we leave," she said.

"If I see dem tomorra I will tell you."

"Finish yo suppa an git ready for bed." Mammy had a look on her face that I had never seen. She was still quiet.

The next morning Mammy and I arrived early at the Farmington house to work. We took a few minutes to make conversation with Mattie and Esther, then got busy in one of the bedrooms sewing Missus Farmington's dress.

After working a short while, I thought I heard the young men outside. I went to the window and noticed that Mattie was talking to the tall one. She clearly liked him a lot. She was smiling. I had work to do so left the window and went back to help Mammy. Later, Mammy sent me to the dining room to see if Esther and Rachel needed help with the dishes.

They were busy cooking and cleaning. I wondered how Mattie managed to get away from her chores. Each of them was more friendly to me now than when I first arrived. Perhaps they thought about how they had behaved earlier. I did not care. I was just happy that they were talking to me.

Soon it was time for the mid-day meal. Esther told Rachel to get Mattie to help with preparing turkey and vegetables for the Farmingtons and the Wilmingtons. Mammy took a break from sewing and came into the dining room to ask Esther if she needed help.

"We kin manich, soon as Mattie git in hure an stop flirtin," Esther said.

"Oh, is de men back?" Mammy asked.

"Yes, dey be comin evry day til de job git done," Esther said.

"Sarah said dere was some yung men workin hure. Where is dey?" Mammy asked.

"Look out de winda."

Mammy was speechless, as she stared through the window for several minutes at the young men. She then ran out of the dining room and into the back yard, as if trying to get a better view. Then, I watched her break into tears, and fall to her knees. I ran to her and held her close.

"Mammy, is you alright?" I screamed! "Mammy, whut is wron wit you?" She slowly stood up, and looked directly at me.

"Sarah," she said with tears flowing, "dats my boy, an yo brotha, Tom. I ain't seen my boy in eight years. Dats my boy, Tom. Lord have mercy, dats my boy!"

8. Raini

OHN AND I BECAME GOOD FRIENDS in the months that followed. We had a great time together. He was fascinated with computers and I was fascinated with politics, but our different interests couldn't keep us apart. It didn't take me long to realize he was the man I wanted to spend the rest of my life with.

We were both highly motivated, goal-oriented individuals. Although John could be very serious most times, he was the most romantic man I'd ever met. I'll never forget the first time he invited me to his home to meet his family. It was Christmas 1998. First, he came to my home to meet my family on Christmas day. The next day we drove to Charlottesville. I spent the day with his family. Before driving me back to Alexandria the next morning, he invited me to lunch.

We drove several miles until we came to a rustic cabin, tucked away in the Blue Ridge Mountains. The view of the city below was breathtaking. I had to take a picture. It was beginning to snow, which only accentuated the picturesque scene. As we approached the cabin, I noticed that it was actually a restaurant. When we walked in, there was no one there except a waiter and a harpist.

"It looks like we're the only customers," I said, as I looked around the rustic, yet tastefully decorated room. There were paintings of wildlife nestled in the mountains.

"This is a restaurant my grandfather built and owned for many years." John pulled out my chair at our table. "Since it was built, only the Carrington family has been involved in its day-to-day operation. I reserved it today for just you and me."

"Why, John, this is so special." The waiter gave us a menu, which was actually a piece of wood engraved with several entrees. John told me all about how his grandfather never worked for anyone in his life. And, although the restaurant was small, it had been, and still was, flourishing. He said his brothers and cousins were very involved in this family business, even though they all had successful careers.

John said his father still called him regularly about the restaurant, to ask for his advice on finances and other details. As we talked, the harpist played several Christmas favorites. The mountain tops were covered with snow, so the view outside only enhanced the cozy setting inside. There was a fireplace close by. The fire warmed my body. There was no one here to enjoy it except John and me, the waiter, the cook and the harpist. This was very special.

We both ordered a pasta dish with seafood. I couldn't stand the thought of having more turkey or ham. I was afraid to think about how much weight I'd gained since I came home for the holidays over a week ago.

John and I chatted more than we ate. As for conversation, our exchanges weren't forced. We had a lot to say. Generally, when I was out with men, I found myself praying for the evening to end because we had nothing to talk about.

The harpist continued to play holiday music, but as we were finishing our meal, suddenly there was silence. Tears began to fill my eyes. The harpist was no longer playing sounds of the season. She was now playing *As We Move Forward,* my favorite song of all time. This was a song about people learning to put the past behind, and focus on the future. I had shared my love of this song with John when I first met him, but never mentioned it again. Now the harpist was playing this most sentimental tune. I was embarrassed for crying, but the tears wouldn't stop flowing. I noticed a smile on John's face, but he didn't look at me; only at the harpist. This man has class, I thought.

Although I was no longer hungry, the waiter brought a chocolate cake to our table, with icing that read "Welcome To My Home." We each had a slice. It was delicious. Then, we thanked the waiter, harpist, cook and left. I felt like royalty!

John and I connected. I liked his family and felt comfortable with them. He felt the same about my parents. He and Dad shared a love of sports, and the two hit it off immediately.

We continued to see each other over the next several months. John and I enjoyed each other's company, and were often together everyday. We never imagined having to be apart. However, in June, 1999, John was selected from several applicants to develop a web-based data sharing repository for universities. The project was designed to connect Brown and other schools in this country with schools abroad, to share information. John was in charge of developing a grid computer network that would connect the schools. The computer grid system would allow each school to share research findings. He knew he would have to travel throughout the country and abroad for this project, and probably spend very little time at Brown during the next 12 months or so. It was a great opportunity for him. Although I didn't want to be separated from him, I knew there was no way he could decline this opportunity.

I was kept busy with my classes and returned to Alexandria that summer. I worked on Senator Cole's re-election campaign, shortly after John began working on the project. My first assignment was to meet with a group of students at Georgetown University to get feedback on social issues for the Senator's re-election strategy. On Thursday night, I brought a stack of information home to comb through, and become fully familiar with, before meeting with the students. The Senator had warned me that I needed to be prepared for all types of questions about his position on various issues. And, be prepared for hostile students who were anti-political. This would definitely be a challenge, so I was determined not to look foolish and unprepared before the students.

I read each page carefully, and made a list of questions I needed to ask the Senator. Although there was a lot of material to review, I found it interesting.

Senator Cole had worked hard to bring dignity back to Capitol Hill. I could speak honorably of him, and the goals he wanted to achieve. My family had known him for many years. He was a man of character.

The students at Georgetown were sharp. They asked questions about the Senator's stand on the value and cost of higher education, and how to eliminate illegal drugs in schools. They wanted to know how he planned to help children who were born with HIV/AIDS. There were questions I couldn't answer, and told them so. But, I made a note to get answers as soon as I met with the Senator.

I left my first assignment feeling like I'd been roasted. These were young people who were sincerely concerned about where this country was headed, and what our leaders had to offer. They believed that character and morals were important factors in our leaders. They wanted honest answers to serious questions, not answers that sounded good or acceptable. There were terrorist attacks here and around the world. These young people cared about national and personal security. They wanted to make a difference.

When I met with Senator Cole the following Friday, I shared everything with him. He was interested in what I had to say. He wanted my opinion on certain issues because I was close in age to the students I had just met with at Georgetown. I talked and he listened without speaking. I told my parents how good it made me feel to know that a United States senator actually cared about my views. I couldn't wait to tell my professors about my experiences this summer, when I returned to Brown.

Before long, it was September, and time to get back into the swing of going to class and writing papers. This was my second year of graduate school. I desperately missed John, and buried myself in books and research to keep busy. He had spent the summer at Oxford University and the American University of Paris in France. He had asked me to join him, but I was too busy with the Senator's campaign.

November brought great news on two fronts. Senator Cole was re-elected, and John was headed back to the U.S. in a week. He was almost finished with the special project. He called on Thursday after the election and asked me to meet him at his family's vacation home in Minneapolis the next day. I dropped everything, books and papers included, and took the first plane out to be with the only man I'd ever loved.

There is no joy that compares to the joy of loving someone, and having that person return your love. Reuniting with John enabled me to forget all the stress of the past several months. There was no phone to answer, no computer to work on, no books or papers to read. I arrived that Friday morning around 10:00. It was just John and me. Nothing else mattered. Later that evening, he prepared a French dish for me, croquet monsieur. That was one of his favorites in Paris. We used no electricity, only candles.

"I have some music I'd like for you to play," he said. He got up to look into his brief case. John knew that I loved playing the piano. It brought a sense of peace and calm to me, so I wondered what he had in mind.

"I met a songwriter while in London. This is my favorite. Would you mind playing it for me?" He handed me sheets of music. John's father had purchased the piano many years ago, because he, too, loved to play.

"I'd love to," I said. I walked over to the piano. He placed a single candle on top of the piano, right above the sheets of music.

"I hope this is enough light for you to see the notes," he said. His smile could melt a candle. Yes, we were very much in love, but still maintained what our parents would say was an "appropriate" courtship.

"This is just fine." I began playing. The room was dark, except for the single candle burning atop the piano. The music and the setting were mesmerizing. John stood over the piano and watched me play without saying a word. He was even more handsome in the candlelight. My fingers seemed to float across the keyboard. It was wonderful. I felt honored that he wanted me to play for him. The scent of the pumpkin spice candle was almost hypnotizing. I had developed a habit of returning to my apartment after a long day and lighting a candle, before changing clothes or doing anything. Tonight, however, the candles were all John's idea of a peaceful, romantic evening.

After playing for a couple of minutes, I abruptly stopped. I felt a piece of metal lodged between two notes on the keyboard. It was sharp to the touch!

"John, there's something on the keyboard. It feels like a piece of metal," I said, reaching for it in the dark. He came around to the bench and sat next to me.

"What is it?" he asked, looking puzzled. "Why don't you hold it up to the light so we can take a look."

I did. I was speechless! I looked at John. He was smiling, staring right into my eyes. Tears fell down my cheeks. I wanted to stop them, but couldn't. John held me close and gently began wiping my face. He then took the small piece of metal and slipped it onto the ring finger of my left hand. The ring had a perfectly clear blue topaz stone, in the middle of six bright, flawless diamonds. I stared at it. He caressed my face with his warm hands, then softly kissed me.

"Raini, will you be my wife? Please say 'yes'."

9. Celia

I WAS UP AND SHOWERING long before the alarm clock went off. I can never remember being more anxious in my life. In an hour, Cole and I were due to meet with Ms. Noland and Mr. Jacobs. We would soon learn what went wrong at our daughter's birth. Cole insisted that I have some breakfast. We had little to say to each other as we ate. We later walked to the hospital, which was two blocks away. It felt like the longest distance I'd ever walked in my life.

"Good morning, you must be Mr. and Mrs. Bentley," a woman said, as we entered Mr. Jacob's office. "He's on the phone and will be right with you. Please have a seat." His door was open. I could see that there was a woman with him. I assumed she was Ms. Noland. I wanted to leave and let Cole bring the news to me, but knew I had to stay to hear whatever they had to say. The secretary's phone buzzed, then she told us we could go in to the office.

Mr. Jacobs appeared to be around 45 years old, with dark hair that had begun to turn gray at the sideburns. He was of average height. He was wearing a striking navy suit, a crisp white shirt and a navy tie with thin red stripes. He had a troubled look on his face, but greeted us warmly. He turned and introduced the woman in the room as Mary Noland. She appeared to be in her mid-to-late 50s, and was dressed in a white nurse's uniform. She also looked troubled. Cole and I sat next to each other. He reached for my hand.

"Mr. and Mrs. Bentley, I know that you must be confused and perhaps disturbed by such a sudden call from Ms. Noland," Mr. Jacobs began. "Let me say that this discovery has been very painful for the maternity unit staff here at Willow Memorial Hospital. And, although I wasn't here during the time your daughter was born, I certainly feel the pain, likewise."

He appeared to have difficulty finding words to tell us what he wanted to say. My heart was racing now. It felt like it had dropped into my stomach. I looked at Cole, but his inquisitive expression had not changed. Mr. Jacobs glanced at Ms. Noland. Then she spoke.

"We've gone through your medical records several times, checking to see if there could have been some mistake in recording the data, but there doesn't appear to be any," she said. She now appeared confident, and clearly was someone who took her position seriously. Whereas Mr. Jacobs seemed uncomfortable with what he had to say, Ms. Noland appeared to be the type who would say what had to be said, then deal with the consequences later. She was staring at some medical charts in her hand.

"Two weeks ago today, a young girl was admitted to this clinic with symptoms that included vomiting, listlessness and some disorientation. She did not respond to several medications that were given to her. After two days of no improvement, Dr. Thad Chiana, a childhood disease specialist from Arizona, came in to take a look at her. He began treating her for a condition known as Reye's syndrome. Tests showed that there was some swelling of the girl's brain. However, tests are still being run."

Ms. Noland continued to discuss various tests and procedures that were being used to verify this condition. As she spoke, I tried to recall if Michaela had shown any signs of being sick, or just tired, recently. Apparently Ms. Noland was preparing to tell Cole and me that Michaela, for some reason, could have, or may be in danger of acquiring, this illness. I was anxious for her to get to the point and tell us if this poor child was going to live or die.

"The child is still a patient here, in intensive care, but Dr. Chiana and his team are optimistic that she will pull through. This process, however, is going to take time and lots of specialized care," she continued. Mr. Jacobs listened intently as she spoke. Somehow I got the feeling that he, too, had some painful things to say to us. I knew very little about Reye's syndrome, but had heard of it. Somewhere I remember reading that the symptoms were similar to those of meningitis. I knew that meningitis could be deadly.

One of my classmates in college had come down with it shortly after school started. Although she survived, she is confined to a wheel chair. She suffered some brain damage as the result of swelling in the brain. My parents wouldn't allow me to stay in that dorm after this incident. I believe there is now a shot that students can get before coming to college, that protects them from this horrible disease.

My heart ached as Ms. Noland talked. I couldn't imagine any of my children having meningitis or Reye's syndrome. After all, I was a stay-at-home mother. I was supposed to protect my children from deadly diseases, and keep them healthy and happy. Perhaps I had failed terribly. I wanted to leave the room and run somewhere, then break down and cry.

Finally Ms. Noland was quiet. She turned the discussion over to Mr. Jacobs, who had been taking notes while she talked. I didn't like the look on his face when he began speaking.

"I'd like to thank Ms. Noland for giving you some medical background on what appears to be a very serious illness. Recently, several children have been admitted here with the symptoms that Ms. Noland described. First, let me ask you if your daughter, Michaela, has shown any signs of being sick or not feeling well?"

Cole answered, "No, I haven't noticed anything. What about you, Sweetheart?"

"No, I haven't, Mr. Jacobs. Please tell me just what you two are trying to say. Is there something about our daughter that we need to know? If there is, tell me, now!" I was upset and wasn't going to suppress my feelings any longer.

We had listened to Ms. Noland's speech. Now it seemed that Mr. Jacobs was about to get started on one. I couldn't sit and listen to another monologue. I wanted to know why Ms. Noland had called me, and disrupted our lives. One of them had better say something, soon. Cole reached out to me, but I didn't want any consoling or comforting. I wanted to know what was wrong with my child, and why we were sitting here in Cleveland, Ohio, at Willow Memorial Hospital, at 8:30 in the morning!

"I'm so very sorry, Mrs. Bentley. I will get to the point. But, there are some preliminary matters that we must share with you," Mr. Jacobs said, slowly. "Over the past few months, we've had six children admitted to this facility with symptoms very similar to those that Ms. Noland described, and they are all the same age. In fact, they were all born right here during the month of December 1977. Of course, we became suspicious, and decided to investigate. We wanted to see what these children might have in common, other than the fact that they were all born here on the same day, or close to the same day. Three of them became very sick, and were rushed here for treatment. I regret to say that we lost two of them. The other three were admitted for observation, but they are fine.

"Did they have Reye's syndrome?" I blurted out.

"No, they did not, Mrs. Bentley."

"Well, what exactly killed those two children, Mr. Jacobs? Did something happen here at this hospital 10 years ago that caused these deaths?" I was standing now, because I could no longer sit while he dragged this on more than necessary.

"Mrs. Bentley, I know you are anxious, but, please, let me finish," he insisted. "We're still investigating. Apparently some of the babies were mistakenly given the wrong medication. But, we don't have any evidence that this mistake caused these children to get sick."

"You mean you don't have any evidence yet, that your staff was incompetent and negligent, and perhaps cost two children their lives? And, our daughter could be your next victim?" I was crying, and felt myself getting sick. I ran from the room. I had to get some fresh air; I felt faint.

Outside the hospital, I found a bench and sat down. I tried to "mentally digest" everything I'd heard this morning. Apparently some staff member had made some life threatening mistakes in the maternity unit when Michaela was born. Now they were calling the parents in, one by one, to tell them to prepare for their child to either die, or become critically ill in the near future. Michaela is now 10. I wondered how long it would take before she began to display some, or all of those symptoms.

I was feeling every emotion imaginable. My darling, sweet daughter was subjected to something during the first days of her life. Whatever it was could kill or make her very sick, and I didn't know if there was a thing in the world Cole or I could do to help her. I wondered if we could bring her here, or take her to a hospital in Nashville, to be examined before the symptoms appeared. But, that didn't really make any sense, or did it? Just the thought that something could be critically wrong with your child has to be one of the most frightening feelings a parent can have. Cole had now joined me. His warm embrace brought a moment of peace.

"Sweetheart, you've gotten yourself all worked up, and they haven't said that Michaela is sick. Why don't you try to calm down so we can go back in and hear them out," he said calmly.

"Cole, how can you be so calm when you've heard them admit that something went wrong back in December 1977, when our daughter was born? Now, innocent children are getting sick, and two have even died. Why do you think they asked us to come here? I know what they have to say to us is going to be devastating. I just can't take this stress any longer. I don't see how you can either. I think they're both cruel for not telling us everything outright. I wonder how many parents have been hurt, or will soon be hurt by this."

"Sweetheart, before I left the room, they told me that, according to their records, they don't think Michaela received the wrong medication." Also, if she hasn't shown any signs of being ill, then she probably isn't."

"Well, if she wasn't exposed to anything life threatening at that time, why did they want us to come here, Cole? It doesn't make any sense to me. Do they want us to bring her here, so that they can check her out? Just what are we supposed to do?"

"If you are okay now, we need to go back in and find out what's going on, and why we're here." I stood up, and we walked back to Mr. Jacob's office. However, I was done listening to speeches. I wanted answers, and they'd better have some. We walked in, but no one was there. His secretary came in to tell us that Mr. Jacobs would be with us shortly. He was called into another meeting. She offered us coffee, which we refused.

While waiting, I noticed a file on Mr. Jacob's desk, with my daughter's name on it. I couldn't resist the temptation to browse through it. Cole asked me not to, but at this point, I had to have some answers. There was medical terminology that I didn't understand. I kept reading, anyway. I knew something would click soon and make sense to me.

There were pictures of Michaela at birth, and of her hand and foot prints. There were pages describing my health problems, and a list of medications that I'd taken during my pregnancy. There was information about medications that were given to Michaela right after birth.

My daughter was very little, but full-term, when she was born, just barely five pounds. I remember that she didn't want to eat. In fact, she stayed in the hospital for two weeks, so the nurses could watch her closely and monitor any change in her breathing. There was also DNA information, which I didn't completely understand, because I didn't have a medical background. I knew from my biology classes, however, that a child inherits one-half of his genetic material from each of his parents.

I continued to skim over the pages. There was more DNA information that I didn't understand, so I put the file back on Mr. Jacob's desk. Then I noticed another file with another girl's name on it. I assumed that Mr. Jacobs would probably be meeting with her parents next. They probably had a list of parents that needed to be contacted, only to discover that this prestigious hospital had been negligent, and their children's lives are at stake. Shortly thereafter, Mr. Jacobs and Ms. Noland returned to the room.

"I apologize for your wait," Mr. Jacobs began, "but I was called out to attend another meeting. There's so much going on around here. I'm so sorry for any inconvenience we've caused you. Well, to get back to where we left off, I mentioned that we at Willow Memorial Hospital are investigating what may have caused several children who were born here in December 1977 to get sick and require hospitalization. We've pulled every child's file, and are reviewing each one carefully. We have a legal obligation to notify the families and inform them about what we discover. After going through Michaela's, we noticed some things that forced us to extend our investigation."

"What exactly did you find in my child's file, Mr. Jacobs? Please be straight with us. We want answers, and we want them now!"

"Yes, Mrs. Bentley, I understand. The reason Ms. Noland called and asked you both to come here is because we have another child here, who, as we told you earlier, is very sick. She was admitted here two weeks ago with symptoms that included vomiting, listlessness and some disorientation. Dr. Chiana is working very closely with her and her family. He is optimistic that she will survive.

"We don't know for sure if it's Reye's syndrome or meningitis. Either way, she is receiving the best of care." Mr. Jacobs looked down, and then continued speaking. He had a pained expression on his face. I knew that whatever he was about to say to Cole and me was going to hurt.

"This child's name is Sidney Williams. We've had to run many tests, try several procedures and do blood transfusions to find out what works best for her system. Through all of this, we have discovered that Sidney's parents, the loving people who raised her, are not her biological parents."

I was praying now, asking God to help me accept whatever Mr. Jacobs was preparing to tell us.

"During the month of December 1977, there was some construction work that had to be done in the maternity unit. The nurses had to temporarily move the babies to rooms outside the unit, so no harm would come to them. As a result of this move, some babies received the wrong medication. We're still investigating to see what, if any, harm may have been done to all, or to some of the babies.

"Sidney Williams was one of the babies moved, and apparently not placed back in the correct bed. We have no reason to believe that any of these babies was misplaced intentionally.

"Unfortunately, there was just a great deal going on at that time, so mistakes were made. We've gone back and examined every infant's medical record, and must now inform all of their parents that mistakes were made. After examining Sidney's records, we have discovered that her blood type and DNA do not match that of her parents, or, as I said, the people who took her home, and raised her as their own.

"Mr. and Mrs. Bentley, we have also reviewed Michaela's records. And, it is with deep regret that I must inform you that Michaela's blood type and DNA do not match yours. It seems that you took the wrong baby home. In fact, the tests and blood samples show that Sidney Williams is your biological daughter, not Michaela."

10. Sarah

WE STAYED IN ATLANTA ONE WEEK, from Sunday to the following Sunday. Early Monday morning we left for Holly Springs. The trip home was quiet, for the most part. Mammy cried softly most of the way, whispering stories about Tom, and how much she missed him.

Tom was only 10 years old when he was taken from us. Mammy remembered vividly the day Tom was taken from his family, in a carriage, with a group of strangers from a town some where in Georgia. Mammy had begged them not to take him. She said Pappy just stared in disbelief as his only son rode out of sight, screaming and crying. That was eight years ago. Mammy's heart was still broken.

I was very young at the time, maybe 5, and did not remember a lot about my brother. I did not remember what he looked like, therefore, I did not recognize him the first day I saw the young men working at the Farmington house. I just knew that at one time I had a brother, then he was gone. I now understood why Mammy did not like talking about my brother. All those years I had wondered what happened to him. Now, I knew. Mammy managed to stop crying long enough to tell me what "really" happened. She whispered softly so the Wilmingtons would not hear her. They had their own conversation in the front of the carriage.

"Sarah, I shoulda told you long befo now whut happen to yo brotha. Mastah Wilmington "hired out" my boy to work for a friend of his some wher in Georgia. You was jes a little girl at da time. I plead wit Missus Wilmington to talk wit her husban, an tell him not to send my boy away. She said she tried to talk to Mastah Wilmington, but her husban neva allow her to intafere in his business. I believe whut she said.

"Slaves is da mastah property, dats all. Mastah Wilmington is a business man. For a long time, I hate Mastah Wilmington, but den I learn dat hatin him was killin me, not him. We did not wanna teach you to hate, baby, so yo Pappy an me decide not to tell you whut Mastah Wilmington did wit yo brotha. Mastah Wilmington said Tom was "hired out," not sold. I always believe my boy would come bak to us some day. I neva give up hope." Mammy began crying again.

She must have known that I would learn the truth. I had so many questions to ask her, but now was clearly not the time. Mammy stopped crying long enough to tell me that the reason she was quiet when we entered Georgia was because she knew that Tom was some place not far from

Atlanta. She had overheard Mastah Wilmington tell one of his friends where her boy was located in general. Just the thought of knowing that her boy could be somewhere close by was heartbreaking for her. The thought of not seeing him was more than she could tolerate.

While we were at the Farmingtons, Tom picked me up and swung me around. He said he thought I was pretty. He told me about how he had to change my diapers, and sometimes rock me to sleep when I was a baby. Mammy was proud that her boy was good with his hands, and did not have to work in the hot fields, as Pappy had done all of his life.

"My boy got good skills an he kin fix anythang." She spoke in a soft voice on the ride back to Mississippi, with tears in her eyes. "I watch him put dat porch togetha, an Ise so proud of him. Da Lord been good to him an have watch ova him caus dats whut I ax Him to do evry day in my prayers. He a fine yung man an he luv his famly. Cain't wait to tell Joshua." More tears flowed down her face.

When Tom saw Mammy at the Farmingtons, he dropped all of his tools, and ran to her without speaking a word. He held Mammy and wiped her eyes. Then I ran to join them. We embraced each other as Rachel, Mattie and the other workers watched. Tom promised Mammy that somehow he would get his freedom and see us again. He told her that he had not been whipped, but Mammy did not think that was true. Maybe he had said this because he did not want to see her cry anymore. Mammy thought all slaveholders were cruel and merciless. She had never met a kind one.

Mammy continued to talk about Tom during the carriage ride. She had a sparkle in her eyes that I had not seen in a long time. She said Tom told her that he had been taught carpentry and bricklaying by Mastah Carnes. When he and the other slaves did not have enough work to do on the plantation, Mastah Carnes hired them out to his neighbors and other white people in need of those services. Sometimes they went with Mastah Carnes to other cities in the South, looking for work. That is why they were in Atlanta working for the Farmingtons. Tom was paid a small amount by whoever he did work for during extra jobs. But, Mastah Carnes did not pay Tom anything, because he was my brother's slaveholder.

On the way home, I could not get Tom out of my mind either. I knew this was wrong, but I hated the sight of the Wilmington family. They were all cuddled together, when my own family had been torn apart. The hurt would probably never go away. Mammy and Pappy had kept this information from me because they did not want me to learn to hate, but their plan had failed. I wanted nothing more than to hurt the Wilmingtons the way they had hurt my family. Mammy had said that Missus Wilmington had tried to talk to Mastah Wilmington, to stop him from "hiring out" my brother. But, had she tried hard enough?

Did white people think Negroes had no feelings, or as strong a sense of family as they did? How could we possibly bond as families, if family members were being sold or traded? I wondered how the Wilmingtons would feel if someone snatched Melissa or Kate, and then not see them again for eight years, or, possibly, never. I know the Bible teaches us to love those who hurt us, but, at that time, I did not think I could love any white person after learning what Tom and my parents had gone through.

The thought of Tom being torn away from us at age 10 made me cry. My heart ached for him. Mammy cried most of the ride back. Even though her son had skills, and *appeared* to be doing well, she had missed out on most of his childhood. Her heart was broken. I wondered how she had survived. Mammy loved the Lord. Perhaps He had given her the strength to endure.

I decided that night that I had to get away from Mississippi, away from its cotton fields and slavery. I was around 13 at that time, could sew quite well and wanted a better life. I did not want to spend the rest of my life as a slave, and risk being "hired out" or sold, like my brother.

Pappy had said that Mastah Wilmington had a good business head, and that business and money were most important to him. I wondered how much money he was getting from my brother's labor. I suddenly hated him, and everything he stood for: politics, slavery and cotton fields. Like Tom, I had skills, and I would find a way to put them to good use.

I had heard about how slaves escaped to freedom to the Northern states, Canada and Europe. I had even heard that some people were willing to risk their lives to help slaves escape. But, how would I get away from the plantation? My parents had often said they thought running away was too dangerous. I also knew how much they wanted to keep the family together. I fell asleep with one thought on my mind – freedom!

The trip back seemed shorter. When we arrived at the big house, I was tired, but anxious to see Pappy. I could not wait to tell him about everything, especially about seeing Tom again. I did not know if hearing this would hurt him or make him happy. I jumped out of the back of the carriage and helped Mammy down. Before I could run to Pappy, who was standing in front of our little cabin, Mammy told me we had to help the Wilmingtons unpack and get settled. This made me angry. Without thinking, I snapped at her.

"Mammy, I wanna see Pappy!"

"Mine yo manners an come on!" she said just as emphatically. We headed to the big house to begin unpacking for the Wilmingtons. It was early on a Friday morning. The sun had not come up. The Wilmington family began preparing to go to bed.

"Sarah, how did you like Atlanta? Isn't it a big, exciting city?" Melissa Wilmington asked, as she brushed her long, golden hair. We were in her bedroom. I was doing the unpacking.

"Yes, Atlanta is a big, beautifa cidy," I said. I wanted to say more, like, "I wush Mammy an me coulda enjoy it de way you an yo famly did." I knew I would have been whipped or punished for getting out of line with the mastah's daughter.

"Thangs go git betta for me," I mumbled as I continued to unpack. I was young, and did not want to be a slave for the rest of my life. I had to believe there was a better life for Negroes some where in this world. My parents and others had told me I was special, and that it would take special people like me to help change things. God had blessed me with kind, loving parents, and a mother who had taught me how to make clothes. I had taught myself to read a few words. Somehow, I had to use these gifts to improve my life and the lives of other slaves.

My brother and I were good with our hands. I could sew, and was learning to design clothing by watching Mammy and how clothes of white women were made. Tom could build and fix things. Mammy had taught me to believe and have faith, by example. She believed and had faith that my brother would return someday. Nothing could stop me from believing. I would be free one day. Some of the slaves did not understand me, my "gumption."   That did not stop me from dreaming.

"You stotin to soun lak dim white fokes, wannin dis an wannin dat," another slave girl on the plantation had said to me. "De Lawd dont lak greedy fokes. Slaves shud be thankfa to hav a ruf ova dere heads an food to eat." I sometimes wondered if it was wrong to pray and ask God to help me have a better life. Yes, I was different. But, Grandma had told me before she died that it was good to be different.

Mammy and I finally finished unpacking for the Wilmingtons and headed home to Pappy. It was still dark that Friday morning. Pappy was waiting for us to get home. He was so happy to see us. I told him all about the ride through Mississippi, Alabama and on to Atlanta. He listened to every word carefully because I spoke with such excitement. Then, I looked down, and spoke more softly.

"Pappy, I saw my brotha." Pappy looked at Mammy in disbelief, then back at me.

"Yes, it true, my husban. Our son is a fine carpenta an bricklaya in Georgia, an so good lookin." She had tears in her eyes. "He said he doin good, an not to worry bout him. He said he luv you an miss you, an to give you a big hug for him." Her voice began to crack. Pappy had tears in his eyes. He looked out the window, toward the cotton fields.

"So, my boy ain't no fiel han. He got skills an he ain't out in da sun all day. Ise proud of dat boy. I knew he was good wit his hans. Our son is sombody, Bertha." He grabbed Mammy and cried on her shoulder.

"Why, Joshua, he built a porch right dere befo my eyes for de Farmingtons. Boy, do he know whut to do wit some tools." She laughed, and managed to get a smile from Pappy. She continued to tell him everything Tom had said to her. Pappy listened carefully to each word.

We had a one-room cabin with a thin partition that Pappy had built from scraps of wood, to give him and Mammy a bedroom. I said good night, and laid on my quilt that covered the dirt floor, on the other side of the partition, which was removed during the day. I tried to imagine what it would be like to be a free Negro. Tom had told us that he hoped to be able to buy his freedom some day. Even though Tom was not free, he had been able to travel to other parts of Georgia with his mastah, working extra jobs. I wondered if I would ever leave Holly Springs again.

Tom told Mammy he was doing good, but he did not look happy. Seeing him again had changed me overnight. I no longer had pleasant thoughts about the Wilmington family. I knew that what they had done to Tom, they could also do to me. Mastah Wilmington was busy with politics and other business matters, and Missus Wilmington was caught up in her social standing. They would never do anything to help me, or my family, have a better quality of life.

One evening in October 1844, about a week after we returned from Atlanta, I sat in a cotton field and stroked two large heads of cotton. They felt so soft and fluffy. I thought it was such a miracle that the dress I was wearing was made from cotton grown here in Holly Springs. Pappy was so good at what he did. He not only planted the cotton, but was a driver in the fields. He knew a lot about how cotton was processed to make clothing. He knew how to grow this product of the earth, and Mammy knew how to cut it up and make beautiful clothes.

My parents were very skilled and intelligent people. So, there was no surprise to me that Tom was good with tools, and I was good at sewing. We were not educated, but if we had been free Negroes we could have fed and clothed ourselves. That night I asked God to help me get out of the South without getting killed. I had dreams of becoming a seamstress who also designed fancy clothing, like Mammy made for the Wilmington ladies. I, however, wanted to be free, and paid for my work. I fell asleep thinking about how I could get away from this plantation, forever.

The next day, while I was washing dishes in the kitchen, alone, Mastah Wilmington walked in and seemed friendlier than usual, and very talkative. Missus Wilmington had gone out on some errands. Mammy was helping Kate and Melissa get dressed for a party they were attending that evening.

"Well, Sarah," he began, "you're growing into a very attractive young lady. "Have you found yourself a boyfriend yet?"

"I ain't got no intres in boys yet," I said, feeling somewhat uncomfortable. "Mammy say I got time for dat."

"Well, you might not be interested in the boys, but I'll bet they're interested in you," he said, with a strange look in his eyes. I did not answer; I continued washing the dishes. I knew he was staring at me, so I avoided looking in his direction.

"You'll soon be old enough to carry on some of the chores without your Mammy being around. That would be a big help to Bertha," he continued.

"Ise sure Mammy would lak dat, but I relly lak workin by her side.

"Yes, I understand, but don't you think your Mammy needs to rest more?" He continued to stare.

"Yes, Mastah Wilmington, I thank Mammy need to rest." If only I could have said more, like, "I thank she need a break, an she need to see her son, so maybe you could give her some time to do all de thangs she done spent her lifetime wantin to do, but could not do caus she stuck hure on dis plantation!" But, I had always been afraid of Mastah Wilmington. He would never have tolerated a slave giving him any smart talk. I suddenly felt sick, and began crying. Mammy heard me and came into the kitchen.

"Sarah, what on earf is wron wit you?" she asked.

"I don't know what came over her," Mastah Wilmington said. "I was simply asking her about working more, so that she could help you out, and she started crying. You need to talk to that girl, Bertha. There's too much work to be done around here for her to be crying, and carrying on about nothing. I won't tolerate any foolishness or laziness from her!"

"Please, forgive her, Mastah. I dont know whut come ova Sarah. I go talk to her right now," Mammy said. "For now, she kin help me wit de cleanin upstairs." Mammy was afraid of what Mastah Wilmington might do to me, as punishment for my lack of control in his presence.

I knew of one female slave who had been whipped by Mastah Wilmington for telling him that she was too sick to pick cotton one day. And, Pappy had seen male slaves whipped by the overseer until their backs bled, because they muttered some "sharp words" toward the overseer. Pappy had said that Mastah Wilmington had made it clear that he would not tolerate any disrespect from any of his 20 slaves, male or female. He had told his white overseers to do likewise. She led me out of the kitchen and into one of the upstairs bedrooms.

"Sarah, whut on earf is de matta wit you?" she asked in her kind, soft tone.

"Mammy," I whispered, "I dont lak Mastah Wilmington."

"Now, you jes calm down, yung lady. It wrong to hate, an you know you cain't desrespec de mastah. He neva done anythang to hurt you."

"Yes, Mammy, he done hurt me." I continued to speak softly. I could not take any chances on Mastah Wilmington or his daughters hearing me. "He 'hired out' my only brotha. An, Pappy gotta work in dose fields from sunrise to sundown, an you gotta work even when you too sick to git outta bed. Yes, Mammy, dey done hurt me, an I hate dem all for it. An, now, Mastah Wilmington stotin to look at me in a strange way. He tol me dat Ise old nuff to come to de house witout you, an dat Ise purdy. He wanna know if I lak boys." Mammy grabbed me and held me close. My tears dropped onto her worn dress.

"Now, Baby, lots of people thank you a purdy girl. Mastah Wilmington dont mean no harm by askin you if you lak boys. Why, you lettin yoself git all work up bout nuttin, Honey." I was sure Mammy understood what I was trying to say to her. But, Mammy was very intelligent. She would never have told me to resist the mastah, knowing that was grounds for severe punishment.

I listened to her comforting words, but I knew I had to find a way to protect myself – my innocence. I had heard stories from other slave girls and women about how their mastahs had violated them, and how the wives hated the slaves, but did not confront their husbands. I knew Mammy loved me dearly, but she was not the type to hate people, especially the ones who owned her. It was time to start thinking about what was ahead for me. Maybe someday I would be in a better position to help myself, Mammy and Pappy.

Sundays were usually "free" days for the slaves. With permission, we could visit with slaves from other plantations. But, we had to have a pass, which was a piece of paper with the mastah's signature, to go from one plantation to another. We ate, danced, ran races, played the banjo, told tales and sang folk songs. The songs often told of our heartaches, work, dreams, oppression, love, culture, ancestors, bravery and courage.

I got a pass to visit relatives at a nearby farm, where another slave girl lived, one Sunday afternoon. Mammy had said Annie was my cousin. She and I were around the same age. We played with my cloth dolls. I overheard some adults talking about slaves who had escaped and made it safely to one of the Northern states. It appeared that some had just "disappeared" from fields and plantations without anybody knowing how, or who helped them. That evening Annie and her Pappy walked me home. This was the perfect opportunity to ask some questions, I thought.

"Mastah Caleb," how do slaves git outta Misippi an live as free people?"

"Well, Sarah, dats a mighty good queshun. Ya see, som is runnin thru de back woods, an some is hidin out in fokes homes, an some even passin as white." Mastah Caleb walked quickly with Annie and me.

"Dere even been stories of slaves who had white fokes dat help dem git way."

"Have you eva wan to be free, an go otha places?" I asked. "Have you eva dream bout whut yo life would be lak if you was not a slave in Misippi?" Sometimes I asked questions that no one expected from a young girl. Mastah Caleb released my hand for a moment, then scratched his head.

"Well, Sarah, I use to thank bout bein free an travlin, but dere was no way I could git outta hure. Dere was always wuck to do when I wuz a chile, den ya git marred an de chuldren come, an befo ya know it, you gotta family to cure for. I cain't leave now if I wan to wit fo chuldren. I guess de time to scape wuz when I was yung, an only had mysef to worry bout. Maybe one day slaves go be free, an we kin aw trava an go places, an not be scured of gittin cart."

Annie just listened as her Pappy spoke. Her big dream in life was to find a mate and have four children, just as her Mammy had done. I wanted to teach Annie the words I had learned to read and write, but was afraid she would tell someone.

Slaves who could read and write were seen as dangerous, and a threat to the institution of slavery. The Wilmingtons had no idea that Mammy and I could read and write some simple words. Mastah Wilmington had made it very clear that any talk or mention of teaching slaves to read and write would result in severe punishment for everyone involved. It was too dangerous to even think of teaching Annie.

Sometimes Kate and Melissa Wilmington would play school, and they would make me sit on the porch with them. That was the classroom. Kate was the teacher and she needed me to pretend to be a student, like Melissa. I was the student who had to clean up the classroom and put everything in order. Kate was two years older than Melissa and me. She would teach Melissa some of the new words she had learned from her teacher. Kate taught Melissa syllable by syllable. I listened carefully, taking it all in, without them knowing it. They had no idea how much I learned by listening to, and observing, them. I absorbed everything I could. Like Mammy, I learned a lot by being a slave in a big house, where the mastah and his family were educated and intelligent.

Kate Wilmington loved to play teacher. She and her sister went to finishing school to learn how to dance, walk and talk. The daughters of wealthy planters were educated for the purpose of marrying wealthy men. Kate and Melissa also had private tutors to teach them social graces, like how to be refined and elegant. I learned so much through my limited interaction with these two girls. But, I learned more from Mammy. I soon realized that the ability to read was a tool that could get me out of the South. Most slaves could not read, so they had no idea what was going on outside of Holly Springs. The few words I had managed to learn to read by looking in the books thrown around the Wilmington house, and in the newspapers plastered on our cabin walls, had turned on a light in me that would never burn out. I thanked God for this blessing each day.

We finally got to my cabin. Mammy and Pappy thanked Mastah Caleb for walking with me. That night I did not sleep well. All I could think about was sewing dainty clothes, and living as a free Negro. I knew that getting away from here would be very difficult. Thoughts of life outside of this plantation frightened me. Yet, I knew I had to leave.

Pappy told us he had recently heard that it was costing slaveholders lots of money to track runaway slaves. People trying to hide slaves were getting killed. I knew it would be too dangerous for a young female to set out for the North, alone. With winter coming, I would probably freeze to death. However, I believed there had to be other ways of getting away from the plantation. God answered prayers. I asked Him to help me get my freedom, so that I could have a better life. Then I could help Mammy, Pappy and Tom.

One cold night in early December 1844 Pappy came home late. He told Mammy and me a most interesting story. He said he had heard his overseer and Mastah Wilmington talking about some slaves that had escaped through an "underground railroad," and made it to Pennsylvania, New York and Canada. Mastah Wilmington then told the overseer that any rumors of slaves planning to escape would result in severe punishment. Pappy said it would be a big mistake for any slave to try to get out of Holly Springs, because the slaveholders were upset and determined not to lose any of them. Clearly, Mastah Wilmington and other slaveholders had probably been meeting, trying to determine how to tighten their control over their slaves. Pappy said they were angry, and prepared to do whatever was necessary to keep their "property." The overseer did not let Pappy or any of the field hands out of his sight from that point on, as long as they and he were on the Wilmington plantation.

I lay in bed that night thinking about what Pappy had said. I knew I had to be extremely careful about how I asked questions about the North. Some slaves could misunderstand my curiosity about other places. There was no telling who you could trust outside of the family.

When Mammy came to kiss me that night, she was smiling, and told me she had some good news.

"An how is my baby?"

"Ise tired, Mammy." I was almost asleep.

"Well, today Missus Wilmington told me dat you will be travlin wit Mastah Wilmington, Kate an Melissa to New Yok Cidy in de spring. He got some portant business to take care of dere. Mastah Wilmington sister live dere, an dats where y'all be stayin. Missus Wilmington wont be goin caus she plannin on havin a party for her lady friends. Corse, I gotta stay hure to help her. She said I gotta clean de house an decurate it wit purdy flowers, an cook lots of good food."

I heard every word, although I was almost asleep. I would get the opportunity to visit the North, although, unfortunately, without Mammy. As I fell asleep, I tried to imagine what New York City would look like. I imagined that it probably looked just like Atlanta. The next morning I asked Mammy about the trip to New York City.

"Mammy, cain't you come? I don wanna go witout you." However, I knew that Mammy nor I had a choice. We had to do what we were told.

"Baby, you know I ain't got no say so ova whut I kin do round hure. Mastah Wilmington said you goin, not me." She stroked my head. "Missus Wilmington need me to help round hure, an I gotta stay. But you, Sarah, you yung an wanna learn. Dis will be good for you."

"But, Mammy, who I go talk to for all dat time. You know how I feel bout Mastah Wilmington. An Kate an Melissa done change. Dey dont ax me to sit on de porch no more when dey play teacher and school."

"Dats cause ya'll big girls now," Mammy said. "An, ya'll too grown for dat. Why, you, Kate an Melissa is suppose to change. Besides, you go be too accited to worry bout Kate an Melissa."

"Take long som of yo sewin, my chile," Pappy added. My parents seemed to think this was a blessing. They were pleased that I would get to see the North.

"Come on, Sarah, it time to work," Mammy said, as she finished dressing. We both kissed Pappy and left for the big house.

It was still early December 1844. There was a lot to do with Christmas coming. I had all winter to get comfortable with the idea of going to New York City in the spring; going without Mammy.

11. Naini

JOHN AND I WERE MARRIED on June 19, 2001. I was 24; he was 29. I wanted to elope and marry him the day he proposed, but we knew it was best to have a wedding ceremony with family and friends present.

We were married in the Episcopal Church I attended as a child and teenager. The reception was held in the nearby Botanical Gardens. I strolled through the colorful, scented spring and summer flowers, in the same gown Mother wore on her wedding day.

John and I spent our honeymoon traveling through South Africa. We had a personable guide to take us around in a jeep, to tell us about his country. It was awesome to see "the big five" running around. Being that close to these animals in their natural habitat was thrilling.

I was reluctant to leave Africa, and didn't want the honeymoon to end. However, I had to finish my dissertation. Two months later, I started law school at Harvard. John went back to Brown. Fortunately, the international data sharing project was finished, at least for now. We rented a small house in Providence to call home. I decorated it with furniture from both of our apartments. I commuted to Harvard each day. I spent many hours in the law library that first year. I found comfort and peace in knowing that I was coming home everyday to a loving and supportive husband. We occasionally had dinner with some of the professors that John and I had grown close to at Brown. They all knew that my professional goal was to teach political science at the graduate level some day. I was confident that a background in law would make me marketable.

Although I didn't plan to practice law, I took part in moot court exercises. This is a mock court setting where law students argue hypothetical cases. I worked hard to have the grades to be on law review. I knew it was wise to take advantage of every opportunity.

By the beginning of my third year, I was feeling bored with law books and papers, and was more than ready to get involved in activities outside the classroom. U.S. Senator Henry Thomas of Rhode Island, whom I had met through Senator Cole, offered me a part-time job in his office; I jumped at the opportunity. I had completed the most difficult courses by now, and had time available to work. I researched the law on many issues for the Senator, and reviewed several of his speeches. He had been in office for six years, and was a polished, seasoned politician. He was as honorable a man as Senator Cole; they both commanded and received much respect.

Both men did their homework. They were well prepared for whatever was on their agenda. Most Americans weren't looking for perfect leaders, but for leaders, who, despite their shortcomings, could be role models for youth. Young people needed guidance and direction. Many had no one to look up to for either. Senators Cole and Thomas weren't perfect by any means, but they had morals, values and principles they tried to live by every day.

I was thrilled to be a 3L, third year law student. Working for Senator Thomas was far more interesting than sitting in a classroom. He wanted every child in Rhode Island to get a good education. He worked hard to improve the educational system for the entire state. I visited some elementary, middle and high schools he had targeted. Feedback from principals and teachers helped him with his proposals to Congress.

I stayed in touch with Senator and Mrs. Cole while I was at Harvard and beyond. I had learned so much from them, and wanted our friendship to last. Although John had little interest in politics, he thought the Coles were fine people. He enjoyed their company.

During the second semester of my senior year, I was offered a position with Strafford, Burke & Long, one of the larger law firms in Providence. The firm handled mostly real estate and insurance fraud claims. I accepted the offer. After almost six years of graduate school, I was ecstatic to switch hats from being a student to an employee, and finally earning a pay check. I graduated from Harvard in May 2004, and went to work for the firm.

In January of 2006, I had lunch with Eric Flynn, one of the firm's partners, to discuss a case we were handling. He then asked me about my career goals. I shared with him my fascination with politics, and my work experience with Senators Cole and Thomas. The conversation shifted to our concerns about Providence, especially what we thought of Mayor Charles Dalton and what City Council needed to do to make improvements in job development and good, affordable housing. His next statement took me by surprise.

"Are you aware that all 36 political offices in the city are up for grabs this year, including the mayoral and City Council seats? Mrs. Carrington, I think you should give some serious thought to running for City Council. You are politically active, knowledgeable and want to make a difference. You could represent the First Ward quite well."

"Thank you for your vote of confidence, Atty. Flynn. But, please remember that Councilman Brian Holt has been in office for two terms. He has no plans to step down from his seat."

"Councilman Holt, I regret to say, is out of touch with the needs of this ward," Atty. Flynn continued. "He doesn't have the support he once had. An aggressive, focused, organized challenger can defeat him."

My mind was racing. I didn't think Councilman Holt had done enough to help make housing affordable for all citizens. But, I'd never thought about challenging him. Could a 29-year-old attorney, who'd only been here a few years, defeat Councilman Brian Holt? In fact, he was something of an outsider too.

Councilman Holt grew up in Concord, New Hampshire. He came to Providence in the late 80s and started a car dealership. That single dealership grew into several dealerships throughout the city and surrounding communities. Needless to say, Councilman Holt was a very wealthy man. I thought it would be next to impossible to defeat him.

"Where on earth would I find the time to campaign for City Council?" I asked. "I'm working on several cases."

"Mrs. Carrington, if you're serious about running for Councilman Holt's seat, I'll adjust your work load to allow you the time you'll need to campaign," Atty. Flynn responded.

"Let me think about it. Of course, I'll have to discuss this with my husband." We finished lunch and headed back to the office. But all I could think about was what Atty. Flynn had said. He actually thought I'd be a good candidate for City Council!

That evening I discussed the subject with John.

"Atty. Flynn thinks I'd be a good candidate for City Council. I've been thinking about it. There are improvements I'd like to see in this ward. Honey, what do you think?"

"I think you have the interest and motivation to be an asset to the council and this ward. I also think it's going to be tough to defeat Councilman Holt. The man is quite rich and well-connected."

"You're absolutely right. But, he hasn't done enough in the last few years for the residents. I want to get out to meet and talk with the people, to see what their concerns are, to find out what can be done to improve living standards here. Atty. Flynn said he would adjust my work load so that I could have the extra time to campaign."

"Then I think you should go for it," John said. And, I did just that. On Sunday I spoke to members of our church. I shared with them my ideas on how to improve our community, and the city of Providence. First on my list of priorities was affordable housing. Second was Children First. This was a state funded program to educate children who are in their pre-school years. Parents of children between the ages of 1-3 could bring their children to select churches in the community for half-and full-day education and personal development programs.

Funds for this program had been cut from the state budget. I planned to work hard to raise money to keep it going. I asked our church members for their support. Several told me they would help me win the City Council seat for the First Ward. My next step was to get enough nominating signatures to qualify to run for the seat.

On Wednesday, I went to nearby colleges to speak to groups of students. I explained that I wanted to represent the First Ward, and why I would be an asset to City Council representing the First Ward. The following two weeks I visited other churches in the area. I presented my platform. I listened to their concerns to understand the needs of the people.

Before long, I had a small group of energetic supporters. I didn't have name recognition in Providence, so we began knocking on doors to talk to ward residents. I listened to more concerns. At the top of the list for most was affordable housing. One of my supporters, Dale Gordon, from my church, did some research and found that children from low-income families stayed in school longer if they lived in a home owned by their parents or guardians.

Stacey Roberts, a senior at Providence College, liked my platform. She asked to join the campaign. Although she was raised in an apartment, her mother's dream was to own a home. They had not given up on that dream. Ms. Roberts campaigned aggressively to get students and young people between the ages of 18 and 23 registered to vote.

One Saturday morning in late February 2006, John and I were having breakfast in a coffee shop near our home. A young lady approached me, and asked if I had a few minutes. I said "yes."

"I hate to disturb your breakfast, Mrs. Carrington," she began. "My name is Selena Rodriquez. I've heard you talk about your ideas and plans for the city. Do your plans include improving living standards for me and my family, or just African-Americans?"

"Hello, Ms. Rodriquez. What ward do you live in?" I asked.

"I live in the First Ward."

"Then, my agenda includes improving the standard of living for you and your family, and others in the city." I invited her to join us for breakfast; she did. Ms. Rodriquez was 26, married and had two children. She wanted someone on the council who was interested in helping Hispanics, an even smaller minority, get a good education and find jobs. She and her husband had lived in Providence for two years. She liked it here, but sometimes worried that her people were overlooked for educational and career opportunities. By the time we finished breakfast, Ms. Rodriquez had signed up to be a volunteer for my campaign. As it turned out, she worked diligently in her community to get Hispanics and Latinos to register to vote.

I asked Ken Akers, a fellow classmate from Brown, to manage my campaign. He enthusiastically accepted. Ken had talked about running for City Council himself when we were students. Some family matters had interfered with that goal. He was still interested, but had put this plan on hold.

Before long, Ken, a large number of supporters, John and I were busy putting lawn signs in yards and placing posters throughout the First Ward. He then began organizing fundraising events. His first priority as campaign manager, however, was strong voter turnout.

The number of registered Democrats greatly exceeded the number of registered Republicans in Providence. I was a Democrat; Councilman Holt was a Republican, but very popular. Mayor Dalton was a Democrat; the majority of the City Council seats were held by Democrats. Ken was confident I could win if we could get the voters out on Election Day.

Soon it was time for my first public debate with Councilman Holt. It was scheduled for 7:00 on March 5, 2006 at the Jefferson Hotel. John, Ken and several of my supporters helped me prepare. Although I was nervous, I had a strong platform. I was advised to stick to my platform, explain to the residents of the First Ward how I would work hard to address their concerns and needs, and let them know they would have a voice on City Council.

Councilman Holt began by attacking me on my credibility and lack of experience. I can still hear his first words: "Mrs. Carrington is a new, young attorney campaigning for a seat on City Council to make a name for herself professionally. She has been a student most of the time she's lived here in Providence. She hasn't been in the real world long enough to know what the concerns and needs of the residents of the First Ward are. Residents of the First Ward, do you really want someone whose first priority is to make partner with her law firm, speaking on your behalf?

"Who is Attorney Raini Carrington? What has she done in the interest of the residents of the First Ward? Once she makes partner, do you really think she's going to stay around and speak on your behalf? I think not." Councilman Holt continued to tear into me, dwelling on my lack of experience in politics. He obviously planned to win the election by trying to roast me. By the time he finished his opening remarks, I wanted to slip out the back door of the hotel, with a bag over my head.

Then, it was my time to speak. I glanced at John and Ken. Many of my supporters were sitting with them. John had his same, comforting smile, that I interpreted as, "You can do it, Sweetheart." Ken had his "stick to the issues" look on his face. I looked at my supporters, but couldn't interpret their expressions. Had Councilman Holt destroyed their confidence in me? Did they think I was just a self-centered attorney, seeking my own interest by running for a seat on City Council? I didn't know; now was not the time to try to figure it out. Everyone was waiting for my opening statement. I took a deep breath, and began to speak.

"Councilman Holt, you're right. I have spent most of my time here as a student. I had educational goals that I've accomplished. Now, I'm ready for my next mission – representing the residents of the First Ward."

"I want to thank my supporters for being here this evening. Many of you met me when you opened your front door, and found me standing there, waiting to introduce myself. I told you what I wanted to do for this ward. At the top of the list is making sure there is affordable housing for all residents. Raising funds to keep the Children First program intact is second."

"Providence has a housing problem. The growth of households has greatly exceeded the growth of new housing units. Statistics show that last year 40 percent of our residents sought affordable housing units, but they were not available. Many of you have told me that owning a home is a dream that may never come true for you and your families.

"Far too many parents also are concerned that the proposed city budget for Providence doesn't include any new money for education, after this year. Some are wondering what's going to happen when the Children First program is cut. Their young children will no longer have the opportunity to spend their days in a classroom, learning. I'm concerned, too. But, if we don't voice our concern, nothing will change. The cost of housing will continue to increase, forcing more people to live in apartments and rental properties, if not on the streets of Providence. More children will enter kindergarten unprepared." I continued to speak. I'd practiced my speech several times. I had an agenda, and stuck to it. I wanted to be elected because of my platform, not because I knew how to tear someone apart. This strategy worked.

Ken had done an excellent job of organizing and motivating my supporters. We had volunteers from various age groups, nationalities and economic backgrounds. He managed to run a high-energy, upbeat, positive campaign. He made me look good.

Atty. Flynn had kept his word about adjusting my work load. I had time to actively campaign. After the campaign started, he offered me a part-time position with the firm, until after the election. I accepted. This opportunity gave me the additional time I needed to convince the residents of the First Ward that I had their best interests at heart.

On election day, November 2006, the weather was perfect for voter turnout, cool and sunny. My volunteers started early that morning calling supporters and reminding them to get out and vote. They stressed the point that I needed every vote possible to win this election. They even added that, based on the polls, the winner could be determined by as few as 100 to 200 votes. We had volunteers on college campuses, at area churches and anywhere else they could camp out, without breaking the law. Ken had raised enough money for us to rent buses to pick up elderly residents, and others without transportation, to get them to the polls.

On election night, John, some of our close friends and several supporters awaited anxiously with me at the Jefferson Hotel for the results.

As expected, the election came down to the wire. I won by just over 300 votes! I didn't realize it then, but, this was the beginning of a long career for me to serve the public. I began my acceptance speech by thanking John, Ken, Atty. Flynn, my volunteers, supporters and everyone involved in helping me get elected. I ended it by assuring the residents that I would work hard to improve the quality of life in the First Ward.

Shortly after the election, I presented a proposal for the annexation of Cedar Lake, a town next to the First Ward. I thought it was important to redevelop this district, to get more recreational and commercial activity in the area. This would help improve the standard of living in the Ward. I believed this would also encourage the construction of middle-tier housing units by providing economic incentives to developers.

The proposal passed the council on second reading. This was a big victory for the First Ward. I felt great, but knew this was only the first step of my plan to make this district a quality place to live.

Three years after the election I continued to work part-time at the firm. At 31, I was earning a good salary practicing law, but my heart was in representing the residents of the First Ward. This was challenging, and, more importantly, more rewarding.

On Tuesday evening at 7:00, a public hearing was held in council to consider a proposal to provide uniform water, sewer, trash and street lighting for the Douglas Street redevelopment district. After the hearing, a group of residents from the First Ward approached me. They told me how pleased they were with my representation. They went on to say they were preparing to get me re-elected for a second term. I thought about this on the way home. After I got there, I discussed it with John.

"They're pleased with my performance, but, I don't think I want a second term on City Council."

"What's on your mind, Sweetheart?" John asked. "I know you. You're not ready to walk away from public service."

"No, I'm not. I've decided to throw my hat in the race for state senator for the Third District. Incumbent Senator Bob Cross announced today that he plans to resign within the next six months. He cited health reasons. His seat will be open for his remaining two-years."

The election would be in November 2010. I had one year to prepare for and win the seat. Once again, I turned to Ken Akers to ask him to manage my campaign. He enthusiastically accepted my offer. Ken was now teaching at Rhode Island College. John and I believed that if Ken used the same strategy for my campaign for state senator, as he did for City Council, I would win.

The Republican candidate, Marilyn Capers, had recently retired from the Providence public school system. She'd spent her last 10 years as principal of a local high school. Joseph Pitt, marketing manager for a large automobile parts company, was running as an independent.

Both candidates were sharp, articulate and eager to represent the Third District. Ken and I had our work cut out for us. However, unlike my run for City Council, I now had name recognition. My first step was to develop and coherently present my platform to a wider range of voters this time. My priorities were health care and children's welfare.

Ken was consistent. He did not deter from his previous strategy, which had proven to be successful. Once again, it paid off. On November 6, 2010, I was elected state senator for the Third District. I was now 33.

I served Senator Cross's remaining two years with pride. It was an honor to represent the Third District. My term ended in November 2012.

12. Celia

SANG IN THE CHURCH CHOIR AS A TEENAGER. One of my favorite hymns was *"One Day at a Time."* This is exactly how I am managing to keep going these days, taking one day at a time. It has been almost a week since Mr. Jacobs and Ms. Noland broke the devastating news to Cole and me. Michaela is not our biological daughter. Our biological daughter is Sidney Williams, who is here in Willow Memorial Hospital, fighting for her life.

After hearing the news, I fainted. Since I've been revived, my brain hasn't processed the fact that the daughter I thought I gave birth to, is not mine. This is the child I have loved dearly since the moment she was conceived. It's very difficult to verbalize to others what I'm feeling. As I tried to explain my emotional turmoil to my mother, I hurt just as I did when my father passed away. I couldn't discuss the news about Michaela without breaking into tears. But Cole and Mother think I should talk about my feelings, so I can heal and move forward.

Cole left yesterday, temporarily, because he had to get back to work. I'm in Cleveland with Mother, who has joined us. She flew in from Charleston yesterday. I desperately want to go home to my children. I want to pretend that this is only a nightmare. But, Mother reminds me that it's real, and that I will get through it. I want to believe her, but I don't. Just the thought of Michaela tears at my heart. This adorable, sweet child that we all thought looked more like my grandmother, than Cole or me, is actually someone else's child! Mother tells me that because Cole and I raised her, she is "our" child. The truth is that she belongs to someone else, at least that was my way of thinking then.

I found the strength to go to Sidney's room shortly after Cole left. I ran from her room immediately in tears. There were tubes all over her little body. She is so very sick. This is my flesh and blood lying here in this hospital, and I can't do anything to help her.

I know Cole is just as hurt as I am, but he's stronger than I am. As he explained, he has a family to love and support, so he had to return to Nashville. It's an effort for me to pray these days, yet I continue to pray for the strength to accept this horrible nightmare. I refused to believe what Mr. Jacobs told us, even though I know blood and DNA tests don't lie. I'd probably lose my mind if I didn't have Mother here with me. Cole's parents have decided to stay with him and the children. They want to help us carry on as usual, to function as the warm, loving family we are.

I need to think about going home, but a part of me doesn't want to leave that little girl in Room 415. She's little more than a stranger to me, yet she's my biological daughter. Mother has visited with her, even met and talked with her "parents." That sounded so odd to me. My biological daughter is critically ill, and my mother is talking to her parents. Mother says they are nice people and are just as hurt and shocked as I am about the turn of events. I guess I've been too caught up in my own feelings, and what this has done to me and my family, to think about Sidney's parents, and what they must be going through. Surely they must be hurting and wondering what their biological daughter is like.

The thought of someone else being Michaela's mother brings tears to my eyes. I feel sick all over. Dear God, how did something so horrible happen to Cole and me?

Mother taught me that out of every experience we endure, there is something valuable to be learned. After almost a week of being here, I could think of nothing valuable about having my child switched with someone else's at birth. It just didn't make any sense. My sister Karen's husband, Fallon, an attorney, has already begun giving us legal advice. However, I have no interest in suing anyone, at least not now. I'm in too much pain.

I spoke with each of my children after we learned the truth. I fought to hold back tears during my conversation with Michaela. We haven't told any of them the news yet. We won't until the time is right, whenever that is. All they know is that Grandma and I are here in Cleveland taking care of some very important business. They know I'll be home as soon as possible.

It's very warm here in early August. Going outside doesn't interest me. I'm content to lie here in the hotel bed, staring at the walls. Mother, however, insists that I get up each morning and eat. Then we walk around the park. I always thought I was invincible. This ordeal has shown me that I'm not. I have to make a special effort to get out of bed each morning, to do simple things, like finish a meal.

Cole is coming back tomorrow; I'm anxious to see him. Mother has vowed not to leave my side until I can accept what has happened. I have no idea when or if I can ever accept this. I talk to Karen, my only sister, every day. She thinks I need psychiatric help. I agree. Mother and Cole don't think I need it.

They have faith that I will learn to accept this painful development on my own, in time. After all, it was no fault of mine, or was it? A part of me believes that I should have recognized my own baby, although Ms. Noland said the babies were mistakenly switched before I ever held Michaela. I wonder if she's telling me the truth, or just trying to ease my pain, or any sense of guilt I may have about not recognizing my own baby.

I remember telling my family and friends that Michaela was so beautiful when she was born. When they asked who she looked like, my response was, "Oh, she has her very own, unique look." That's certainly not so unusual because infants rarely look like either the mother or father. Still, I believe there was something I could and should have done before leaving the hospital 10 years ago, but didn't.

After our walk around the park today, I came back to the hotel and took a nap. My doctor in Nashville prescribed some medication to help me relax; I desperately needed it. Cole wanted me to cut back on the dosage, but I don't think I can get through a day without it. This worries him. I know he has a lot to deal with right now, but I need my medication. While I was asleep, Mother went back to visit Sidney. This has to be very painful for her, but she still wants to get to know her "granddaughter." Although Sidney is not able to speak right now, Mother has talked to her parents, and learned some things about Sidney Williams.

She is one of six children, "born" to Ralph and Cynthia Williams. The Williamses have four sons and two daughters. Sidney is the fifth of their children. Ralph and Cynthia were born and raised in Cleveland. Their children range in age from 19 to 7. Ralph works for a large automobile manufacturer here, and Cynthia is a school teacher.

Their oldest son attends Ohio State University, on a football scholarship. The other children are at home. Mother said they appear to be good, hard-working people, who love and care about each of their children. They want to meet Cole and me.

I know that is the decent thing to do, but, oh, so difficult. The thought of meeting "my child's parents" was very frightening. I couldn't help but wonder if they had loved and nourished "my child" as Cole and I had loved and nourished "their child." Is Sidney a loving and sweet girl like Michaela? What are her likes and dislikes? What morals and values have Ralph and Cynthia instilled in her? The questions were running through my head. I knew I had to stop them or I'd drive myself crazy! That was easier said than done.

Ironically, Cole and I had decided to leave Cleveland when Michaela was 6 months old, because he had a great job offer in Nashville. Plus, we wanted to raise our children in a smaller, less congested city, with good educational and cultural opportunities. Now, we learn that our "daughter" was born and raised here by people we don't know anything about.

Now, I had to find the strength to meet these people, and actually spend time with them. Since Sidney is my flesh and blood, I had a right to know what type of people raised her.

Cole's flight arrived shortly after noon. I was thrilled to see him. He looked thinner. He would never admit that he was troubled. I have had to tell him that it is okay to cry on my shoulder, just as I have cried on his. This had to be as difficult for him as it was for me.

I also hadn't seen Matthew, Michaela and McAlister in three days, and I was anxious to hear about each of them. School would be starting in a week. I would have to pull myself together so I could get home to get them ready. Matthew is a freshman this year; Michaela is in the sixth grade. They couldn't be happier about returning to school. They are both excellent students. I made a conscious effort to teach my children something new each day when they were younger.

Cole gave me an update of what was happening at home. "When Mom arrived, I told Mrs. Davenport she didn't have to stay with the kids. Mom and I took Matthew and Michaela shopping for school clothes. You wouldn't believe some of the outfits they chose," he said, smiling as if everything was okay. "Michaela said her Grandma has good taste, and she wants to go shopping with her more often. She chose a red skirt that you'd probably choke over, but Mom liked it, so I bought it."

"I hope you voiced your opinion, and didn't just buy everything they asked for. You know their school has a strict dress code. I'm afraid to look in their closets when I get home," I said.

"Speaking of home, Sweetheart, the kids really miss you, and McAlister has been pretty quiet since you left. You know when he's quiet, something isn't right. Maybe it's time for you to go home." Cole was telling me in a nice way that it was time for both of us to go home. He was absolutely right. I had responsibilities, so I had to get myself together.

"I'm going home with you, Honey, but I want us to spend some time with Sidney and her family before we leave. Mother has met her parents. I know it's time for us to do likewise." The words came out before I could process them.

"I think you're absolutely right. Do you want to go over now, or wait until tomorrow?" Cole asked.

"I want to wait until tomorrow morning. You just got in, and I need to spend some time with you. Mother and I have been walking daily and talking endlessly. I'm starting to feel better, but I can't leave here without meeting Ralph and Cynthia Williams." I proceeded to tell Cole everything Mother had told me about the Williams family. He listened intently. I could tell from his expression that he was just as interested in knowing more about these people as I was.

Cole, Mother and I went out for dinner to a soul food restaurant that had recently opened on Shaker Square. One of Cole's clients had told him about the food. We decided to try it. I ordered a fish sandwich, but Mother and Cole wanted to try the chicken and pancakes. This was certainly a treat. Cole got to chat with the owner, Larry Thompson.

Mr. Thompson grew up in Cleveland, went away to school, and returned with an MBA, determined to start his own business. His determination paid off in a big way. The restaurant was packed. He was doing well.

After dinner, we drove around the city to show Mother some of the new attractions in Cleveland. She had visited Cleveland often when I was a student at Case Western Reserve University, but she was thrilled when we decided to move to Nashville. It was much closer to Charleston, where I was born and raised. That's also where most of my family still lived. Karen, and my two brothers, Ronald and Sandy, decided to make Charleston their home after they married and started families. Mother was heartbroken when Cole didn't find a job there that paid enough. She had wanted all of her children living near her and each other. Nevertheless, she was happy that we were in Nashville. She had gone to Tennessee State, which is in Nashville, and really enjoyed living there.

I am proud to say I have the best mother in the world. I don't think I could've gotten through the past three days without her. She planned to go with Cole and me to meet Ralph and Cynthia Williams.

Needless to say, I didn't sleep much that night. I was up early the next morning, feeling anxious. I had absolutely no appetite for breakfast. A part of me was anxious to meet the Williamses, however, the other part resented the very idea of having to meet and make conversation with these people. I felt as if they had stolen my child from me. Then it dawned on me that maybe I had stolen their child from them.

I knew I would not begin the healing process until I got to know the Williamses. Mother, Cole and I walked to the hospital that morning, and waited in the family visiting room in the unit where Sidney was located. It was close to 9:30. I became more anxious as I waited. Early on, Mr. Jacobs and Ms. Noland had offered to set up a meeting between Cole and me and the Williamses, to help ease any stress or tension between two heartbroken families. I declined their offer and told them we would work it out.

I was very angry at that time, and didn't want Willow Memorial Hospital arranging or setting up anything for my husband and me. I felt like they had done enough harm. However, I was much calmer now. Maybe the set-up wasn't such a bad idea after all. Well, we were here now, and I expected the Williamses to walk in at any moment. Cole and Mother were each holding one of my hands; that was comforting.

What on earth will I say to these strangers? I could feel my heart pounding. Cole left the waiting area to see if Ralph and Cynthia were in Sidney's room. Mother pulled me close to her. I felt like a frightened child on the first day of school, who didn't want her mother to leave.

"Now, Celia, everything is going to work itself out, Honey. You are a strong, special person. God will see you and Cole through this. This is not the end of the world."

"It sure feels like it, Mother." I was determined not to break down again this morning. I had to make the most of this meeting, because tomorrow I was going home with my husband, to three children who needed me. God had always guided me through every ordeal in my life. Mother was right; He would also see me through this.

Cole returned and told us that Ralph and Cynthia Williams were in the room with Sidney. I slowly got up, and walked hand-in-hand with Mother to meet the people who had taken my child home from the hospital 10 years ago, and raised her as their own. As I entered the room, I noticed that a nurse was attending to Sidney. A woman, who I assumed was Cynthia Williams, was watching. Her husband was sitting in a chair next to the bed.

Cynthia Williams turned to look at me. My eyes filled with water. I fought hard to keep the tears back, but couldn't. This woman had Michaela's features! She was a very attractive woman, who appeared to be in her mid-40s. She was full-figured, and dressed in a casual black pantsuit that fit her well. Her hair was the color of Michaela's; it fell just above her shoulders. Her eyes were large, and filled with compassion. To my surprise, she reached for me.

We embraced tightly, because she, too, was crying. Mother came forward and rubbed my back. I guess Cynthia Williams was feeling just as hurt and confused about what had happened. She continued to cry, and didn't speak a word.

"I think I need to leave you alone," the nurse said, then slowly left the room. I turned my head to look down at Sidney. I knew instantly that Ralph and Cynthia Williams had taken "our" baby home. The nurse had uncovered her face. Anyone could clearly see that the little girl lying in the bed, with tubes everywhere, had Mother's round face, my keen nose, and Cole's pointed chin and curly hair.

Mother must have thought the same thing because she began weeping softly. Matthew, McAlister and Sidney looked almost identical to each other!

13. Sarah

SPENT MOST OF THE WINTER THINKING about New York City. I did not know anything about this place, and did not have the opportunity to learn about it.

Being in the presence of Mastah Wilmington, alone, was difficult. I remember the day in April 1845 when Mammy was sick and could not stop coughing. I had to do her house chores. Kate and Melissa were with their private tutor. Missus Wilmington was visiting some of her friends when I arrived at the big house on a sunny morning. I was washing dishes, when someone touched my shoulder. Frightened, I turned around. Mastah Wilmington was looking me straight in the eyes.

"I hope you're getting those dishes clean, just like Bertha does. How is she feeling?" he asked, with a look on his face I had never seen.

"Mammy cain't stop coughin. I hope she gonna git well. I wish I coulda stay wit her today," I answered, trying to avoid looking at him.

"You know, Sarah, you're doing a real good job around here. I see no reason why you can't do more house chores. Bertha is getting older, and could really use the help." He rubbed my shoulder. I felt very uncomfortable, again.

"Mastah, you right, Mammy do work real hard, but she luv you an yo famly, an she gonna always work hard, cause she is a good person." I prayed he would go away. The Bible taught us to do unto others as we would have them do unto us. But, Mammy had not been treated the way she treated other folks, I thought. I turned from him to pick up another plate. I could feel the tears welling in my eyes.

"You're fortunate, Sarah, to have a mother like Bertha. She can teach you to sew, cook and clean. He tilted my head to look at him. I felt sick to my stomach. I wanted to run from the big house, into Pappy's arms, but knew I would be punished by this awful man.

"My wife and I are pleased to have Joshua and Bertha on our plantation. And, thanks to them, we now have you, Sarah." He folded his arms across his chest.

I hated this man. So now they "had" me, as he so proudly spoke. He stood there looking me up and down. I was afraid, but continued to wash dishes. All I could think about was that, aside from being their slave, I had to stand here in his presence and feel ashamed. I was about 14, and quite tall for my age. I had long, thick hair, Mammy's big smile, and Pappy's large, bright eyes. My light brown skin glistened when moist. Several other slaves had said that I was pretty. Mastah Wilmington was making me feel ashamed because of the way he looked at, and, now, touched me.

"Sarah, I've been thinking. I want you to help your mother more. You can clean, wash and iron as well as she can. I think I'll use Bertha more for cooking and sewing." He moved toward me. He looked at me as if I was a woman, not a child. I clearly sensed the difference in his stare.

"Mastah Wilmington, is you happy bout goin to New Yok Cidy?" I asked, trying to get him to talk about something other than me.

"Yes, I am. We'll be leaving the first of June. You're coming along only to help with Kate and Melissa. My daughters will need to be coiffured during their stay in the city." God must have heard my prayers, because there was a knock at the back door. Someone was calling his name.

"I'll be right back." He walked away to answer the door. He looked disappointed about having to leave. I recognized the visitor as one of Mastah Wilmington's political friends. They walked from the back porch into the back yard, talking. I prayed the visitor would stay until Missus Wilmington returned. I was old enough to know what my mastah's intentions were.

When I was younger, I thought one of the boys I had seen from a nearby plantation was really handsome. I told Mammy about him. That was when she told me everything. I had asked her why some of our people, like him, looked almost white. She told me that some of them had white fathers. I had finally figured out what must have happened in order for this to be the case with him.

Mastah Wilmington never rubbed my shoulders when Mammy or Missus Wilmington was around. I felt strange, almost like I was going to get sick when he did. I wanted to run to our cabin and hold onto Mammy.

I left the big house and asked Mastah Wilmington if I could check on Mammy. He said "yes," but told me to hurry back to finish my work. When I got to the cabin, Mammy was sitting up in her bed. She said she felt better. Mammy suffered from asthma, so sometimes had difficulty breathing.

"How is my baby girl?" She gave me a big hug. As I hugged her, I started to cry. I had held these tears for more than an hour. Now nothing was going to stop me from letting them flow.

"Sarah, baby, whut is de matta?"

"Mammy, I wanna be wit you. I miss you. Dere ain't no one ova dere but Mastah Wilmington," I said, wiping my eyes. Mammy looked weak. I did not say any more, for fear I would upset her. She gave me a hug and kiss, then told me I had to get back because Missus Wilmington would expect the chores to be finished.

The plantation mistress's major responsibility was to care for sick slaves. Missus Wilmington made daily rounds to cabins if there were sick slaves on the plantation. She often complained about the trouble of dealing with slave illnesses, yet doctored them as best she could. This was one way she could see to the wellbeing of her husband's property interest.

More than ever, I wished my brother was here. I had only spent a few hours with him in Atlanta. I barely knew him. But, he was blood kin and I loved him. If only I could tell Tom about what Mastah Wilmington was trying to do to me. He would understand. He would not have any power to stop the mastah, but Tom would understand. Male slaves had to endure the sexual abuse of slave women, or face severe punishment from the mastah if they tried to help their women.

As I entered the big house through the back door, I heard voices. It sounded like the visitor was still there. I finished the washing and ironing, then set the table for dinner. Mammy was teaching me to cook, but I did not cook for the Wilmingtons yet. While Mammy was sick, Missus Wilmington had told Hattie, another slave, to do the cooking. I cooked meals for Pappy when Mammy had to work late at the big house. Pappy had said I was a good little cook.

I heard another voice; Missus Wilmington had returned. Thank God she is here, I thought.

"Sarah, have you finished your chores?" She pulled her shawl off and looked around the house.

"As soon as I sweep de flo I be done." I stared at the dress Missus Wilmington was wearing. It was made of pale green patterned silk, with two-flounce skirts worn over wide crinoline petticoats. The sleeves were full at the shoulders and gathered onto a cuff. The V-shaped bodice came to a point at the waist. The matching bonnet was decorated with embroidery. She had paid a lot of money for it in Atlanta. I heard her telling her cousin how much it cost, and how she just had to have it. I studied it, trying to see how it had been put together. I believed I could make it.

That evening when I got to our cabin, Mammy was feeling better, but still weak. I sat and talked with her. Mammy was looking better. I did not want to burden her with my troubles with Mastah Wilmington, so I talked about the dress Missus Wilmington was wearing.

"Mammy, de wais was tight but de skirt was big an full. De sleeves was long an gathered at de cuffs."

"Baby, I made a dress lak dat for Missus Wilmington. One day you go be ready to cut fabric den put it back togetha to make purdy dresses all by yoself."

Mammy had heard Missus Wilmington say to a friend that most plantation mistresses were very busy with the production of cloth, and the manufacturing of clothing, a demanding task. Some mistresses made most of their own clothing, with help from slaves. They also made clothing for slaves. Each slave required a winter and a summer set of clothing, and little else. However, Missus Wilmington did not enjoy sewing. She was not very good at it anyway. She thought Mammy was a gifted seamstress, and rarely ever helped her with this chore.

"Mammy, thank you for believin in me." I knew that some day I would be just as good a seamstress as Mammy. I had heard Missus Wilmington talk to her husband and daughters about making trips into town to buy clothing. That is how I first got the idea of making clothes and selling them as a free woman, not a slave. I believed this was possible, even for a slave girl like me. Also, for years I had heard Mastah Wilmington talk about business matters to his friends and house guests. This knowledge was priceless. I absorbed it all.

By Sunday, Mammy was feeling much better. We went to church as usual. Mastah Wilmington had built a chapel on his plantation many years ago. Most slaves worshiped in these churches, where they could be supervised.

We looked forward to Sundays. With passes, we got to visit other plantations. With permission from the mastah, Mammy sometimes invited family from nearby plantations to have suppa with us. She cooked pork loins, smoked ham, corn, sweet potatoes and beans. Food was rationed to the slaves by the mastah. I enjoyed getting together with family and other slaves on Sunday afternoons. After suppa, the children would play and dance, while the grown ups sang spirituals and told folk tales.

Family was very important to us. One Sunday, when families gathered at our cabin, Mammy found the strength to talk about Tom. Everyone had tears in their eyes, but she told them not to cry because her boy would make it through. She said that somehow she would see him again. She told them about his skills as a carpenter and bricklayer, and how proud she and Pappy were of him.

Then Mammy changed the subject to me, and told everybody that I would be traveling to New York City in June. I remember everyone laughing and calling me "travlin girl." Lord knows I wanted to be a "travlin girl." But, even more, I wanted to be free.

On this Sunday, we were eating, dancing and singing when the sound of somebody moaning broke up the laughter. It was Samuel, my cousin on Mammy's side of the family. We loved that boy because he was like a brother to me. When I had asked about him earlier, his Pappy had said that he was at home resting. Then, the truth came out. His Pappy said Samuel was in a lot of pain, because he had been mercilessly whipped. His back had deep cuts. It was covered with dried blood. There were blisters every where. I cried softly as I listened to him tell what had happened. He had come to the cabin anyway, but stayed outside. He leaned against a tree and told us why he had been whipped, and pulled up his shirt to show the proof.

"De massa queshoned me an beat me fer not tellin de truf bout som slaves who had ran way in de early monin." His body appeared to be almost limp.

"Boy, why is ya even out hure?" his mother asked, as she pulled his shirt down.

"Mammy, today is Sunday an I wonts to be wit my famly," he said, rubbing his head. Mammy came over and hugged him. I knew she was thinking about Tom. She helped him into our cabin. She then rubbed a potion made from pork fat and herbs on Samuel's back. Mammy did this over and over. I heard her tell him that he would feel better in two or three days.

After Mammy finished, Samuel, who was 18 or 19, and I took a short walk behind our cabin. This gave me a chance to talk to him.

"Samuel, why did yo mastah do dis to you?"

"Caus I ded not tell de truf bout som slaves dat ran way. I knew dey was planin to run, but I jes cud not tell on dem."

"But dats no reasin to tear yo back open," I said.

"I kin take it, Sarah, dont you worry. Ise a man now."

"But, Samuel, dis ain't bout bein a man. What yo masta done to you was cruel. Whut you gonna do?"

"Ain't much I kin do. He de massa." Several slaves thought like this. Like me, they wanted their freedom, but were afraid to talk about it. I was not the only one who wanted to escape the harsh, brutal life of being a slave.

"Did you know dat I go git to go to New Yok Cidy in June? Mastah Wilmington takin me long to help wit Kate an Melissa. He wan his daughters lookin purdy in New Yok Cidy. Mammy cain't go cause Missus Wilmington said she gotta stay hure." I tried to think of something pleasant to talk about, to get my mind off his wounds.

"My cuzzin gwine to a big place? I sho hope to git to see som of dis worl. I ain't neva lef Misippi."

Mammy came out to check Samuel's back. I joined some of the other young people my age. They were still singing and dancing around the cabin. They did not like what had happened to Samuel, but did not want to talk about it.

It hurt to see Samuel in such pain. He did not tell the truth because he was trying to protect other slaves. I knew we would be punished for not telling on others. I had heard Mastah Wilmington talk about it sometimes when Mammy and I were working in the big house. He had said some niggers needed to get some sense whipped into their heads.

Soon it was Monday morning. Mammy was strong enough to go back to the big house. It really did not matter how she felt. Missus Wilmington had told her that she had to return to the big house on Monday. I was cleaning Mastah and Missus Wilmington's bedroom when I noticed her dress thrown across a chair. As I was hanging it, I carefully studied how it was put together. If only I had enough fabric to try to make this dress. Of course, the few pieces of scraps that Mammy had would be put to good use. I finished the bedroom, and went to help Mammy with the washing and ironing. Missus Wilmington was telling her about a dance Kate and Melissa were invited to, and that Mammy had to make their dresses.

"Dat ain't no problem, Missus Wilmington, cause Sarah kin cut an stitch bout as good as I kin," she said, as she hugged me. Missus Wilmington carefully described to Mammy how she wanted the dresses to look. Mammy was smart enough to do the rest.

"This is a wonderful occasion. Kate and Melissa are so excited. Why, this will be their first formal dance. I want them to be the prettiest young ladies there. Tomorrow, I'm going to town to find the fabric," Missus Wilmington said. She looked happy as she spoke about her daughters.

"Bertha, I don't know what we'd do without you. And, now, Sarah can do all the things that you do. Your sewing continues to get better. I'm so glad you've taught Sarah to work as hard as you do. Sarah's cooking and sewing are improving. That's important to us because..."

Missus Wilmington continued to talk about what she needed us to do for her. I thought about my family. I thanked God every day that Mammy and Pappy were in good health. I loved them. We were a very close family. I knew of several families that had been torn apart by slaveholders. Although my brother was not with us, we loved him dearly, and he knew it.

Mammy and I had worked together everyday in the big house for as long as I could remember. Mastah Wilmington had other female slaves, but Mammy and I were the only two who worked in the house. This caused problems for us with the other women. They said we thought we were better because of this, but Mammy and I thought no such thing. Mammy said we were chosen to do house chores because of our skills, but some of the field slaves said it was because we had lighter skin.

The gossip bothered Mammy, but I did not care what the others said about us. I knew Mammy had great skills. Sometimes I wondered if Mastah Wilmington had intentionally planned to cause problems among his slaves, through this division of labor. I wished everybody could be in the house. But, if I had had my way, no one would be a slave. Negro men and women would be able to work for pay, and for white people only if they chose to work for them.

I had met slave women and men who had light or brown skin. Some even had facial features like those of white people. Mammy and Pappy had said that some Negroes could, and did, pass for white people.

Pappy had said we were proud people, with a rich heritage in Africa. But, that pride seemed to be slowly fading away. I had heard some of my friends teasing each other about having nappy hair and thick lips. I thought Pappy was the most handsome man I knew, even though he had darker skin and more African features than me or Mammy.

My parents would not let me forget my African heritage. Almost everyday I heard a story about Kenya and eastern Africa, and what life was like there. Even though my parents were born in Mississippi, they had learned a lot about their history from their parents, who were brought over as slaves. We often sang spirituals and talked about how life here was so different from what my grandparents had known in Kenya.

Mammy had never been whipped by a slaveholder, although I suspect that Pappy had. I had seen some marks on his back. When I asked him about the marks, he had said, "Som day I go tell you aw bout bein a Negro man slave. But fer now, my chile, I wan you to thank bout de good thangs in life. We dont wan you to hate nobody."

Knowing that our people had been forcibly taken from their African homelands, and shipped forcibly to a new land, was enough to make me hate all slaveholders. We were being treated like animals.

Maybe I was wrong, but I could find no reason to thank Mastah and Missus Wilmington. If my parents were free, they would have a good life because of their skills and intelligence. But, they would never have that life as slaves. Having lived on the Wilmington plantation since my birth, I saw white people enjoying and loving life. This was natural for them. I wanted the same for me and my family. I thought about this often. Nothing was more important than a human being being free, answering only to God, and maybe a paying employer. If I had my freedom, I would not trade it for anything in this world.

That night at suppa, Pappy talked about a slave who ran away from the fields, and how this had made Mastah Wilmington very angry. Pappy said the slave was a big money loss for Mastah Wilmington.

"He was worf a lot caus Mastah Wilmington paid a lot fer him. He was yung an stron an I know he got halfway cross de state, as fast as he was runnin," Pappy said, cutting into his fried pork. "We go miss him caus he cud rully plont an pick cotton."

I could not hide my joy, and shouted without thinking, "Run, run, run as fas you kin. I hope you neva git cort!" Mammy and Pappy looked at me without saying a word. I did not know this slave. All I could think about was that he could now live his life the way he wanted to, without any slave driver watching over him again.

"It kin be dangrous out dere fer some of dese slaves. Sometime it jes ain't whut dey thank it is," Pappy continued.

"But, Pappy, maybe he ran caus he believe he was born to be free." Although we were taught differently in church by white preachers, I still had a hard time believing that God created us to be servants for white people. There just had to be more in this life for us than working in cotton fields. I did not say anymore, just picked at my food.

"Sarah, finish yo suppa. Ain't no need for you to be gittin so upset. He ran an I hope he make it safe. But, yo Pappy is right. I hear deres a bunch of slaves gittin beat up an evan kulled tryin to git to de Norf," Mammy said calmly.

"Mammy, I wush I cud tell Tom bout goin to New Yok Cidy," I said, trying to calm down. "I wush I cud see my brotha agin. I so proud dat he is my brotha." Mammy and Pappy looked down. Talking about Tom made them sad. I said nothing else.

I must have been about 13 at the time. If I lived to be 100, I would never understand how my parents could not hate the Wilmingtons for what they had done to their only son. Yes, Mammy and Missus Wilmington had a somewhat special relationship, because Mammy grew up with her. Mammy had even wet-nursed Melissa, and Mammy had never been beaten. But, this could not possibly excuse the Wilmingtons for "hiring out" their only son. Perhaps Mammy and Pappy's faith in God had taught them not to hate. I, on the other hand, was not my parents. I did not think as they did.

It was now May 1845. Kate and Melissa were busy deciding what to take to New York City. They were planning to join their aunt in a lot of activities, so decided to take along some of their finest clothing. Pappy had overheard Mastah Wilmington tell his overseers that he needed to go to New York City to borrow money for his businesses, all of which were becoming more prosperous. He specifically wanted the money drawn from Northern banks to expand his interests to that region. We were going to stay with his sister, Katherine. She had married a young man from New York City a few years ago. They had met when he visited Mississippi with his father. His family was in the cotton manufacturing business.

Mastah Wilmington was taking me on this trip only to attend to Kate and Melissa's needs. They were very attractive girls, with light blue eyes and long, golden curly hair. I was good at coiffuring their hair and helping them dress. Mammy said Mastah Wilmington was bringing his daughters to introduce them to New York City society. It was important that they meet and marry men of wealth. Mastah Wilmington and his sister had both married well. He wanted nothing less for his daughters. This was the perfect opportunity for him to "present" his daughters. Their aunt would be proud to see how lovely her nieces had become.

After they married, Katherine's new husband wanted to return to his home in New York City. Mastah Wilmington was quite fond of his brother-in-law, Robert Baxter, even though he was a Northerner, because his family was wealthy. And, Mastah Baxter was kind to his younger sister. Mastah Wilmington had an older sister who lived somewhere in the South, but he didn't have any brothers.

Pappy was quite busy in the fields these days, preparing to harvest a rich crop of cotton. Mammy was working hard at making new window coverings for the big house. Missus Wilmington had decided to redecorate while Mastah Wilmington and her daughters were away. Missus Wilmington had told Mammy that she could have the scraps of fabric left from the window coverings. Mammy was always grateful for this.

Mammy found the time to make me two calico dresses for the trip. Someone had given Missus Wilmington discarded calico fabric. Missus Wilmington had given it to Mammy, because Kate and Melissa did not wear dresses made of calico. Mammy had to stay up late each night to finish my dresses. She wanted me to look nice while I was away. Pappy and I were very special to her. She had taught me that nothing was more important than family.

When she left the big house each day, Mammy was always tired, yet never failed to let Pappy and me know how much she loved us. She always had something kind and pleasant to say to us. I knew there had to be a God, from watching my mother and seeing her courage and faith. She taught me to believe that anything is possible. There was no telling what she could have achieved if she had had her freedom.

Mastah Wilmington had hired another overseer to help run the plantation, and keep the slaves in line. Pappy had heard him say that he would have to take more business trips as time went on because of his cotton and banking businesses. He must have trusted his overseers to supervise the plantation in his absence.

Some nights while I was in bed I wondered what was ahead for Negroes in the South. Would things get better or worse for us? I especially wondered about female slaves. Mammy had said that she could never run away from the plantation and leave her family. She knew nothing about being free, or the North. She had said she was too old now to find out. I did not agree with her. She certainly was not old. But, I respected her; I would never have argued with her.

I often wondered how free Negroes lived. Were they comfortable in nice homes? Were they happy? Could they read and write? Did they get to go to different places? How did they earn money? What kind of food did they eat? Did they live in big houses or small cabins? What skills did they have? What kind of clothes did they wear? So many questions ran through my young mind. Maybe one day I would get answers.

There was so much I wanted to do, but could not, because I was not free. I prayed often, and believed that one day all slaves would be free. And, with freedom, we could make choices. I knew that African women were strong, and would always be strong. Mammy and Grandma had told me about their ancestors, how they had always overcome obstacles or hardships. Grandma had said African women were all connected by a strong bloodline and sense of pride. She had said there was no telling what we could do if we did not have the chains.

The day before we left for New York City, I felt a deep sadness. I had never been away from Mammy. We worked together everyday. It was really difficult for me to leave. But my parents were excited for me. When Mammy finished packing my luggage, we talked, hugged and cried.

"I luv you, Baby. Mastah Wilmington will look afta you. You be carful, an dont git outta dere sight." Mammy stroked my head. Pappy told me he loved me. He said he was proud of me because I was a good girl and had learned so much. He was proud and thankful that I could cook and sew almost as well as Mammy.

Finally, Mammy said, "Joshua, we actin lak dis chile ain't comin back. De time will pass quick, an our baby will be home." We laughed and talked a while more, then went to bed. Mastah Wilmington planned to leave early in the morning.

It was warm and sunny on the morning of June 18, 1845. I had no more tears to cry, because they were all on my quilt. I kissed my parents again and again. Mastah Wilmington, Kate, Melissa and I left early for New York City. We rode through Holly Springs in the carriage to Memphis, where we would take the train to Philadelphia, then go on to New York City. I stared at the cotton fields as we began our long journey. Slave men, women and children were working in them. The sight filled me with deep sadness.

14. Celia

AS I WALKED THROUGH THE FRONT DOOR of our home that Wednesday evening, I felt as if I had been away for months, instead of a few days. McAlister jumped into my arms and gave me the biggest hug. He had two new stuffed animals in his arms that I'm sure his grandparents had bought for him. He had plenty of stories to tell about each one. It was refreshing to sit in the family room and listen to my baby, who didn't have a care in the world.

Listening to him, I was able to totally tune out all the madness I'd been forced to deal with since last Thursday. It was 5:30. Matthew was probably in his room doing homework. Michaela was probably on the telephone. She usually finished her homework early. They apparently had not heard us come in. That was good; the sight of Michaela would be too much for me to handle.

I listened to my baby son chat about his adventures while I was away. Cole, Mother and Cole's parents were in the living room talking. I could tell from the painful expressions on their faces that they were discussing Sidney, and all that we'd learned about our "new" daughter and her family. Listening to McAlister was an escape; I didn't want his stories to end.

I heard steps, and turned to find Matthew standing in the doorway of the family room. Cole and I had decided that today was not the time to tell Matthew what we'd discovered. How would he react to the news that Michaela was not his biological sister? How would Michaela cope with the knowledge that we were not her biological family? A part of me wanted to keep this a secret, forever, to spare my children the pain that Cole and I were feeling. But, I knew in my heart that they had to be told the truth. The question was when. Was there a best time to discuss such a matter?

Cole wanted to tell both Matthew and Michaela tomorrow, after school. However, I asked him to wait a few days. This was for my benefit, not theirs. Matthew came over and gave me a hug. My teenage son wasn't too grown to show affection to his mother, and I wasn't too old to enjoy it.

"So, when did you guys get back? I didn't hear you come in."

"We just got in, Sweetheart. How are you, and what have you been up to?"

"I'm great, Mom. I was waiting for you to get back to tell you the good news. Where's Dad? He needs to hear this, too." Matthew's eyes were filled with excitement. I was anxious to know what had made my son so happy.

"Hey, Dad, I've got some good news for you guys." Cole and his parents came into the family room and gathered around to hear what Matthew had to say. The Bentley grandparents loved their only three grandchildren dearly. I knew how they must be feeling right now, yet they managed to smile warmly as Matthew began talking.

"Well, as you all know, I've been playing tennis since grade school. Now, I'm proud to announce that I made the tennis team today. And, we have our first match on Friday, so I expect to see each of you there. That's all for now." My son was wearing the biggest smile. There was no way I was going to spoil this moment for him today.

"Son, I knew you could do it!" Cole said, looking as excited and thrilled as Matthew. "What time are you playing? I'll be right there!"

"The match starts at noon. We'll be playing at St. Joseph's Academy."

"I'll be there. Maybe you and I can hit some balls before Friday, just to get in some extra practice." Cole was the best father in the world. His kids loved him dearly. He had played tennis most of his life, and couldn't wait to take Matthew and Michaela with him onto the courts.

Matthew, like his father, was focused, and took the game seriously, as he did his schoolwork, and everything else that captured his attention. Michaela also enjoyed tennis. She often talked about playing professionally. Cole and I instilled in our children the belief that they could accomplish any goal, if they stayed focused and worked hard. That's what we believe and practice. I couldn't help but wonder what Sidney's "parents" had instilled in her.

"What's all the noise about?" Michaela asked, as she bounced down the stairs. The very sight of her brought tears to my eyes. I turned to walk away, but Cole hugged me. I knew that meant for me to stay, to talk to my child.

"Your brother just announced that he made the tennis team. We're all excited about this great news," Cole said. "I knew all of those tennis lessons weren't in vain. And, Sweetheart, one day you, too, will make the team."

"I sure will. Even Matthew has to admit that I'm a good tennis player, don't you Matthew?"

"I think I said something more like, 'You've got potential, kid, but you definitely need to keep practicing'." Matthew loved to tease his sister. The more he teased her, the more she tried to get his approval. Matthew loved playing the big brother role with both Michaela and McAlister. However, although he enjoyed teasing his sister, he was quick to come to her defense at school.

As I listened to them bicker with each other, I wondered how Matthew would react to the news that his beloved Michaela was not his biological sister. Would he still tease her, or would he distance himself from her? The thought of them not horsing around with each other morning and night brought tears to my eyes.

"Mom, I missed you." Michaela gave me a hug. I tried hard to keep from breaking down. This was my daughter, biological, or not. No blood test or DNA could ever change that. I wanted to hold onto her, and never let go, but she had a lot to talk about.

"You must have had some pretty important business to take care of in Cleveland. You didn't call home a hundred times like you usually do when you're away. I didn't hear you come in, because I was on the phone with Courtney. Can you believe that she had the nerve to go to the mall today, and buy the very same skirt that I have? I wore my skirt on Friday. I saw her staring at it most of the day. Now she tells me that she was planning to buy it all along.

"And, Mom, she's going to wear it to school tomorrow, right after I wore mine on Friday! I don't like her anymore. I told her so, because she's nothing but a copy cat." My daughter continued to talk about Courtney and her week in school, even though I wasn't listening.

When and how was I going to tell her the truth? At this moment, I couldn't even imagine getting the words out of my mouth. I'd loved and nurtured this child from the moment they brought her to me in the hospital. Now, I had to find the words, the courage, to tell her that her "natural parents" are Ralph and Cynthia Williams. What would she think of Cole and me? Would she run away, have an emotional breakdown, or demand to leave us and go to Cleveland to be with her "real family?" She noticed the tears in my eyes. I wasn't able to keep them back any longer.

"Mom, what's wrong? Why are you crying?" she asked. Cole answered for me.

"Sweetheart, your mother has had a long week. She isn't feeling well. I think she needs to get some rest. In the mean time, I want you guys to get ready for dinner. Michaela, why don't you help your grandmother in the kitchen." Michaela gave me a puzzled look, but did as her father asked. Mother held my hand and guided me to our bedroom.

"Mother, what am I going to say to my daughter? Michaela is my daughter. Nothing can ever change that! I feel as if my world is starting to crumble, right before my eyes, and there isn't a thing I can do about it. What did I do to deserve this?" I was sobbing now. Mother told me to cry to get it all out. The problem was, I couldn't get it all out, ever. I wanted to sleep, and forget it all.

I asked Mother to get me something to help me relax. She brought me a warm cup of milk. Mother never believed in taking medication, because she believed all medication was addictive. She sat in the chair next to my bed and watched me slowly sip the milk. She then started talking about how much she enjoyed the performance by the Charleston Symphony two weeks ago.

I was invited to join the Nashville Symphony a year ago, which was one of the proudest moments of my life. I had played the violin and cello since I was a little girl. The instruments and music had been a source of relaxation for me. Mother knew of my love of symphony music. Just listening to her talk about the performance calmed me down. I knew three members of the Charleston Symphony, and visited them whenever I went home. We would talk for hours about the music we enjoyed, conductors and upcoming performances.

Mother had a gift for putting people at ease, especially her children. Before long, I was nodding. In addition to listening to Mother's soothing voice, I was tired. I was also stressed to the max, so falling asleep quickly was inevitable.

I didn't wake up until after 10:15 that night. I felt confused and disoriented, but went to check on my children. McAlister was tucked in, dressed in his favorite pajamas and sleeping like an angel. Matthew was still doing homework. He was an excellent student, but was usually late doing his homework. However, Michaela was adamant about finishing hers early.

"How's it going, Sweetheart? Do you have a lot to do?"

"Hi, Mom, I thought you were in bed for the night." Matthew responded. "You looked out of it when I went to your room to say goodnight. I'm almost finished, but Mr. Taylor got carried away when he started assigning math homework. He didn't know when to stop. This guy doesn't think that students have a life outside of school. He has no mercy on us when it comes to doing homework. I sure hope he leaves next year. That's the word around campus."

"Well, he gives a lot of homework, but you must admit, he is one of the best math teachers at the school. Most of his students go on to do very well in their junior and senior years. They usually go on to college. One day you're going to come back and thank him for all the nights you had to solve math problems."

"I hate to disagree with you, Mom, but I can't imagine thanking Mr. Taylor for anything." Matthew continued working his math problems. I kissed his forehead and said goodnight. I then headed to Michaela's room. I didn't hear her on the phone, so assumed she was asleep. Instead, she was lying in bed reading.

"Mom, I thought you were finished for the night. You were fast asleep when I went to your room an hour ago. Are you feeling better? Why were you crying earlier?" Her questions brought the tears back. I took a deep breath, and tried to compose myself.

"Sweetheart, I love my children more than anything in this world. Just the thought of losing one of you is very, very painful. I had some very important matters to attend to in Cleveland last week. I don't know how to best deal with some information we received."

I knew Cole wanted to be present when I broke this difficult news to our daughter, but I felt I had to try to start talking about what was wrong with me. I wanted to explain why I was crying so much. Michaela was looking directly at me, waiting for answers. She was mature for her age. I'd always been honest and direct with my children, so I had to talk frankly with her.

"Michaela, as you know, you were born at Willow Memorial Hospital in Cleveland on December 10, 1977." I began slowly, not sure exactly how to approach this painful subject.

"Yes, Mom, I haven't forgotten my birthday, or where I was born. I'm not that old, yet!" This child was full of personality. She had the ability to make anyone laugh. I'd always thought she inherited that quality from my father, but, I guess not. I continued.

"I got a call last week from Ms. Mary Noland, the Director of Nursing at Willow Memorial Hospital. She said she needed to talk to your father and me, that it was very important. Well, that's why we left so quickly. We met with Ms. Noland and Mr. Cary Jacobs the next morning. They informed us that the hospital was under construction during the time you were born. They said the nurses made some terrible mistakes." I could feel my heart pounding!

"First of all, Mom, who is Mr. Jacobs, and what in the world does all of this have to do with me? And, Mom, I don't mean to be rude, but I have a big English test in the morning with 'The Witch.' I really need to get some rest, so if this is going to take a long time, why don't we meet for lunch or dinner. Then we can really talk without being interrupted. You know, that's what you and Dad do sometimes when the two of you really need to talk." This statement made me laugh and I felt more relaxed.

"Sweetheart, Mr. Jacobs is the Hospital Administrator, although he wasn't there when you were born. Ms. Noland was." Michaela was starting to yawn. Either I was boring her, or she was sleepy. I asked her if she wanted me to wait until a better time to talk.

"Sorry, Mom, but I'm really tired," she said, sounding exhausted. "Some other time, please." I respected her request, but didn't leave her bedside. I stroked her head until she fell asleep. She looked so peaceful, almost angelic as she slept. Real or not, I could see some of my features in this child.

As I sat staring at Michaela, I suddenly wondered how Sidney was doing. The nurse had uncovered her face before we left. I assumed she was getting better, although I didn't ask. A part of me wanted to go back to

Cleveland, snatch my child from that hospital, and bring her here to a hospital close to her "real" parents. I wanted both Michaela and Sidney here with us, because Cole and I cherished our children. But, that was a selfish thought.

I decided to call Cynthia Williams the next day to check on Sidney. Then it dawned on me that Cynthia was probably concerned about Michaela. Would she want Michaela with her in Cleveland? Would Michaela want to go? I kissed her cheek, and hugged her when I thought about this possibility. Would she want to leave Cole and me to join her biological family in Cleveland? There was a knock at the door; Cole entered.

"How are you? What are you doing?"

"Just sitting here, staring at a child I have loved and nourished from the moment I set eyes on her." We headed toward our bedroom.

"Honey, you know we have to sit her down and tell her the truth. The sooner the better. The longer we put this off, the more difficult it will be to tell her about all that happened."

"I know you're right. Actually, I started to tell her tonight, but she was so sleepy. She asked me to continue the story tomorrow. I think the preliminary details were much too boring for a 10-year-old."

"I'm so proud of you. However, I want to be with you when you break the news to Michaela. She's going to need all the love and support we can give her."

"What do your parents think about all of this?" I asked.

"They're shocked, of course, but you know my parents. They're tough; they don't fall easily. Actually, they would like to stay around to help us get through this. I told them that would be okay. I hope you don't mind."

"I don't mind, Cole. But, let me add that I'm not going to be the most pleasant person to be around over the next few days. I'm certainly not up to entertaining anyone."

"My parents aren't expecting to be entertained. They just want to help." I didn't mean to hurt Cole's feelings, but the truth was that I had my mother here. She, Cole and my children were the only people I needed during this difficult time in our lives. I knew his parents meant well. They loved Michaela just as much as Mother did. I was probably being selfish to not want them around. But, I needed time to deal with all of this, with those closest to me. The truth was that I hadn't fully accepted the fact that Michaela was not our biological daughter. My brain hadn't fully processed how this all came about. I didn't know if it ever would.

"Sweetheart, I want you and me to sit down with Michaela tomorrow, after school, and tell her the truth. As much as this hurts all of us, she has to know. The sooner we tell her, the better we'll feel. Once we're feeling

better, we'll be stronger, better able to help our daughter get through this."
I knew that what my husband was saying was the truth. It was the best
course to take. Cole, his parents and Mother stayed up talking. I was
exhausted from all of this, so I took a hot shower and went to bed. I opened
a book that I'd been reading, but fell asleep pretty quickly.

I woke up around 12:30 a.m. Cole had not come to bed yet. I got up to
check on him. They were all still talking. I still didn't feel like joining the
conversation, but sat with them in the family room and listened to some of
what was being said about what had happened. Cole was saying that he had
hired an attorney to look into all of this, to determine how we should
proceed. He hired the attorney after he left Cleveland temporarily to return
to work. Fallon, my sister's husband, and an attorney, also was advising us.

His father asked him if Mr. Jacobs was absolutely sure that Michaela
was not our biological daughter. Cole assured him that the information was
accurate. He explained how David Turner, a well respected attorney in
Cleveland, had already gone through all of Michaela's medical records, and
spoken with several doctors and hospital staff. Everything appeared to be
as Ms. Noland and Mr. Jacobs had explained. This news saddened me
because I'd been praying and hoping that this was all a big mistake.
Unfortunately, it wasn't.

Cole also told them that he and I planned to sit down with Michaela
after she got home from school later that day to tell her the truth. Mother
and his parents agreed that this was the right thing to do. His parents added
that they wanted to get to Cleveland as soon as possible to meet their "new"
granddaughter. Cole explained to them that Sidney was very ill, so this was
not the best time.

Thank God he told them to hold off. They continued to talk. I went
back to bed. This time I slept until McAlister came into our bedroom later
that morning and jumped onto the bed. He had a book with him that
Grandma Katie had given him. He wanted me to read to him. I sat up in
bed to read to my baby son. His excitement over his new book brought a
measure of peace to me. Then it was time to get up and start a new day, a
day that would change Michaela's life forever. Mother was in the kitchen
preparing breakfast for everyone. She told me to sit and enjoy it with
everyone else. I did just that.

"Well, you both look bright and very much prepared for your tests
today," I said to Matthew and Michaela, who were already enjoying a
breakfast of pancakes, sausage and milk.

"Some of those math problems were tough, Mom, and Mr. Taylor is
known to pull a few surprises on us. But, I'm prepared to do my best."

"Your best is all that we want from you. I love you and know you'll
do fine."

"I'll be home late, Mom, because we have tennis practice after school," Matthew said. "I'll try to get a ride home. I've got to run because Kevin is pulling up. Love you." He kissed me on the cheek, then dashed out the door. I watched him get into the car with Kevin and his mother. Jennifer Scott and I took turns taking our sons to school. I actually missed not taking him everyday, because that was special time we spent together. I had cherished it.

"And what about you, Sweetheart, are you ready for your English test?" Mother asked, as she refilled Michaela's glass of milk.

"Yes, Grandma, I studied hard. But don't you think it's unfair to have tests twice a week? None of my other teachers give tests that often."

"Now, Michaela, teachers are free to test their students whenever they want. Miss Redden is trying to prepare you for life."

"How is giving a difficult English test twice a week preparing me for life, Grandma?"

"Because in the real world there are challenges and tests that we must deal with daily, like it or not. Life isn't a well-written play that we get to rehearse and practice until we get it right. We can't always follow a schedule, or do what we want to do, Honey."

"Grandma, that's pretty deep for so early in the morning. We can talk about this some other time. Mom, who's taking me to school, you or Dad?"

"I'm taking you, Sweetheart. I'll be ready in a minute, just let me get my purse," I said. Actually, Cole had planned to take her. But, I thought this would give me a few special moments with my child before we broke the news to her after school. A part of me wanted to take my daughter and run away with her, so I could protect her from this devastating news. I wanted to protect her from a world that could be so cold and cruel at times. I wanted to protect each of my children from ever getting hurt or experiencing disappointment. But, I knew I couldn't. Even if I could, what kind of people would they become if they didn't experience adversity?

Michaela was pretty worked up about her English test this morning. I was careful not to say anything that might upset her even more. I had always made a practice of making my children feel like they were the most important people in the world. If they were down, I had no problem finding something special to say that would lift their spirits. Helping my children build a healthy outlook on life, and a sense of self-esteem, had always been a priority for me. I worked at this daily.

"You look absolutely lovely in that outfit, Sweetheart. You'd better be glad I can't wear your clothes. If I could, you'd be missing some items from your closet," I said, jokingly.

"Sure, Mom, I can just see you in this outfit. Mom, after my piano lessons, can we go shopping today? I need a white dress for the induction ceremony in two weeks." We had recently been notified that our daughter was to be inducted into the Beta Club. This was a club for high achievers. We were very proud of her.

"Why, of course we can. By the way, last night I started to tell you about why I spent a few days in Cleveland. You were almost asleep, so I would like to finish my conversation with you later today."

"Okay. I just hope this isn't going to be a long story. Love you, Mom. See you after school." Michaela jumped out of the car and ran to join two of her friends. I wondered if this would be the last time I'd see my child so happy and full of life. Somehow I had to get myself together enough to tell my daughter the truth about her "parents."

I went home and helped Mother clear the kitchen. Then I got McAlister dressed. Cole's parents were taking him out for the morning. With the children at school, I had too much time to sit and think. I had to keep busy and my mind occupied to ease the pain, so I decided this was a good time to go to the attic and clean out Dad's old trunk. We found it after he died five years ago. I loved antiques and this was truly a treasure. I had planned to sort through the items, then put the trunk in the study to store books. However, with raising three children, and my other responsibilities, I had never found the time to even begin this project. Now was certainly a great time to get started.

I began digging through the old trunk, and found worn quilts and dresses, some dishes and a very old Bible. Inside the Bible was a stack of papers. I began reading through the papers, to see if they were important enough to save. Soon, I realized that this appeared to be a journal, or the story of someone's life. Her name was Sarah Johnson. I didn't know of any Johnsons in our family. I continued to read. It was a most interesting story. I didn't want to put the papers down, but the phone was ringing. It was Ms. Noland.

"Hello, Mrs. Bentley, how are you today?"

"I'm fine, thank you." My heart began racing. Just the sound of this woman's voice made me anxious. What on earth was she calling to tell me now?

"I'm calling to inform you and your husband that Sidney's condition has gotten worse. You may want to get here as soon as you can." I took the Bible and papers with me, and left the attic.

15. Sarah

On THE MORNING OF JUNE 18, 1845 we left Holly Springs for New York City. We traveled to Memphis in a carriage, then on to Philadelphia by train. Mastah Wilmington referred to the train as a "sleeping car." The coach, section of the back of the train, had three tiers of bunks, with pillows and mattresses. There was a front section for sitting. It was not very large inside. Each side of the coach had two small windows. Mastah Wilmington, Kate and Melissa sat near the front of the train. I sat in the back, near the coach. I sewed, practicing different stitches that Mammy had taught me. Mastah Wilmington talked to an older man.

The train ride was long. Kate and Melissa complained about not being able to sleep comfortably. Although I missed Mammy and Pappy already, it was a blessing for a young slave girl to have the opportunity to get away from the plantation.

I could not wait to see New York City. I wondered if all of our people in the North were free, and if white people there were kind or cruel to us. Did they have any respect for us? Perhaps I would get some answers during my short visit to the city.

Some slaves on the Wilmington plantation believed that Negroes in the North could read and write. I wondered if that was true. My reading and writing skills were limited, but I knew I was special. Grandma and my parents had taught me to believe in myself. Mammy had taught me to have faith in God, and to be patient. And, she had taught me to sew. This was a great way to pass the time on the train.

Mammy had packed dried meat and bread for us to eat. Mastah Wilmington passed some to me from time to time using workers on the train. Kate and Melissa ate and enjoyed the company of other young people on the train. They also brought books to read.

When we finally reached Philadelphia, a young male and female boarded the coach, with two adults who appeared to be their parents. Kate and Melissa soon began chatting with the young people. I heard them say they were headed to Boston. I would have loved to have had someone my age to talk to on the trip. But, it did not really matter because I had my sewing to keep me busy.

When they were ready to go to bed, I helped Kate and Melissa change their clothes and get settled. After I finished with them, Mastah

Wilmington showed me where I would spend the night. It was a small storage area near the back of the train.

The area was cluttered with boxes, but I did not care. I just wanted to get some rest. There was another Negro lady in the storage room. She was resting on a bed that was simply a quilt thrown over two chairs in the room. She appeared to be around Mammy's age. She said she was traveling with her mistus. She told me to call her Missus Luella. She lived on a large farm owned by her mistus in New Orleans. She said they were traveling to Richmond, where her mistus had some family business to resolve.

Missus Luella went on to say that, if she was a younger woman, she would run away rather than spend a lifetime in slavery. Her husband had died several years ago from pneumonia. Her three children were grown, but not free. She talked about an "underground railroad" that had helped hundreds of slaves escape to freedom. She said she could neither read nor write. She also gave me the names of two Negroes who lived in New York City. According to Missus Luella, these people had helped slaves in many ways.

"My dear chile," she said, "you is so yung and curius. I bleev thangs is gonna be betta fer you dan dey was fer me." She wiped her eyes with a piece of cloth. I showed her some of my stitching. She said people in the North paid well for a skilled seamstress. She asked about my family. I told her all about Mammy, Pappy and Tom, and about life as a slave in Holly Springs. I told her that my brother had been "hired out" to a slaveholder in Georgia, but had not returned to us.

She said her heart had been broken many times, but did not say how. I did not ask. She shared stories with me about her ancestors in East Africa. She discussed many of the traditions she wanted her children to learn, and never forget. What hurt her most was that many slaves did not know enough about the traditions and culture of their homeland. She was afraid that future generations would completely forget about Africa. She told me to never forget who I was, or where I came from, meaning Africa. I could tell Missus Luella was tired. She and I talked a long time. We then fell asleep.

The next morning Missus Luella left the storage room early to help her mistus pack to continue on to Richmond. I hugged her and asked her to pray for me. She said she would. I was already dressed when Mastah Wilmington came to get me, to help Kate and Melissa get dressed. The Wilmingtons ate breakfast with other people in another part of the train. I ate, then returned to my sewing.

One of Mammy's friends had recently taught me to make fancy stitches. This long trip gave me the time I needed to practice them. Mastah Wilmington, Kate and Melissa appeared to be enjoying talking to different people. I enjoyed my sewing.

After several hours on the train, we finally reached New York City. I had no idea how long we had been traveling. However, I remembered stopping in Philadelphia at some point.

Mastah Wilmington's sister, Missus Baxter, and her husband met us at a train station. She hugged her brother, kissed Kate and Melissa and said "hello" to me. Mastah Baxter then put Kate and Melissa's luggage into their horse-drawn carriage. Mastah Wilmington and I carried our own.

As we rode to Missus Baxter's house, I paid little attention to what any of them were saying. I was too busy looking at all the people. This was more exciting than Atlanta. I saw some Negroes, but many more whites. There were shops with people walking in and out. This was such a change from Holly Springs. Negroes were walking without white people by their sides. I could hardly believe what I was seeing!

We soon arrived at the Baxter home in a section of the city called Manhattan. Their home was not nearly as large as the Wilmington plantation. The exterior of the house was narrow; the house had two stories. There were other houses very close to it on both sides. They did not have the land and space that the Wilmingtons enjoyed in the South. We entered through the front door into the living room. Several works of art covered the walls. The windows in the room were large, which provided a great view of the shops and people on the streets below.

Kate and Melissa would share an upstairs bedroom. After I helped them get settled, Missus Baxter showed me where I would be staying. It was a small room next to the dining room on the first floor in the back of the house. A cot, wooden table and chair were the only furniture in the room. I was thrilled, but did not let her see my excitement about having a place to rest after such a long trip. I quickly unpacked my bag, and asked Missus Baxter what she needed me to do. Kate and Melissa said some of their clothing needed to be ironed, so I got busy with that. Missus Baxter showed me where to do the ironing and washing. These chores would be done in another small room next to the room I would be staying in. They all went outside to sit in lawn chairs in the back. I could hear, through an open window in the kitchen, Missus Baxter talking to Mastah Wilmington.

"Frank, I can't believe this is Sarah, Bertha's daughter," she said at one point. "My, she has grown to be quite tall.

"Yes, she has," Mastah Wilmington agreed.

"So, how are her parents?"

"Oh, Bertha and Joshua are just fine. They have no health problems. I guess they'll be around for many years." His words made me angry.

"Sarah is now at an age where she can help around the house, I would think," his sister continued.

"Oh, Sarah is a good worker. We have plans to relieve Bertha of some of her duties in the house soon, so that Sarah can take over. Charlotte and I think she is ready."

Mastah Baxter had always lived here in New York City. He asked questions about how slaveholders controlled slaves who wanted their freedom. Mastah Wilmington told him that he was lucky because he had responsible overseers on his plantation. He then added that he had few problems with runaway slaves. He said some of his friends had hired more overseers to watch their slaves both day and night. I left the window and continued with the ironing. I guess they continued to talk about slaves, and other interests they shared.

When I returned to the open window, they had changed the subject to dinner. I heard Missus Baxter say she needed some food items from the market around the corner. She made a list. Kate and Melissa volunteered to go. Mastah Wilmington came into the house and told me to go with them to carry the bags.

The market was actually quite close to Missus Baxter's home. Kate and Melissa decided to walk a little farther first, just to look around the city. As we crossed a street near the market, I could see Negroes in the market. After we entered the market, Kate and Melissa told me to stand in one spot while they got the goods. They said they would be ready to leave shortly, and that I was not to move from that spot. I noticed an older, Negro lady buying some canned goods. I looked around to see if Kate and Melissa were looking. I did not see them, so took a chance and asked the lady if she knew Reverend Charles Baker. Reverend Baker was one of the individuals that Missus Luella had told me to ask about. I had carefully tucked his name into my memory.

The lady said she knew Reverend Baker, that he was a minister with the American Missionary Association. She said his church was not very far from the market. She also said Reverend Baker was at the church most of the day, and that he would be happy to talk with me. Apparently Reverend Baker was well known. I was excited and thanked her. She walked away.

Soon Kate and Melissa said it was time to leave. I took the bags they had to carry from them. We headed back to the Baxter house. After the food was taken out of the bags, and some put away, I began cooking the chicken and vegetables that Missus Baxter told me to prepare for dinner. I then set the table and called everyone to eat. Kate and Melissa were upstairs admiring their aunt's beautiful dresses and jewelry, and the presents she had bought them. After they came into the dining room, I heard their aunt tell Kate and Melissa that she was taking them out tomorrow. If only I could find Reverend Baker, I thought. I could ask him about the city, and the Negro people who lived here.

The next morning I got up early, prepared breakfast, then cleaned the dining room. Mastah Wilmington was drinking hot tea and reading the newspaper. Then he spoke. "Sarah, I'll be leaving here soon. You're going to clean this house and do whatever my sister needs you to do. Kate and Melissa's clothes need to be washed. My sister will tell you what she wants you to prepare for the mid-day meal and dinner."

"Yes'um, Mastah Wilmington. I kin stot wit de cleanin as soon as y'all finish yo breakfus." I noticed that he was staring at me again, the way he had stared when Missus Wilmington was not around. I kept busy working in the kitchen, pretending not to notice. He continued to look at me from head to toe. I quickly finished cleaning and left to start washing Kate and Melissa's clothes. After I finished washing, I went upstairs to start cleaning the house. I just had to get out of Mastah Wilmington's sight.

Before long, Mastah Wilmington was dressed and ready to leave for his meeting. I overheard him tell his sister that I was good with all household chores, and to give me lots of work to keep busy. He then said he would be back later in the day, around 5:00. That was the best news I had heard since I left Holly Springs!

The weather in New York City was mild, not as warm as June was in Holly Springs. Missus Baxter and her nieces were sitting outside in the back of the house in chairs, laughing and talking. I had to stop cleaning and start preparing their mid-day meal. Missus Baxter had told me earlier to prepare ham with cheese, bread and milk.

I called them to come in to eat. Kate and Melissa only picked at their food. They were too excited about going out with their aunt to enjoy their food. After they finished, Missus Baxter told me what needed to be cleaned in the house. I went out in the back of the house to sit, quickly ate what was left over, then began cleaning the kitchen.

Missus Baxter told her nieces that it was time to leave. Before leaving, she told me, "My brother will be home later today. I think I've given you enough chores to keep you busy until we return. I want beef and vegetables for dinner. We'll have dinner as soon as my brother and husband are home."

"Yes'um. I do de chores an have dinner ready befo you git back." Kate and Melissa left the house looking lovely in their bright-colored dresses, talking and laughing. I could not remember seeing them more excited.

It did not take long to finish in the kitchen. I had finished the other cleaning chores before they left. I had learned to work quickly, because Missus Wilmington was so demanding about the appearance of her home.

With my work done, my mind began to wander. I began thinking about what Missus Luella had said about Reverend Charles Baker. She had said he was a kind man, who loved helping his people. If only I could meet him. The lady in the market had told me that his church was not far from the market. I knew that Missus Baxter's house was close to the market. I also knew this was a dangerous thing to do, but I decided to take a chance. I was going to try to find Reverend Baker. I had heard Mastah Wilmington tell his sister that he would be back later in the day, around 5:00. Missus Baxter had said it was just after noon then. I could not tell time with numbers, but knew what time of day it was in Holly Springs by watching the sun. Slaves also knew about the different seasons because of the frost, whether warm or cold weather was on its way.

It was risky, and foolish, but I left the Baxter house without permission. I could have been severely punished for this, but, I had to take a chance. I desperately wanted to meet Reverend Baker before I left the city. There was so much I needed to ask him. As I left the house, I wondered just how far the church was from the house. Surely someone could direct me there. I did not know where Missus Baxter's house was located in the city, and could have gotten lost. As I slowly walked in the direction of the market, I saw two elderly Negro women walking. I approached them and asked if they knew where I could find Reverend Charles Baker.

"He ain't too far, just keep wolkin dis way. It's right down yonda," one of the ladies answered. She pointed in the direction of the church.

"Thank you very much," I answered, and quickly walked away. I kept walking until I saw a red brick building. I prayed it was Reverend Baker's church. I had to get back before Mastah Wilmington, or his sister and daughters, returned. A Negro woman was leaving the front entrance. I ran to her, and asked if this was Reverend Baker's church.

"Why, yes, my chile, it is," she answered. "Might you be looking for the Reverend?"

"Yes'um, Ise lookin for Reverend Baker." I was trying to catch my breath. I was overwhelmed with excitement.

"He's right in dere workin in his office," she said.

"Thank you." I turned and walked into the church. The church was much larger than the chapel on the Wilmington plantation. It had pews, a preacher's stand and a section for the choir. The windows were painted yellow, green, red and white. There was a bright red carpet on the floor. Lots of people could worship here, I thought. As I slowly walked down the aisle, I felt special, like a free person. Just then I heard a door shut. I saw a large man walking from the back of the church. I asked him where I could find Reverend Baker.

"Hello, young lady, I am Reverend Baker," he said, in a heavy voice. "I don't think I've seen you in my congregation. Are you new to this community?" I was speechless. I could not believe I had found this man! Missus Luella had told me that he was an important man. She said that he had helped his people in many ways.

"Ah, hello, Reverend, Ise...my name is Sarah." I could hear my voice cracking. "Ise, Ise here wit my mastah. I met somebody on de train who told me to try to fine you." I was so frightened, I looked away.

"Did you say 'master'?" He came closer to me. "Are you telling me, young lady, that you are a slave?"

"Yes'um, Ise a slave from Misippi." My voice continued to crack.

"My child, where is your master?"

"He do not know dat Ise here wit you." I avoided his eyes. I did not know what he might say to me. I was about to cry. Now, I desperately missed Mammy, and she was so far away. I was scared. I wished I was at home.

"My child, please come and sit down." His tone was softer now. "My wife is in the back. We would like to talk to you. Please, come and talk to us."

He led the way, and called out for his wife. She was an attractive lady, small frame, fair-skinned with keen features and a warm expression.

"Isabelle, Isabelle, come meet our young visitor from Holly Springs, Mississippi." He sounded excited.

"Why, Charles, where did you find such a pretty young lady?" She gave me a big hug. "Hello, sweetheart, I am Isabelle Baker. Do you need anything, my child?"

Talking to Missus Baker brought tears to my eyes. Her tone and demeanor reminded me of Mammy. As much as I did not want to, I began to cry.

"Why, what's wrong, angel?" Missus Baker hugged me tighter.

After wiping my eyes, I spoke slowly and softly.

"My name is Sarah. Ise from Holly Springs, Misippi." I tried to pull myself together. "I betta be goin now cause Mastah Wilmington might be back. He said he wud be back round 5:00. Dey have no idea dat I lef de house." I told them where Missus Baxter lived. I remembered hearing Mastah Wilmington mention the name of the street. There was so much I wanted to say to them. But, I was nervous and should not have left the house.

"You need not worry, child. We'll get you back long before 5:00, and see that no harm comes to you," Reverend Baker said. "Tell me, why did you come to see us?" His voice was calm and caring. It was so different from the one he had when I first met him, just minutes ago; it was less formal. I think they both wanted me to feel that I was safe here.

"As I said, Ise a slave from Misippi." My head was bowed as I told my story. Like most slaves with some education, I displayed my better grasp of English when I was around other, trusted Negroes. "I kin read an write some words, but not many. I heard bout de North, an wont to know whut life is lak for our people hure. Mammy an Pappy was born into slavery. Dey have accep dat life an believe dat is how dey will die. I do not believe I gotta accep it.

"My brotha was "hired out" many years ago by our mastah, an he ain't come back yet. I saw him agin las Septemba. It been eight years since I seen him befo den. I met a Negro lady on de train name Missus Luella. She told me to try to fine you cause you cud tell me bout what it lak to be free. I jes wanna know if dere is any hope for us in de South, to have a betta life." I could hear my voice cracking again. I stopped talking, and held my face in my hands. I felt Missus Baker's arms around me. She then sat next to me.

"Freedom is everybody's God-given right," she said in a soft, calm voice. "You are very blessed, my dear child, that you can read and write some words. Reading only a few words can open doors to a world that many of our people in slavery have no idea exists. We were born and raised here in the North. But Charles and I have risked our lives helping our brothers and sisters reach free soil. Sarah, you are a very intelligent young lady. You don't have to spend the rest of your life in slavery. Charles and I can help you, my child. But, you have to be sure you want your freedom, at any cost." I had no idea what she meant by "any cost," and asked her to explain.

"I mean, are you willing to say goodbye to your Mammy and Pappy in Holly Springs, at least for now, then try to adjust to life as a free person?"

How could I possibly say goodbye to Mammy and Pappy? They meant the world to me, and I to them. I stared straight ahead and did not speak. There was a scary silence in the room. I knew they were waiting for me to answer.

"I thank it time for me to leave cause Mastah Wilmington will be angry wit me." I said, as I stood up. "I dream bout bein free, but do not thank I kin hurt Mammy and Pappy lak dis. Dey have already loss one chile." I was struggling with what the Bakers had said, what I wanted to become, and leaving the people I loved most in this world, Mammy and Pappy. The Bakers were complete strangers. I did not want to be a slave, but that life was familiar to me. I did not know anything about New York City, the Bakers or being free. I felt so helpless.

"I'm so sorry, my child," Reverend Baker said, in almost a whisper. "Are you talking about your brother?"

"Yes, my brotha, Tom. Mastah Wilmington "hired him out" when he was only 10 years old. Mammy still waitin for him to come back to us. I hate whut slaveholders do to us slaves." I had not meant for this to come out. But I was so full of anger at the thought of going back to Mastah Wilmington, that I could not control myself. The Bakers did not say anything for a moment. Missus Baker hugged me tighter.

"My child, we will walk with you. I'm not afraid of Mr. Wilmington," Reverend Baker said. He had a not-so-pleasant look on his face as the three of us headed out to the streets of New York City. On the way back to the Baxter house, I told the Bakers about Mammy and Pappy, and how wonderful they are as parents and as people. I also told them about how I sometimes had the opportunity to look through books lying around the big house, and old newspapers plastered to our cabin walls. I explained how I had absorbed all the knowledge I could from listening to and watching the Wilmington family over the years.

Finally, I told them how Mammy had taught me to sew, and that I could make dresses and window coverings. I told them I was learning to make quilts. They laughed, hugged me and told me I was a special gift from God. As we approached the Baxter house, they asked me when I was leaving New York City. I told them that Mastah Wilmington said we would be leaving on Thursday morning. Today was Tuesday.

When we reached the Baxter house, I could feel my heart racing. I had planned to run in and start suppa. I prayed that Mastah Wilmington had not returned. Reverend Baker knocked at the door. Mastah Wilmington opened it.

"Girl, where have you been?" he shouted. "I didn't know what on earth could've happened to you. You are my property. You don't leave my sight without permission!"

"This child hasn't done anything wrong," Reverend Baker said calmly.

"Mastah Wilmington, I need mo vegebles for dinner, so I ran to de markit to git dem. I got confuse an went to a church for hep. I ain't been gone long." He knew I was lying because I did not have money to buy anything. I wondered how long he had been waiting here for me.

"You didn't have permission to leave! I came home expecting dinner to be ready. I don't tolerate this foolish behavior from any of my slaves! I'll deal with you when we get back to the plantation. You won't leave my sight again. I'm glad you *found* her and brought her back," he said, looking at the Bakers.

I knew what Mastah Wilmington meant when he said "deal with you." Pappy had heard him say that to other slaves. It meant that I would be whipped. He could change his mind and do it right here at the Baxter home. I had no one to blame but myself. I had asked for this punishment by foolishly leaving the house.

I thanked the Bakers for bringing me back. I said "goodbye" to them. As I hugged Missus Baker, I could feel her slipping something into the pocket of my dress, out of the sight of Mastah Wilmington. I turned and hugged Reverend Baker. He smiled at me. Missus Baker discretely winked at me as she turned in the direction of the church. I had a feeling that, by the grace of God, I had met two people who would somehow become a part of my life.

Once in the house, I noticed that Mastah Wilmington and I were alone. Kate and Melissa were still out with their aunt. I went to the kitchen to start preparing dinner. Missus Baxter had said she wanted to eat when her husband and brother returned. I did not know what time it was, in numbers, but knew it was late in the day.

I wanted desperately to stay with the Bakers and talk. They were intelligent, kind and caring people. Then, with my back to him, I felt Mastah Wilmington's arms fold around me. I was in deep trouble with him for leaving the house. Plus, I did not know what he had in mind. I was at his mercy. White men did as they pleased with slave women. I prayed that he would leave the kitchen so that I could finish preparing dinner. I knew exactly what he wanted. I continued to pray silently as he began moving his hands along my body. Then, I heard Kate and Melissa's voices.

"I hear Kate and Melissa," I said, with a forced smile. He looked angrier than I had ever seen him look. I politely pulled away from him and ran to help Kate and Melissa with their bags. They were happy and excited about all that they had seen and bought.

"Let me take yo thangs an put dem away." They both ran to hug their father, and began telling him about their day. I took their bags upstairs, then returned to finish preparing dinner. Their day had not been as exciting as mine, I thought. I could not forget the caring look in the Reverend and Missus Baker's eyes. I sensed that they really wanted to help me.

I was more afraid of Mastah Wilmington now than ever before. He was angry with me for leaving the house. I did not know when he would punish me. But, I knew I would be punished. He had obviously made plans to have his way with me today, when no one was around. I had tried to tell Mammy how uncomfortable he made me feel. But I knew that neither she nor Pappy could stop Mastah Wilmington from having his way with me.

Grandma had told me that all of the answers to life's problems were in the Bible. I wanted to save my body for my husband. If I had been able to read it, perhaps the Bible could have told me how to keep Mastah Wilmington away from me.

I continued to prepare dinner. Kate, Melissa and Missus Baxter were sharing the fun they had had today with Mastah Wilmington. I left the kitchen and went to the upstairs bedroom where Kate and Melissa were sleeping to fold some of their clothes. I felt something tucked in my pocket. Suddenly I remembered that Missus Baker had slipped something in there when we were hugging goodbye. I reached in and found a piece of folded paper. I tried my very best to read the words. It was difficult.

Dear Sarah:

We want to help you and we can help you if you decide to stay here in New York City. However, this has to be your decision. We would never tear you or anyone away from their family. If you decide to stay, you will always have a home here with us. We love you.

Reverend Charles and Isabelle Baker

I could read enough words to understand what they were trying to tell me. I began to cry. Someone actually cared enough about me to offer me a place in their home, cared enough to try to help me escape slavery. I liked these people, even though I really did not know them. What would Mammy and Pappy think? This could kill them! They loved me so much. I was all they had, because Tom might never get his freedom and come back. What would God want me to do?

I kneeled by the bedroom window and prayed like I had never prayed before. I asked God to help me, to give me strength. I told Him that if He would only send an answer, I would not question Him and would do as He said. I then got up from the floor and went about my work. I decided not to worry about this anymore. Perhaps I should make the most of being a slave, and accept it, as Mammy and Pappy had done. Maybe some day I would find a mate, and we could work hard to buy our freedom. I had even heard about families buying relatives.

But, for now, my big concern was Mastah Wilmington's new interest in me. Unlike Kate and Melissa, I would never be able to go out and meet men who could provide for me. None of the boys I knew were free. And, Mastah Wilmington would never allow me to get close to the male field slaves. He had said more than once that my place was in the house, not the fields, talking to boys. I heard someone calling my name. It was Mastah Wilmington.

"Sarah, come on down here," he said in a harsh tone. "Kate and Melissa are hungry. We are ready for our dinner. When you finish that, my sister has more chores for you to do." I was now certain that everything I thought about Mastah Wilmington was true. He was a cruel man, with evil thoughts and desires.

"Ise comin, Mastah." My voice was strong, although I was hurting inside. Grandma had told me that there would be times in my life when I would have to be strong, no matter what. This was surely one of those times. She had said there would be times when I would not have anyone, other than my Creator, to tell me what to do. She said that would be enough to help me make wise decisions.

I had to be pleasant to the Wilmingtons, no matter what I was feeling. I had no choice but to do what Mastah Wilmington told me to do. I was strong, and knew I would get through this somehow. I came from a generation of strong women. Now was the time to prove it.

I came downstairs to finish preparing dinner, while they all sat around talking. Mastah Baxter had returned home by this time. Mastah Wilmington boasted about his political career, and the influence he had in Mississippi. He also talked about a big party he and Missus Wilmington were giving soon. He said he wanted to buy some things here for the event.

"You're coming with me tomorrow, Sarah. I'll need your help carrying the bags.

"Yes'um, Mastah."

"I plan to leave early. Make sure your chores are done."

I served everyone dinner. I was feeling better. Mastah Wilmington had apparently calmed down, at least, for now. Still, I knew my punishment was coming.

The family enjoyed the beef, carrots, potatoes, beans and bread that I had made. They asked for more. It was pleasing to know that I also had Mammy's cooking skills. After dinner, they all went outside to sit on the front porch. I sang two of my favorite spirituals, "Walking With Jesus" and "God Loves His Children" as I cleaned the kitchen and put everything away. These songs had always been a source of strength for me. After my chores were done, I went out back and sat in the chairs on the lawn. I enjoyed the mild June weather and the breeze. I thought about the Bakers. I wondered if they were still at the church, or if they had gone home. Missus Luella had told me that they spent long hours at the church trying to help our people with jobs, education, their legal rights and their freedom.

As I sat thinking, I knew I could grow to enjoy this city. I did not know what life was like here for Negroes, but it had to be better than Holly Springs. I could not fall asleep on the cot that night. I had so much on my mind. I wondered what tomorrow would bring.

The next morning, I got up early to prepare breakfast for the family. Although Mastah Wilmington was only taking me along to carry bags, I was excited about getting out of the house.

"I have a busy day ahead of me. I don't want any foolishness from you today." He revealed a smile I hated.

"Yes'um, Mastah." I continued to set the table. I was afraid and wary of him, but tried to stay calm. He watched me closely, as I moved around the room in the pink and white calico dress Mammy had made for me. It had a white collar with short, puffed sleeves. The white apron was the length of the dress. I felt special in it because Mammy had worked hard to get it finished for the trip. I wished she could see me in it.

"That's a lovely dress," he finally said, and continued to stare. "Did Bertha make it?"

"Yes'um," I said proudly. "She finish it de day befo we lef. Breakfas is ready. I betta git Kate an Melissa up." I desperately wanted someone to come into the kitchen. I was wary of talking to him.

"No, don't do that," he said quickly. "Everyone is tired. They probably want to rest."

"Yes'um." I began placing food on the table. Mastah Wilmington asked for more tea.

"Are you excited about leaving for home tomorrow?" He sipped his tea.

"Yes'um. I wanna see Mammy an Pappy."

"Your Mammy should be proud of you. You speak well, unlike other slaves." His words hurt. I took two deep breaths before speaking.

"Thank you, Mastah." I wish I could have said what I was thinking, like, "You right, sir, I do speak well. It sad dat mos of my people ain't had de oppatunity to learn to speak English. But, dey all cud, wit de oppartunity." Maybe some day I would be able to say those words to his face, with no consequences. But, today was not the day. I turned and finished buttering the bread. Mastah Wilmington said nothing else.

The rest of the family came into the kitchen. I was relieved to see them. After they had everything they needed, I took my food outside in the back to sit and enjoy the sounds of a big city. I did not hear birds, as I did in Holly Springs. Instead, I heard people talking and streetcars moving around. I thought about Tom, and wished he could be here with me. I did not know whether Mammy and Pappy would like it here. This was a large place, unlike Holly Springs.

I could learn to like living here. The thought of learning to read and write, well, and working for money, made my heart jump. People had called me a dreamer. But, if you did not dream, would you ever have anything? I finished eating, put the plate on the ground, and stared at the sky. I smiled at how clear and peaceful it looked. I wondered what it was like up there in the clouds.

"Sarah, get ready. It's time to go," Mastah Wilmington said, as he looked up to see what I was staring at. "I've got a lot to do today." So much for the clouds. I picked up my plate and went inside to clean up.

I changed into the blue and white calico dress Mammy had made for me. He and I walked down the street, then got onto a streetcar. This was quite an experience for me, because I had never seen one. We had to sit close because it was crowded. That was when he began talking.

"My wife and I think your Mammy and Pappy are hard workers. In fact, we would never sell them, ever. We feel the same way about you. You'll never have to worry about being separated from your family."

"You mean, de way my brotha was?" I said without thinking. I did not want to make this man angry again. The words slipped out. I was not trying to be disrespectful. Mastah Wilmington looked at me. It appeared to be a look of guilt, and perhaps anger.

"What happened to your brother is no concern of yours, Sarah," he snapped. "I don't want you discussing him, ever. It's none of your business. Do you understand me?"

"Yes'um, Mastah." I shut up, and stared at the people on the street, enjoying another day of freedom.

We were now in a different part of New York City. I did not know exactly how far we were from Missus Baxter's home. My eyes got bigger as we entered the first shop. There were all kinds of goods, even more than we had seen in Atlanta. I touched different types of fabric. Missus Wilmington would have loved some of the cloths. I imagined how lovely she and her daughters would have looked in dresses made from these fabrics.

Mastah Wilmington bought some fancy glass items for his wife. He also bought clothing for himself. He gave me several bags of his purchases to carry, and said it was time to get back to his sister's house.

As we traveled, he told me that I had to start packing their clothes for the trip back to Holly Springs in the morning. He then reminded me that it was very foolish of me to leave his sister's house without his permission. He said his slaves knew better than to disrespect him. I sensed that he was still angry about what I had done yesterday. Once we were back at the Baxter house, I prepared dinner. Later I began packing for the Wilmingtons. I was tired, but there was a lot to do before leaving in the morning.

After I finished cleaning and packing, I gathered my few things and went to bed. I had the most wonderful dream that night. It was the same dream I had had when I was younger. I dreamed I was in a big city, but Mammy and Pappy were not there. I saw a shop with beautiful dresses in the window. I wanted this dream to go on and on. But, I woke up suddenly, and could not get back to sleep.

There was some paper and a pen on the table in the room. Since I could not sleep, I decided to try to write. I had so much on my mind, and realized that that was why I could not get back to sleep. I needed to talk to Mammy.

mamy

new yok is big dere is lots of peple hure I wush yu an Pappy cud se it dere is shops wit fance dreses an bonits dat yu wud luv I evin got to rid a sretcar

mamy for de firs tim in my lif I se owr peple wit no mastahs dey is fre I talk to to of dem dey sa dey wanna hep me dey is good peple.

I aint cumin bak hom I kin not caus I wanna be fre I belev dis is whut God wan for me yu an al of us I belev dat we was mad to surv God an not mastahs mamy if yu crien plese stop I wan yu to undastan dat Ise a big girl an yu taut me good I kin red an rit som an sew caus of yu God is gonna tak cur of me mamy yu wont eva hav to wory bout nobode selin or hirin me out I wuz scard mamy but not no mo I hav fath an corag dat evrythan is gonna be alrit I aint sayin goodby mamy caus yu wil hure frum me agin I luv yu an papy

sarah

By now, the paper was wet. I wiped my eyes, folded the paper and put it in my bag. Somehow, I had to find a way to get this paper to Mammy. I then, quietly, picked up my bag, slipped out of the Baxter house and headed for the church. It was very early that Thursday, June 18, 1845. There were some people on the streets. I was walking quickly and looking around. Yet, I was not afraid. This day was a new beginning for me. Fear had no place in my life on this warm summer morning.

16. Raini

IN THE FALL OF 2012, John came home with some wonderful news. I was still at Strafford, Burke & Long. I'd been working diligently, preparing for a complicated insurance fraud case. Finally, it was time to go to court. It was after 8:00 when I got home, all prepared to tell John about my day at the office. Before I could discuss that, he broke the news that Professor McWherter wanted to see me in his office as soon as possible. According to John, there was a part-time position for an Associate Professor of Political Science at Brown.

"Sweetheart, that's all I know about it," he said. "When can you get in to see Professor McWherter?"

"Not until Friday, unless he can see me before I get to the office in the morning. I'll call him and see what we can work out." That night I couldn't sleep. I had the case on my mind, but, more importantly, I couldn't wait to speak with Professor McWherter. I really admired this man, and had the utmost respect for him as a person, and a professor. I had learned so much from him. The thought of being one of his colleagues was overwhelming.

I called him before going to court the next morning.

"Mrs. Carrington, how are you?"

"I'm just fine, Professor. John said you wanted to see me. I'm calling to ask if we can meet this morning."

"How soon can you get here? I've got class in 30 minutes."

"I can't get there in 30 minutes because I've got to be in court, and I don't know what time I'll get out. Could you possibly see me early tomorrow morning?"

"Yes, that'll be fine, Mrs. Carrington. Why don't we plan to meet around 8:00."

"That sounds great. I'll see you then." I knew that getting there by 8:00 was pushing it, but I wasn't going to let anything ruin my chances of getting this position.

I had a difficult day in court. Things didn't go as well as I'd hoped they would. But the thought of meeting with Professor McWherter cheered me up. The next morning I arrived at his office at 7:45, and waited for him.

"Mrs. Carrington, it's so good to see you," he said, as he walked into his office. "Do you miss being a state senator? John tells me you're still working at Strafford, Burke & Long."

"Yes, I miss representing my district. However, there are other goals I want to pursue at this time. And, yes, I am still with Strafford, Burke & Long."

"I asked for you because we have a position that will soon be available for an Associate Professor of Political Science. You told me that you wanted to teach. I didn't know if you were still interested, or if you wanted to stick with practicing law."

"Professor, I'm very interested. We want to stay in this area. John is happy here."

"Well, Mrs. Carrington, this is a part-time, associate position. It could possibly become full-time one day, but there is no guarantee. Would you be interested in applying?"

"I most definitely want to apply, Professor. I've wanted to teach since my undergraduate days. That hasn't changed." I didn't say too much because he hadn't offered me the job, however, I certainly wanted him to know that I was interested.

"Good, Mrs. Carrington. Go ahead and apply. We'll see what we can do. There are others who are being considered as well, so I can't make any promises."

"Thank you for thinking of me. I'll get my application to you by Friday. It's so good to see you." I left his office and raced to mine, not even thinking about the case I'd been working on for weeks. I could only think about the possibility of teaching the subject I loved.

I called John as soon as I got a break to tell him everything Professor McWherter had said. He tried to calm me down. After talking to him for 30 minutes or more, I calmed down. I tried to focus on my insurance case. This was going to be a long afternoon, so I ran out to grab a sandwich. Then I rushed back to the office.

It was late afternoon by the time I got out of court. I still had a ton of things to do. I needed to win this case, but had to find the time to update my resume and get it to Professor McWherter by Friday. The next day we won the case, but I was too tired to celebrate with the others. I rushed home in the early afternoon and crawled into bed. I didn't hear John come home. The next morning he laughed about how I was "out" at 4:00 in the afternoon. We spent the weekend at home, in bed, enjoying each other. It had been a hectic, but exciting week. I intended to spend what little energy I had left on my husband.

The following Friday, I was interviewed by three professors at Brown. This was stressful because they each had taught me. Now I was applying to become one of their colleagues. I left the interview feeling confident. I went straight to John's office and offered to take him to lunch.

"Well, Sweetheart, you don't expect me to turn down a free lunch, do you? There's a new restaurant over on Park. Let's give it a try." We didn't discuss the interview over lunch. Instead, John shared some of his plans and asked for my opinion. He wanted his own Information Technology consulting firm. He felt he had enough experience and knowledge to accomplish this. His parents were willing to help him financially. He, of course, planned to pay back every dime.

"Honey, you've wanted to do this for some time. I think you should go for it. Once you get it off the ground, it should be quite profitable. You've proven that you are brilliant when it comes to computers and software. It's time to do your own thing."

"I'm glad to hear you say that, because if you weren't behind me, I'd probably bury the idea. I've taken notes from day one on all of the projects I've worked on at Brown. If I can make it happen for Brown and other universities, then I can make it happen for the federal government. I've dreamed of owning a business for years. I think the time is ripe to give it a shot."

John was ready to make a go of it; he had my full support. I took him back to his office, then headed for mine. We both had big dreams, and the support of strong, loving families. I knew he had too much going for him to be employed by someone else indefinitely, but it was his life, and he had to make his move when he was ready. I was committed to him. I would always be there for him, no matter what happened.

I got back to my office and reluctantly began preparing for the next case. Practicing law wasn't my long-term goal in life, even though it certainly had its good points. Winning in the courtroom was the best feeling. Afterwards, you got the utmost respect in the office. I was absorbed in research on a new case when the phone rang.

"Mrs. Carrington, this is Susan Weens from the Political Science Department at Brown. I want to let you know that you are scheduled for a second interview on Thursday at 10:00. Will you be able to make it?"

"Yes, Ms. Weens, I'll be there at 10:00. Thank you for calling." I used every ounce of self-control to keep from screaming! A second interview meant they might want me as the new Associate Professor. I tried to calm down, but had to talk to John. I called him at his office.

"I got a second interview! Isn't that great?"

"Yes, it is. But please try to calm down. You've got another big case to prepare for," he said, laughing at my girlish excitement.

"Honey, have you heard anything about who they might select?" I asked, knowing how John would answer.

"No, Raini, I haven't. But, remember, you'll get the job if it's for you."

"You're right. I need to work on this case. What time will you be home?"

"I'm trying to get out early because I want to work in the yard while there's still daylight.

"Well, thanks for listening. I need to get back to work. See you when you get home." I managed to put the interview out of my mind. There was nothing I could do to prepare for it any way. John was right. They would either select me, or someone else. It was pretty much out of my control.

I had an appointment with my client in an hour, so I needed to be prepared. He was one of our well-to-do clients, and extremely demanding. I couldn't make any errors on this case. However, I worked equally as hard for all of my clients. This is the reputation I was trying to build. John understood my dedication to my work. Some of the older, more seasoned attorneys told me to slow down and take it easy. That was easy for them to say. I was new at this. I was determined to learn as much as I could, as quickly as I could.

When I got home that chilly November evening, John was still working in the yard. I had begged him to hire someone to help, but he said working in the yard helped relieve the stress he got from his work. He had made a great deal of progress establishing his own company. His parents had come up to look at several buildings he had considered purchasing. We chose one that was fairly new and close to our home. It wasn't a very large building, but just the right size for John, who wanted to start small and work his way up.

Thanksgiving was a week away. We decided to spend it in Charlottesville at John's parents' home. My parents and John's siblings were joining us. I was excited about seeing everyone. John and I shared the holidays with both of our families, which kept the in-laws happy.

Thanksgiving was a blast. My grandparents were able to join us. John's mother did most of the cooking, but Mother brought several dishes. It was a real feast, which included turkey, duck, ham, hen, garlic potatoes, collard greens, macaroni and cheese, tomato aspic, several salads and desserts, just to name a few. John and I had strong family ties. This was one quality that brought us together, and, perhaps, would help keep us together. Our families got along well. This made holidays even more enjoyable. Mother had grown closer to John since our marriage. Even though she thought he was somewhat complicated, she knew that he made me very happy. That was all that mattered to her and Dad.

My dear friend, Larkin Landers, came to Charlottesville to spend the day with us. She's a veterinarian in Fairfax, Virginia. She hadn't settled down with anyone. She was consumed with her work, and found most men boring. Larkin is so very selective. As a prerequisite, her "dream man" has to love animals, be well educated and established, good-looking, well dressed… I thought she'd found him two years ago when she and the newest man in her life came to Providence to spend some time with John and me. But, a week later, she discovered that he was allergic to cats. That was the end of that sweet relationship.

Larkin and I grew up together. We had been friends for as long as I could remember. She lived down the street, only a few blocks from me while we were growing up. We went to the same schools. She was the sister I never had. We'd always found the time to support each other, through personal and professional drama.

Larkin has always adored animals. Whenever I came to her house, I was prepared to hold a cat, dog, bird, hamster, rabbit or any one of her "babies." My favorite was Chester, her pig. In fact, when I was 10, she asked me to be his godmother. I said "yes." I took really good care of him when he was with me.

I also remember the time she called me when she was in her second year of veterinary school. I was a second year graduate student, preparing to come home for the summer. I could tell by the tone of her voice that she needed a big favor.

"Hello, best friend. How have you been? I can't wait to see you."

"I'm just fine," I said. "What's up?"

"Well, I have a dog we've been working on here at school. He's homeless. I was wondering if you could take him in, you know, give him a nice home."

"I really don't have time for an animal. I plan to work for Senator Cole this summer."

"Please, just hear me out, Raini. His name is Oliver; he is a Yorkie. I would take him, but I honestly don't have the space for another animal at home. If I don't find a home for him soon, he'll be sent to a shelter. He'll never make it there.

"Why not?"

"Because he likes to cuddle, and he won't get any attention here at school. Please, be an angel, help me out. I promise to vote for your boss in November."

"Larkin, I don't have time to come to Auburn University to pick up a dog."

"You don't have to come here. My parents can bring him to your home. They're here visiting."

"You have no idea how busy I'm going to be with my job this summer. I won't have time to lie around and play with a puppy."

"Oliver is 6 months old and you don't have to change your schedule. He desperately needs a loving home."

"Okay, I'll take him, but what exactly is wrong with him? If you all have been working on him, I need to know what I'm getting into."

"Oliver had cancer. Notice I said 'had' because we are 90 percent sure we've gotten all of it out of him. In time, he'll get his strength and energy back. He'll make a great friend and companion."

"Great, that's all I need, a puppy with cancer! What kind of medical expenses are we talking about, my dear veterinarian friend?"

"Actually, none. The school will cover any medical expenses for him for the rest of his life, since we've learned so much about cancer in animals while treating him."

"Okay, send him. I'll do my best. But, if I find that I can't take care of him, because of his medical problems, I'm sending him back!"

"You're a doll, Raini. Tell the Senator 'hello,' and that he has my vote this fall."

I could not believe I had allowed Larkin to talk me into caring for a recovering puppy. But, that was the kind of relationship we'd had since we were kids. To this day, I couldn't think of anything I wouldn't do for her. By the way, I grew to love Oliver dearly. I kept him until he died three years later.

Larkin thought John had become more exciting since our marriage, but she still believed that anyone who understood computers and software as well as he did couldn't be normal. Still, she visited me, and I spent time with her whenever I was home. I knew sisters who weren't as close as we were. We still talked and listened to each other often.

When John and I got home from Charlottesville, after Thanksgiving, there was a message for me to call Professor McWherter. Perhaps he wanted to tell me that I hadn't gotten the job. Several well-qualified individuals had applied. I was prepared to accept whatever decision the team had made. There would be other opportunities.

The next morning I called Professor McWherter before leaving for work, but he wasn't in. I tried again after I got to the office. He asked me to come in as soon as possible. I returned some phone calls, then left to meet with him.

"Mrs. Carrington, I hope you and John had an enjoyable Thanksgiving. John told me you spent it in Charlottesville with your families."

"Yes, Professor, we had a wonderful time, but it's good to be back." I kept the conversation short because I wanted him to get to the point.

"The team has made a decision. I want to be the first to say welcome to our staff." He continued to speak, but I didn't hear anything else. I'd been offered the position of Associate Professor of Political Science! I was speechless, but tried to compose myself.

"Thank you so much, Professor. You don't know how much this means to me. I feel honored to be on your staff. You and the other professors have taught me so much, and been great inspirations to me. Those are some of the reasons I want to teach."

He reminded me that the position would be part-time, but could possibly become full-time at some point. I didn't care. I left Professor McWherter's office and raced to John's.

"I got it! I got it!" was all I could say as I ran to him with open arms. After I calmed down, I noticed that John had the slyest grin on his face.

"Congratulations, Sweetheart, you got what you wanted. I'm happy for you." He gave me a big hug. "I knew you were a finalist, but I was asked not to tell you. Then I was told you'd been selected, but Professor McWherter wanted to break the good news to you. I couldn't take that away from him." I playfully punched him in the stomach and hugged him again. I wanted to take the day off to celebrate. Unfortunately, there was work to be done at the office. I had enjoyed working here and I'd learned a lot. If I ever decided to practice law again, this firm would be my first choice.

John and I celebrated my new job that night with some close friends. We went to our favorite restaurant and had a great time. I wouldn't start teaching until the following spring. Everyone wanted to know what John and I thought about working at the same university.

"Actually, I won't be there with her very long," John began. We hadn't told our friends about John's plans to start his Information Technology consulting firm. This was not the time to go into details.

"For years I've dreamed of owning a business, and my dream is about to come true," John did say. This evening is a celebration for my wife, because teaching is something she has wanted to do since I've known her. I don't want to take away from her party, but to answer your question, I think I'll love having her on campus. Now we won't have to drive across town to meet for lunch."

With that, John gave a toast, kissed me and we ate dinner. He was so sweet not to want to discuss his dream-come-true on the evening I was celebrating mine. That was just one of the many reasons I loved him. He was so considerate of others, never wanting to upstage anybody. I wanted him to share his good news with our friends that night, too. He, on the other hand, didn't want his business to be the focus of our conversation. He wanted this evening to be a celebration for me. That's exactly what it was.

17. Celia

COLE AND I CAUGHT THE FIRST AVAILABLE FLIGHT to Cleveland. I had prepared to tell Michaela everything after school that afternoon, but it was more important to be with our biological daughter, to spend what could very well be her last hours of life with her.

The thought of losing Sidney deeply saddened me. Although I didn't know her, she was our flesh and blood. That was enough. I'd been in so much pain over the past week, now I felt like I was going to explode. I wondered how much more I could physically and mentally handle. I was torn between being here for Michaela, and at Sidney's bedside in Cleveland. Although Sidney didn't know me, I am her biological mother and she needed me.

Much to my surprise, there was no one in the hospital room with Sidney when we arrived. I'd expected to find nurses and doctors hovering over her, and her immediate family present. She looked like she was asleep. Was she even alive? I held her hand. It was warm. When I leaned in close to her, I could see that she was still breathing. Thank God, my baby was alive! I decided right then that I wasn't going to leave her again until she was conscious and no longer in critical condition.

"Where has everyone gone?" I asked. "I can't believe no one is here."

"I'm sure they're close by." Cole was also holding Sidney's hands. I held his and began praying. I thanked God for allowing Cole and me to learn the truth about what happened here in December 1977. If Sidney had never gotten sick, we would have never known the truth. Although the pain of knowing was almost unbearable, I was thankful that we had learned the truth. I asked God to let Sidney live. I prayed that she would grow into a healthy, happy young woman.

At that moment, I didn't care about trying to figure out what was going to happen with two families claiming her as a daughter. All that mattered was that my child got better, that she be able to live a normal, healthy life.

Suddenly, as I was praying, I realized that this tragedy wasn't just about me and the other three parents. It also was about two innocent children, who were victims of a mistake made by hospital staff. Cole and I, along with Ralph and Cynthia Williams, had to decide how to best handle a difficult situation. That was the bottom line, nothing else. After I prayed, Cole and I kissed Sidney on the forehead, then warmly embraced each other. We loved each other. Nothing was going to change that.

"Hello, Mr. and Mrs. Bentley. I didn't think you'd be here so soon," Ms. Noland said, as she entered the room.

"Why not, Ms. Noland? You left a message saying that our daughter had taken a turn for the worse. Why didn't you think we would come up as quickly as possible?" Ms. Noland looked embarrassed that she had asked the question.

"You're right, I should've known that you both would be here. Actually, shortly after I called you, Sidney's temperature dropped. Dr. Chiana said her condition is slowly improving. It's as if she got worse only to turn around and get better. This sometimes happens with very sick people. Still, we told you that we would call whenever there was a drastic change in her condition, and that's why I called," she explained.

"I was somewhat alarmed when we walked in and didn't see anyone with Sidney. Where are her parents?" I felt strange saying "her parents," but that's what Cynthia and Ralph Williams had been to this child. Nothing could change that.

"Mr. and Mrs. Williams are here daily with Sidney," Ms. Noland assured us. "You can imagine that they both are physically and mentally exhausted. After hearing the good news that Sidney had improved, Dr. Chiana convinced them that it was okay to go home to get some rest. They had been sleeping here at the hospital."

"I'd like to call and tell them that my wife and I are here. I'd like to tell them that we would like to spend a few days with our daughter." Cole tightened his arm around my shoulder. He planned to get to know his daughter; the sooner the better.

"I'll be happy to call the Williamses and tell them you're here, if that's okay with you. They'll know that Sidney is not alone," Ms. Noland said.

"I'll call and let them know that we're here," Cole said. "They can decide if they want to stay at home and rest, or be here with Sidney. It's their choice, but regardless, Celia and I will be here with her." Cole left the room to make the call. I sat and stared at this beautiful child. Tears started flowing. This time, they were tears of joy, not sadness. My little angel was improving. This was a miracle. It was time to celebrate.

Cole returned to the room. He said he had spoken to Ralph Williams, who said he and his wife were very tired, so would stay at home tonight. They would return in the morning to be with Sidney. I was glad because this would give us some time to be alone with our daughter. I was ready to get to know Sidney Williams. I wanted to know everything about her, her favorite food, color, style of clothing, subject, music, movies. I was anxious to know everything about my daughter.

Although she hadn't grown up with us, there were certain traits and characteristics that would surface at some point, regardless of the environment. I wanted to know where she went to school, what type of student she was, learn about her personality. Cole and I were excellent students, so are Michaela and Matthew. Surely Sidney was an excellent student also.

Dr. Chiana entered the room to examine Sidney. I introduced myself and asked him to tell me everything I needed to know about my daughter's condition.

"Mrs. Bentley, I've been informed about the mistake that was made here when your daughter was born. It was unfortunate, and you have my sympathy. I've spent time with Mr. and Mrs. Williams. They both seem to be very kind and caring people. They are just as hurt and shocked over this as you are. I'm sure Michaela is a lovely young lady, and I look forward to meeting her. As for Sidney, she is a very sick child. However, the good news is that she is improving. We expect her to live a healthy and normal life, in time."

"Doctor, how did Sidney get such a deadly disease?" I wanted to know what caused this illness. Did she inherit it from our families? Did the hospital give her medication that led to this condition? Was the disease a product of her environment? I had to know the truth. I also wanted to know what had caused the death of the other children who were born during this period. But that could wait for now. Cole and I had an attorney who would get to the bottom of all of this.

"We have determined that Sidney has Reye 's syndrome. We are not certain about what causes this disease. We do know that some children have contracted it following a viral illness. Studies have shown that certain medications, such as aspirin, that are used to treat viral illnesses, can increase the risk of developing Reye's syndrome."

"Dr. Chiana, could the staff here possibly have given Sidney a medication during the first days of her life that could have caused this?"

"Again, Mrs. Bentley, we are not sure of the cause, however, research is still being done." I didn't expect him to say anything that could incriminate the hospital for negligence.

He continued, saying, "The good news is that, for Sidney, there was an early diagnosis. We were able to reduce brain swelling early on, which protected her brain from irreversible damage. This also prevented complications in the lungs. Sidney has received the very best of care here. She has been watched closely to prevent any onset of cardiac arrest, which has caused the deaths of some children who developed Reye's syndrome."

"Did cardiac arrest cause the deaths of the other children born in December 1977?" Cole asked.

"I didn't treat the children, but, it is my understanding that they both had meningitis. It wasn't diagnosed early enough, so, unfortunately, there was a delay in treatment, which contributed to their deaths."

The question and answer period between Dr. Chiana, Cole and me continued for more than an hour. I felt strongly that Dr. Chiana was a competent physician, who was knowledgeable about Reye's syndrome. But, he was careful not to speak negatively about the hospital. Maybe he was trying to protect Mr. Jacobs and the hospital. Perhaps he simply didn't choose to speak ill of them.

He then pulled Sidney's chart and showed us the improvement she had made in only 24 hours. I wanted to know how long she would have to stay here. He said that depended on how quickly the medications worked, and the strength of her body. This disease had weakened her, so it would take time for her to regain her full strength. Dr. Chiana said he would be available in the morning to answer any other questions we might have regarding our daughter. He then left the room.

"What else did Ralph Williams say to you?"

"He told me that he and his wife would be here some time in the morning. One of their younger children is in a play at school, so they are pleased that we will be here with Sidney this evening."

"I'm flying back on Saturday to talk to my staff. I've got to make some decisions about who will cover for me until I get back to the office full time," Cole said. "I am Sidney's father, and I intend to be here for her." Cole thoroughly enjoyed Matthew, Michaela and McAlister. Now it appeared he had decided that Sidney would be treated no differently than our other children. We didn't leave Sidney's bedside that night, except to eat, shower and dress. Each time a nurse or Dr. Chiana entered the room, we asked questions. We wanted to know everything we could do to help Sidney, now that we knew she was going to live a normal life.

Ralph and Cynthia Williams arrived the following morning, looking fresh and well rested. The four of us began talking about our daughters, Sidney and Michaela. Cynthia Williams, displaying pain and discomfort, disclosed to us that she had heard a few years ago that there were problems at the hospital back in December 1977. She had heard that children had suffered because of some mistakes, but she had decided not to look into it because Sidney appeared to be healthy. She believed that what she didn't know couldn't hurt her or her daughter. She also acknowledged that Sidney had been sick with a viral illness shortly before she developed Reye's syndrome. I wanted to ask her how she treated the viral illness. However, at this point, it didn't matter if she had given her aspirin or some other medication. Sidney had developed this horrible disease, and was fighting for her life. She needed all the love and support she could get.

Cole left the next day to return home to check on our children, and to make those announcements at his office. I spoke to Matthew, Michaela and McAlister daily on the telephone. It appeared that Mother had everything under control. Cole's parents had gone home, but planned to return when we decided to break the news to Michaela. They wanted to be there for their granddaughter; wild horses couldn't keep them away during a crisis. Ralph Williams also had to get back to work. That left Cynthia and me alone, to talk and cry about our children. There was something about Cynthia Williams that I liked. She appeared to be genuine. I asked her to tell me about Sidney. She did.

"Sidney is an honor student, and has been one since grade school. She is so detail-oriented. With her, everything always has to be just right." Cynthia paused, and laughed to herself. As she continued to describe Sidney, I knew, without a doubt, that this was Cole Bentley's child. "Sidney would rather stay in and study for an exam, or practice the piano, than go to the mall with her friends.

"She is somewhat of an introvert. There were times when I wondered who she had taken that from, because Ralph and I are outgoing. Still, I know that children are individuals, and I simply brushed this off. As you can see, she is a beautiful girl. But, there are beautiful people in both of our families, and children sometimes don't look like either parent." I listened intently to every detail. Cynthia described some difficult times that she and Ralph had gone through, financially.

They had not been able to expose their six children to some of the cultural experiences they wanted for them. Last year, Sidney was chosen by her school to be one of four children to go to Europe to participate in a math and science conference. The Williamses weren't able to send her, because Ralph's job was cutting back on staff. They were afraid that he would get laid off, and didn't want to spend the extra money they had saved.

Their oldest son, Edward, attends Ohio State University on a football scholarship. Cynthia added that there were still expenses for parents even when you have a child in college on scholarship. The second son, Randall, is a freshman at the University of Kentucky, on a basketball scholarship. Cynthia had taught school all of her life, and enjoyed it, but she wanted better opportunities for her children. She told me that each child was special in his or her own way. They each had unique talents. She described each child as only a caring parent could, with warmth and love.

Then she asked me about Michaela. I showed her Michaela's most recent picture, and she broke into tears. Apparently she felt the way I did when I first set eyes on Sidney. There is something about a child that touches a mother's heart. No one can explain it except the mother. I reached out to Cynthia Williams and held her close. I believed I knew exactly what she must be feeling. When she calmed down, I began telling her about Michaela.

"Michaela is absolutely wonderful. She is an excellent student, loves to talk and is very sociable and athletic…" I went on and on about my daughter because our children are very special to Cole and me. As I was speaking, I noticed that Cynthia Williams continued to stare at Michaela's picture. She then excused herself and left the room. I didn't follow her because I knew she needed time to herself, to mentally digest all that she was hearing.

Here were two mothers, looking at photos, and discussing their biological daughters for the first time in 10 years. Words could not adequately describe what we were feeling. We were both struggling with the bond we have with the daughters we've raised, and the years we've lost with the daughters we were separated from. How could this ever be fixed? Would these young girls ever be the same, once they knew the truth? Would Michaela and Sidney cling to the parents who raised them, or would they choose to be with their biological parents? The questions were running through my head. I took a deep breath, and asked God to give Cynthia and me the strength to keep moving forward. We both had other children as well, so we had to be strong.

Cynthia didn't return, so I had time alone to sit with Sidney. I tried to figure out what the best course of action would be for these young lives. They were both 10 years old. This could sometimes be a tough age for girls, even more so when they have to deal with drastic change in their lives. I was lost in my thoughts, and fell asleep in the chair next to Sidney's bed.

The next morning I left to go to the hotel to shower, freshen up, get some breakfast, then return to my daughter. I missed Cole so much. Today was the last day of July 1988. I wanted to be home with my family, but a part of me was lying here in this hospital bed. I just couldn't leave, at least, not now. I held Sidney's hands and started talking to her. For some strange reason, I believed she was listening. I told her that I loved her very much, and how sorry I was that we were separated at birth. I took a deep breath, and continued to talk to her.

"I would never have left the hospital if I'd known the nurses had given you to someone else. I feel so guilty about what happened to you, and it really hurts. But, I have to be strong, because what's important now is that you get better and grow strong. You are such a lovely young lady. You don't know it, but you look just like my mother when she was your age. Your mother has told me some things about you. She is so proud of you. She has told me what a good student you are, that you were chosen to represent your school in a math and science conference in Europe. What an honor! Your biological father, Cole, is brilliant with numbers. I'm sure that's where you got your ability, however, I've always enjoyed math, too.

"You have two brothers that you'll simply love. Matthew is a freshman in high school. He just made the tennis team. You'll love having him as a big brother. He's very protective and won't let anybody pick on you. However, I'd better warn you that he's also playful at times and likes to tease. Your father travels quite often. While he's away, Matthew tries to step into his shoes. He keeps an eye on all of us. Your younger brother, McAlister, is 2 years old. He gets up with the birds each morning with a book in his hands. He is trying to read and loves to have someone read to him. When you meet him, be prepared to sit and read a story. You also have a sister, Michaela.

"We were supposed to bring you home from the hospital, but, instead, the nurse gave us Michaela. We raised her, and your parents raised you. Michaela is also a lovely young lady. I just know you two will like each other. Michaela, like you, is an excellent student. Biology is her favorite subject. She plays the piano, and recently started taking tennis lessons. Michaela's favorite color is pink. Your mother told me that your favorite is also pink. You see, you both have something in common. I'm sure there are other things that you both like."

I stopped talking to Sidney and began rubbing her forehead. She started moaning and moving her head. She appeared to be trying to wake up. I didn't know what was happening with her. I finished telling her about her new family.

"Your father was here earlier this week, but he had to leave to get back to work. He'll be back soon. We are so thankful that we have found you. I don't want you to be sick, but at least we know the truth now. Let me tell you a few things about me. My name is Celia. I am one of four children. I grew up in Charleston, South Carolina. I have a younger sister and two older brothers. All three still live there. My mother lives there too; my father passed away five years ago. He was such a wonderful person. I wish you could have gotten to know him. He would've loved you dearly. My mother has been here to visit you, and she already loves you.

"Your father, Cole, is an only child. He grew up in Denver, Colorado. His parents recently came to visit us. They are anxious to meet you. Your father and I met when we were graduate students here at Case Western Reserve University. It didn't take us long to get to know each other, and realize that we had common interests. Before long, there were picnics in the park, then a marriage proposal. He's a great guy, my best friend in the whole world. Shortly after you were born, we moved to Nashville, and we've been there since. Nashville is a nice place to raise a family. I think you'll like it."

I felt so much better, now that I had talked to Sidney. It was as if a heavy weight had been lifted from my shoulders. Now that I'd revealed the truth to Sidney, maybe it wouldn't be so difficult to tell Michaela when I returned home. Suddenly, I didn't feel as sad as I had last night. I felt the presence of someone else in the room.

I grabbed both of Sidney's hands and prayed to God for strength for Cole and me, Ralph and Cynthia, and our daughters, to get through this ordeal in a way that would help us all to be able to help our children. I prayed long and fervently. I asked God to fill our hearts with love, so we would not be selfish or cruel when dealing with Ralph and Cynthia, regarding Michaela and Sidney.

After I finished praying, I felt an unusual sense of peace. I thought about Sarah Johnson, the young slave girl who had captured my attention with her strength and faith. I wondered who she was, and why Dad had never mentioned her. Why were those old papers about her in a trunk in the attic? She was a stranger, but I was learning so much from this young girl. I was anxious to finish reading her story.

I then opened my eyes. To my surprise, Sidney's eyes were open, and she was smiling at me! I desperately wanted to believe that she had heard the words I'd spoken to her, and heard my prayer. I reached for her and held her close. I wanted to hold on to her forever, because I had never held my baby. My child would always have a special place in our lives. I would never lose her again. It was time for Cole and me to sit and talk with Ralph and Cynthia Williams.

18. Sarah

SEVERAL WEEKS HAD PASSED since Mastah Wilmington left New York City and returned to Holly Springs.

Reverend and Missus Baker had opened their hearts and home to me that warm summer morning in June, 1845, when I decided not to go back to Mississippi. They hid me for fear that I would get caught and sent back to the Wilmington plantation. Several church members had spoken of white Southerners asking around about a young slave girl from Mississippi. I was sure Mastah Wilmington had sent them.

I gave Missus Baker the note I had managed to write to Mammy. She and Reverend Baker said they would somehow find a way to get it to Mammy. They told me they knew people here who had purchased land and cotton in Mississippi. They said they would do everything in their power to get the note to Mammy. I asked God to take care of Mammy, Pappy and Tom, and to keep them well until I could see them again.

The Bakers wanted me to be tutored in reading and writing at their church, but they were afraid the white Southerners would find and take me back. Missus Baker and another church member taught a small group of young people at the church each day. They taught the young and the old how to read and write. Missus Baker decided to teach me at their home each evening after she returned from the church. She and Reverend Baker thought it was too dangerous for me to leave the house each day.

Missus Baker was an excellent teacher. She spoke and read very well. I did not know, but she appeared to be an educated woman. Missus Baker said it was a pleasure teaching me because I was so eager to learn. I caught on quickly. During that first week, I learned the alphabet, how to pronounce and spell new words, and how to correctly pronounce many of the words I already knew. I also learned to count. It was hard work, but this helped distract my mind from Mammy and Pappy.

For more than a month I did not leave the Baker house to go anywhere. The Bakers did not live far from the church. They did not want to take any chance on someone recognizing me. Lots of Negroes came to the Baker's home and church for different reasons. Some came to get food and clothing, while others came for instruction on how to get jobs or a place to live. There were always new faces. The Bakers thought it was just a matter of time until someone questioned my presence.

As the days passed, I did very well in reading and writing, but struggled with numbers. However, I knew that if I continued to work hard, I would be good at that also. I spent all of my time studying because I could not leave the house. The Bakers had a few books in their home. Sometimes I tried to read until my eyes hurt. Living here with them was a dream-come-true for me. I had a teacher, a room with a "real" bed and did not have to sleep on a cold, dirt floor. A table and chair were in the room. I often worked at the table until the early hours of the morning. I still had a lot to learn, but believed that my life would be prosperous. The Bakers tried to teach as many of our people to read and write as they possibly could. They were truly good people.

I sewed for Missus Baker to earn my keep, even though she told me they wanted nothing in return. But, Mammy had taught me that nothing was free in life, so I insisted on paying them back, by sewing for them. Missus Baker's taste in fabric was as good as Missus Wilmington's. Like Missus Wilmington, Missus Baker was a refined lady. I wanted to go with Missus Baker when she purchased fabric, but she and Reverend Baker still did not think it was safe for me to leave their home just yet. Missus Baker showed off my dresses throughout the church and city. She said people thought my work was good.

One day in August 1845, Missus Baker decided to take me with her to look for fabric. She thought it was safe for me to leave the house now. It had been almost eight weeks since Mastah Wilmington left the city. I wore a shawl and bonnet to cover up. We stopped in a dress shop. The shop was not too far from where the Bakers' lived. The owner, Missus Crane, a white lady, and Missus Baker, appeared to be close friends. Missus Baker was looking at hats. She soon began talking to Missus Crane about my work as a seamstress. Missus Crane asked to see some of my work. Missus Baker told her that we would be back in a few days. She and I selected several pieces to show.

On a Saturday morning we left early, headed to the shop. Missus Crane was amazed at my work. She asked Missus Baker if I could work for her on Saturdays. Missus Baker told Missus Crane that she would get back with her after discussing it with Reverend Baker and me.

I thought it was a great idea, but Reverend Baker was afraid it would interfere with my studies. More importantly, he thought that I would be discovered by someone from the South. However, Missus Baker and I thought working in the shop would be a way for people to see my work, and help me start a business some day. The Bakers wanted me to learn as much as possible, to put me in a better position to make choices for my life. Reverend Baker reluctantly agreed to allow me to help Missus Crane, on Saturdays only. I was thrilled and determined not to let this interfere with my studies. If I wanted to own a business some day, I would have to be good in reading and writing, and with numbers.

There were still days when I cried. Although I was comfortable living with the Bakers, and learning so much, my heart ached for my parents. I missed them terribly, especially on Sundays. Mammy loved cooking for Pappy and me, and having family and friends gather at our cabin for suppa on Sundays. I often wondered how they were getting along without me. Had Mastah Wilmington transferred his anger toward me onto my parents? Were they being whipped because of their runaway daughter? Some days I was noticeably sad to the Bakers. Missus Baker would fix a special suppa and invite people my age over to eat with us. This always cheered me up, which was her hope. If only Mammy and Pappy were here with me.

Whenever I saw Reverend and Missus Baker together, I always thought about my parents. The Bakers were a close, loving couple, like Mammy and Pappy. I worried that Mammy had even more to do in the big house, now that I was not there to help her. If only I could talk to her and tell her I was safe. Whatever she had to face, I somehow knew she would be alright, because she was strong personally and in faith.

Some people around my age had asked me if I was from the South. I told them that I indeed was a Southerner. No one knew that I was a runaway slave. Some of them had asked me what it was like living in the South. They also wanted to know how I got to live in New York City. I knew it was wrong to lie, so I told them I was staying with the Bakers for now, and planned to return to the South. This was true. I planned to go back for Mammy and Pappy, someday, somehow.

I began working in the dress shop the first Saturday in September 1845. I had been in New York City for more than two months. Missus Crane gave me dresses to hem or lengthen. Some needed to be altered. She was quite pleased with my work. She paid me $2.00 each Saturday. I thought about all the sewing Mammy had done for the Wilmington family, with no pay. I was thrilled to get those two dollars!

It was great having my own money. The Bakers taught me how to count, and the value of money. I could now buy most of the things I needed without having to go to them. They now knew that I was a young lady who wanted a better life than I had had in Holly Springs, and did not mind working for it. I thanked God every day for my new life. All the things I had dreamed about and prayed for seemed to be coming true.

One Saturday morning at the shop, in late September, as I was measuring a customer for a fitting, I overheard her tell Missus Crane to beware of some slaves who had run away from their mastahs. She said the slaves were believed to be dangerous. Missus Crane said the slaves had no reason to harm her. The customer, however, said the slaves might do so because they were hungry, and were looking for food and clothing.

Missus Crane was aware of my past, because of her friendship with Missus Baker. So, I did not feel uncomfortable or unsafe with her. The customers, on the other hand, thought I was just another Negro girl, born and raised here. This particular customer continued to talk about how the slaveholders were angry, that they wanted desperately to find their slaves. She talked about how some people in the North were actually trying to help these runaway slaves.

Missus Crane tried several times to change the conversation, but the customer kept returning to the subject.

"I think it is just wrong for people to take these slaves into their homes, when they belong to someone else. Why, that's just not right. Slaveholders pay lots of money for slaves. Their crops cannot survive without them." I wanted to stick her with one of the pins. Finally, I was finished pinning her dress. Thank goodness, she left the store.

"Sarah, I am so sorry that you had to listen to that," Missus Crane said. "You must understand that all people are not the same. Everyone doesn't think alike. I personally think slavery is wrong. I will do every thing in my power to keep you from going back." I had tears in my eyes by now, and gave Missus Crane a big hug. She hugged me back, and told me I was one of the sweetest girls she had ever met.

I soon forgot about what the customer had said. I was too busy with my studies and sewing. Everyday I thought about my friends in Holly Springs who could not read or write. My heart ached for them. I had learned so much in the three months I had been in New York City. Grandma had taught me to be a dreamer. Now, my dreams were coming true. I was living with and learning from free Negroes. I deeply missed Mammy and Pappy, but not enough to go back to Holly Springs and the Wilmington plantation. I had to believe that God would take care of Mammy and Pappy.

Reverend Baker's church was big, compared to the little cabin we worshipped in back home. The Bakers had decided that it was now safe for me to go to church on Sundays. I loved singing and clapping with the others. Reverend Baker taught his congregation that it was God's will for us to be free, not slaves. If only every slave could hear him speak. He taught things that I knew to be true, but could not say openly in Holly Springs. I tried to remember everything he taught us. Perhaps one day I could help him spread his message.

Missus Baker played the organ and piano for the church, and for her enjoyment. She began giving me lessons at their home. At first the lessons seemed very difficult, but she encouraged me to practice daily. Before long, I was playing quite well. Living in New York City was exciting to me, but many Negroes here did not share my excitement. Reverend Baker preached that, although some of us lived in the North, our people still were not "free." He said we were an oppressed race throughout the country. According to him, white people had decided that there were limits to what we could achieve and accomplish as a people in America. He talked about how most Negroes lived in worse conditions than white people throughout the country.

I soon learned that our people could not ride public transportation here, attend theatres or go to other public facilities. Most of our people did not have good jobs, because they lacked the skills and education, which led to them living in ignorance and poverty. Many white people considered us to be inferior because of this.

Reverend Baker was disturbed that Negroes were accused of committing most of the crimes in the city, and did not receive fair or equal protection in the courts. He preached each Sunday that it was wrong to make judgments about people based on the color of their skin.

I also learned that New York City society was divided into upper and lower class citizens. Some educated, hard-working Negroes were even considered lower class. Reverend Baker preached that many of the white churches were teaching and spreading the same ideas held by white slaveholders in the South. I had not been here long enough to understand all of this. Still, I was thrilled about not having to go to a "big house" every morning, and being owned by someone else.

I learned so much while living with the Bakers. Next to my parents, they were the best people I had ever known in my life. They did not want me to be ignorant about freedom, or New York City. Missus Baker feared that our people would never overcome some of the demeaning labels that white people used when discussing us. But, she also wanted me to know that there were white people who were helping our people escape slavery in the South. The slaves were able to start new lives in the North. Missus Crane was one such white person. Although there was still much work to be done to help our people survive, living in the North was much better than being owned and controlled, not to mention beaten, by slaveholders in the South.

Holly Springs was becoming a distant memory, although I longed for Mammy and Pappy to join me. I dreamed of becoming a prominent Negro woman, born and raised in the South, who would rise to be prosperous, and help my people get their freedom.

One Friday afternoon, after I had been in the city for four months, Missus Baker came home in a state of panic. "Sarah, you can not go to the shop tomorrow to work!" she said in a tone I had never heard before. "In fact, I may never let you out of my sight again!" I listened, not knowing what to say to her.

"Missus Baker, what is wrong? What has upset you so?" I was finally able to ask.

"Missus Crane said three white men were asking her questions at her shop, and other nearby businesses, about a young Negro girl. The description fits you, so you are not leaving the house!"

I could feel my heart drop! Could they still be looking for me? How did they know that I was still here and had not moved on to Canada, or some other state, or even Europe? I was afraid, but did not want Missus Baker to know. This would only upset her more. I was quiet as she talked. I wanted to run to my room upstairs and shut the door. After she finished speaking, that was exactly what I did.

If caught and brought back to Holly Springs, I would have been punished severely, or even sold. Just the thought of it made me cry. I began praying, and prayed until I calmed down. That night the Bakers brought my dinner to my room. Missus Baker said she would rather die than let them take me away.

Reverend Baker was very active in the anti-slavery movement. He knew several prominent white people around town, and said he would try to find out about these white men. Things didn't look good for me in the days that followed. It appeared that Mastah Wilmington, and two other men, were in the area looking for me. I knew he would not give up easily. To him, I was a valuable piece of property. I would rather have died than go back and face whatever he had planned for me. I still hated this man.

Although there were provisions against slavery in New York City, it was reported that white Southerners were able to come here to reclaim their runaway slaves. Reverend Baker had said there were even incidents where Negroes born and raised here were kidnapped, and falsely accused of being runaway slaves. Not only was I, a runaway slave, in danger of being returned to the plantation, but free Negroes were at risk of being snatched away from their families! The Bakers knew of free Negroes who had been taken back to the South, after having lived here for several years.

In New York City, and throughout the North, vigilance committees were being formed. They were made up of Negroes and some whites in the anti-slavery movement. These committees provided food, clothing and shelter to fugitive slaves. They also worked to help prevent free Negroes from being enslaved, and runaway slaves from being re-enslaved. The Bakers were actively involved with several of these committees. They were fighting hard to stop any further kidnapping of Negroes. Many of our people were being arrested and falsely accused of being runaway slaves.

Under the amended Federal Fugitive Slave Law, any hard-working, respectable Negro was subject to be taken to the South and enslaved. And, in many instances, the charges about being runaways were false. The

Bakers thought its purpose was to protect fearful white people at all costs. In many cases, the testimony of Negroes was not even admissible to determine their status. Reverend and Missus Baker did not believe there was any real freedom, or justice, for our people anywhere in this country!

Fortunately, our people came out to attend committee meetings in large numbers to fight for their rights. I wanted desperately to join them, but the Bakers would not let me out of the house. It had now been two weeks since I had left their home. I desperately missed church, and my work at the shop. Because Missus Baker taught me at home, I kept up with my studies. In my spare time, I made dresses for her and her daughter, Cora, who was married and lived in New Haven, Connecticut. Missus Baker wanted me to have a lifestyle that was as prosperous as that of her own children. Their son, Jonathan, also lived in New Haven with his family.

Reverend Baker returned one night from one of his meetings and announced that Mastah Wilmington was still in the area, asking questions about a young slave girl named Sarah. Some of the Bakers' friends thought they should let me out of the house to lead a normal life. They said if I was captured by Mastah Wilmington, or seized by a United States Marshall, there would be proceedings, and perhaps I could win the right to stay here. But, the Bakers did not trust the law, or the court system. Even with a good attorney, the testimony of a Negro was prohibited in court by the Fugitive Slave Law. No matter how prominent or well-respected the Bakers were, they could not speak in my defense. I was a fugitive, who was not entitled to a trial by jury.

One evening the Bakers came to my room with dinner. They were quite upset. Reverend Baker said he and other ministers with the local American Missionary Association were teaching their congregations to fight the Fugitive Slave Law, with whatever means they could. But, many white ministers were teaching just the opposite. They were teaching that Christians were bound by all laws, even those that encouraged slavery. As for me, something had to be done, soon. It did not appear that Mastah Wilmington was going anywhere, until he had me with him!

The following week, about five months after my arrival, Missus Baker was helping me with my writing. There were tears in her eyes. I asked her what was wrong. She said nothing. The tears turned to sobs. She left the room. I followed her, because I had never seen her so upset.

Finally, she calmed down and said, "Baby, the Reverend and I have decided to send you away." I know the blood must have drained from my face. It was like the world had shut down. They were actually going to send me back to Holly Springs, Mississippi, the place I had come to associate with pain and suffering. I could see the cotton fields, as I looked through Missus Baker in a daze. I could even feel the whip across my back!

I saw Melissa and Kate laughing because I had been caught. They had me back to do all of their chores. I saw Mastah Wilmington approaching me in an inappropriate manner. That was all I could think of before falling onto Missus Baker's shoulders and sobbing. We cried together for several minutes. Then, Reverend Baker entered the room.

"Sarah, Boston is a nice place, and Aunt Clara is about the kindest person you would ever want to meet," he said. I heard the words, but did not really understand what I was hearing. "Why, I spent several years there. It's a fine place to live. Furthermore, my wife and I will come to see you often." Slowly, I stopped crying, and looked at both of them. Why was Reverend Baker talking about Boston? They were both hugging me now. Missus Baker had calmed down.

"You mean, you ain't, you ain't sendin me back to Holly Springs?" I asked in disbelief, or maybe relief.

"Child, have you taken leave of your senses? Do you honestly think we would send you back to that hell hole?" Reverend Baker said, as he stroked my head.

"Baby, I'm sorry I didn't say more to you before I broke down," Missus Baker added. "I just couldn't hold back the tears. Since it doesn't look like Mr. Wilmington is going to give up on finding you, we have a plan. Mr. Wilmington and his men are almost certain you are in this area, so we have decided to send you to Boston, to live with my sister, Clara. You will love her. I'm more of a mother figure to you. Aunt Clara will be more like grandma to you. I've told her all about you. She can't wait to meet you."

I listened, and did not speak. This wonderful place I had grown to love was about to become a memory. Once again, I was about to leave a mother and father that I loved. It all seemed like a dream. Maybe I was dreaming, and would wake up tomorrow morning in Holly Springs, where I was born and raised. The Bakers talked on about my leaving.

Suddenly, I wanted to crawl into bed and go to sleep. I did. That night I prayed and thanked God that I did not have to go back to the South. He had blessed me with yet another home, and another chance at freedom. If Grandma were here, she would tell me to be strong, to count my blessings. That is exactly what I did.

The Bakers did not waste any time. The next day we were on a train, headed to Boston. I was dressed to look like a much older woman, so that I could not be recognized. No one questioned the Bakers about my identity. We all gave a sigh of relief when we were out of the city. I had lived in it for five months. My dream was to be free and prosperous. This trip to another city was just another bridge I had to cross. The Bakers were both happy and sad. They did not want to lose me, but, more importantly, they did not want me to be brought back to the South, to be sold, or severely punished.

The trip to Boston was not very long. Missus Baker had prepared chicken and bread for us to eat. We spoke softly to each other during the trip, for fear someone was listening, or watching for me. Even if I had to leave the country, I was determined not to live in slavery.

We finally reached Boston. Aunt Clara greeted us at the train station. She indeed reminded me of a warm grandmother. We traveled to her house by horse and carriage. It was a one-story house made of wood and painted white. It had windows with sparkling glass, like the Bakers' house. The curtains were white and very clean. There were four rooms, a parlor, Aunt Clara's bedroom, a kitchen area and a room with a decorative wooden table and chair. This room also had books, and paintings on the wall. I still remember the beautiful metal door knocker as you entered the house. However, it was not the size of Aunt Clara's house that still captivates me, but the quality of her possessions.

The Bakers stayed for five days to help me adjust to Aunt Clara and my new home. They promised to write and visit soon. I loved them dearly. As much as it hurt to see them leave, I knew I was a lot safer here than in New York City. Aunt Clara had already arranged for me to continue with my studies. She had hired a teacher to come to her house to work with me. She had also found a shop for me to work as a seamstress. It was a small shop, very much like the one in New York City, where men and women came to get their clothing altered.

I knew nothing about Boston. I was in a new city, with no family. But, I had to make the most of it. I had a choice. I had to either build a new life here in Boston, or, return to Holly Springs. That was not a difficult decision.

19. Celia

CANNOT GET SIDNEY'S EYES OUT OF MY MIND. Could she have heard and understood what I said to her when we were alone?

When I saw her eyes open, I screamed. The nurses rushed into her room to see what was wrong. Well, there was nothing wrong. Actually, everything was right, because a miracle had just taken place! Ralph and Cynthia rushed to the hospital. They embraced Sidney with warm, loving arms. We were all in tears. Cole returned early to embrace his daughter. He wanted to tell her how much we all love her.

The trip home to Nashville the next day was sad for both Cole and me. We wanted to be close to Sidney, to watch her slowly improve each day. We had already fallen in love with our daughter. I wished there was some way I could bring her home with us to recover. I felt as though I owed her so very much. She had been deprived of her right to grow up with her family.

Cole reminded me that she did grow up with her family. Ralph and Cynthia Williams are the only parents she knows. Still, I believed she could have had a more comfortable lifestyle with her biological parents. Ralph and Cynthia had five other children. It must have been a struggle for them to provide for them all. Cynthia told me they had not been able to send Sidney to Europe after her school selected her to go, because they could not afford to send her. It all hurt so much. But my wonderful husband reminded me that what's most important is that she was loved. Ralph and Cynthia appeared to be kind, loving people.

During this ordeal, I couldn't get Sarah Johnson out of my mind. If only I had her strength, I could get through this situation with the same strength she showed. My problems seemed trivial when I thought about everything she had gone through. And, she had only been 14 years old when she left her parents in Holly Springs, Mississippi. Mother and I had begun asking questions about and researching our roots, because we wanted to know who this amazing woman was. I was determined to find the time to finish reading her story.

Michaela met us at the door. Once again, she asked why I had been spending so much time in Cleveland. Although I was tired, I didn't plan to put my child off again. I told her that we needed to talk to her right now. Matthew was out playing tennis and McAlister was asleep. Mother left the room to give us time alone with our daughter. It was a warm August afternoon. Cole, Michaela and I headed to the sunroom.

Cole knew that was my favorite room in the house. I guess that's why he led us there. I sat in the sunroom often when I read, or simply needed time alone. There was a great view of my flower garden from there and it was easy to get lost in my thoughts. It was so peaceful and calm there. When we were house hunting, I knew immediately this was the house for us when I saw this room.

It was an old, colonial style house. Cole and I worked hard to restore it to its original charm. After we finished inside, I spent nearly every free moment developing a garden. I read about various plants, to discover which ones would do best in Nashville. I chose holly hocks, shooting star hydrangea, shasta daisies, lavender, astilbe, coneflowers, pincushion flowers, various types of lilies and rose bushes, to name a few. Finally, the garden was complete. Every time I came into this room I enjoyed nature. Cole called it "my room" because I spent so much time here. So, it didn't surprise me when he led Michaela and me into the sunroom to talk.

Amazingly, I was calm. There was a sense of peace I couldn't explain. I'd been under a great deal of pressure for over two weeks, and had been dreading this moment. However, I was now ready to open up to Michaela. I wanted to tell her how much we loved her, and that she would always be our daughter, no matter what. I began talking to her calmly.

"Sweetheart, last month I received a call from a lady named Mary Noland, the Director of Nursing at Willow Memorial Hospital in Cleveland. I started to tell you about this earlier, but you were sleepy at the time. Then I've been busy too. As you know, we've had to go to Cleveland to take care of some very important business. Honey, this business concerns you. As you very well know, you were born on December 10, 1977, at the hospital." Michaela looked at her dad and giggled. I knew she was thinking, *of course I know when and where I was born.*

"Well, Sweetheart, the maternity unit at the hospital was under renovation during that time. The doctors and nurses wound up making some terrible mistakes that involved you, and some other babies."

"What kind of mistakes, Mom? Am I really a boy, and I've been passing as a girl for 10 years?" Now she was laughing. Cole was trying to laugh with her, but I could see the pain in his face.

"No, Sweetheart, you are very much a pretty girl, and there isn't anything in this world your father and I wouldn't do for you. I think you know that," I said, still calm and peaceful.

"Does that include letting me spend the weekend with Carla and her parents at their beach house in Florida in two weeks, when we're on fall break?" Michaela winked at Cole and me, as she used this particular time to tell us that she had been invited. This child had a magnetic personality. I loved every moment of being her mother.

"We'll have to talk about that at a later date, dear. Anyway, let me get to the point. You've waited long enough to know what's going on. When your father and I got to Cleveland, and sat down to talk with Ms. Noland and Mr. Jacobs, the Hospital Administrator, they said some children born during that time had been getting very sick, and two had even died.

"A week before we received the call, a young girl named Sidney Williams was admitted to the hospital. She was very sick. She was born on the same day that you were at the hospital. Because she was so sick, the doctors had to run several tests on her to determine what illness she had contracted. In the process of examining her blood samples, and DNA, which I know you've studied in your biology class, they discovered that she was not the biological child of the parents who raised her."

"Mom, what are you trying to tell me? Are you saying that the two people she thinks are her biological parents, really aren't? What does this have to do with me, and with your having to go back to Cleveland?" This was the moment of truth. I took a deep breath. I was still calm. By now Cole was almost squeezing my hand. He jumped in to rescue me because this was long overdue.

"Michaela, what your mother is trying to tell you is that we love you dearly. You are our daughter, and will always be our daughter, no matter what." Michaela was no longer smiling. Instead, she had a shocked, almost gaunt expression. This is a very bright child. She had to have figured out what we were trying to say.

Then, the tears started, and she reached out for me. She laid her head on my shoulder. She was very quiet. I prayed to God to give me strength because I had to be strong for me. If I fell apart, then she would too. Then, Michaela softly asked, "Mom, you are my mother, aren't you?" I had tears now. Thank God she wasn't looking at me.

"Yes, Sweetheart, I am your mother, and always will be. We have loved you from the moment you were born. We will never stop loving you. I have been going back to Cleveland because the hospital informed us that Sidney Williams' blood and DNA match ours, and that yours match Ralph and Cynthia Williams."

I stopped talking to give her time to digest what I had said. The announcement had been a blow to Cole and me. I knew it would be very difficult for my baby girl. This was, by far, the most difficult moment of my life! I wasn't hurting for me, but for my child. Michaela was sobbing now, and Cole was embracing her. We held her close. No one said anything. I knew she would speak when she was ready. Finally, she did.

"Mom, how could this have happened? Didn't you know that you had the wrong baby when you came home? Mom, are you going to send me away?" I looked directly at her and said, "No, Sweetheart, I did not know that the nurses hadn't done the job they were trained to do." I was careful with my selection of words and avoided using the term "wrong baby," because Cole and I had not brought the "wrong baby" home. We simply did not come home with our biological child. There was nothing "wrong" about Michaela, and I didn't want her to start thinking there was. Michaela was no longer sobbing. She was silent. That was just as painful.

"Honey, we love you more than you can ever imagine. There's nothing in this world your mother and I wouldn't do for you," Cole said, as he stroked her hair. "You are our daughter, and we are your parents."

"Who is Sidney Williams?" Michaela asked. "If I'm your daughter, then who are Sidney Williams' parents?" Michaela began crying again. Cole and I held her closer. Mother understands people very well. She had told me it would be best to let Michaela do the talking at this difficult time, and that we should be good listeners. I was listening, trying to answer her questions. My heart was pounding. Michaela must have felt the vibration!

Cole, Michaela and I held on to each other for more than an hour. I did just as Mother had advised me to do – let Michaela lead the discussion. Michaela cried, asked questions, cried some more, then asked more questions. Cole was as calm as ever. When he sensed that I was struggling with an answer, he would jump right in with a response that calmed Michaela and me. Apparently he had anticipated every question that she could possibly ask, and had an answer.

I felt strongly that both Michaela and Sidney would need psychological counseling, to cope with this traumatic discovery, but Mother and Cole disagreed. They firmly believed that our unconditional love and support for Michaela was what she needed to cope with this news. We prayed that Sidney would get the same love and support from Ralph and Cynthia.

After more than an hour of crying and asking questions, Michaela said she was tired and went to bed. I went with her and stroked her head until she fell asleep. Cole and Mother came in later to kiss her. We held hands and prayed for both of our daughters. Although I was drained emotionally, there was a sense of relief that the truth was out. We didn't have to live a lie any longer. Michaela didn't go to school the next day, or the next. We didn't try to force her. She could stay in bed as long as she needed to, to digest what she was learning.

Cole's parents, my sister and two brothers, all wanted to be here with Michaela, to let her know how much they loved her. They wanted to assure her that she was family, no matter what anybody had discovered. However, they decided to give her some time, first to let this revelation sink in, before making their visit.

Cole and I sat down with Matthew later that day to tell him everything. His response brought tears to my eyes! I'd always known that he was a fine young man, but now discovered how brave, loving and compassionate he truly was.

"Mom, Dad, Michaela is my sister, and I will always love her and be there for her. If I have another sister, I can love my other sister too. It's hard to imagine this family without Michaela, and that's just what I'm going to tell her. I can't wait to meet Sidney." The impish, big brother side of him came out. "Although, I know I have my work cut out for me. Can you imagine how long it's going to take to train her, so that I get the same respect from her that I get from Michaela?"

We all laughed. That was just what we needed to hear. I'm sure Matthew had sensed the pressure that his father and I had been under for the past two weeks. This obviously was his way of trying to help us relax. He was such a good son. I thanked God that McAlister wasn't old enough to understand any of this. I didn't have to have this conversation with another child.

Michaela slowly began to get stronger. Three days after being given the news, she finally started asking questions about Sidney. I told her what I knew, which wasn't very much. Then she started asking questions about Ralph and Cynthia Williams. I knew this was coming. I was very uncomfortable. I knew it was only natural for a child, or adult, to want to know about their biological parents. But, this didn't make it any easier to hear her ask about them. I knew there was nothing but fear about my child wanting to meet her biological parents. I knew that on an intellectual level, however.

What if she fell in love with them, and wanted to leave us? Mother reassured me that Cole and I had been warm, loving parents. Michaela wouldn't want to leave us, she said. We had showered each of our children with love. Still, Michaela might want to spend the rest of her life with her "natural parents." It was all too difficult to deal with at the moment. I decided that now was not the time to think about whether or not my daughter would choose to leave us. I had more important matters to deal with, like Michaela learning to cope with all of it, and Sidney getting stronger and healthy again.

Michaela joined us for dinner on Friday night. She had been eating in her room since she was told the devastating news. During dinner, Cole received a call from David Turner, the attorney in Cleveland we hired to investigate this mix-up. They talked for more than an hour. Cole didn't appear to be pleased when he asked me to come onto the back porch. He had this look on his face that suggested something wasn't right.

"That was David Turner. He's coming here to meet with us next week. He has questioned the staff on the maternity unit about events that took place during the time Michaela and Sidney were born. Do you remember Ms. Noland and Mr. Jacobs telling us that the maternity unit was under construction when Michaela and Sidney were born? Well, David has learned that an addition to the hospital was under construction during that time. However, the maternity unit was not under renovation. Everything appeared to be normal in the maternity unit. There was no construction or other renovation being done there during those months. There were 10 nurses assigned to the maternity unit, working different shifts. He has met with some of them. But he has learned that while the everyday work environment appeared normal in the maternity unit, the three nurses that he has met with tell a different story. He'll be here on Tuesday to tell us what he has discovered."

"What are you trying to tell me?" I asked, anxious about what David Turner had said. It now appeared that this "mix up" in babies may not have been an innocent mistake. I'd been too caught up in disbelief and pain to even think about what could have caused such a horrible thing to happen in the first place.

"It's possible that David's investigation will disclose information that will prove negligence on the part of Willow Memorial Hospital," Cole explained. "He has met and spoken with three nurses, and their stories are pretty much the same. There's one thing he's convinced of – this wasn't some innocent mistake. He's determined to get to the bottom of it."

David Turner arrived in Nashville around noon on Tuesday. I picked him up at the airport. From the moment we hired him to look into this matter, he had been very concerned about our well-being. He had been a source of support for my family. Cole met David several years ago when he was a student at the Case Western Reserve University Law School. He was a focused, bright young man, determined to finish at the top of his class, which he did. He was definitely going to leave his mark on the legal profession. Several large national law firms were after him, but he had decided to stay in Cleveland.

David was born and raised in Cincinnati. He came from a family of attorneys with a reputation for working hard for their clients, and winning their cases. When Cole called to ask him to take our case, he jumped at it. David had children close to the ages of our children. He told Cole he couldn't imagine having to go through anything like this. He wanted to find out why this happened, and who was responsible. He had kept his word. Cole was pleased with his work.

After dinner, David, Cole and I talked until the early hours of the next day. I had no doubt that we had hired someone who could solve this puzzle, but I also knew that it wouldn't erase the pain my family and other families had to live with. David told us what he had learned from and about three of the nurses who were at the hospital's maternity unit at the time.

Beverly Fields is African-American, 56 years old, born and raised in Cleveland. She had worked as a nurse in the maternity unit for 10 years. She resigned seven years ago because of health problems. She then started working as a private nurse, caring for elderly people in their homes. She distinctly remembered that there was no renovation going on in the maternity unit during the time that Michaela was born. Ms. Fields was pretty certain that she was on duty the morning that Michaela was born, but couldn't remember anything unusual taking place. Several babies were born that day. She had absolutely no idea that anything had gone wrong.

David didn't tell her what had happened with Michaela and Sidney, because he didn't want to compromise the investigation. However, he did tell her that children born during that time were now sick, and two had died. He was trying to find out what went wrong. He did learn from Ms. Fields that there had been a power struggle among some of the nurses. Apparently, Ms. Noland had just been tapped to fill the vacancy for head nurse, and two other applicants weren't happy about that. Ms. Fields gave him the names of some of the other nurses she had worked with, and said she would contact him if she thought of anything else important.

David next met with Stephanie Anderson. Ms. Anderson is 43, Caucasian, and had worked as a nurse in the maternity unit for only three years. She then relocated to Detroit after getting married, but was still working as a nurse. Ms. Anderson couldn't remember if she actually had been on vacation during that time, because she usually took her vacation in mid-December. She did recall that there had been a lot of tension in the unit because of the vacant position for head nurse.

Also, a young male nurse had recently been hired, and some of the other nurses didn't think he was competent. They said he made their jobs more time consuming because they had to cover his shortcomings. She described Cedric Alston as a nice guy, but he didn't want anybody telling him what to do. She said he and Ms. Noland were at odds from day one, and that he probably would never have gotten the job if Ms. Noland had been the head nurse when he was hired.

When asked if Cedric Alston was competent at his job, Ms. Anderson replied that he was as competent, or at least appeared to be as competent, as the other nurses. Ms. Anderson denied that she was interested in the head nurse position. She said she didn't apply for the job, but Ms. Fields had said Ms. Anderson wanted nothing more than to be the head nurse on the maternity unit. David didn't tell Ms. Anderson that he'd already met and talked with Ms. Fields.

Cedric Alston was now living in Atlanta, selling real estate. He told David that he had become disillusioned with the nursing profession, after he realized that his true love was showing and selling homes. He had worked in the maternity unit for only a year and a half before deciding to leave. Cedric Alston is African-American, born and raised in California, and now 36 years old. He spoke highly of Ms. Noland. He didn't mention any problems between the two of them, or that there had been any tension in the unit.

He did say that there had been one nurse, Nola Simpson, who simply didn't know what she was doing, and should not have been hired. According to Mr. Alston, Ms. Simpson was going through a divorce during that time. Most days she walked around like she was in another world. He said she'd been put on probation twice, and was finally dismissed. But, he didn't know exactly why. He wasn't sure, but he thought she might have been dismissed around January 1978.

David was determined to meet with and talk to anyone who might have been involved with the maternity unit when Michaela and Sidney were born. We all agreed on one point – Ms. Noland and Mr. Jacobs weren't telling all they knew, and that there were problems in that unit that could have led to Cole and me, and Ralph and Cynthia, going home without our biological daughters. Still, I was too hurt to be angry with anyone. Although I wanted David to get to the bottom of this tragedy, I had too many concerns about our daughters to worry about that now.

Michaela went back to school on the following Wednesday. Our talkative, outgoing little girl had now become very quiet. She didn't want Cole or me out of her sight, except when she was in school. Perhaps she was afraid that we were going to leave her again, and run to Sidney, just as I was concerned that she might want to leave us and run to Ralph and Cynthia.

Cole had some of his staff members traveling for him, because he didn't want to leave his family at this time in our lives. Even Matthew was spending less time on the tennis courts, and more time at home. He loved his sister. He was supportive and protective of her. I began to miss his teasing and playing around with her the way he used to, before we told him about the mix-up.

Cole and I spoke with Ralph and Cynthia daily to keep up with Sidney's condition. Apparently she was getting stronger each day. She was now talking. Cynthia, like me, was dreading the thought of having to tell her daughter the painful news. She didn't want to tell her just yet, because of her health. I could certainly understand her decision.

As I continued to read through the papers about Sarah Johnson, there was a note at the bottom of one of the pages that read: "Through our pain, we gain strength and wisdom." I didn't know if these were Sarah's thoughts or someone else's, but I couldn't have come across them at a better time.

Michaela was beginning to talk more openly about what had happened. Mother thought this was a good sign, proof that she was coping with the situation. She had so many questions. We answered them as honestly as we could, even though there was still so much we didn't understand ourselves.

Then one afternoon after I picked her up from school, she asked *the* question: "Mom, when can I go with you and Dad to Cleveland to meet my birth parents?"

20. Sarah

AUNT CLARA WAS A WONDERFUL PERSON to live with as well. I had now lived in Boston for a month. I came to understand that the color of one's skin pretty much determined where that person could work, how much education he could get and how he was treated. In these respects, Boston was not so different from New York City.

Reverend and Missus Baker wrote to me often. Their letters helped me stay optimistic about my future. They strongly encouraged me to continue to learn as much as possible.

Missus Baker wrote that Mastah Wilmington and his men had apparently left the area, because she had not heard any more talk about whites trying to find a young slave girl from Holly Springs. But, Missus Baker wanted me to stay in Boston. She did not think enough time had passed for some of the white people to stop asking questions. Reading their letters, and certain verses in the Bible, strengthened me.

It was now November 1845. In two months I would turn 15. The Bakers and Aunt Clara were committed to helping me learn as much as possible. I saved all of the money I earned from sewing in New York City and Boston. I now had saved $60.00. I made dresses for Aunt Clara and Missus Baker. I even made some for Mammy. I strongly believed that, somehow, I would see her again.

One of Aunt Clara's friends, Missus Loretta Cross, taught me each day at her home. She lived on Tulip Street, which was only a short distance from Aunt Clara's house. Missus Cross appeared to be close to Aunt Clara's age, perhaps around 60 or so. She had taught young and older Negroes how to read and write. After her husband died, Missus Cross devoted most of her time to teaching. Before my arrival, she and Aunt Clara had worked out a plan for me to continue to improve my reading and writing skills. Missus Cross loved to teach as much as Missus Baker did. I could not have had better people in my life. My speech improved significantly after only a few months with the Bakers and Aunt Clara. They all worked with me on how to correctly pronounce words.

Aunt Clara took me around the city with her to different events. She was proud of how much I had learned and of my skills as a seamstress. Her friends did not ask about my past. I was proud of my roots, but deeply hurt that slavery had destroyed much of the dignity and pride my family, and other slaves, had back in our homeland.

Missus Baker and Aunt Clara were born and raised in Boston. They knew quite a lot about the South. They knew people who had actually lived in Mississippi. Like the Bakers, Aunt Clara was very active in the anti-slavery movement. She said many times that her last wish before she left this world was to see all of her people free. Aunt Clara told me about the injustices our people had to endure, even in the North, where there were no slaveholders. I told her about my brother, how he had been "hired out" at a young age and never returned. I also told her about slaves who had lost fathers, mothers, sisters and brothers to different slaveholders. She had heard all about Mastah Wilmington from Missus Baker. She thought I was the bravest person she had ever met.

In early November 1845, Aunt Clara gave me a letter from Missus Baker. She was coming to Boston, and had a surprise for me. I was so happy I began to cry. I did not care about the surprise; I just wanted to see Missus Baker. I started counting the days to her arrival. I had a special present for her also.

When I was younger, I believed I would get out of Mississippi, but had no idea how it would happen. Many of our people had suffered, even lost their lives, trying to escape the brutality of slavery. Through the grace of God, Mastah Wilmington had brought me to New York City, and God had led me to Reverend and Missus Baker. They, the Bakers, led me to Aunt Clara. If only I could share all of this with my family. Surely they would be proud that I had had the courage to stay behind in a large, strange city, with no family. I would teach my children everything Grandma and Mammy had taught me about faith and courage.

Reverend and Missus Baker arrived early that Thursday morning. They brought hugs, kisses and gifts. I gave Missus Baker her dress, and Reverend Baker a poem I had written especially for him. We all had a wonderful time. Aunt Clara and Missus Baker told stories about their childhood, how they played tricks on their mother and on each other. As I listened to them, I wished I had a sister. More importantly, I wished I had had the opportunity to grow up with my brother.

The Baker's son, Jonathan, and daughter, Cora, both of whom were married and had families, joined us for dinner. They both lived in Connecticut and had come to Boston to visit Aunt Clara. They were just as loving and kind as their parents. The sight of them together made my heart ache for Mammy, Pappy and Tom. After dinner, Missus Baker walked with me to my room to tell me about the special surprise.

"You have given me so much, Missus Baker. What else could you possibly have for me?"

"My dear child, we know someone who is going to Mississippi to take care of some business. He's involved in the manufacture of cotton here and in Europe. He is white, but active in the anti-slavery movement. We have worked closely with him for several years. You met him when you were living with us. His name is Samuel Trent. Do you recognize the name?"

"No, I do not, Missus Baker. What does Mastah Trent have to do with me?"

"Well, my child, he knew all about you from the day you came to live with us. He worked hard to distract Mr. Wilmington and his men when they were looking for you. He is the person we have asked to try to deliver your letter to your mother. He recently told the Reverend and me that he is returning to Mississippi on cotton business. He has plans to stop in Holly Springs. We have asked him to try to find your parents, and tell them that you are safe and doing well."

I began to cry. Someone was going to Mississippi and might actually find my parents. I wondered if they were well, or if perhaps they had taken ill after I left. So many thoughts ran through my mind. What did they think of their little girl, who ran off and left them? I could not speak for several minutes. Missus Baker stroked my head and held me close.

Finally, I found the strength to speak, "Can Mastah Trent be trusted not to turn me in to Mastah Wilmington?" I still did not trust white people, and did not know if I ever could.

"Baby, Mr. Trent is a good, decent man. He has risked his life because of his activity in the movement. Yes, my child, I do trust him. We would never allow anyone to hurt you. Furthermore, he doesn't know where you are now, and has never asked. For all he knows, you're still somewhere in New York City."

"But, Missus Baker, surely Mastah Wilmington will get suspicious of anyone asking about my parents. Why would a white Northerner be interested in finding Mammy and Pappy? Mastah Wilmington is no fool. I was valuable to him. He would never allow a slave girl to make a fool of him. Once Mastah Wilmington even suspects that I am in Boston, he will surely come for me!"

"I certainly understand your concern, Sarah, but if Samuel Trent wanted to turn you over to Mastah Wilmington, he had plenty of opportunities to do that when you were in New York City. Now, if you don't want him asking questions, or trying to get information about your parents, I will tell him that," Missus Baker said. I knew she only wanted what was best for me.

Suddenly, I did not care about my safety. I just wanted word that Mammy and Pappy were alive and well. I hugged Missus Baker and asked her when Mastah Trent was leaving for Mississippi. She said he was leaving within the next three days. She told me to wash my face and come downstairs to join the family for some cake she had made especially for me.

I rejoined the family, but was quiet the rest of the evening. I could not stop thinking about Mammy and Pappy. How I wished I could go with

Mastah Trent, and possibly see them. I knew that could not happen. Missus Baker said she had told him that if he was able to find my parents, to tell them that I was safe, that I was living with a wonderful person who loved and was taking good care of me. He was to also tell them that I was learning more each day. I knew I would not be able to think of anything else until Mastah Trent returned from Mississippi with some report about his ability to contact my parents.

Soon I began going to various anti-slavery movement meetings with Aunt Clara, to learn more about how I could help our people. Aunt Clara was involved in many activities. She always looked eloquent wherever she went. Although I could make my own clothes, she bought dresses for me, and insisted that I wear them. The social groups she belonged to raised lots of money to help our people learn skills and find jobs. Aunt Clara believed that Negroes had to be educated, so we would be less dependent on white people.

I met kind people in Boston through Aunt Clara. She seemed proud to introduce me as "my Sarah." She said many times that she would love to meet Mammy and Pappy, because they had done a wonderful job raising me.

Because I was so eager to learn, I did not mind struggling to finish all the study work Missus Cross gave me each day. She said I was an excellent student. Although I was tired when I left her home each day, I refused to give up my sewing job. I needed the money. The Bakers and Aunt Clara had given me a place to live and food to eat. I was very thankful for that. Allowing them to give me money was out of the question.

While Aunt Clara and Missus Baker were sociable, gracious ladies, active in their communities, I preferred staying in to study or work on my sewing. Still, Aunt Clara insisted that I come to some meetings and social gatherings with her. I usually felt uncomfortable, at these gatherings, but Mammy had taught me good manners. I was polite, even when I did not feel like socializing with their friends. There was no way I was going to do anything that would hurt Aunt Clara or Missus Baker's feelings. If they wanted me to socialize, then I would socialize.

It was almost Christmas now, and Missus Baker was coming back to Boston. Christmas would be difficult without Mammy and Pappy. It would be my first without them. I had so many memories of our times together. I laughed and cried when I thought about all the wonderful times I had shared with my parents and other slaves.

The mastah, on any plantation, determined whether or not his slaves could celebrate Christmas. Slaves on the Wilmington plantation could; they did not work on Christmas day. How much celebration the slaves – if they were allowed to – could do depended on the master. After the Wilmington family celebrated Christmas, Mammy and I were allowed to leave the big house and celebrate with Pappy and other slaves. No matter what the future held, those good memories will stay with me.

Memories of my family came flooding back when the day I had so desperately waited for arrived. We received word from Missus Baker that Mastah Trent had good news. Missus Baker would tell me all about it when she came to Boston again. I prayed each night that Mammy, Pappy and Tom were alive, and that we would see each other again. Missus Baker's letter had very little information. I wondered if Mammy had forgiven me for what I had done. But I knew I would always be Pappy's little girl.

Mammy and I had always spent Christmas morning at the Wilmingtons, preparing a delightful breakfast for them, their friends and family. Missus Wilmington always had her home decorated with a big Christmas tree, and presents underneath. Melissa and Kate would get up early to open their presents. They all seemed so happy.

After everyone had eaten Christmas breakfast, dinner was prepared. When all of the cleaning was done, Mammy and I were allowed to go home and spend time with Pappy. Missus Wilmington always shared various meats with us when the hunting was plentiful. She also gave us loins, entrails, chops, feet, necks and livers after the hogs were killed. Some of these meats were part of our Christmas dinner.

Mammy worked hard to make our Christmas special. We had presents to exchange with each other. Mammy made useful things for Pappy and me, like clothing and quilts. Suppa was always good. She cooked fried pork, sweet potatoes, beans, corn bread and pies. We invited cousins and other slaves to our cabin to eat. After suppa, there was singing, praying, dancing, banjo playing and lots of laughter. I wondered what their Christmas would be like this year.

Reverend and Missus Baker arrived early the day before Christmas. Aunt Clara and I were there to meet them at the train station. Everyone could see the excitement in my eyes. Missus Baker gave me a big hug. She told me that everything was going to be just fine. On the way back to Aunt Clara's house, Missus Baker handed me a folded piece of paper. I opened it and realized it had a message from Mammy. Someone had written it for her, but Mammy had scribbled her name. Tears filled my eyes. What did she have to say to me? I decided not to read it until after dinner. I was afraid I would not have the strength, or appetite, to get through the special meal Aunt Clara and I had worked so hard to prepare, if I read it now.

The four of us had dinner. After I helped clean the kitchen and wash the dishes, the Bakers and Aunt Clara went into the parlor by the fire. They talked about their memories of past Christmases.

I excused myself and went to my room to be alone. They all understood why I needed to be alone. I sat on my bed and carefully opened the piece of paper. I would cherish it forever. Mammy and I had not talked in months. There was so much I wanted to say to her. But, now, it was time to listen.

To our Sarah:

We love you and we miss you. Yes, we still cry for you. But I never stopped believing that God would take care of you. We are just so thankful that you have found good people to help you. You are so brave. Pappy and I are proud of you. Pappy and I take care of each other. We want you to have a better life than we did. You are a gift from God. We have faith that we will see you and Tom again.

Mammy

After I read the note, I held it close to my heart. I sat on the bed with my legs folded, staring at the words. I stared at those very special words from Mammy! She did not hate me after what I had done to them, left them behind on the plantation. She thought I was brave. I knew she and Pappy had cried and worried about me, but now they knew that I was doing well. A heavy load had been lifted from my shoulders. I could breathe easier, after so many months of worrying about them. I still had a lot to accomplish, but at least Mammy and Pappy knew I was safe and well.

They also believed that one day we would see each other again. Mammy and Pappy should have been proud. They had taught us to believe in God, in ourselves. They had taught us that nothing was impossible. If I ever had children, I would teach them that they are very special, descendents of strong, gifted people. My children would be proud of their heritage. This would show in the way they walked and talked.

I did not feel like rejoining the others, so stayed in my room. I read Mammy's words over and over. At some point, there was a knock at the door. It was Missus Baker. She wanted to know if I was alright. I let her read the note; she cried with me. She explained that Mammy had asked Mastah Trent to write the note for her.

Mastah Trent worked for a large company in New York City that manufactured and marketed cotton. The company purchased hundreds of bails of cotton from Holly Springs each year. According to the Bakers, Mastah Trent was not a personal friend of Mastah Wilmington. He was sent to Holly Springs as a representative of the company.

Missus Baker said Mastah Trent had a difficult time finding Mammy and Pappy at first because he did not want anyone to suspect that he knew where I was hiding. He had to be careful about asking questions.

Fortunately, Mastah Wilmington returned home from a trip and was able to meet with him.

Mastah Trent found Mammy in the big house, washing clothes. When he got the opportunity, he followed her outside and told her the news about me. He said Mammy cried, and said this was the moment she had been praying for, to hear that I was safe. She pleaded with Mastah Trent not to say or do anything that would bring harm to me. I guess Mammy had to go on blind faith that Mastah Trent was an honest white man.

Mammy then asked him to write a message from her to me. She told him what to say; he wrote it. He did not see Pappy, but Mammy told him that Pappy was well. He also said Mammy asked him to tell me that I should still be very careful. I assumed she meant that Mastah Wilmington and his men had not given up on finding me.

Missus Baker asked me to show Aunt Clara and Reverend Baker the quilt Mammy had sent to me by Mastah Trent. I was proud to show off her work. They all said I got my gift of sewing from a good teacher. We all held hands and said a prayer for Mammy, Pappy and Tom. We then sang songs and opened presents. I could feel Mammy and Pappy's spiritual presence. I felt joyful. This was all I needed to keep going. That night I slept well, with Mammy's quilt and note close to my heart.

The days that followed were colder than I could ever have imagined. I longed for spring. I was still learning new words and how to work with numbers. I was amazed at how my reading and writing skills had improved since my lessons began six months ago. Missus Baker, Aunt Clara and Missus Cross had helped me learn to enunciate words more correctly. Although I grew up listening to the Wilmingtons speak perfect English, I still had difficulty pronouncing certain words. However, that was quickly changing.

I also kept busy helping Aunt Clara, and other Negroes, organize to fight for rights for our people. The few businesses owned by Negroes were failing from lack of support. Aunt Clara and others were fighting to save them. At meetings, they argued that if we did not buy goods and services from each other, no one else would. It was now 1846, yet many of us still did not have jobs to support our families. In the mean time, people from other countries were coming here looking for work. Some were better educated and had more skills than most Negroes.

Because they were not skilled, Negroes were being overlooked for jobs that were going to whites and foreigners. Aunt Clara was careful to do business with white people only when it was absolutely necessary, when she wanted something not found in businesses owned by Negroes. She said it was not because she did not like whites, but she wanted Negroes to make progress and become prosperous. People from other countries came to

Boston to earn a living, and in a short time, became prosperous. We wanted the same for our people.

Negroes in Boston were not wealthy, like white people, but some were well-to-do, relatively speaking. They donated money to programs to help educate and teach skills to less fortunate Negroes. But, so much more was still needed, to buy books and help with teachers' salaries. We still had a long way to go. If only I could tell Mammy and Pappy that free Negroes had struggles, too.

In church the following Sunday, Aunt Clara and I heard about an entire slave family that had escaped from Georgia to Boston. We were told that they were hungry, sick and had no clothes for their two young children. Our minister asked the congregation to contribute food, clothing, money and anything else to help them begin a new life here. Aunt Clara and I visited them the next day at the temporary shelter opened by an anti-slavery group where they were staying. It broke my heart to see how weak and discouraged they were. They talked about the danger they faced in escaping to have a better life. They could not believe that I had once lived in Mississippi.

"Ya dont look nere soun lak ya been no slave," the father, Daniel Cumby, said to me. "Why, ya speaks good, an ya is dress real purty. Howd ya git hure?" I told them my story. They listened to every word. I also told them about Tom.

"I give anythang if my babies could read n writ," the mother, Eve Cumby, said. "Elijah hure is fo years ol, an Ruth is six. Dey ain't neva seen a book, less mo read one. Ya is mighty bless to know so much, my chile, comin from Misippi."

Aunt Clara and I discussed the family over dinner. There were lots of people donating food, clothing and furniture to them. I told Aunt Clara I wanted to do something different. I wanted to teach Elijah and Ruth to read and write. Aunt Clara did not think I had the time, because of my studies and sewing. I told her I would find the time.

I decided to spend Sunday evenings teaching Ruth and Elijah. Meeting this family brought back painful memories of Holly Springs. I had never taught before, but I remembered how Mammy had taught me to sew. I also knew how much my reading, writing and speaking had improved since meeting and being taught by Missus Baker, Missus Cross and Aunt Clara. The Cumbys wanted what most of us wanted, a better quality of life for themselves and their children.

I began working with Elijah and Ruth by talking to them using correct pronunciation of words, and by listening to what they had to say and the way they expressed themselves. We slowly moved to learning letters and numbers. Ruth had a cloth doll that she loved dearly, so I made a dress for the doll. We talked about the different parts of the doll's body, how to pronounce each part, then how to spell those parts.

Aunt Clara and her friends found a house near our church for the family to live in temporarily. They also found someone who needed a carpenter. Jake Tillman, a construction worker, was active in the anti-slavery movement. He hired Daniel Cumby. Mastah Cumby was grateful to find work. He said he had worked hard all of his life and did not plan to stop just because he was free. Mastah Cumby had done some carpentry work in Georgia, so was well qualified for the job.

Aunt Clara was soon able to help him get more training in carpentry. Eve Cumby turned the small, three-room house into a warm, loving home for her family. Aunt Clara and her friends kept this family "hidden" as much as possible, because there were slaveholders roaming through Boston, looking for runaway slaves, just as there were in New York City.

Spring arrived, and I watched this frightened, almost starved family gain weight, and slowly become comfortable with strangers who wanted to help them find some happiness in this life. Missus Cumby began sharing her dreams, and fears, with Aunt Clara and me. I had always thought things had been tough for me and my family in Holly Springs. But, the Cumby family's life had been tougher than I could have imagined for any slave family.

Mastah Cumby had been whipped on several occasions by his mastah, in Macon, Georgia. This same mastah had also violated his wife. Mastah Cumby told us that he would rather be dead than remain a slave on that plantation. He showed us scars and bruises on his body that would never heal completely.

Missus Cumby said Ruth and Elijah loved coming to me on Sundays to learn more words and numbers. The lessons had brightened all of their lives. They were getting stronger emotionally and physically each day.

It was now June 1846. I had been away from Holly Springs for one year! Missus Baker came to visit, and we all celebrated. The pain of being away from home was not as sharp anymore. I was confident that I would have a better life. I had also saved quite a bit of money, almost $270.00.

Missus Cross "pushed" me to do my best in reading, writing and working with numbers. I also worked hard to help Ruth and Elijah learn as much as they could. I was very pleased with how much they had learned at this point. However, they still had a long road ahead of them, for more education and training for jobs.

That summer, Aunt Clara planned a trip to Canada to visit some of her friends. They were former slaves who had settled in Boston temporarily, then moved farther north. She invited me to come with her. I was so excited I could barely think of anything else. I gave Ruth and Elijah enough work to keep them busy until I returned in two weeks. If only I could tell

Mammy about this. She would be so proud of me, because she knew how much I wanted to see other places.

It was good to get out of Boston, at least for a few days. Our people were being accused of crimes they had not committed. And, their overall standard of living was much lower than that of white people. There was obviously growing hostility between Negroes and white people.

As we traveled, I got lost in my thoughts. I was thankful to have met so many interesting and helpful people since I left Holly Springs more than a year ago. As we approached Toronto, I closed my eyes, and counted my blessings. I knew I now had far more blessings than troubles.

21. Raini

BEGAN MY PART-TIME POSITION as Associate Professor of Political Science at Brown in June 2013. Facing a room full of college students, trying to keep them interested enough to ask questions and engaged in conversation, was a challenge. However, I have loved every moment of it. Although many of them are not political science majors, I wanted each of them to learn something and enjoy my class.

Our Information Technology consulting business has grown and prospered. John managed to negotiate a contract with the Office of Homeland Security. He left his position at Brown four months ago. Some of his co-workers told him he was making a mistake, but he never doubted his ability to make this business a success. In the early months, he spent most of the day and night at the company, trying to get it off the ground. There were days I wished he hadn't left Brown. I missed having lunch with him, or simply dropping by his office to say "hello."

As the business began to grow, we had to begin scheduling our personal lives. We had to check our calendars to arrange time for each other just to do the simple things we enjoyed. This was difficult. I realized I'd taken so much for granted. John was determined not to fail. I certainly didn't want him to, but I also wanted my husband at home. I coped the only way I knew how, by burying myself in my work. I spent most of each day in the Political Science Department, preparing for classes or grading papers.

Some days it was difficult to be home alone, so I would go to John's office. He was usually busy, however, working or training staff. During this time, I turned to Mother for support. As always, she was there for me. I'd expected her to say that John was a computer genius, who loved his work more than he loved me. I could imagine her saying that I should've seen this coming when we were dating. Instead, she told me about some of the difficult times she and Dad had gone through, and how she was thankful that she'd stuck by him. She said John could be spending his time doing worse things than trying to build his own business.

She and I became close all over again, the way we were when I was growing up. After I married, we hadn't seen or talked to each other as often as before. I was so busy trying to be a good wife, and establish a career. Now, I needed her more than ever; she was there for me.

Mother had grown to love John as a son. Anyone who made me happy was okay with her. Dad had always liked John, and thought he was smart to build his own business. He and mother encouraged me to be supportive, because the hard work would pay off someday. They were right. That day had arrived.

Before long, John had reached the point where he could do a lot of his work from our home. This was perfect, because that made it possible for me to continue to teach part-time. He in turn became a full-time father to our twins. Yes, we became the proud parents of a son and daughter, now 4 months old. I'm still nursing, and look forward to coming home each day to feed my children. John thoroughly enjoys his new role as a father. He even gets up with the little angels at night to feed or comfort them.

I had complications with my blood pressure during the pregnancy, so I'm done with child bearing. John is excited to have a son and a daughter. He shows more interest in the children than he does in the business these days. He delegates some of his responsibilities to his staff, as opposed to trying to do everything himself.

We share the responsibility of bathing and dressing our children. I often wonder how he manages so well with them when I'm not around. I'm exhausted whenever I have them by myself. John, on the other hand, never seems to get tired. He has even put cribs in his office at home, so that he can be close to them while he's working.

Our children were born prematurely, but are healthy babies, except that our daughter, Haley, has respiratory problems. She has to be monitored closely. She has been diagnosed with Respiratory Distress Syndrome, and sometimes has rapid, labored breathing. She only weighed four pounds at birth, and was unable to initiate breathing. John and I are very much aware that this condition can result in multiple organ failure, if not properly handled. Fortunately, Harry, our son, has healthy lungs.

I love my babies and husband. I also love my career. I've managed to build a reputation as an enlightened, concerned professor and politician. John's devotion to our children has given me the freedom to be actively involved in local politics.

A friend from law school, Anna Southerland, decided to run for U.S. Congress from our district two years ago. She had asked me to manage her campaign. I accepted, and was able to put together a strong team for her. I used the knowledge I gained from working with Senator Cole, and my personal knowledge as an elected official, to help get Anna into office.

I read about how past presidents and other prominent elected officials campaigned, and were able to win elections. I learned that the successful ones surrounded themselves with smart people. This information was fascinating. Many nights John came home and found books scattered across our bed. I had taken notes and passed the information on to Anna.

I had some guilt about leaving our children each morning, especially Haley, because of her illness, but not enough to give up my career. I always resolved it by telling myself that our children were with their father, so they were in good hands. Still, I wondered if they needed me more. John, by the way, began delegating more of his duties at his company to spend more time at home.

My mother did not work until I was in the second grade. She strongly believed that the early years were critical to a child's development. John was a devoted father, but I sometimes wondered if I was a devoted mother. We discussed this issue at times. I was nursing my children, and spent my free time with them. Was this good enough?

My mother, Sharon Hamilton, is an amazing person. She's my hero, and I love her dearly, but we're so different. Fortunately, there's no law that says a daughter must be a carbon copy of her mother. She chose to stay at home with me, but I didn't think it was necessary to stay at home with my children. John's mother had also chosen to stay at home with her three sons. I sometimes wondered what she thought about me leaving my family every morning, especially since we didn't need a second income. John wanted to be home to take care of our children. At the same time he was very supportive of my career. Perhaps the day would come when we would switch roles. For now, though, we were enjoying our lives. We saw no reason to change anything.

Anna Southerland called quite often for advice after being elected to Congress. I gave her as much advice as I could. She was brilliant, having finished at the top of our law class. She was married to a successful architect. They didn't have children. Anna was quite pleased with how I managed her campaign. She felt that she won the election because of the team strategy I developed, and the hard work of volunteers.

Anna asked me to chair a committee that would study the number of babies born in this country with HIV/AIDS. She wanted a report on how to provide successful ongoing treatment to them. I wanted to accept, but didn't know how John would feel about the decision. After all, I was a working mother with two children and family obligations.

One afternoon I came home and found John asleep, on his back, on the sofa in his office. Both babies were cuddled in his arms. I stood and watched them. All three had the most peaceful, the most pleasant expressions on their faces. I wondered if our children were bonding more with John than with me. I wondered what I was missing when I left home each morning. John was so content to be at home with them. They clearly adored him. I didn't know if it was jealousy or feeling guilty because I wasn't here during the day. I sat and stared at the three of them, lost in those thoughts.

I wondered what my children would think of me when they were grown, after I told them their dad cared for them while I worked. Larkin thought it was great that I worked and John stayed home. But then, Larkin wasn't a mother. She was a dear friend who had not given birth to two beautiful babies. Perhaps if John had to work outside of the home, I would have stayed home with our children. Fortunately, he didn't have to leave them to go to the office, and his pay check was still a lot more than mine. I was proud to be their mother, and John's wife. I also was proud of my career.

As I sat watching my husband and babies sleep, I prayed for guidance to be a good wife, mother and professor. I asked God to help me keep my priorities straight, to be the kind of mother and wife He would have me to be for the family. I knew how important the role of wife and mother was in a family. I didn't want to be a disappointment to my family.

Dad had always asked for, and valued Mother's advice; so had I. Mother was and is strong, and we knew it. We loved her for her strength. I didn't want to be any less than that to my family, even if it ultimately meant giving up a career. As I sat thinking, John woke up.

"Hi, Sweetheart, what are you doing home so early? I was lying here playing with these little guys, then all of us passed out," he said, sounding as if he'd enjoyed every moment of the day.

"I finished grading papers early, so decided to pop in to spend some time with my favorite people." Our voices startled the children. Soon they too were awake. "Let me feed them, then let's take them for a stroll," I suggested. As we pushed our babies in their carriage through a nearby park, I talked to him about our role as parents.

"Do you ever wish I was home, and you could get up, dress and get out in the mornings?" I began.

"Raini, I love being home with our children. If I didn't, I would hire someone to come in and take care of them."

"You wouldn't ask me to do it?"

"I would ask, but it's certainly your decision. You enjoy your work, which is great."

"But, don't you think a parent should be with the children, as opposed to bringing in a stranger?"

"I wouldn't bring in a stranger to keep our children. I know several staff members who have retired from the university. They would be more than happy to spend their days with two beautiful children. Now, why all of the questions? Are you thinking about coming home, about giving up the career you love?"

"No, I'm not thinking about that. I'm just curious to know what you *really* think about having to be here with the children all day, while I work. And, Haley has to be closely monitored to ensure that her treatment is appropriate for her respiratory condition. The doctors have said her respiratory distress may gradually resolve, but they don't know when it will happen. Don't you feel overwhelmed at times?"

"First of all, Raini, we're both raising the children. You're not here most of the day, but you're still their mother. You come home right after work. I'm not complaining, so what's the problem?"

"I came home and found you and our babies asleep on the sofa. The three of you looked so peaceful. I've been wondering if I'm missing out on too much, perhaps not bonding with my children the way I should be. I want them to know that I am their mother, no one else."

"I doubt they'll mistake me for their mother," John said, laughing. "Mothers don't have to be with their children around the clock to bond with them."

"But, your mother stayed home with you, and mine with me. Don't you think that I'm less of a mother to our children than they were to us?"

"I certainly don't. In fact, I admire you for being able to work, come home at lunch to feed your children, then go back to campus. If you're happy as a person, then you'll be a great mother to our kids. I like being here with them, that's why I have so much fun with them. If I didn't like being here, then you, the kids and everyone I work with would know it."

I was silent. John was making sense. I knew he was content to be at home. Although he had built a prosperous business, his children were, in his words, "my greatest success story."

"So, what else is on your mind, kid?" he asked, breaking the silence. This was the perfect time to discuss my career plans. The weather was unusually mild. It was a great afternoon for walking. Our babies were awake and appeared to be enjoying the fresh air.

"John, Anna has asked me to chair a committee that would study the number of babies born in this country with HIV/AIDS, and report on how to provide successful ongoing treatment for them. This is a project she often talked about when we were law students. Now that she is a member of Congress, she is preparing to introduce a bill on the issue. I believe Rhode Island, and every other state, needs a program of this nature. I'd be honored to chair this committee."

"You should be," John responded. "So, have you given her an answer?"

"No, because I wanted to discuss it with you first. This project will require some travel." John looked down at the babies. I waited for him to say something, anything, but he didn't. I continued.

"I'm not sure how often I'll be away, so before I made a decision, I wanted to get some feedback from you. Then I'll get back with Anna. If I accept, I'm going to devote a lot of my spare time to this project. I will do everything possible to see it through. I'll have to check with Professor McWherter, to see if I can keep my teaching position."

"Sweetheart, I've never tried to stop you from growing, or doing what you want to do. However, you must think about your children, and, of course, your job. I can take care of myself."

"Yes, I know. I appreciate you. It hasn't been easy trying to decide. That's why I have to know what you think about me as a mother and wife. You and our children are my first concern. If you wanted me to come home tomorrow, I would. However, if I can help Anna get funding for the project, think about what this could do for children here, and around the country."

John knew me well enough to know that I had given this a great deal of thought. However, this was not an offer I could accept without talking to my husband and parents. Once I knew what John thought, I'd then talk to my parents. Larkin is my children's godmother. She would be coming to visit us in two weeks. I planned to discuss it with her after she arrived."

"John, if I accept, would you promise me one thing?"

"What is it?"

"If ever you think I'm slipping as a wife or mother, will you please tell me?"

"Yes, if you promise me one thing?"

"And what's that?"

"That you won't accuse me of trying to run your life, or stop you from reaching your goals."

"I promise. I still haven't reached a decision, but thank you for allowing me to be me."

"You're going to do that anyway," he said with a smile. "So, if you accept, does this mean that my wife will be a public figure again?"

"I wouldn't say that, but Anna wants this project to get a lot of coverage in the papers and media. She wants the public to know what she's trying to do, and who's helping her do it. John, if I accept, and if this requires a lot of travel, I don't see any reason why you and the children can't travel with me. Although, I have some concerns about packing Haley's ventilation support."

"Don't worry, we can manage. Just tell me when we need to start packing. I've got two little helpers now. We can handle anything."

It didn't take long for me to reach a decision. Anna called the next day. I told her I would chair the committee. My husband had given his approval. Now I had to clear my plans with Professor McWherter. He needed to know. There might be times when I wouldn't be able to teach some of my classes. Surprisingly, he was very encouraging. He thought it was great for the staff to be involved in local and national politics.

"This is good for the university, Professor Carrington. I strongly encourage the staff to publish articles and get involved in government and causes. The more we experience, the more we can talk about the real world to our students. You have always been active in local politics and community affairs. This is one of the reasons you were chosen for the position over several applicants, who had far more teaching experience.

"I like your hands-on approach in the classroom. It is apparent that your students do, too. Please be sure to give enough notice of your travels and other activities so your classes can be covered. You're going places, Professor Carrington. You are an asset to this university. I am proud to have you on my staff." I certainly hadn't expected a speech from Professor McWherter, but it was one I thoroughly enjoyed.

Anna and I planned to meet over lunch the next day to discuss the goals of the committee, and how we could reach them. It didn't take long for me to get busy with this new assignment. There were two other women and three men working with me. They were just as busy as I was with family and career obligations. However, we all had one common goal beyond our families, – to raise funds for this program. There were children who were very sick, and many had been abandoned because of HIV/AIDS. If they couldn't count on their elected and appointed leaders for help, then where would they go? Everyone on the committee was determined to make this project a success.

Politics wasn't John's favorite subject, yet he wanted to get involved in this particular cause. He typed letters and made several phone calls for me, when I was at work. I had to go to Washington, D.C. to testify before a Congressional committee; John and our children joined me. A week later, the committee met with Anna to give her a briefing on our progress.

We had discovered that 1,000,000 children, from birth to age 12, had HIV/AIDS in this country. There were 12,000 in Rhode Island alone. What was more heartbreaking was that 8,000 were orphans. Many of them had lost their parents to this disease. Our next step was to get busy raising money for the care and treatment of these children.

Anna met with Governor Joel Benton and state legislators to try to get the state to cover the cost of care and treatment. She was informed that if the state funded the cost for every child in need, other important state programs, such as education, would suffer as a result. Some children who qualified for Medicaid could be covered for treatment. So, we had to find other ways to get money for the children with no insurance.

I made a list of corporations and prominent individuals in the state that we planned to submit our proposal to, to show them our plan of action. We would ask them to be sponsors of the program, to help alleviate the financial burden on the state. Our goal was to get companies and individuals to make donations and to "adopt" children and families of children suffering from the disease. We would ask them to provide food, clothing, shelter and money. The money would be used to educate their "adopted" children and families on prevention and comprehensive care and treatment.

We met with children and the families of children infected with the HIV virus. Some of the children were lying in hospital beds, waiting to be placed in a home with a loving family, or an orphanage. We gathered information on several of these children to help present our case.

The response was overwhelming! Within a matter of weeks, money was coming in from all over the state. We were ecstatic. Governor Benton met with and commended us on a job well done. He said governors from several other states had contacted him, wanting to know how they could get similar programs started in their states.

There was still work to be done. We didn't think our work should end here in Rhode Island, or the United States. We wanted to take it abroad, to Asia and Africa where the number of children with the disease was outrageous!

In early September 2013, we learned that an International Summit would be held in Lagos in November, to discuss how the world could come together to fight the spread of HIV/AIDS. Anna was going. She asked the members of the committee to join her. I wanted to go, but knew I had to talk it over with my husband. If he didn't approve, I wouldn't go. John had been more than supportive of me. I would honor my husband's opinion.

"How long would you be in Africa?" he asked.

"I'd be gone for a few days, not very long. Please understand, I don't have to go. I just want to know how you feel about it."

"Your committee has gotten national attention," John began. "People like and support what you all have done. Think about all the children who will have a better life, or even *a* life, because of what your committee is doing. And, you're absolutely right, your work shouldn't stop here in Rhode Island and the States.

"I read recently where children in Africa and Asia are struggling to survive on their own, without parental care. Their life expectancy has been cut in half because of this disease. Orphanages are over-crowded. Some children are living in streets. Classrooms that should be filled with children eager to learn, are close to being empty in some countries. But, this epidemic can be stopped."

"This country alone has donated millions to various preventive and treatment programs," I added. "But, we need to do more. Our focus is to provide treatment that would prevent infections, and provide care for orphans. Far too many children have died; they each deserved the right to grow up and have a normal life. I'm confident that, with enough funds, Africans, Asians, Americans and people around the world can be educated on how to prevent and treat this dreadful disease."

"Did you know that 10 years ago, HIV infection rates were much lower in Nigeria than in other African countries?" I asked. "Now, unfortunately, it has one of the highest death rates from HIV/AIDS in all of Africa."

"I think you should join Anna at the summit," John said. "But, I have one request."

"What's that?"

"Do you mind if I tag along? I've never been to Nigeria. I'd like to visit the country."

"Are you serious about coming with us?"

"Absolutely."

"I'd love for you to come. What about our babies?" I asked.

"My parents would be thrilled to come up and care for them. I know yours would too. I don't plan to stay in Nigeria any length of time," John said. "I just want to spend a few days there."

I was overwhelmed with joy! I was going to Nigeria to attend the summit, and John was coming with us. I discussed this with Mother, and she insisted on coming up to keep her grandchildren. In the days that followed, I did some research on HIV/AIDS in Nigeria. I learned that most of the infections were transmitted by heterosexual sex. Often, blood used for transfusions had not been tested. Far too many Nigerians did not understand how the virus was transmitted. There was a national effort to reduce the incidence of the disease. The government, however, needed more funds, and educational and treatment programs to conquer this deadly disease.

Several international organizations were providing funding for HIV/AIDS. I didn't know how much our committee could help yet. We certainly were prepared to step in to try to make an impact on improving the lives of those infected.

Anna, two other members of the committee, John and I arrived in Lagos, Nigeria three days before the summit began. This gave us an opportunity to visit hospitals and shelters. We wanted to learn more about the care and treatment of those suffering from the disease.

What we saw was heartbreaking: babies, children, teenagers and adults too weak to move their bodies, and doctors and nurses working long hours, trying to ease the pain and suffering. We heard stories about how thousands of people died daily, about how children growing up to become teenagers, was more of a goal than an expectation. Yes, money was coming in from around the world, but not nearly enough. And, often, the money was mismanaged.

We talked with one of the doctors caring for children in an orphanage. Dr. Quince Nuru took the time to discuss this tragedy with us.

"We need more money to support programs that are already in place," he began. "We are working hard to educate our people on prevention. This is the number one priority. Second, the children must be cared for. They cannot care for themselves. They need to be touched, loved and nourished, like any other child. If something isn't done quickly, many African and Asian cultures will become extinct."

The summit began promptly on Thursday morning at 9:00 in November 2013. Leaders and health care professionals from around the world were there. As I listened to each of them speak, the word "extinct" stuck in my mind. Cultures could become extinct because their children were dying from HIV/AIDS. Some of the most recognized names in health care were present at the summit. Surely somebody had a solution on how to put an end to this human tragedy.

The afternoon of the second day of the summit, everyone was asked to divide into discussion groups. I was separated from Anna and the other members of my committee. During one of our breaks, I met a most interesting individual, Dr. Essien Bakari.

Dr. Bakari was Director of Microbiology at Stanford University. He was born in Botswana, and had lived there until he was 12. Since he had family in the States, he had moved there to live with them. He later won a scholarship to study at Stanford for undergraduate school. He went on to study at Yale University. Dr. Bakari held degrees in microbiology and zoology. To my surprise, he had read about the work our committee had done to fight the HIV/AIDS epidemic.

"Mrs. Carrington, it is so nice to meet you. Your committee has been quite successful in meeting the needs of those in Rhode Island, who are infected with this disease. Before you leave Lagos, I would like to meet with you and your committee members, to tell you about the progress we have made toward finding a cure for HIV/AIDS. I have been consumed with finding a way to end the suffering here and around the world. I believe my colleagues and I may have found the answer. Would you and the others be willing to meet with me?"

"I most certainly would like to meet with you. I will mention this to Representative Southerland and the other members of the committee. But, you mentioned you might have the answer. I assume you are talking about medications that would ease the suffering and prolong the lives of those infected, is that correct?"

"No, Mrs. Carrington. I believe we have found a cure for HIV/AIDS. Please let me know tomorrow if you all can meet with us. Perhaps we can have lunch together." I told him I would get back with him.

Later that evening I told Anna and the other members what Dr. Bakari had said. They were eager to hear more about his research. That night I also told John what Dr. Bakari had said.

"He certainly has the credentials to do the research. I'm curious, though, about why his work hasn't received more recognition. Still, I think you all should meet with him," John said.

John flew back home the following Saturday. Anna and my committee members met with Dr. Bakari and his team for lunch that afternoon.

"We have been working diligently to find a cure for HIV/AIDS for several years," Dr. Bakari began. "The U.S. government has funded the pre-clinical discovery. Six years ago, in Phase I of the research, we discovered that this drug not only killed bacteria, but also killed viral infections in rabbits. Two years later, in Phase II, the government gave us permission to use monkeys in our research. We discovered that this treatment protects monkeys from becoming infected. We also discovered that symptoms of the virus disappeared when infected monkeys were injected with this drug. We are confident that it will likewise protect humans from becoming infected, and that symptoms will disappear from those who are infected with the virus."

"What do you need us to do?" Anna asked.

"We need a pharmaceutical company that will sponsor the clinical trials needed for the FDA approval, and, ultimately manufacture the drug.

"So, you're looking for a pharmaceutical company to sponsor the clinical trials and manufacture the medication," I repeated.

"Yes, that is correct."

"Have you presented your research findings to any pharmaceutical companies?" I asked.

"Yes, we have. Unfortunately, none of them have the funds to cover the high costs of testing the medication. We're talking about millions of dollars. They don't have that kind of money to spare for this project."

We continued to question Dr. Bakari and his team members. We were satisfied with their answers. Anna and our committee believed his proposal was worthy of us spending time to look into the matter. We assured Dr. Bakari that we would get back to him with a plan of action.

The summit ended on Sunday. We headed home that afternoon. I couldn't get the children that we'd seen lying in hospital beds out of my mind. They didn't, or couldn't, speak. Nonetheless, their eyes communicated that they were suffering. I knew we had to at least try to get a pharmaceutical company, with the financial resources, to meet with Dr. Bakari. I was sitting next to Anna. She broke the silence.

"I got a message from my secretary earlier today," Anna began. "She said Senator Washington has decided not to run for a third term. Apparently the negative media has worn him down."

Clifton Washington is the democratic U.S. senator from Rhode Island. He had almost completed two full terms in office. However, he had been the subject of a recent scandal centered around the sale of stock from his prosperous family-owned business. I didn't know Senator Washington well, but thought he'd done a good job.

"Raini, I think you are the perfect person for that seat. The election is exactly one year away. You have plenty of time to prepare for a victory in November 2014. You have my full support."

"Me, a U.S. senator? Anna, you must be kidding!"

"Well, I'm not kidding. You'd be perfect for this spot. You've served twice as an elected official, and done a great job. You're an Associate Professor of Political Science, you've practiced law and you've always been actively involved in politics on some level."

"And, what about you, Anna? Why don't you run? You're the congresswoman, not me."

"I won't run because I haven't reached my goals in this position yet. Perhaps down the road I may consider running, but not now. I still have things I promised the citizens I'd accomplish as their congresswoman. I always honor my promises."

"And what about my committee, and all the work that needs to be done for victims of HIV/AIDS? I can't just turn my back on these people."

"I'm not asking you to turn your back on them. Serving as a U.S. senator will enable you to have a stronger voice to speak on their behalf. Raini, I honestly can't think of anyone else who'd be better for the seat."

"Well, Anna, thanks for your vote of confidence. But, for now, I only want to get home to see my babies. I miss them terribly."

When I got home the next day, I grabbed my children, and didn't want to let go. They had grown since I last saw them. During dinner I told John and my parents everything Dr. Bakari had discussed with us. They agreed that we had to somehow convince one of the larger pharmaceutical companies to meet with Dr. Bakari.

I went to bed early that night, exhausted from the trip. While preparing breakfast the next morning, I told my family that Anna had suggested that I run for Senator Washington's seat.

"I'm not surprised that he's stepping down," John said. "The investigation into his family business is getting pretty ugly. The media is having a party with this."

John and I explained to my parents that Senator Washington had been accused of inside trading. We also told them what he had accomplished.

"My daughter, a U.S. senator. I'd love to see that happen," Dad said, with a big smile. John and my parents talked about that possibility most of the morning. They thought it was a great idea. I, on the other hand, got busy with more important matters. I had to make an appointment for my children's seventh month check up with Dr. Ashley Curry, their pediatrician. For now, I was thrilled just to be at home.

22. Celia

COLE AND I DECIDED NOT TO FLY to Cleveland this time because Michaela was with us. We wanted her to have time to get her thoughts together before meeting Ralph and Cynthia Williams for the first time. So we drove.

Michaela had asked a week ago if she could go to Cleveland to meet her biological parents. Just the thought made me uncomfortable. I am Michaela's mother, the one who brought her home from the hospital and cared for her. Just the thought of someone replacing me made me feel weak and helpless. It has been more than a month since we learned about the baby mix-up. Each day I try to put my feelings aside and think about the emotional ups and downs Michaela must be going through. As soon as Sidney is stronger, Ralph and Cynthia are going to tell her the truth. The pain will continue.

Cynthia and I have been talking daily. She appears to be a loving, concerned mother. She returned to work once Sidney's condition began to improve, but goes to the hospital each day. The only peace I have is the assumption that my biological daughter has been raised by a woman who appears to be kind and loving. Still, I believe I would have been a better mother to my child. I suppose Cynthia is having similar thoughts about me, and how we raised her biological child.

It has been difficult to "reach" Michaela since she learned the disturbing news. She and I used to talk about everything, from clothes to girlfriends. Now she spends her free time in her room, with the door shut. I often wonder if she has decided to shut me out of her life. Perhaps she's angry with me for mistakenly taking her away from her biological parents. I can understand this.

My heart aches for my daughter to come back to me, because I feel as if I've lost her. But there's nothing I can do, except wait, and see how she comes through this. And then there's Sidney. What will she think about Cole and me when she learns the truth? My faith in God and the love of my family have enabled me to keep going. I certainly couldn't have continued on my own.

Matthew has been a real trooper. He spends time with Michaela, playing games and helping her with her homework. Fortunately, she has not shut him out. He says his sister is hurting, but that she will come through this situation just fine. Matthew is so much like Cole. He'll tell you what he wants you to know about a given subject. Then, he says everything is going to be fine. It's a blessing that I'm surrounded by so many strong people. Mother is still with us. One of these days I'm going to have enough strength to let her go home, but not today.

Michaela read books almost the entire drive to Cleveland. She didn't ask any of the questions I thought she would. She only wanted to know if she looked like the Williamses, and if they were nice people.

Cynthia and I decided that the five of us would have dinner together at a restaurant, rather than bring Michaela to their home for that initial meeting. Upon our arrival, we checked into a hotel, then took Michaela to visit the Rock and Roll Hall of Fame and Museum. We wanted this to be a pleasant, positive visit. She enjoyed the museum and asked to see more of Cleveland.

She was very young when we left Cleveland, and didn't remember anything about the city. She wanted to know where we met. We took her to Case Western Reserve University. She bought a cap and a T-shirt from the campus book store. By then it was time to meet Ralph and Cynthia for dinner. Michaela wanted to look her very best for the first meeting, so I took her shopping before the trip. I bought her a bright pink dress and shoes that complemented the dress. I had her hair styled professionally.

It had taken some time, but I had resolved to try to make this the most special moment of her life. I didn't want to do anything that would strain the relationship between Ralph, Cynthia and Michaela. Although it was going to be painful for me, I wanted her to love her biological parents.

Ralph and Cynthia were already at the restaurant when we arrived. I could actually see the blood drain from Cynthia's face when she looked at Michaela. I knew exactly what she was feeling. I didn't look at Michaela, for fear I would break down. Ralph Williams appeared to be calm. He helped his wife out of her chair. We were all speechless for a moment. Then Cole made the introductions.

"Michaela, I want you to meet your biological parents, Ralph and Cynthia Williams." I felt numb. Cole and I were her parents. Nothing could change that, not even blood and DNA samples. I knew in my heart that Michaela would always be my daughter. However, for now, I had to put my feelings aside, and help our child cope with this major development in her life.

"Michaela, it is so nice to meet you. You are such a lovely young lady," Cynthia said, with tears in her eyes. She gave Michaela a big hug. Michaela looked lost and confused. A part of me wanted to grab her and run out of there. I could feel my heart pounding. Cole held me close, as if he knew what I was feeling.

Michaela reluctantly hugged Cynthia Williams. I had raised my children to understand that they didn't have to hug or embrace everyone they met, if the act made them uncomfortable. We all sat down. At first, the meeting was a bit awkward. Cole, bless his heart, struggled to relieve some of the tension. He tried to make conversation with Ralph about the upcoming season for the Cleveland Browns. But, Ralph was almost speechless as he stared at Michaela. When I first set eyes on Sidney a month ago, I, too, had been speechless. Words can not explain what it feels like to see your flesh and blood for the very first time in 10 years.

Finally, after several minutes, the waiter came. We all placed our orders. Michaela said she wasn't hungry, and I didn't try to force her to eat. I could feel her little hand clutching mine, and I was squeezing hers. Then Cynthia began asking questions.

"Michaela, your mother tells me that you are an excellent student. I think that's wonderful. You may already know this, but I teach the sixth grade. I know some of the classes are difficult. Do you have a favorite subject?" I was pleased that Cynthia was trying to start a relationship with Michaela by asking simple questions. Michaela answered her softly. "Yes, my favorite subject is biology. I also love math. Sometimes the teacher can make math real hard, though."

"How is that?" Cynthia asked.

"Well, sometimes her explanation is totally different from the one in the textbook, and much more difficult. It's almost like she wants math to be our hardest subject." Both sets of parents laughed. This exchange helped us all to relax.

"You're very special, Michaela, because most students say that math is their least favorite subject," Cynthia continued. "Teachers should try to be as creative as possible when explaining math. Next year there's going to be a national math and science competition in New York City. You should think about entering. First prize is $15,000.00, and second prize is $10,000.00. Plus, there will be great gifts for all participants. Your school should be getting the information soon."

Cynthia seemed to have calmed down, tremendously. She couldn't stop smiling as she spoke. She had every reason to smile. She was talking to her biological daughter she had never seen. That daughter was intelligent, polite and beautiful. It was obvious to anyone that Cole and I had spent a lot of quality time with Michaela. We were proud of her.

"My teacher hasn't mentioned it to us yet, but I definitely would like to participate," Michaela answered. "If I win, I could use that money to travel around the world." We laughed again, even though Michaela was serious.

"Michaela, the money is in the form of scholarships, but that's still a lot of money," Cynthia explained.

"Yes, it is. I'll talk to my teacher when I get back to school."

Then Ralph Williams began to ask questions. "Michaela, I understand that you're taking tennis lessons. I've never played tennis. Does it take as much work and effort to be good as it appears?" Ralph had worked hard to support his family. I'm sure it hadn't been easy to clothe and feed six children. One would think that he would have no interest in meeting another child, however, he seemed to be as joyful as his wife, talking to his *new* daughter.

"Well, yes, it is a lot of work, because you're always running around the court trying to hit the ball. I still miss a lot of balls, but I'm getting better. My brother has also been working with me. Matthew is really good, if I must say so." Ralph and Cynthia laughed again. In fact, they seemed to have already fallen in love with Michaela. I guess it was because she was *their* daughter. Plus, she was charming.

They were reluctant to leave the restaurant, but Michaela was tired and needed some rest. Before saying goodnight, we all decided to meet at the hospital in the morning. Cole and I were anxious to spend time with Sidney. I was certain that Ralph and Cynthia wanted time alone with Michaela too. They asked her if she had plans for tomorrow. After she said she didn't, they offered to take her to the zoo. I was pleased that Cynthia asked her to think about the offer. She would let them know in the morning.

Michaela was quiet for most of the evening after leaving the Williamses. She thought they were nice people, but said she didn't want to live with them. She also said she didn't want to go to the zoo without us. We told her it was strictly her decision how she wanted to spend tomorrow.

Before falling asleep back at the hotel, Michaela wanted an answer to a question that had obviously been on her mind.

"Mom and Dad, since they're my biological parents, can a judge order me to leave you, and move in with them?"

"Sweetheart, we don't think so, but we've hired an attorney to help us out with all of this," Cole replied. "You are almost 11 years old, so I think any reasonable judge will allow you to choose where you want to live." The truth of the matter was that Cole and I didn't know for sure. We had never been in a custody battle. I think it would kill me if anyone tried to take Michaela from us. I couldn't help but wonder if she would some day change her mind. Maybe one day she would choose to live with the Williamses. She didn't want to live with them now, but would that change after a few months, or weeks. I could hear my mother's words ringing in my ears, *Celia, just love and listen to Michaela, and this will all work itself out.*

Mother had warned me not to say, or even suggest anything negative about the Williams family, because these words could come back to haunt me. I needed that warning. Actually, there was really nothing negative to say. After all, Ralph and Cynthia were her biological parents. To criticize them would be to criticize Michaela, since she had biological ties to them. I would only use my words as a powerful, positive force in my life, and in the lives of others.

The next morning Sidney was sitting up when we got to the hospital. Ralph and Cynthia were already there. I gave Sidney a hug. This child was the spitting image of my mother at that age. Michaela stared at Sidney, without saying a word. Then Cynthia made the introduction.

"Sweetheart, I want you to meet Celia, Cole and Michaela Bentley. They have come from Nashville to visit you. They will be spending more time with you once you're strong and healthy again." Sidney gave us a big smile that covered her face. Then, for the first time, we heard her speak.

"Hello. I am *so* happy to have visitors. I've been sick, but I feel much better now. My doctor says I'm going to live." Although I fought hard, I couldn't keep the tears back, and neither could Cole. Our child was talking, and she knew that she was going to live! She had beat the horrible illness. She was becoming herself again. She was eager to talk, to anyone.

"Hi, Michaela, how old are you? I'm 10, and I'm five feet tall, the third tallest girl in my class. I'm in the sixth grade, but I might have to repeat a year because of all the time I've missed." Cole and I were smiling, just as Ralph and Cynthia had smiled at Michaela last night.

"Well, Sidney, I'm also 10, and I'm five-one, an inch taller than you, sorry." We were all laughing now. Cynthia suggested that we leave the girls alone, briefly, to get acquainted. We went to the hospital cafeteria to get something to drink. After we were seated, Cynthia said she was waiting for Sidney to get strong enough to come home, before she and Ralph broke the news to her. She wanted her home before she learned the truth about her biological parents.

Cynthia was just as protective of Sidney as I was of Michaela. She told us that Sidney should be able to come home within the next two weeks, but wouldn't be able to return to school for another month or so. Cole asked if they had looked into getting a tutor. Cynthia said she had, but didn't know if the family could afford a tutor. Cole offered to pay, or help pay for one, so that Sidney wouldn't have to repeat the fifth grade. They thanked him, and said they would let him know.

"Michaela is such a lovely young lady," Cynthia said. Tears were in her eyes. "It's so hard to believe that we had a child in this world we didn't know anything about. I often wondered why our Sidney got so sick and suffered so much. Now, I know. God wanted the truth to come out." There was silence. We were all probably thinking the very same thing.

"We want to get to know Michaela, as I'm sure you want to get to know Sidney, Cynthia said, in her soft voice. "Did she mention to you whether or not she wants to go to the zoo with us today?" I didn't want to hurt

Cynthia's feelings. I tactfully explained to them that Michaela didn't want to go to the zoo, unless Cole and I were present.

"Certainly you can understand why," I continued. "She has just learned the truth, and only met you yesterday. There's so much going through her mind these days. I'm an adult, and I'm having a tough time trying to digest all that we've learned over the past weeks. Give Michaela some time. She's a good child. She'll work through all of this."

"Yes, I'm the mother of six, and definitely know that kids need their time and space. At least you've had the opportunity to inform Michaela. It's been very difficult for Ralph and me, waiting and praying for our daughter to survive. Then, once she's strong, we have to break this painful news to her. I just don't know what this is going to do to her. I do know that she has to know the truth. Ten years is long enough to be in the dark. However, we definitely want Sidney to come home first and get settled, then tell her everything."

The four of us talked about our daughters, and how to help them. The bottom line was that we first had to wait to see how well the girls coped with this painful revelation.

I felt a certain connection, or bond, with Cynthia. Her large, brown eyes were compassionate and caring. She spoke softly. I wondered how she could have raised six children, using such a soft tone. I hadn't met her children, but Cole and I wanted to visit their home, to learn as much as possible about the family. They had raised my daughter. I wanted to know what their priorities were, and how they spent their time away from work and school. I had so many questions, but this wasn't the time to ask. Our families needed to grow close. If Michaela decided to leave us, I would be able to keep in touch with her, because of the foundation being laid now between the two families.

"What do you think could possibly have gone wrong at the hospital that could have led to this mistake?" I asked Cynthia, wondering how much they knew about all of this.

"We know very little about what went wrong in the maternity unit when Michaela and Sidney were born," Cynthia responded. "I have a friend whose husband is an attorney, and he's trying to build a case for us. But I don't want a law suit. I simply don't want anything as painful as this to ever happen to other parents. It just isn't right. Only God knows how long it will take our daughters to learn to cope with this, and move on with their lives."

"They are young, Cynthia. They will find a way to handle this, and go on with their lives," Ralph said. "Sidney was raised in a loving home, and all of our children are warm and caring. Cynthia and I wouldn't have had it any other way. We have never turned a child away from our home, and we certainly won't turn away Michaela, our flesh and blood." Ralph was of average height, with a thin body frame and medium brown skin. His hair was thinning on top. His hands were thick-skinned, like hands that had worked hard. He clearly loved his family dearly.

"One thing is certain," Cole said. "We all love Michaela and Sidney, and are going to do everything in our power to help them. The best thing we can do for the girls now is to show strength in our resolve to get to the bottom of this. We must also cooperate with each other, so that they don't have to suffer any more. They're going to be watching us to see how we react to them, and to each other. Neither of them needs to be hurt any more."

"Cynthia and Ralph, whenever you're up to it, Cole and I would love to have you come to Nashville to visit us. We want you to meet Matthew and McAlister," I said.

"Thank you, Celia. And, the next time you and Cole are in Cleveland, we want you to stay with us. We've got five children at home now, but we can certainly make room for you. It's so important for the girls to be allowed to slowly integrate into their new families," Cynthia said.

"Thank you very much," I said. "Well, I think we need to get back to check on the girls to see how they're doing. I hope they've had a chance to at least begin to get to know each other." I led the way back to Sidney's room.

To my surprise, and I guess everyone else's, Michaela and Sidney were wrapped up in each other's arms, crying their hearts out. Sidney looked directly at Cynthia and Ralph.

"Mom, Dad, tell me it isn't true. Please tell me it's all a mistake! Please tell me that you are my real parents. Tell me, Mom, please. It isn't true, is it?"

I immediately knew what had gone wrong. In our excitement over Sidney's sudden improvement, Cole and I had forgotten to tell Michaela that Sidney didn't yet know about the mix-up.

23. Sarah

I AM 22, AND IT IS JUNE 1853. It has been eight years since I ran away from Mr. Wilmington. I have finally broken the habit of saying "mastah." Thank God, it has been years since I have had a master. The Bakers, Aunt Clara and Miz Cross made it possible for me to get an education. My work as a seamstress has enabled me to earn my keep and not depend on others financially. Over the years, in addition to getting an education, I have developed social skills.

I have learned, through my association with the Bakers and Aunt Clara, that not all white people are in favor of slavery. I no longer hate white people; not even Mr. Wilmington. One can never be truly "free" as long as he or she hates. God has worked on me over the years.

Although I hate what some white people have done to our people, hating them is not the answer. Because God has blessed me to get an education, I have been able to help our people in many ways. While I realize that hating white people accomplishes nothing, I still cry about my parents and Tom living in slavery. Mammy, Pappy and Tom would be so proud to know how much I have learned, how well I can read and write. I still have not given up on seeing them again.

Because I earn money from sewing jobs, I am able to pay Aunt Clara boarding expenses. She does not want my money, but I insist that she take it. She and the Bakers have helped me so much. I am an adult, determined to support myself. I make dainty, colorful dresses for young girls. I can still remember the beautiful dresses Mammy made for Kate and Melissa Wilmington. I remember how badly I wanted to wear dresses like that, but could not. Although I design and make dresses for women too, my passion is making dresses for girls. Some of the more prosperous Negroes pay me well for these dresses. I also have a few wealthy white customers.

I operate my business out of Aunt Clara's home. I am a perfectionist when it comes to sewing. Aunt Clara takes me to fine shops to purchase fabrics for my dresses. I work long, hard hours to get the detailed stitching just right.

I have enjoyed living in Aunt Clara's lovely home. She has a small garden and berry patch behind her house. She makes the best fried berry pies, and wine, from the berries we pick each summer. We eat and drink out of beautiful china and glasses.

Aunt Clara and Miz Baker are among the exception for our people, because they are pretty well-to-do and educated. Their father left them quite a bit of money when he died. He owned a small grocery store in Boston, in the Negro neighborhood. They have no other siblings. They invested their money wisely, by buying small houses and renting out rooms in them.

I planned to someday move out of Aunt Clara's house and open a dress shop. There was no need to rush into this, though, because Aunt Clara and I had grown to be very close. We enjoyed each other's company. She and the Bakers were my family away from home.

Over the past eight years I had been cautious and afraid of being shipped back to the South, so I had held on to my money as if it were gold. I kept my money in a savings club that was started at our church. There were no banks owned by Negroes in Boston at the time. I had only spent my money on basic necessities. Because my dresses were selling well, I believed I could have the prosperous life I had dreamed of since I was a little girl.

Aunt Clara, the Bakers and Miz Cross encouraged me to continue to study and learn as much as possible, even after my eight years with them. I knew how to make money, and Aunt Clara was teaching me how to invest some of it. She has good business sense, and does not miss an opportunity to teach me something new. I am very fortunate to have Aunt Clara and the Bakers in my life. Mammy had taught me how to sew like a perfectionist. Now, they were teaching me how to turn this skill and talent into a prosperous business.

I found time in my busy schedule to get involved in anti-slavery groups, which helped fugitive slaves. There was no way I could not, considering the help I had received since coming to the North. In my limited spare time, I continued to teach Negro children and adults to read and write. Without those skills, their lives would be so limited. There were far too many illiterate and unskilled Negroes in this country. But more groups were being formed to help our people.

Through Aunt Clara, I was fortunate enough to mingle with some of the more prominent Negroes in Boston. I also worked with some of the less fortunate people in the city. Aunt Clara and I helped several children and adults learn to read and write. The greatest joy was to watch and listen to my students read.

One night that following October, Aunt Clara and I attended a party held at the home of some of her friends. The goal of the party was to raise money to help Negroes find housing. She introduced me to members of the Harper family. They owned a small printing press, and circulated a community newspaper called *The Herald Progress.* This paper had many articles about the needs and hopes of free Negroes.

"Clara, how are you? This must be your lovely granddaughter," Thaddeus Harper said that night.

"This is Sarah, my pride and joy," Aunt Clara responded. She never said I was not her granddaughter. As she had explained to me on several occasions, unless people specifically asked, my relation to her was none of their business.

"Where is Henry?" Aunt Clara asked. Thaddeus and Henry Harper, his brother, were born and raised in Boston. They had owned the community newspaper for several years. They, like Aunt Clara, were relatively well-to-do Negro Bostonians, active in the anti-slavery movement.

"Henry is around here somewhere. Sarah, you are such a lovely young lady," Thaddeus Harper continued. "You must meet my nephew, William Harper. He is here tonight. Oh, there he is. William, I need to see you." His nephew came over to where we were standing. I had no idea he would be so young, or handsome. He was around six feet tall, thin, with dark skin. He shook my hand, then told Aunt Clara that he would like to introduce me to some of the other people our age. As I walked around the room with him, and listened to him, I could tell that he was a gentleman.

I was 22, and had given little thought to meeting a male companion. With my studies and sewing, there was no time for anything else. The party was at William's home. We decided to walk outside to get some fresh air. I was surprised at how easy it was to talk with him. He was born and raised in Boston. I was from Holly Springs. Despite those differences, I actually felt comfortable with him.

"I never knew that Miss Clara had a daughter," he said, as we enjoyed the fresh air.

"She does not, and I am not her daughter," I said. I was proud of my roots. There was no way I was going to dishonor Mammy and Pappy by allowing him to think that Aunt Clara was my mother. He looked surprised, but did not ask any more questions. If he wanted to know more about me, I would tell him; if not, I would not. We talked most of the night about our goals. I learned that he was 25, had been educated in Massachusetts at some of the finest schools that accepted Negroes, and was an editor for his family's newspaper. We talked about injustice toward our people. He thought some of the Northern white people, but certainly not all, were as cruel as the slaveholders in the South.

"You seem to know a lot about the South, and Mississippi in particular," he said, after we had talked for more than an hour.

"That is because I was born and raised in Holly Springs, Mississippi. My parents, Bertha and Joshua Johnson, are slaves. I would still be one if I had not escaped eight years ago, and met the Bakers and Aunt Clara." He was speechless. He looked puzzled.

I could see inside the house that the party was apparently over. Everyone was starting to leave. Aunt Clara was looking for me, so I said goodnight to William and quickly joined her. I knew I would never see or hear from William Harper after that night. Surely he would not want to be seen in the company of a former slave from Mississippi. But, the next day he came over and told Aunt Clara he needed to talk to me.

"You left so abruptly last night. I was concerned that I would never see you again," he said.

"I did not think you would want to see a former slave again," I said. He said that was the most ridiculous thing he had ever heard. We began talking about the newspaper, the articles he was planning to print and how he wanted to use the paper to help our people in various ways.

It was Sunday afternoon. This was usually the only free time I had during the week, so he invited me to his office to show me some of his plans for the paper. William was quite intelligent. We became very close over the next few weeks.

He criticized white people who said they were against slavery, but tolerated it through their actions. He printed articles calling for prominent Negroes to come together to help our less fortunate brothers and sisters, by finding homes and jobs for them.

William was supportive of my love for sewing. He introduced me to several prospective clients. I told him about my dream to have my own dress shop some day. He thought it was a great idea. His mother cried when I told her my story. She had seen me with Aunt Clara on several occasions. She had always thought that I was either her granddaughter or a close relative.

William asked for my opinion on some articles he was preparing to print. This made me feel special, like I was someone important in his life. I considered him a friend, a special friend. For the first time in my life, I began thinking about sharing my life with someone. I enjoyed his company very much. My past did not seem to concern him. He escorted me to several social events, even though there were attractive, prominent Negro women in Boston he could have invited. Thanks to the Bakers, Aunt Clara and Miz Cross, I had the social skills to feel comfortable amongst his family and friends.

By April 1854, I had enough money saved to lease space to use as a dress shop. The owner wanted $9.25 a week. The building was only four blocks from Aunt Clara's house, so I could walk to and from the shop. William and Aunt Clara helped me set up the shop. Before long, I had several of my fanciest dresses hanging on display. I spent most of my free time at the shop working, or talking to clients I would meet throughout the city.

William published an article in the newspaper announcing the opening of my dress shop. I soon had orders for several dresses for a wedding. This was a great business opportunity. Aunt Clara wanted me to get some help with the sewing, but I could not afford to pay anyone at this point. I thought about Mammy, and how much she would love to help me out. She would be so proud to see me in my very own dress shop!

In late April, I received word that Reverend Baker was very sick. He was 67. I had not visited him and Miz Baker since I left New York City nine years ago. There was always the fear that I would be discovered, and returned to Mr. Wilmington. Now, however, I didn't care if I did get caught! Reverend Baker had been like a father to me when I ran away from Mr. Wilmington. I was determined to get to see him again. Aunt Clara made arrangements for us to travel to New York City by train. Although it was difficult for me to leave my shop and sewing behind, I was anxious to see the two people I loved as much as my own parents.

New York City looked the same as the day I left. My heart felt heavy as I entered the city that was once my home away from home. I remembered all too clearly that warm morning in June 1845, when I slipped away from the Wilmingtons and headed to the Bakers' home. I was scared, very much alone. I did not know if I was doing the right thing. I knew how much my decision would hurt Mammy and Pappy, but I had prayed about this opportunity for so long. I believed that was what God wanted for me. We took a carriage to the Bakers' home. Miz Baker met Aunt Clara and me at the door. She and I hugged for several minutes. She was crying softly. I did not know if she was glad to see us, or if Reverend Baker had taken a turn for the worse.

"Praise the Lord, my family is here," she said. She embraced both of us. "The Reverend isn't doing well. He has a terrible fever. The doctor is with him now." We all held hands and prayed for Reverend Baker. I began to cry. The Bakers' son, daughter and grandchildren were in the parlor. They were all quiet. Finally, the doctor came out and told Aunt Clara that she could come in to Reverend Baker's bedroom. She grabbed me by the hand, and took me with her.

Reverend Baker looked thin and weak. He stared at me. The brightest smile then covered his face.

"My baby, my baby is home," he said softly. We embraced. I wiped my tears away, and held his hands tightly. He asked how I was doing. I told him about how I had managed to open a small dress shop to design, sew and sell dresses.

"You were always a highly intelligent child. The Lord sent you to us. It broke my heart when you had to leave, to go to Boston. But, we just couldn't risk having you sent back to that cotton plantation, to be mistreated by that Wilmington man. We love you like a daughter, Sarah. Don't you ever forget that."

"I know, and I love you both like family." My tears were flowing again. I moved away so that Aunt Clara could speak with him. Miz Baker and I left the room.

"What is wrong with him?" I asked Miz Baker.

"The Reverend's heart has always been weak. It's a blessing that he has been with us this long," she answered. She was trying to smile, but the pain was obvious. "I am so glad you could come, my child. He has been asking for you. You know, Sarah, we are so proud of you. We thought of you as our own, and still do. We even considered moving to Boston to be closer to you and our children. But so many people here depend on us to run the church and help our people. The Reverend believes he was called to stay here to do God's will."

Miz Baker looked exhausted, but refused my offer to sit with the Reverend so she could get some rest. That night the three of us talked for hours. Miz Baker told us about all the Reverend had done to bring people to Christ, and help fight for equality for our people. She told us about the many Negroes he had clothed and fed with his own money, and how he left early for the church each morning, knowing that someone would come there looking for food, peace and rest. She told me, for the first time, that she and the Reverend had planned to go to Mississippi to offer to buy me from the Wilmingtons, if I had gone back.

She and Aunt Clara then talked about happier times. They talked about when the Bakers first met, about how happy they were together. Miz Baker said she never dreamed she would marry a minister. Reverend Baker changed that when he came into her life. They married 47 years ago. She left Boston and her family to start a new life with the man she loved.

The Reverend worked hard to build a small church. Over the years it grew into one of the larger Negro churches in New York City. She said people loved and respected him because he loved and respected people. Finally, she told me how they cried over their decision to send me to Boston to escape those who were looking for me. It was one of the hardest decisions they had ever made.

It was very early Thursday morning, but no one wanted to go to bed. The doctor had left, but said he would return. Sometime during the early hours of the morning, before the doctor made it back, Reverend Baker died peacefully in his sleep. This was very difficult for everyone, especially Miz Baker. I thought about my parents. His death made me want to go home to my family, even if it meant being a slave again. Aunt Clara and I stayed on to help with the funeral, and support Miz Baker. Pretty soon, however, I had to get back to Boston to finish the wedding dresses. I reluctantly left Miz Baker and the others.

William was waiting to meet me at the train station, but I was too depressed to be excited about seeing him. In the days that followed, I withdrew physically and emotionally by burying myself in the dresses I had to finish. I did not want to see anybody, and only spoke with the people who needed my services. I desperately wanted to see my parents. I did not care about getting caught! I could not get Mammy and Pappy out of my mind. Suppose they were sick and needed me, or had passed on like Reverend Baker. I suddenly felt guilty for having left them. I felt selfish for wanting my freedom and a better life.

I somehow managed to finish all of the dresses over the next five days. Then I decided to close the shop for a while. I needed a break from sewing. William came to see me one night after I closed the shop. I told him how I felt. Aunt Clara was still in New York City.

"It is time I went home to take care of my parents. I have had a taste of freedom, and like it, but I love my parents more," I said, fighting to hold back the tears.

"Sarah, do you know what you're saying? You want to go back and allow the Wilmingtons, or some other white person, to control your life? You didn't come this far just to give up and go back!"

"It is easy for you to say that, seeing how you spend time with your parents every day! I have no one except Aunt Clara and Miz Baker. Suppose something happens to them? They are not going to live forever. Then, what would I do?"

"You have me, Sarah. Haven't we been the best of friends since we met?"

"Friends and family are two different things. It has been nine years since I have seen Mammy and Pappy. I am not sure I want to stay away any longer. I miss my family. I want to go home!"

"To be severely punished, or beaten by Frank Wilmington?" William was almost shouting now. He appeared to be quite upset. He held me close. I began to cry on his shoulder. I was hurting inside, and wanted the pain to go away. William stroked my hair and continued to hold me close.

"You can't go back, Sarah, at least not now. Tension is rising between white people and Negroes, especially in the South. Frank Wilmington hasn't forgiven you, and probably never will, for leaving him. This man wanted you. He will probably take that strong feeling to his grave!"

I listened to William, and slowly calmed down. Reverend Baker's death had obviously upset me more than I had realized. William invited me to have dinner at his home with his family that evening. I said "no," but he insisted that I join them. It turned out to be a delightful evening, with only him, his mother and father. They talked about all the good things they had heard about my dresses, and how I was truly gifted. They also talked about my courage, and how much they admired and respected me.

I wondered if William had told them about my depression because the evening seemed to have been planned around making me feel better. Their plan worked. I left their home feeling much better, but told William I still planned to go back for my parents, soon. He said he understood, that he would go with me. There were many risks involved. We knew we had to be prepared for anything.

Aunt Clara was still in New York City with Miz Baker. I missed her dearly. William was determined not to let me get depressed again. He invited me to spend more time with his family in the days that followed. I was still emotionally exhausted, but decided to re-open the shop anyway. I also continued to teach young and older Negroes to read and write. This was a source of great joy in my life. I had closed the shop, but never stopped teaching. That was too important.

William was very much an activist with several anti-slavery groups. Many of his articles bashed the laws that kept Negroes from moving forward by having equal opportunities. I thought the best way to help our people was to educate them. If they could read and write, this would surely open doors for them. I knew I would always find the time to teach, no matter what I was going through. This was my way of giving something back, and showing my appreciation for all of my blessings.

24. Celia

REFUSE TO GO TO THERAPY or have a pity party. I know there is a God and I have inner strength, so I have begun the difficult task of getting my life back in order without the involvement of a third party. I won't have the life I once enjoyed; clearly some things won't be the same, but I'm slowly learning to accept this.

Fall is here, finally. That had to be the longest summer in history. October has always been one of my favorite months, so I'm glad it's here. Each morning, after the kids and Cole leave, I take a long walk, alone. This gives me time to meditate and count my blessings. There is a part of me that's still as feisty and determined as ever. I'm 37, and, like the leaves around me, I've fallen a bit. My spirit has been broken a little. But, unlike those leaves, I will get up, brush off the debris, and regain my color, beauty and strength.

At first, I honestly thought I was being punished for some past behavior. I spent days wondering what I'd done to deserve such painful news. Now, three months later, I know I'm not being punished. That is not how God operates. Instead, I'm being tested. I must put my faith, strength and will power in high gear, to get through this dark tunnel. I refer to this ordeal as a tunnel, a long tunnel, because the journey has been dark, and the path has been narrow. I've worried about getting custody of Sidney. I've wondered about whether Michaela will want to stay with us, or choose to live with her biological parents.

There were times when I actually gasped for breath. I felt like I'd never see daylight again. But I know that tunnels have a beginning and an end. The driver must keep going, not stop and get out, until daylight appears. The air is fresh and the sun is shining bright after you leave the tunnel. I have a destination, a purpose in this life. If I allow fear and despair to take over, I'll get stuck in the tunnel and never come out. I don't need a therapist to tell me this.

Nature is therapeutic. I love trees and leaves, flowers and bees, oceans and rivers, plants and vegetables, mountains and hills, rocks and sand, and walking in the grass. Nature has always been a source of peace, calm and healing for me. All I have to do is take the time to enjoy it. Well, I haven't taken the time to reap the benefits of this God-given gift in several weeks. I'm now rediscovering its beauty and healing powers.

I got so caught up in day-to-day living, and trying to be everything to everybody, that I forgot who I was and that I have a purpose in this life. That purpose goes beyond caring for my children, and loving and supporting my husband. I realize I must reach out and touch other lives, bring something positive to their world. I just need a way to do it.

I had felt that my life was complete, because I was fortunate to be able to stay home and care for my family. I could do all the things I enjoy, like gardening, playing in the symphony, playing tennis and being involved in the community. Now, I realize I must broaden my thinking if I am to survive and move forward.

This is an especially peaceful fall morning. I want to walk, and keep walking in this park near our home. I don't have to rush back today because Cole and Mother insisted that I enroll McAlister in an early childhood program, so I could have some free time. I argued with them, saying that I didn't need any more free time. Then, reluctantly, I agreed to let him attend two mornings each week. Surprisingly, I've discovered that I do need time for me. To be truthful, I need time to get back in touch with the "real" Celia, because I've been playing several roles over the last several weeks. Now, I'm starting to forget some of the lines. The roles weren't real. They weren't really me.

Walking through the dried, crisp leaves brings back memories of a sad incident that occurred when I was a child in Charleston. My grandpa built an outside playhouse for me for my 8th birthday. I was the happiest little girl in the world. I invited all of my neighborhood playmates over to enjoy some snacks and tea. Every little girl on my block wanted to be best friends with me.

Two days later, while in the house cleaning up tea cups and getting ready for another full day of fun with my friends, I heard something hit the playhouse. I rushed out to find the most beautiful red bird lying on the ground, flapping its wings. It was unable to get up and fly. I decided it was a female bird. I picked her up and held her in my arms. I sang a lullaby to her, then put her in the playhouse to care for her until she was stronger and could fly again. I didn't want anybody to know about this little bird. There were boys in my neighborhood who had been known to kill birds with BB guns. I loved birds.

I felt terribly guilty about this beautiful bird being hurt, because in my young mind, I reasoned that she was probably on her way home. If the house had not been built in her pathway, she wouldn't have flown into it. If Grandpa hadn't built the house for me, this little bird could've been at home in her nest, with the rest of her family. I took good care of her. She had food, water and even toys. I placed them in a nest for her that I had made with cotton.

My Uncle Walter had brought me the cotton because I needed it for a science project. Also, there were about 10 children in my class who had never seen or touched cotton straight from the vine. These children had moved to Charleston, South Carolina, from other parts of the country, including New York and California. It was truly a show-and-tell day for me when I pulled out this soft, white product of the earth, and passed it around the classroom. Uncle Walter graciously brought enough so that every child could take a piece home.

I carefully nursed the little bird, and didn't tell anyone about her, except my parents. She didn't have to do anything, except eat and rest. I wanted her to be strong enough to fly away, to join her family one day. I ignored my parents when they told me that this little bird needed to be out in the sun, trying to walk and fly. They said this would help her get stronger. I simply refused to think about taking her out of the playhouse, because I thought she was much too special to have to do anything for herself.

Then, one morning before leaving for school, I found her in her cotton nest, eyes closed and body limp. I screamed and cried, and finally understood what my parents had been trying to tell me. This beautiful bird wasn't created to be locked up in a playhouse, living in a nest of cotton, unable to do anything for herself. She was made to fly, soar, gather her own food, build her own nests and care for her babies. I'd only made things worse by depriving her of her God-given ability to provide for herself. Memories of that little bird are saving me.

My mother has returned to Charleston. I had insisted. I'm here in Nashville, trying to find the strength to soar above the challenges in my life, to walk and strengthen my body, to use my God-given gifts to find answers to questions that have puzzled me for weeks. Although Mother wanted to stay and continue to help us cope, it was selfish of me to keep her here with my family for so long. Yet, there was a time when I didn't think I had the strength to go on after learning that Michaela was not our biological child.

Mother had done everything for me, including cooking and helping the kids get ready for school each day. She talked to Michaela when I didn't know what to say to her. She crippled me, just as I crippled that little bird. But it was out of love, not intentionally. That little bird couldn't tell me to go away, and mind my own business. I meant well, but she didn't need me.

Mother loves me dearly and wanted to help. I took advantage of her big heart. However, after I started walking each morning, I came to my senses, and gradually realized that I will get through this tunnel and see daylight again. The sun will shine again. The Bentley Family will move forward.

Cole already had moved forward. He's been right here, in the midst of this turmoil with me and our children. But he has an escape through his job. There were mornings when I kissed him goodbye, wishing that we could trade places. I wanted him to stay at home all day, struggling with trying to find the strength to keep going. I used to take Michaela to school, but it soon became too difficult to see the pain in her eyes when I kissed her, then sent her off to her classes. So Cole agreed to take her. Then I felt guilty about being a "cop-out" mom. For weeks I thought I was fighting a battle I could not win, as I watched my husband and son move on with their lives.

I'd always been grateful to be a stay-at-home mom. Suddenly the idea of returning to a career I once cherished seemed very attractive. I even talked with executives at several financial institutions, and submitted resumes, but then realized I didn't really want to return to work. I wanted an escape from the pain and hurt I'd felt since that dreadful phone call from Ms. Noland. My parents had taught me not to run away from anything. I've taught my children that there's nothing worse than a coward. Now that I'm walking daily, I'm finding the strength to stand my ground.

Matthew has moved on with his life. He's in high school now, playing tennis and developing an interest in the opposite sex. He says Michaela is his sister, blood or not, and that he loves her. He has met Sidney. He thinks she's nice and looks like a Bentley. He says he's going to have to "train" her as he has "trained" Michaela on how younger sisters are supposed to behave. Surprisingly, this ordeal hasn't slowed him down.

Both Matthew and Cole were a source of strength for me with their attitude about life. But, they are not Michaela and Sidney's mother. It's simply not possible for them to feel what I feel. Neither of them has carried a child for nine months, only to face the possibility of losing that child. Thank God McAlister is too young to understand any of this. He talks on and on, without a care in the world. I find the strength to talk and play with him, just as I did with Matthew and Michaela. After all, I'm his mother, too. He needs me as much as they do, or did.

Seeing the light of the end of this dark, emotional tunnel began one night, before Mother left. I was sitting in the sunroom, trying to focus on a book a friend had given me. It was a self-help book that I was having trouble getting into, but I had promised her I would read it word for word. Cole was out of town on a business trip. Matthew had gone to a football game at school. Michaela was in her room with the door closed. She said she wanted to be alone. That was her usual response these days when I asked her if she wanted to talk, or do something special with me. I was getting used to being rejected by her.

The phone rang. It was the conductor of the Nashville Symphony, Allen Connally. He said they all missed me, and wanted to know if I was ready to return. I told him "no," but after talking with him for more than an hour, I realized I wasn't ready to curl up and die, either. Yes, I had fallen, in spirit. Undoubtedly, if I didn't get up, I was going to dry to a crisp and fade away, like the leaves. I had much too much to live for to do that.

I started counting my blessings instead of the heartaches. I realized that nothing had been taken away from me. Instead, Cole and I had received another blessing, Sidney Williams. She was ours, and we would accept her into our lives. We, in turn, would share Michaela with Ralph and Cynthia. We could choose to continue to grow as a family, or walk around bitter and angry with the world, because of the baby mix-up.

I chose the former. The next morning I thanked Mother for having moved into our home and putting her life on hold to help me. I then told her to get her things together. I was taking her home, so that she could enjoy her life and the rest of her family. I apologized for being selfish, and told her how much we loved her. I assured her that she always had a home here whenever she wanted to return.

I then went to the beauty salon and got a haircut. I went shopping for new clothes. I was ready to start living again! I was ready to see daylight again. Unlike the little red bird that died in her nest of cotton, her cushion from life, I had the opportunity to get out in the sunshine. I was going to walk and flap my wings, and meet and overcome challenges, so I could heal and grow stronger. Mother had made a nest of cotton for me, but thank God I finally found the strength and had the voice and wisdom to tell her it was time to leave. It was time for me to fly.

I thought about Sarah Johnson, the young slave girl. She had moved on to a big city without a mother to lean on, and she was only a teenager. She'd started a new life. She refused to accept her former status in life. Sarah had no family to turn to; she was walking by faith. She was such an amazing young woman. If only I had her strength. If only I knew why these old papers were in Dad's trunk. Could I possibly be related to her? My paternal cousin, Darlene, a history professor at Clemson University in Clemson, South Carolina, had now gotten involved with helping Mother and me research our family history. She started her research one month ago.

The next morning I started walking, and kept walking. In the beginning, I thought I wouldn't be able to handle having McAlister away two mornings each week. I'm now thinking about enrolling him in the early childhood program four days a week. I need time to practice playing the violin, because my conductor says the symphony *needs* me. I'm sure he wouldn't have any trouble finding a talented violinist to replace me, but he wants *me* back. It's such a good feeling to know that you're missed, that someone wants you. I want only the very best for Matthew, Michaela, Sidney and McAlister. But, I also want what's best for me.

Michaela and Sidney talk every day on the telephone. Obviously, they care about each other. Michaela was the one who broke the news about the mix-up to Sidney in the hospital. From that moment on, they have bonded. Sidney is now at home with her family. Her health is continuing to improve.

Cole, Michaela and I have been back to Cleveland to visit her, and to give Michaela an opportunity to get to know her "natural" parents. Michaela has decided that she will spend some time with the Williams family, as soon as Sidney is strong enough to get around. Then the two can do fun things together.

The great news, however, is that Ralph and Cynthia are bringing Sidney to Nashville to spend a week with us. She has a fall break from school. This is the perfect opportunity for her to visit with us. This will be her first trip to Nashville.

Sidney is a pleasant young lady. From what I can see, Ralph and Cynthia have done a good job with her. She is shy and not very talkative with Cole and me. On the other hand, she and Michaela can talk for hours. Michaela says they are sisters, because of what they've gone through. They have almost 11 years of life to catch up on with each other.

Finally, Michaela is starting to open up to me again. She told me that she and Sidney talk about their families, that's why they're on the phone so much. She's trying to help Sidney get to know us, and Sidney is trying to help her to get to know the Williams family. She said Sidney has described Cynthia as a nice person, but very strict when it comes to grades. She said Sidney sometimes feels pressured to do well, because her mother was recently voted "Teacher of the Year."

According to Michaela, Sidney would like to be more outgoing, but doesn't have a lot of time to socialize. Her schoolwork and chores at home keep her very busy. Also, Sidney is very fond of her dad, Ralph, but thinks he works too hard. He wants his children to have nice things. He tries to earn extra money so all of them can get a good education, because he was unable to finish college for financial reasons. I didn't ask Michaela how she described Cole and me to Sidney. We love our children dearly and that should speak for itself.

One Friday morning I received a call from Ralph saying that he would be bringing Sidney to Nashville as planned. He said that Cynthia wouldn't be able to come. He didn't say why. I told him we were grateful to them for allowing Sidney to visit for a week. I couldn't help but wonder why he didn't mention the reason why Cynthia wouldn't be coming. She had told me earlier that she had never been to Nashville, and was looking forward to coming to our home. Both families would have been able to enjoy Michaela and Sidney. Perhaps something had come up at work, or maybe she had other obligations. I brushed the thought off, and got busy decorating the room that Sidney would move into during her stay.

I desperately wanted everything to be perfect for this special child, who had suddenly come into our lives. A part of me wanted this visit to be so special for Sidney that she wouldn't want to return to Cleveland. I knew that was a selfish thought. I tried to put it out of my mind.

Matthew and Michaela were just as excited as Cole and I were about the visit. We spent the next week getting everything in order. Michaela made bright-colored posters welcoming Sidney to our home, and Matthew actually helped with the decorations. Michaela knew a lot more about Sidney than I did, including her clothes and shoe sizes, so we were able to shop for items for Sidney.

"Mother, there's no way Sidney would wear this dress," Michaela would say. "Let me select the clothes and you can write the check." We started shopping Friday after school, and didn't finish until around 9:00 that evening. I almost collapsed when I walked into the kitchen.

"Looks like you two girls had a busy day," Cole said. "Did you buy everything in sight?"

"No, Dad, but Sidney described the kinds of clothes she likes, and we had trouble finding some of the styles. I really wish Nashville had larger malls." Michaela continued to talk about what Sidney liked and didn't like. These two young ladies had clearly connected.

Sidney and her father arrived that Saturday morning. We all gave her a hug as soon as she got out of the car. Michaela took her to her bedroom for the next week. While Michaela showed her around the house, Ralph, Cole and I sat in the sunroom and talked about our families.

He said Cynthia was sorry that she couldn't make it to Nashville. He said they both felt good about Sidney spending time with us. They were praying that Michaela and Sidney would adjust to their new families, and move on with their young lives.

I managed to get Ralph to have lunch with us, but he declined to spend the night because he had to get back home. He didn't say what the rush was, and we didn't ask. Sidney shed a few tears when he kissed her goodbye, then Matthew and Michaela led her into the family room to watch a movie. It didn't seem to take long for her to be okay in her new environment.

Cole and I hugged each other, and I cried. After weeks of worrying, and traveling back and forth to Cleveland, we now had all of our children here with us. We could share our love and lives with each other. Michaela and Sidney had bonded so well that their relationship had brought the two families together. Michaela had believed she could help Sidney recover more quickly by talking to her daily. She also wanted to let her know that she wasn't alone with what she was going through. Sidney felt weak and sometimes had trouble breathing. Michaela called her faithfully. Sidney did begin to get stronger, and started calling Michaela. It was as if they were each other's therapist.

Once they grew closer, I felt more comfortable calling to speak with Cynthia to try to get to know her better. I was thankful that kind people had raised my daughter. I hoped they felt the same about Cole and me. It didn't matter that Cynthia and Ralph couldn't afford a fancy life style for their six children. What mattered was that they had brought their children up in a loving home, with good morals and values.

Matthew and Michaela only had a three-day fall break, Wednesday through Friday. So, Cole and I had the opportunity to spend time with Sidney, while those two were at school. We tried to focus our conversations with her on subjects that we knew she was interested in, such as math and painting.

My father loved to paint. I knew Sidney was blessed with his talent when Cynthia showed me two of her paintings of nature scenes. She even had my father's smile. If only he could've gotten to know her before he passed away. Mother had met and fallen in love with her at the hospital in Cleveland. She is coming to spend a few days with us, so that she can spend some time with her "new" granddaughter. This time I'm not going to hold her captive like I did before.

On Monday, after Matthew and Michaela had gone to school, Sidney asked Cole and me how we wanted her to address us. We told her that it was fine for her to call us Cole and Celia. We took her downtown. Her favorite site was the Frist Center for the Arts. She enjoyed the painting exhibits and we had discussions about some of the work. She was quite knowledgeable for her age. I was almost embarrassed that I couldn't answer some of her questions about art.

We then had lunch at the center's café. Sidney explained to us that she hadn't developed a big appetite, since the surgery, and that she mostly enjoyed different kinds of soups. She ate slowly. I noticed that she was staring at Cole and me from time to time. I'm sure she was looking to see which one of us she resembles more. I wanted to tell her that she is the spitting image of my parents, but I didn't. Needless to say, Cole and I thought she was beautiful. I had to fight back the tears when I realized we might never have met her if she hadn't gotten sick. God has His way of making things happen when the time is right.

As soon as Michaela walked into the door after school, she and Sidney were off to Michaela's room. Even Matthew came straight home from school, so he could be a part of this unusual family gathering. Little McAlister followed Sidney everywhere, asking her to read to him, which she did. She was used to having lots of siblings around, and didn't seem to mind. I left the kids to enjoy each other. I decided to call Cynthia to tell her that Sidney was adjusting just fine.

I was surprised that she hadn't called to check on her daughter. Ralph answered the phone and said she was resting. It was only 5:00 on a Monday evening. I wondered why she couldn't come to the phone, but didn't make an issue of it with Ralph. Teaching sixth graders had to be a challenging job. I told Ralph to tell her that Sidney was just fine, and that she seemed to be enjoying herself. He thanked us for inviting his daughter to our home, and said he would give Cynthia the message.

On Thursday we took all of our children to the Opryland Hotel complex, and had dinner there. Sidney said she had never seen such a huge hotel, and joked that she would need a bicycle to see it all. The week was over long before we wanted it to end. Ralph arrived early Saturday to get her. I wished I could've hidden her, and kept her with us. She said she really enjoyed being with us, but I could see that she missed her family. She was ready to return to Cleveland. She told Michaela, as she was getting into the car, that she would see her at Thanksgiving.

"So, have you two made plans for the Thanksgiving holiday?" I asked, as soon as Ralph's car pulled out of our driveway.

"Yes, Mom; Sidney invited me to come to Cleveland for Thanksgiving. I said 'yes.' I hope that's okay with you and Dad."

"Sweetheart, don't you think you should've discussed this with your father and me, before giving Sidney an answer?"

"You're right, Mom, but Sidney likes me, and I didn't want to say 'no' to her."

"Who said you had to say 'no?' All I'm saying is that you don't make plans to be away from home, especially out of the state, without discussing them with your father and me. Your dad and I have decided to spend Thanksgiving in Denver, and we are taking all of you with us."

"I'm sorry, Mom. When can I go to stay with Sidney, and… and… with Ralph and Cynthia? They've invited me to come, and I want to go."

So here we go, I thought. I'd been waiting for the moment when Michaela would ask to spend time with the Williams family. But now I was emotionally strong enough to deal with the issue.

"You can go when there's not a conflict with school, or a conflict with plans that your father and I have made for the family." I wasn't about to freak out and get upset, because she wanted to spend time with her "natural" parents. She had every right to spend time with them. However, I raised her. And, at 10 years old, she had to have my permission to leave this house. I had to make that very clear, before she got any crazy ideas about doing her own thing.

"Okay, Mom, calm down. When would be a good time for me to go to stay with the Williamses for a few days?"

"Since you get two weeks at Christmas, your father and I can take you there the day after Christmas. You can stay until school starts in January." I thought this was reasonable. I didn't ask for Michaela's opinion. I was sure Cole wouldn't object to this arrangement.

"I'll call Sidney when she gets home to tell her when I'm coming," Michaela said, and left the room.

It was the middle of October. I had two months to get used to the reality that my daughter would be spending time with her "new" family. I wanted Michaela to get to know and enjoy the Williamses, but didn't want to lose her to them. I also wanted Sidney to grow to love Cole and me.

Thanksgiving came. We enjoyed time with Cole's parents in Denver. Cole is an only child, so his parents love spending time with us. They wanted Sidney to come with us, but I didn't think Cynthia would want her away for Thanksgiving. Yet, I wish I had at least asked. I was amazed at how well his parents, and Mother, had adjusted to having a "new" granddaughter.

I began Christmas shopping soon after we returned from Denver. I usually finished early, but this year there were too many things to deal with that were far more important. I called Cynthia to find out if there was anything Sidney especially wanted for Christmas. She gave me some ideas, but Cole and I decided to give her a nice art set, and a book about the lives of several famous artists. We were impressed with her knowledge of art and thought she would enjoy the book. We also bought her a heavy coat, because I could still remember those harsh Cleveland winters.

Christmas day was a week away. Sidney called to tell us that she had received her gifts from us, and couldn't wait to open them. Michaela was thrilled about being able to stay with the Williams family for five days after Christmas. Before she could get to Cleveland, I received a call from Ralph that hurt Michaela deeply. He told me that this wasn't a good time for her to visit, that perhaps we could bring her up later. When I asked to speak to Cynthia to discuss when would be a good time, he simply said she was not available. He added that he would get back to me later.

This was another strange incident involving Cynthia recently. I was beginning to wonder what was up with her. Was she the loving mother she appeared to be, or had I simply misread her?

25. Sarah

I AM PASSIONATE ABOUT DESIGNING CLOTHING for free Negro women. Success is inevitable when you do what you enjoy in life.

Two years after Reverend Baker's death, Miz Baker came to Boston to live. That made me very happy. She moved in with Aunt Clara in May 1856.

I moved out of Aunt Clara's home that following June, and put a bed in the back of the room I was leasing for my dress shop. My moving out of her house broke Aunt Clara's heart, but she had done enough for me. It was now time to stand on my own. Although she would have preferred that I had stayed, Aunt Clara understood.

I hired three women to help me with the sewing. These women, like me, had escaped slavery. They were desperate to remain free and independent. I felt good about being able to offer them the opportunity to work in my shop.

William, like Aunt Clara, has a good business head. They have helped me make my business a success. My employees and I work long hours. They cut and sew fabric, while I design. I work late each day to get the paperwork done. William, Miz Baker and Aunt Clara are concerned that I am spending too much time at the shop, but I have not come this far to fail. I still remember having dreams about being in a large city, walking toward a shop. I would always wake up before the dream ended, though. *I* was the lady in those dreams, walking toward *my* dress shop. God brought young Sarah from Holly Springs, to New York City, then to Boston to do great things. I did not intend to let them down, or ignore those who needed my help.

I continue to teach reading and writing to Negro adults and children. It is heartbreaking to look into the eyes of a child, or adult, who can not read or write. Their yearning to do both is so great. I try hard to keep Sunday afternoons open for teaching, and only go to the shop if it is absolutely necessary.

William and I are still very close. We spend lots of time talking about social issues in Boston and other places. His father and uncle are proud of him. They have given him the authority to make major decisions about what should or should not be printed in the paper. One evening after dinner at William's home, he and I discussed a very sensitive topic of an article he wanted to print.

"I don't think there's a lot of difference between the North and the South, that is, when it comes to attitudes about our people. Some Negro

Bostonians, unfortunately, view the Southern Negro as being inferior because of slavery. But, just how free are any of us? I think we need to wake up and realize that all of us are subject to laws created by white people. We aren't as free here in Boston as some of us like to think. Most of us can't read and write, don't have any skills and can barely speak the English language. This keeps us down as a group and out of touch with political and social issues. The day will come, Sarah, when slavery will no longer exist. How prepared are we, the "free" Negroes, to help our deprived brothers and sisters?

"We can't continue to pretend that we are safe, that injustice only exists in the South. I want to help our people by printing articles that will force us to think about things realistically. Some Negroes don't want to talk about slavery because it's Southern. But, there are white people, many of them right here in Boston, with slave and plantation mentality."

"I understand, William. Remember, I am a former slave. If I get caught, I will become one again. When I first came here, I did not tell people I was a slave, because I did not want them to feel uncomfortable, or pity me. Then, I thought about everything Mammy and Pappy had taught me, and realized I had so much to be proud of about my heritage. I am no fool when it comes to white people, and how they see us.

"We are Africans, and many white people will never see us as any more than that. I was truly amazed when I met the Bakers, Aunt Clara and you, because all of you are free Negroes from families that have accomplished a lot. You all are educated and own property, but you still make the effort to help your brothers and sisters. I am so thankful to have met each of you. I truly believe God had it all planned out for me."

"You are a very special person, Sarah. No, you are no fool when it comes to white people. That's one important thing we have in common. You had so little when you left Mississippi, now, look at you."

"Actually, William, I had a lot when I left Holly Springs. God gave me wise and talented parents who taught me almost everything I know. Yes, they have spent their lives in slavery, but they *will* know what it is like to be free. I will see to it that they have a taste of freedom, even if it costs me my life. I have been saving money since my first job in New York City, after the Bakers took me into their home. The Bakers and Aunt Clara refused to accept money from me for boarding, so I was able to save all of it."

"And, so have I, Sarah. My father taught me the importance of saving money when I was just a child. I always saved the money he gave me for helping with the paper. I have two brothers, but I'm the one most like my father. He knows I will do everything I can to keep the paper circulating throughout the Negro community, if anything happens to him or my uncle. I love it because it's a part of me and my family."

"So, Mr. Harper, what exactly are your plans for the future?"

"Well, Miss Johnson, I plan to stay here in Boston, to work hard to make *The Herald Progress* bigger and better. That's my professional goal."

"That is a pretty big goal," I said.

"Why set small goals? You certainly didn't set small ones for yourself." It was a peaceful evening. William and I were talking more openly than we had before. He had helped me get through my moments of depression about being away from my parents, and Reverend Baker's death. He was very special to me; I told him so. I thought about him a lot and knew that I loved him, but could not imagine ever saying this to him.

He was strong, intelligent and compassionate, which was partly why I loved him. He was also quite handsome. I loved his dimples when he smiled. His dark skin was flawless. His smile revealed perfectly placed white teeth. He was from a prominent family, but like Aunt Clara and Miz Baker, he was interested in the less fortunate Negroes here and in other places. There was a long silence. Then, William spoke.

"Sarah, I have given this a lot of thought, and think the time is appropriate to ask you to be my wife. I love you, enjoy your company and we have so much in common. I know I could be happy spending a lifetime with you." There was another long silence. I could not speak. William Harper had just asked me to be his wife! Surely I had misunderstood him.

"Sarah, I would like to have an answer tonight, whatever it may be." I turned away from him, so he could not see my tears. I was overcome with joy. I could not believe he felt the same way about me! William Harper could have his pick of beautiful Boston society Negro women, yet he had asked me, Sarah Johnson, a former slave, to be his wife. He pulled me close and kissed me softly on my lips, cheeks and forehead.

"Sarah, why are you crying? Are these tears of joy or sorrow?"

"Both," I said. "I cannot believe that you want me, of all people, to be your wife."

"And, what's wrong with you?" he asked, with a big smile.

"You are a Harper, a society man, born and raised in an affluent family. We are from different worlds, William."

"Different how, Sarah? You were born in the South, and I in the North. You refer to yourself as a former slave. Does that make you any less of a person than me, or anyone else? Just how free are any of us, anyway?" I could hear the pain in William's voice, and knew he could hear it in mine. I did not think I was any less of a person, but I was being realistic. I wanted him to think about what he was asking me to do.

"Sarah, I have given this a lot of thought. I'm quite capable of thinking for myself." He appeared to be irritated now. I certainly had not intended to hurt or upset him. We did not speak for several minutes.

"William, you are very intelligent, and certainly capable of thinking for yourself. However, I never dreamed that anyone like you could fall in love with me."

"Why not? Is it because you were born in Holly Springs, and I in Boston? If I'm correct, I do believe that both of our ancestors came from the same place. Just so happens that some of us ended up in one place, and some in another. Sarah, in case you don't know, you are a very attractive woman, who happens to be kind, sincere, genuine, intelligent and very talented. What's there not to love about you?"

I could not hide the big smile that covered my face. William was sincere. I could hear it in his voice, see it in his eyes. We embraced and kissed as we never had before. I could feel the strength of his arms around me, and knew that he cared deeply. My very best friend in the whole world had asked me to marry him. I did not know how to respond. Perhaps if he had given me some warning, I could have been better prepared. The thought made me laugh.

"What's so funny? Is that a 'yes' or 'no' to my question?"

"William, I had no idea you would propose to me tonight."

"Should I have written you first, then asked you in person?" We were both laughing now. William had a great sense of humor and always seemed to be able to lift my spirits. We were definitely good for each other. Whenever he wanted to talk, about anything bothering him, I always listened intently. I only gave him my opinion if he wanted it. If I did not think he wanted an opinion, I said nothing. By now, I knew the difference. That was something I learned from Mammy. William obviously needed, and appreciated, that quality in me. Mammy had taught me far more than she realized. I could not wait to tell her that she had taught me how to attract, and win, the man I loved.

"Am I going to get an answer tonight, or are you going to make me wait?" William asked, affectionately. I knew my answer, but was careful to phrase it tactfully.

"William, I would love to be your wife. I feel honored that you have chosen me. However, I made a promise to myself some years ago that I would not marry until I had gone back to get my parents. I am committed to seeing Mammy and Pappy, and honestly cannot commit to say 'yes' until I have done this." I saw the hurt in his eyes, but that was my answer. I had to tell him the truth. The truth sometimes hurt. William held me close, stroked my hair, and said he understood. But, I think my answer surprised him.

"Sarah, I will wait for you. Tell me, though, when do you plan to go back for your parents?"

"Within the next two months. Although I can not talk about it much, I have been thinking about this for years. The time has come for me to take action."

"Sarah, believe me, I know how much this means to you. But, have you thought about the consequences of what you are about to do?"

"Yes, I have, and I am still going back. The worse that can happen is that Mr. Wilmington will reclaim me as one of his slaves."

"Or, severely punish or kill you! What do Aunt Clara and Mrs. Baker think?"

"They do not want me to go. They want a white person with whom they are acquainted to go to try to talk Mr. Wilmington into selling Mammy and Pappy to one of them. My parents have gotten on up in age. I am not so sure how useful they are to the Wilmingtons anymore, so they may be willing to sell them."

"Then, why do you have to go and risk your life, Sarah?"

"Because I want to see my parents!" William looked at me with deep sympathy, but my mind was made up. There was nothing he or anyone else could say that would change it. I was 25. I had not seen my parents in over 10 years. I had to know for myself if they were well. Plus, I wanted them to see the woman I had become. Aunt Clara and Miz Baker did not think it was wise for me to write to my parents, because Mr. Wilmington seemed so determined to catch me when I was younger. Now, I prayed that he had forgiven me. Hopefully he would allow me to buy my parents. Based on what I had been told by other former slaves, I had enough money to buy them.

"Sarah, I can't let you do this, alone. One day you will be my wife. Now is the time to start protecting you. We have to come up with a safe plan that will work for us. What concerns me is that your parents may not want to leave Mississippi. It has been very difficult for some of our people to adjust to a new way of life, once they leave their masters."

"That is because many of them do not have skills other than picking crops. They find it hard to get work elsewhere to support their families. My parents will not have to work because I can take care of them. I have my own dress shop. If Mammy wants to, she can work with me."

"Your mind is clearly made up. I obviously can't change it. Just promise me that you will let me help you. Please promise me that you won't leave, or do anything drastic, before discussing it with me. I love you, Sarah, and don't want to lose you."

"I promise, William. But, please understand that I am ready to act. I am not going to put this off any longer." We then began talking about our future together as man and wife. We both wanted children. I asked him how he felt about me keeping the dress shop. He said he would help make *Sarah's Dress Shop* bigger and more profitable. His mother had worked with his father and uncle to make *The Herald Progress* a success. He said he would do the same for my business.

It was late when William and I said goodnight. I felt great! The man I loved had asked me to be his wife, and, I was going back to Holly Springs to try to buy my parents from the Wilmingtons. This was not going to be easy. On the other hand, I had the kind of faith the Bible said "can move mountains!" Over the years, I never stopped believing that my family and I would be reunited, that we would spend the rest of our lives together.

Everything was looking good for me. My business was growing. I was designing and creating more unique ladies' clothing. There was a demand for more creativity. I made more money on ladies' dresses than on girls' dresses, so began concentrating on clothing for women. I had begun going to some of the larger stores in the city to see what women were wearing. More importantly, I needed to know what they wanted to wear. Although I worked long hours, I enjoyed every one of them. This was truly what I was born to do in life.

I gave credit for my talent to Mammy. After all these years, I can still remember the delicate, colorful dresses she had made for Miz Wilmington and her daughters. Mammy was always happy when she had the time to make pretty dresses.

The orders for women's dresses from my shop increased; so did the work load. We had to meet the growing demand. I spent most of my time designing and creating styles. I had prayed that my business would become a big success, but had not expected it to happen so soon.

The shop was small, but we made the most of the space. I was quite pleased with the ladies who worked for me. It was a wonderful feeling to be in a position to help my own. I had received much. Now I was able to give back to help others.

Despite the increase in orders, I found it hard to concentrate on sewing or anything else at times. William and I were thinking of ways for me to reunite with my parents, without getting caught. He, Aunt Clara and Miz Baker did not think I should show my face to Mr. Wilmington. I was still a young woman, so very valuable to him and his household. Mr. Wilmington was no more than 50. He had many good years ahead of him.

William came up with a plan that he thought would work. We all discussed it at Aunt Clara's house. Miz Baker and Aunt Clara were acquainted with white people who worked for companies that did business in Mississippi. Some were in the cotton and banking businesses, and some had purchased land in Mississippi. Some were in the insurance business. However, none of them were personal friends of Mr. Wilmington. William wanted one of them to go to Mr. Wilmington and ask to buy my parents. Of course, Mr. Wilmington would want to know why either of the businessmen would be interested in two older slaves. The answer would be that the businessman needed someone to care for his young children, and keep the house.

Kate and Melissa Wilmington were as old as I was now, so I could not think of any important reason why the Wilmingtons would still need my parents. Pappy was close to 60. He could not possibly be as strong and useful in the fields as he once was. If Mr. Wilmington was a decent human being, he would give my parents their freedom. They had worked very hard for his family for years. Personally, I knew he was not decent, so I was prepared to try to buy Mammy and Pappy from him myself.

No one wanted me to go along with the one businessman to Holly Springs, but they could not stop me. I had to see Mammy and Pappy, to see for myself that they were well. I was not going to accept any more messages from anyone. This time I was going along.

I knew Mr. Wilmington probably still hated me, but, I had a plan. I would disguise myself as a man, traveling with a white businessman; I would pretend to be his body servant, valet or gentleman' gentleman. Aunt Clara and Miz Baker had the perfect clothing for me to wear. I knew how to play act the rest. We had to have someone who had done business with Mr. Wilmington, but was not his personal friend. We needed someone who believed that Negroes had a right to be free. However, Aunt Clara and Miz Baker had to be very careful about who they asked to do this. After inquiring for several days, they thought they had found the right person.

"Sarah, dear, you know we do not think you should go, but, I guess we can't stop you now," Miz Baker said, with resignation.

"No, Miz Baker, no one can stop me now. It has been 11 years since I left home. Before I can marry William, or get on with my life, I have to go back for Mammy and Pappy. Tell me, please, who you have found to help me." I could not allow myself to feel the deep concern shared by Miz Baker or Aunt Clara. They had always stood up for what they believed. Now I had to take a stand for my beliefs. I believed that Mammy and Pappy deserved to spend some of their lives as free people. I was prepared to risk mine for theirs.

"Sweetheart, we've known Daniel Broughton for many years. He has been in the cotton business for several years, representing a company that manufactures and distributes cotton to European countries. I'm almost certain that he has done business with Frank Wilmington, but they are not personal friends. He is known as a respectable man. He says he will try to help you. Daniel said Frank Wilmington has no knowledge about his views on slavery. Their relationship is strictly a business relationship.

"His mother has been quite ill lately, and he has really been looking for someone to help care for her. He wants to buy your parents to hire them.

He wants them to stay with him to help with his mother. He will pay them for their services."

"I do not know, Aunt Clara. It sounds like Mammy and Pappy will have a new master, except that it will be here, and not in Holly Springs."

"My dear child, Mr. Broughton is not in favor of slavery. He has spoken out against it."

"And, what if my parents do not want to work for him? Would he tell everybody about our little plan? I want to buy my parents. I want them to have a choice. For once in their lives, I want them to be able to decide what they want for themselves." I did not like what I was hearing. I was about to say forget about Mr. Broughton, when William interrupted.

"Sarah, please, just listen. My father knows the Broughton family. He thinks they're decent people. It sounds to me like Mr. Broughton wants to approach the Wilmingtons with a genuine request. He needs someone to look after his mother, to help him out."

"We've told him that your parents are good people," Miz Baker said.

"*I* want to buy *my* parents. I do not want anyone else buying them for their own personal gain. Can't you all understand this?"

"We can," William said. "But, we have to have a plan that's going to work. Frank Wilmington is no fool. You of all people should know this, Sarah." They were all staring at me. I was getting more irritated as they talked on.

"We are discussing my parents, not just some elderly couple. I am not about to agree to anything that may cause them more pain and suffering." I was visibly upset now. I sat down and stopped talking. There was silence all around.

"Sarah, you've never met Mr. Broughton. I think it would be a good idea for you to talk with him before you turn down this plan. Mrs. Baker, Aunt Clara, is there any way we can arrange a meeting with him tomorrow, or very soon?" William asked.

"Why, dear, I don't see why not. I'll try to reach him and see what he has to say. I'll let you know something as soon as I hear from him," Aunt Clara said. She grabbed my hand.

"I think that's a great idea, William," Miz Baker added. "Sarah is right. These are her parents. She is concerned about their well being and dignity. I think she and Mr. Broughton need to meet soon."

I remained silent and grabbed my purse. It had been a long day. I was ready to go home. I needed to work at the shop, but was too tired to think about sewing.

William took me home in his carriage that warm summer night in August 1856. He asked me to look at the stars, and see how bright they were that night. My mind and heart were in Holly Springs, not the sky. I had not been very pleasant over the past few days. This was not my personality by any means. It was as if there was some uncontrollable force telling me to go back for Mammy and Pappy. I had not been able to sleep well the past few nights. I wondered if something had happened to my parents. Something must have happened to them. Why else would I have felt so sad and alone these past few days? If only I could see them.

If they had died there was no way anyone would have known how to contact me. During the ride home, I began to cry softly because I did not want William to hear me. He wanted a romantic night, but I just did not feel that way. Looking at the stars only made me sadder. I wanted to be alone, to think about the past 11 years of my life. There were still times when I was sorry I had left Mammy and Pappy. There was a price for freedom. I had surely paid it.

I said "goodnight" to William when we arrived at my shop, which was still where I lived. I could see the hurt in his eyes as I almost pushed him away. That night I thought about going back to Holly Springs alone, without telling anyone. I could disguise myself as one of Mammy's older relatives, visiting from a nearby plantation.

My mind drifted back to those Sundays after church when family members visited with us and everyone had a good time. Mammy cooked lots of good food. Relatives came by from other farms and plantations. Mr. Wilmington sometimes gave the slaves permission to gather and socialize on Sundays. If I went back, dressed as one of Mammy's relatives, who just happened to be visiting on a Sunday afternoon, Mr. Wilmington probably would not get suspicious. The challenge was getting Mammy and Pappy back to Boston. They were older now. It would be too difficult for them to try to escape as runaway slaves. The thought of them getting whipped or killed if they were caught, was too much to bear. The thought of leaving them behind, again, was even more painful to consider. Perhaps William was right. I would have to go along with someone else, to try to get my parents back to Boston.

I lay in bed thinking about home. My education, dress shop and even William's proposal for marriage could not take away the pain. I cried when I thought about all the families that had been separated because of slavery. I spent the first 13 years of my life with my parents, when so many other children had been separated from their parents much earlier. I could not imagine how deeply Mammy's heart must have ached for Tom, when he was snatched from her and Pappy at such a young age.

I prayed that night for strength and courage to go through with the plan with Mr. Broughton. I needed the faith of that grain of mustard seed mentioned in the Bible to make it work. I made a promise to God that night that if He helped me get back to see my parents, I would do whatever I felt He wanted me to do with my life, whether it was teaching, preaching, sewing, whatever. I would do it. After that prayer, my heart felt lighter. I fell asleep.

26. Naini

AM TRAVELING TO CITIES AND TOWNS across the state, campaigning for the U.S. senate, in February 2014. It didn't take long for me to realize that this opportunity might never come my way again. I took a leave of absence from my teaching position to concentrate on the campaign. I asked Ken Akers to manage my campaign again. But, he is serving on City Council and teaching full-time. Anna suggested that I talk to Laura Gates.

Ms. Gates is Director of Human Resources for a large corporation in Providence. She is known for her sharp organizational and motivational skills. After my initial meeting with her, I was convinced she was the person to manage my campaign.

I haven't raised as much money as my Republican opponent, Brent Kirkpatrick. However, the donations are pouring into my camp. I now have name recognition here and across America because of my work with HIV/AIDS.

Within two weeks of leaving Lagos, I met with executives of four pharmaceutical companies. My goal was to try to convince them to meet with Dr. Bakari; to hear his proposal. I was not successful. They each were concerned about the cost of such a project. By the end of December 2013, however, I had managed to persuade the CEO of Acacia, one of the largest pharmaceutical companies in the country, to invite Dr. Bakari to Boston for a meeting. I'm still amazed at how it happened.

Around the first of December 2013, a member of my church, Dr. James Woodard, invited me to speak at the annual Good Health Day. Dr. Woodard is principal of a high school in our district. He had read about my work with HIV/AIDS, and asked me to talk to the students about the progress we'd made. I really didn't have any free time on Wednesday, but accepted the invitation anyway.

Good Health Day is an event the PTA began sponsoring several years ago, to help young people improve the quality of their health. Each year it is a success. Doctors and health care professionals in Providence and nearby cities attend. They distribute information and close the event with a question and answer session. I felt honored to have been invited.

The following day I got a call from Grant Hunter. Mr. Hunter is the parent of a student who attends the high school.

"Mrs. Carrington, I want to thank you for your presentation on HIV/AIDS yesterday. My son needed to hear every word of it. I've recently learned that he is sexually active. He thinks HIV/AIDS is a disease that only 'other' people can contract. At 17, my son thinks he's invincible.

"I found him in his bedroom last night reading the material you gave to him. He finally understands that HIV/AIDS doesn't discriminate when it comes to age, race, gender or economic background. My wife and I have been trying to communicate this message to him for months, with no success. Thank you for taking the time to come to speak to a group of high school students."

"I'm pleased to know that I at least helped one of the students. That motivates me to keep working, to get this message out," I said.

"Mrs. Carrington, I think I may be able to help you with your project. I am an executive at Acacia. I'm meeting with our CEO, Jack Tinsley, in the morning. I want to tell him about Dr. Bakari and his work. If you have a few minutes, I'd like to get some additional information before presenting this to Mr. Tinsley…"

I could not believe what I was hearing! I'd gone to speak to a group of high school students, to help them become more aware of HIV/AIDS, and this was my reward!

Mr. Tinsley asked to meet with me the day after he met with Mr. Hunter. And, the rest is history.

Dr. Bakari flew in from Stanford the following week to meet with Jack Tinsley. Mr. Tinsley was clearly impressed with Dr. Bakari's research. The following week, this historical meeting made headlines in The Boston Herald: ***Acacia To Provide Millions To Sponsor Clinical Testing For Drug That May Cure HIV/AIDS.*** Just below the headline was a picture of Dr. Bakari, Mr. Tinsley, Anna, the Committee To Help Hurting Children and me. Within a matter of days, this picture and related articles were printed in newspapers around the country!

My campaign for the U.S. senate is going well. At the top of my agenda is treatment and placement of orphan children with HIV/AIDS. Secondly, I focused on the placement of elderly people in need of long-term care, into affordable facilities. Most women are now expected to live to age 85, and men to age 80.

John informed me that he had a seminar to attend in Santa Fe, New Mexico, from Friday through Monday. He wanted me and the children to come along, but I decided to keep the babies at home. I took a week-end break from the campaign. This would be a great opportunity for the three of us to bond.

John is so funny. He made a list of things they liked and disliked, and told me he would call often to check on us. He sounded like a mother hen. Harry and Haley are fraternal twins, and are the spitting image of John and his family. I almost feel cheated when I look at them. My daughter looks more like John's mother than me. They both have my brown eyes, but that's all. Perhaps this is one of the reasons their father enjoys them so much.

John caught an early flight out of New Mexico on Monday. He couldn't wait to get back to his babies. I enjoyed having them to myself, but was ready to get back to campaigning.

After months of traveling, debating and making speeches, I won the election for U.S. senator in November 2014. Needless to say, I was excited, motivated and eager to begin serving. I had goals, and a plan to accomplish them. However, I did not get to complete the remainder of my term.

One Friday morning, in early May 2016, I got a call that would change my life forever! I was dressing to go to my office, when John called out for me to get the phone.

"Hello."

"Hello, may I speak to Senator Carrington."

"This is she. How may I help you?"

"This is Senator Christian. How are you, Senator Carrington?"

Senator Steven Christian, a powerful politician from Pennsylvania, was a candidate for president of the United States. The election was in six months. We would have a new president. Both parties had sharp, competent candidates running for the most powerful position in the world. I was on the phone with one of them. Senator Christian had recently won the Democratic primary.

"Senator Carrington, I will be in Providence tomorrow, and would like very much to have dinner with you and your husband."

"Please call me Raini. We would love to have dinner with you."

"That's wonderful. My secretary will make the arrangements and contact you tomorrow. It's good talking to you."

"Thank you. I look forward to seeing you tomorrow. Goodbye." I went back into my bedroom to finish dressing.

"That was Senator Steven Christian. He wants to have dinner with us tomorrow evening." John gave me a puzzled look.

27. Celia

MATTHEW AND MICHAELA are already beginning to talk about their plans for the summer; it's early March 1989. Matthew is talking about tennis, and would play all day if he could get away with it. Michaela is anxious about visiting with the Williams family in two weeks.

Our attorney, David Turner, is busy with the investigation. He is trying to find Barbara Cramer, the Director of Nursing at Willow Memorial Hospital in December 1977. David recently learned that Ms. Cramer was fired. She was asked to leave the hospital some time around the end of February 1978. Apparently some medications were missing from the hospital around that time. It was discovered later that several employees were involved, including Clarese Evers, the head nurse on the maternity unit at that time.

David desperately wanted to talk to Ms. Cramer, but couldn't find her. Every lead to her whereabouts yielded nothing. She apparently skips around the country, not keeping the same job for very long. David is determined to prove that the hospital was aware that there were drug-related problems with the nursing staff, but tried to keep it hidden. Now, a decade later, two children may have lost their lives because of this negligence. And, two families must learn to live with the knowledge that their biological daughters were switched.

I should be more interested in the investigation, but I'm too busy being a mother to Matthew, Michaela, McAlister and Sidney. It's a challenge when they're under your roof. When one is several hundred miles away, it's almost impossible. I talk to Sidney several times a week to keep in touch, to let her know that we love her. Unfortunately, I don't know what's going on with Cynthia. Ralph called in December to tell us that the week after Christmas wasn't a good time for Michaela to visit with them. He didn't give an explanation. Michaela is counting on a visit this summer.

Giving no explanation for the change in December seems almost cruel to me. They've just learned that they have a biological daughter who lives in Nashville with another family, and Cynthia seemingly has shown little interest in getting to know her. Michaela doesn't understand; neither do I.

I've tried to smooth this over so that my child doesn't have to hurt any more than she already has over this unfortunate situation. Michaela wants to get to know her new family. I've finally accepted this, and want only what's best for her. Sidney has begun to bond with Cole and me, even if it is through telephone calls. I, likewise, want Michaela to bond with Ralph and Cynthia.

Sometimes I wonder if they see Michaela as another body to feed and care for. If that's what's going on with them, I could politely inform them that Cole and I are quite capable of providing for Sidney. Michaela has never experienced rejection from her family, and I'm not going to stand by and watch her get rejected by her biological parents.

I make a conscious effort to talk to Sidney each week to see how she is feeling, and how she's doing in each of her subjects. Last week, by Wednesday, I hadn't called her so she called me to find out why I hadn't called her. I was overwhelmed with joy! I've been careful not to force myself into Sidney's life, just be there for her. I do want her to know how special she is to all of us. I believe Cynthia should be doing the same with Michaela.

Finally, it was spring break. We packed Michaela's clothes and headed for Cleveland. I was nervous that Ralph or Cynthia would call to cancel again; they didn't. Michaela was greeted with welcome signs that Sidney and her younger sister, Allyson, had made. Sidney and Allyson shared a room that was decorated with an artist's touch. There were mobiles, bright posters and several of her drawings hanging around the room. They showed Michaela her bed, and where to put her belongings.

Cole and I joined Ralph and Cynthia in the family room. I was amazed to see that Cynthia had lost quite a bit of weight. She was probably on some diet. Clearly, it was working. Cynthia was an attractive woman, who appeared to be in her late 40s. She probably had to buy a new wardrobe, perhaps one size smaller. I thought she looked great and told her so.

Cynthia had prepared an appetizing dinner. We all sat down to enjoy a tasty grilled chicken dish. By the time we finished eating, I had fallen completely in love with Allyson. Allyson is the 6-year-old baby of the family, and it shows. She talks as much as Michaela. I could now understand why Sidney was so quiet. She probably didn't have the opportunity to get a word in with her younger sister around.

Cynthia talked at length about each of their children. Edward, the oldest, is a sophomore at Ohio State University, on a football scholarship. Randall is a freshman at the University of Kentucky, on a scholarship for basketball. Cynthia's eyes lit up when she talked about each of them. She was clearly a proud mother. I could hear it in her voice, see it in her face. Next in line is a set of twin boys, Cade and Cary, who are juniors in high school. They both play soccer and also hope to get scholarships. Then, there are the girls, Sidney, 11, and Allyson, 6.

Cynthia appeared to have the patience of Job. I wondered if she was always so calm. Then common sense told me that there was no way she could be the mother of six and always be this calm.

By the time Cynthia finished describing her six children, we had finished dessert. Cole and I were ready to head to the hotel to get some rest. We kissed the girls good night. I felt comfortable leaving Michaela with this family. My instincts assured me that she would be fine.

With Michaela away for spring break, we had decided not to go to Florida as planned. Mrs. Davenport stayed in our home to care for McAlister and cook for Matthew until we returned from Cleveland.

Matthew spent most of his time on the tennis court practicing. He has worked hard at his game, and it shows. Cole and I attend all of his games. He says he can't imagine playing without us watching. McAlister loves the preschool he attends three mornings each week. He almost pulls me out of the house as soon as he is dressed. I can't help but feel that none of my children needs me anymore.

Thank God for the symphony. I spend my mornings practicing the violin. When possible, I have lunch with two other ladies in the group who enjoy playing the violin as much as I do. With Michaela gone, the house was pretty quiet. I certainly wasn't ready for an empty nest.

Michaela called this morning to say she was enjoying Sidney, but that Allyson talks much too much. She went on to say that Allyson wakes them up in the middle of the night when she remembers something she forgot to tell them. For the first time in her life, Michaela is experiencing what it's like to have a sister, and a younger one at that. She said Matthew's teasing is no comparison to Allyson's talking.

Then Sidney got on the phone. She said Allyson listens to their conversations, then runs to tell Cynthia. Michaela finally told me how much she misses us. This brought tears to my eyes. Here my child was staying with her "blood" relatives, and she was telling me how much she loves and misses all of us.

Soon it was time to go back to Cleveland to bring Michaela home. Cole had a business trip, so I flew up. I got a big hug from Michaela, Sidney and Allyson as soon as I got out of the cab at their home. Michaela didn't let go of my hand. I didn't want her to let go. I was ready to have all of my children home again, under my roof, teasing and bickering with each other.

It was already Saturday afternoon. I spent the evening with the Williamses at their home, then went to the hotel. Michaela asked if she and Sidney could stay with me. Of course I said "yes." We watched a movie together in bed, then sat up and talked about everything from their going to middle school next year, to pretty clothes and braces. I knew it was going to be difficult to say goodbye to Sidney in the morning.

That night I slept with my arms around both of my daughters. It was definitely time to talk to Ralph and Cynthia, to make arrangements for Sidney to spend more time with us. Michaela, of course, would spend more time with them. I wondered if they would agree to let Sidney spend the first half of the summer with us.

The next morning the three of us had breakfast together, then took a cab to Sidney's home. It was time for Michaela and me to leave. I could see the pain in Cynthia's eyes as she embraced Michaela. It was painful to be separated from a child, not knowing when you'd see her again. Sidney and Michaela had grown to love each other. Their embrace was long and heartfelt. This love had brought two families together.

Matthew, McAlister and Cole met Michaela and me at the airport. They acted as if she'd been away for a month, rather than a week. Matthew immediately began teasing her, but this was just his way of telling her that he missed her. McAlister gave her a doll that he picked out himself.

I hadn't had a chance to talk to Michaela at length about her visit. I wanted to hear all about the Williams family, without asking too many questions. I didn't want to alienate Michaela again. Some things had to be done tactfully; this was one of them.

While I "tucked" Michaela into bed, we talked for a few minutes. She told me she enjoyed her visit, emphasizing that Ralph and Cynthia were very kind to her. They took her to visit both sets of grandparents. They too were very kind. But Michaela complained that they kept staring at her. I explained that they were excited about having another grandchild in their lives. I asked if she wanted to go back to visit soon; she said she wanted to spend time with them this summer. She seemed to be thrilled to be at home, though, in her own bed. I kissed her good night.

I joined Cole in the sunroom and told him some of the things that Michaela had shared with me about her visit with the Williams family. Michaela didn't seem to be as excited about this visit as I thought she'd be, for someone meeting her biological parents. I wanted to be fair, though, so I tried not to read anything more into her seeming lack of enthusiasm. Yet, for weeks, all she'd talked about was going to Cleveland. She had wanted to get to know her natural parents. Mother had told me to encourage her to talk about her new family, and I had, even though it was difficult at times.

Sidney and I talked sometimes several times a week. Mother and Cole thought it was important for me to help Michaela reach out to Cynthia. It was more difficult for Michaela to contact Cynthia, however, because she was a schoolteacher. Cynthia sometimes had to stay at school late. I, on the other hand, was usually home and available to listen to Sidney.

There were times when I simply asked Michaela to hand me the phone so that I could say hello to Sidney, and tell her that I loved her. All children needed to hear those words. Or, I would give her words of encouragement, like "You are so very special." I wanted to make it clear to Sidney that this was also her home, and that she could come here anytime.

Cynthia was a warm person. I knew she loved Michaela, but she had seemed somewhat distant from us during the last few months. I guess if I had six children, and taught public school, I'd probably seem distant too. I decided to let the "distant" issue go.

Michaela had said Cynthia told her, during one of their infrequent telephone calls, that she had planned to do more fun things with her during her stay. But she said she hadn't been feeling well lately. Apparently there was some virus going around at her school; she hadn't been able to fight it off. Still, Michaela got to do some fun stuff and she really liked the Williams family. She still had not met her two older brothers, but they would be home when she returned in the summer.

Cole changed the topic to David Turner. Apparently David was quite sure there was an illegal drug operation at Willow Memorial Hospital, during the time of Michaela and Sidney's birth. He also had several theories about what could've led to Michaela and Sidney being switched. Cole was just as determined as David to get to the bottom of this. I wished them well. I was focused primarily on our four children growing up to be well-adjusted, confident and productive individuals. There was absolutely nothing any of us could do to undo the past.

The next morning I felt especially calm and relaxed during my walk in the park. Mother was right, this was going to somehow work itself out. I could clearly see that now. In retrospect, I wish I'd stayed calm after first learning that Michaela was not our biological daughter. But, hind sight is always so much sharper.

Cole had encouraged me to keep a journal. Each day I forced myself to write about my feelings. It was difficult in the beginning, but I'm now amazed at how much this exercise has actually helped me. Writing also helped me realize that my faith in God, and love for my family, are integral parts of my strength.

As I continued to read through the old journal, I learned that Sarah Johnson wrote about her feelings, as she struggled with her new status as a "free" runaway slave girl. This young woman lived in another era. I still had absolutely no idea who she was, but I had learned so much from her, through her writings, about coping with adversity and pain. And, most importantly, Sarah didn't have her mother to lean on and talk to during her journey. In fact, she didn't have any blood relatives to pour her heart out to. But, she survived. Yes, she was more than a conqueror.

I have a dear friend who lives in Phoenix, who has been with me in spirit through the trials of my own family. Ally and I have been very close since our first year of college. Neither of us could get along with our roommates that first semester, so we ended up being roommates the second semester. Ironically, that didn't work either. Our tastes then were so different. We have remained as close as blood relatives anyway. Ally is married to a physician, but they never had kids. She is godmother to all of my children. She hasn't met Sidney, but has talked to her several times on the telephone.

Ally came to visit me twice last summer, because my family thought I was on the verge of a nervous breakdown. I managed to pull through my personal turmoil. She's been begging me to come for a visit. Finally, I've decided that my family is stable enough for me to leave them for a few days.

Cole's parents are flying in on Wednesday; I'm flying out Thursday morning, and will return on Sunday. I'm actually excited about this trip. I don't even feel guilty about leaving the nest. My husband and children, including McAlister, have shown me that they will go on in spite of what comes our way. And, so will I.

I hadn't visited Ally in a while. Although we talk often on the telephone, there is nothing like sitting with a close friend and sharing experiences. She owns a boutique. The décor simply invites you to come in and spend money. She is a people person, well-connected socially. Her customers look to her not only for advice on fashions, but also on subjects ranging from problems with significant others, to how to stay physically fit and healthy. When she isn't at home or the boutique, Ally spends her time teaching physical fitness classes.

She is 6 feet tall, pencil thin, has naturally curly hair that she keeps cut short, olive skin tone and facial features that look like they were borrowed from a porcelain doll. Her husband, Taylor, absolutely adores her. But then it's difficult not to adore Ally. She has a genuine beauty both inside and outside. Her personality attracts people. Then once you're in her boutique, you can't leave without buying something. Once you attend one of her classes, you have to join because most women want a body like hers.

Ally loves my children. She and Taylor wanted children at one time. It didn't happen, so they moved on to other things, like building successful careers and flying around the world. Our lives went in totally different directions, but we remained very close friends through it all.

After giving birth to three children, I'm not pencil thin like Ally. She always looks like she should be on the cover of a magazine. Her boutique and fitness classes have taken off like rockets. I put my career on hold, which may last forever. We spent four days together at her home, talking about everything. This is as good as it gets for therapy.

"You drove me crazy just sitting around studying all the time," Ally said, as we reminisced that first day about college. "There was this wonderful world out there, a scenic campus and a huge city to explore. All you ever talked about was your GPA! There were guys who really liked and wanted to get to know you. You brushed them off like you were a member of England's royal family.

"And, if that wasn't enough, my parents adored you. They thought you were such a positive influence in my life. Well, that did it. I was determined that, not only was I not going to room with you, I wasn't even going to associate with you!" Listening to Ally brought back so many memories of college life, some good and some bitter. She had certainly described me to a tee. Now, it was my turn.

"Please don't forget that obnoxious group that you were a part of," I began. "All of you were loud and didn't care about others, who were trying to study or just relax. It was as if you all came to school for one purpose, to be seen and heard. I was relieved when you packed your things and moved out of the room. I didn't miss your music, arrogant friends or junk!" We continued to dump on each other. Once it was all out, we calmed down. We talked about how we reconciled, and have been loyal, loving friends for 19 years.

"You know, Lacy was actually a very shallow person. It took me forever to see through her," Ally continued. "It's just that I was so happy to get away from St. Catherine's, and all those confused girls, that I didn't take the time to really get to know people. My parents insisted that I stay at St. Catherine's and graduate, because Mom and Grandma had. Each day was a struggle for me. I simply couldn't wait to get away to college and run wild. So I hooked up with this group of women who didn't share any of my values and beliefs. I hung out with them just to be defiant.

"Celia, you represented the person I was raised to be. But, there was no way I was going to let anybody else tell me how to act, or what to say. I was almost 18, and ready to take on the world. I wasn't about to let you or anyone else stop me."

We were sitting on Ally's terrace, sipping one of her health food drinks, and enjoying the warm Phoenix sunshine. I tried to reach Cole and the kids to see how everyone was doing. Matthew answered the phone. He said he was walking out the door to go play tennis, and that everyone else had gone to see a movie. The second time I called I didn't get an answer. So I decided to take Cole's advice and enjoy myself. Taylor was at his office. Ally didn't expect him home until much later. We had nothing but time to reminisce and unwind.

"Whatever happened to that group?" I was totally relaxed. I didn't feel like I had a care in the world.

"I think Lacy went back to New York, but I'm not sure. Thank God I finally came to my senses. I realized I had nothing in common with any of them. None of them cared about me, or each other. I'm so grateful you and I rediscovered each other after all of that drama. I still think you're pretty stiff, Celia, but you're truly a decent human being. I respect you. And the way you've pulled through this incredible ordeal and developed a relationship with Sidney is absolutely phenomenal!

"Well, I certainly didn't pull through without the love and support of my family, and you. I honestly wanted to run away from it all last July. I wanted to go somewhere and pretend it hadn't happened."

"I begged you to come here, but you wouldn't. Taylor and I even tried to get Cole to send you here. He, understandably, wanted you close. He and your mother were trying to help you regain your mental strength. By the way, you look great; I'm so very proud of you." Ally leaned over and gave me a big hug.

"So tell me, is Cynthia's behavior still strange?" she continued. "It sure sounds like she isn't quite ready to take on another child. I can certainly understand that. It's hard enough out here if you don't have any children. Trying to feed and cloth six children must be tough."

"It is, but Cynthia and Ralph have done a great job with their children. I haven't met the two older sons, but you would absolutely fall in love with the twins, Cade and Cary. They are all good students with warm personalities. Getting to know Cynthia and Ralph better has helped me heal and move on."

We finished our drinks, then dressed and headed for the boutique. Ally hired Caroline a year ago to manage the shop, and is quite pleased with her. Caroline has a lot of experience in retail buying. In fact, she has brought in a number of affluent customers. Taylor wants Ally to spend more time in the shop handling day-to-day matters, and spend less time at the fitness club. But Ally's income from her classes alone is quite lucrative. Women take one look at her and sign up.

Caroline showed me several very popular pieces that had just come to the boutique. I couldn't remember the last time I'd been shopping for myself. I actually felt strange trying on different outfits and modeling for the two of them. Ally wasn't the type who'd lie to make a sale, so I valued her opinion on what looked good on me. I bought four outfits as a special treat for me, and two dresses for Mother.

The next day we worked out at her club, then went to get our hair done. Ally talked me into cutting my hair. Fortunately, I had enough common sense to know that I couldn't get away with her shorter, daring look. With my new haircut and clothes, Cole would be in for a surprise.

Before long, I was at the airport, ready to get home to my angels. I felt rested and peaceful. I was ready to resume my roles as mother, wife and housekeeper. Cole and the kids met me at the airport. This confirmed that they missed me.

"Boy, Mom, you're a knockout! What did you do in Phoenix?" Matthew asked, as he looked me up and down. Then it was Michaela's turn.

"Mom, why don't you come to school and have lunch with me?" My daughter hadn't invited me to have lunch with her at school in months! Even McAlister smiled and played with my hair.

"Yeah, sweetheart, what did you and Ally do in Phoenix?" Cole asked, as he helped me into the car. "If I didn't know any better, I'd think the two of you had a great time."

"We did have a great time, but I was ready to come home before you all forgot about me. I called twice and only got to talk to Matthew, who, by the way, was on his way out. I'm not ready to be replaced yet."

I kissed them all and listened to what everyone had done over the past four days. Cole's parents loved coming to Nashville to spend time with us. His mother had a delightful dinner prepared when I walked into our home. After dinner Cole told me that Cynthia had called, and said she needed to talk to me as soon as I returned. I was tired from the trip, so decided to call her in the morning. She probably wanted to make arrangements for Michaela to come up for a visit. Michaela's school closed for the summer on May 21. It was now April. We had ample time to prepare her for a visit with the Williams family.

We were also preparing for Sidney to visit with us. I wanted her to spend the entire summer here in Nashville, so that Cole, our children and I could have some quality time with her. We wanted to really get to know her. I knew she probably wasn't always sweet and polite. Like Michaela and her friends, she probably could be difficult at times. Sometimes the least little thing could set off Michaela. She would get in a testy mood if her hair wasn't falling into place perfectly. I'm sure the same was true with Sidney.

But unless she actually spent some time with us, we would probably never see that side of her. I was prepared to ask Cynthia to let Sidney spend the summer with us. But, Sidney would have to be comfortable with this, and agree to come.

I also had to prepare for Cynthia to ask the same of Michaela. Of course I would have to say "yes," if Michaela wanted to go. This had to work both ways or not at all. I wanted both girls here with us for the summer because they get along well together. They have been so very supportive of each other.

I'd even begun making plans for how we would spend the summer. First of all, Ally asked me to bring the girls to Phoenix because she wants to get to know Sidney, and because Michaela is her goddaughter. Ally has been waiting for me to say they're coming, so she can plan a pool party in their honor at her home. Both Ally and Taylor have teenagers in their families. The girls would surely have a great time.

Then Cole and I would take our children to visit our relatives in Denver and Charleston. Later we would go to Washington, D.C. to take in all of the sites. We would perhaps end the summer with a trip to one of the islands to enjoy the water and sand. Just thinking about having all of our children together was exciting.

I got up early the next morning to call Cynthia. One of the twins answered the phone. He said his mother wasn't in, but that he would tell her I called. Cade said he was doing fine and asked about Michaela. Sidney was not in so I asked him to say "hello" to everyone.

It was Saturday morning. My "things to do" list was full, so I reluctantly got started with the washing. Cole was taking the kids to see a play that evening. I couldn't join them because I had to practice with the symphony. While the clothes were washing, I took our dog to be groomed. Then I stopped to do some grocery shopping. As I entered the store, I suddenly remembered that I left my list on the kitchen table. I hastily walked down each aisle, trying to remember what I needed. Not only did I forget my list, but also my cell phone. I couldn't call to ask Cole or one of the kids to read the list to me. As I breezed down each aisle, trying to remember what was on the list, I ran into the guidance counselor from Michaela's school.

"Mrs. Bentley, how are you? Michaela seems to be doing so much better. I'm so happy to see that bubbly personality resurfacing," Dana Winters said. Cole and I had several meetings with her last year. At the time, Michaela was having such a difficult time with the news about her biological parents. Mrs. Winters had been absolutely wonderful with her. Michaela spent time in her office almost every day for weeks, before she opened up to her.

"I don't know if Michaela has told you or not, but St. Ann's is offering an excellent summer program this year. There will be math, science and computer classes. I think Michaela would enjoy it. If you're interested in encouraging Michaela to sign up, please get an application in early because it will be quite competitive to get in."

"I'd like to know more about it. I'll stop by later for an application. Michaela hadn't mentioned the program. Thanks for letting me know." I cut the conversation short. I had so many things to do today. I quickly grabbed a few more items, checked out and was on my way home. I decided to call Cynthia again to ask if Sidney could spend the summer with us. If she agreed to it, I would get two applications for the summer program at St. Ann's. I knew the girls would absolutely love it.

"Hello, Cynthia, how are you? I'm sorry I missed you earlier."

"Hello, Celia, I'm, well, I'm making it," she answered. "I called you to discuss Michaela's visit with us this summer. I'm so sorry, Celia, but I'm not going to be able to have Michaela here to spend time with us this summer." Here we go again, I thought. Once again, the woman who gave birth to my daughter is saying she cannot spend time with her. I tried to stay calm; it wasn't easy.

"Since Michaela can't come to Cleveland, do you mind if Sidney spends the summer here in Nashville with us?" I began. "Michaela was really looking forward to spending time with you, but, once again, you have other plans. First, you said that you would come to visit her here in Nashville in November. Michaela was so excited about this, then Ralph calls and informs us that you couldn't make the trip.

"Then you cancel her trip to Cleveland for the Christmas holidays. This hurt her. Michaela isn't used to being rejected by family, and I don't ever want her to get used to it. This past year has been very painful for her, Cynthia. I would think that you certainly would understand why." Before I could continue, Cynthia cut me off with some choice words of her own. The conversation had gotten heated.

"Excuse me, Celia Bentley, but just who do you think you are? I've raised six children, six wonderful children, and I teach children. So, please don't tell me what I should understand about a child. I couldn't come to Nashville in November, but Ralph made sure that Sidney was there to spend time with you all. I don't think we owe you an explanation about why I wasn't there."

"Cynthia, Michaela wants to get to know you. She doesn't think that you are reaching out to get to know her. Also, she doesn't understand when you don't follow up on what you say you're going to do. I make the effort to talk to Sidney every week because she is my flesh and blood. I want to get to know her. This has been a traumatic experience for both girls. I believe that, as their mothers, we must do our part to help them continue to cope."

"How and when I choose to get to know Michaela, Celia, is my business. I don't tell you how to bond with Sidney, so please don't tell me how to bond with Michaela. She is my *natural* daughter. We will bond and establish a wonderful relationship, just as I have with my other children. Our role as mothers is to guide our children through this, not dictate to anyone how it should be done."

"Cynthia, I know that you are busy, because you work outside the home. But, none of that is important to Michaela. What's important to her is that she has just learned that you and Ralph are her biological parents. She wants to be accepted by all of you, including your other children. Sidney is beginning to open up to me. That's because she knows that I love and care about her."

"Are you insinuating that because I work outside the home I am too busy to get to know Michaela, that I don't love and care about her?"

"No, I wasn't insinuating anything, but I am saying that Michaela needs some of your time. I'm not going to keep telling her that your plans have changed, and she's excluded."

"Celia, Michaela is *my* daughter. I can tell her what I want her to know. Yes, she and Sidney have been through a difficult time. It's unfortunate, but if you live long enough, you're going to experience much more pain. I'm sure that Michaela's life hasn't been perfect with the Bentley family, and neither has Sidney's with this family. But Ralph and I have taught our children how to cope with adversity."

"This isn't about what we've taught our children, Cynthia. It's about a child who doesn't understand why she wasn't raised by her natural parents. It's about why they aren't reaching out to her. We are the mothers. We have an obligation to help Michaela and Sidney learn to cope with this big pain in their lives. That's what Cole and I are trying to do." Our pent up emotions were finally boiling over!

"Once again, Celia, I've raised six wonderful children without any help from you, and I don't need your help now with Michaela. If you want to talk with Sidney weekly, that's your choice. Ralph and I love Michaela dearly. In time, she will love us dearly. Now, back to your question. Yes, I do have a problem with Sidney coming to Nashville for the summer. I want Sidney and all of our children to stay here at home this summer. I would like for Michaela to be close to all of us, but this may not be the best time for her to get to know Ralph and me now. You can't bring a child that you've just met into a difficult situation, and expect her to understand, and then bond with you.

"You have absolutely no idea what my family has been through over the past year. I have wonderful plans for Michaela, but my health hasn't allowed me to follow through. I guess I should have told you and Cole much sooner, but there was so much going on with Sidney's health. I was waiting for the right time to share this painful news."

Cynthia sounded as if she was struggling to get her breath. I wanted to end the conversation, but it was much too late for that. I had opened the door for both of us to explode. Now I realized that perhaps this hadn't been the time, or manner, to confront her with what I perceived as her rejection of Michaela. I had always defended my children if I thought they were being mistreated. This situation with Cynthia was no exception. I had clearly upset her. Now I wondered how we could put our feelings aside and get on with the business of helping our children. Cynthia spoke in almost a whisper.

"Celia, I have breast cancer. My doctors don't know how long I will survive. I could possibly beat this and live a long life, or this could very well be my last summer. I don't think Michaela would want to spend her summer with a mother who might be dying."

28. Sarah

MR. BROUGHTON AND I LEFT for Holly Springs, Mississippi, in August 1856. Aunt Clara and Miz Baker arranged for me to meet him prior to our departure. He and I talked several times to discuss how I would hopefully get my parents back to Boston with me. He actually wanted to buy Mammy and Pappy to work for him, to care for his mother. He wanted to buy them to hire them. Having been hired, they would be free to stay or leave his employ at their will.

This was fine with me. I certainly was not going to risk getting caught by Mr. Wilmington, only to see my parents enslaved by somebody else. I simply did not want my parents answering to anybody else, unless it was their choice. They had done that all of their lives. Now it was time for a change. I was prepared to risk everything to set them free!

William asked to come with me, but I did not want him or anyone else to come. I had wanted to do this alone, my way. However, Aunt Clara and Miz Baker insisted that I take Mr. Broughton out of fear that I would get caught. They did not think my plan to disguise myself as one of Mammy's elderly relatives would work. Instead, I would disguise myself as a man – Mr. Broughton's body servant. He would offer to buy my parents to hire them. I would buy them back from him once we got back to Boston.

He agreed to try to help me, after Aunt Clara and Miz Baker had a long talk with him. There was no way he could not see the pain in my eyes as he listened to my story. I had run away not only for my freedom, but also out of fear of what Mr. Wilmington would do to me if I had gone back. Although Mr. Broughton was not in favor of slavery, and had spoken out against it, he honestly needed an elderly couple to care for his mother and help with house chores. He decided to help me, to go along with the plan.

Surprisingly, I am quite calm on this August morning. We traveled by train from Boston. I was lost in my thoughts, thinking about seeing my parents. Eleven years ago I had come to New York City with the Wilmingtons, wondering what the North would be like. Now, I am wondering what the South will be like. Through the grace of God, I have accomplished much more than I ever dreamed I could. However, nothing was more important, or difficult, than getting my parents out of the South. This would truly be the greatest challenge of my life!

Aunt Clara and Miz Baker spent a lot of time dressing me for the trip. When they finished, I looked much older, and nothing like Sarah. William tried to help me with some male mannerisms. Aunt Clara and Miz Baker told me to try not to speak in the presence of the Wilmingtons, so no one would recognize my voice. I had no problem playing this role. I was prepared to do anything to get my parents away from the Wilmingtons and the South.

William was hurt because I did not want him to come. I, too, was hurting because I was leaving people I loved dearly. I did not know if I would ever see them again. Still, I knew I had to do this. If I did not at least try to get my parents, I would never have any peace of mind.

Mr. Broughton and I engaged in little conversation during the trip. I was lost in my thoughts most of the time. He appeared to be consumed with some business matters he had to take care of in Mississippi. The company he worked for purchased more Mississippi cotton than any other company in the North.

"Mr. Broughton, if this plan works, I will always be grateful to you."

"Sarah, if this plan works, I will be very pleased for you and your family. You don't know me well, but I believe slavery is wrong. Negroes, like all human beings, should be able to chart their own destiny. I am appalled by what slaveholders have done to your people. I have often spoken out against slavery. I am not so much doing this as a favor for anyone, but I sincerely believe that keeping human beings in bondage is against God's will. I also believe that slavery could someday destroy this country. At some point, slaves are going to rebel, and fight for their God-given rights. That will not be a pleasant time for this country."

"Why would someone like you, Mr. Broughton, who has so much, take a risk to help slaves?"

"The answer is simple, Sarah. Freedom is a God-given right. I believe everyone knows this, even slaveholders in the South. However, to acknowledge it would not be advantageous for many people."

"Well, thank you for helping me."

"Sarah, my other reason for helping you is that I want to hire your parents, because I really need someone to care for my mother, who is very ill. At the same time, I respect your concern about not wanting your parents to work for anyone. If the Wilmingtons are willing to sell them to me, and, if they choose to leave, I'd be more than pleased to have them in my home to care for Mother. I know they will be very caring and compassionate. Of course, they'll be generously compensated for their services. I will also respect their decision not to work for me, if they choose that course."

"Thank you, Mr. Broughton." Having said that, he went back to reading papers, and I to my thoughts. I believed he was a decent man, which made this plan a little easier to accept.

We traveled for many hours, and were expected to arrive in Mississippi the next day. However, the calmness I felt when we first boarded the train in Boston was slowly slipping away. Although I did not sense that Mr. Wilmington and Mr. Broughton were friends, they apparently had been involved in some of the same business ventures. According to Aunt Clara, Miz Baker and William's parents, Mr. Broughton was a decent man, respected by most people. Whether they liked him or not, they appeared to respect him. I prayed that Mr. Wilmington had enough respect for Mr. Broughton to allow him to buy my parents.

We got off the train in Memphis, then rode in a carriage to Holly Springs. As we approached Holly Springs, the sight of cotton fields brought back painful memories. As a child, I loved to touch cotton, and rub it against my skin. It was so soft and warm. I would sometimes take a piece and stick it in my hair. It was the softest thing I had ever felt in my life. However, as I grew older, I began to understand that this soft, beautiful product of the earth was one of the reasons Mr. Wilmington, and other white people, were wealthy. It was also the reason Pappy worked so hard and we had no freedom. He and other slaves were responsible for the success of that crop.

Pappy spent most of his days in the field. I can still remember him working in the sun and sweating until his hands were sore. Mammy or I would leave the big house to take water to him in the fields several times a day. Through it all, he never complained. It was so cruel of Mr. Wilmington to hire out Pappy's only son. My brother could have been a big help to Pappy.

I could feel my heart pounding as we got closer and closer to the Wilmington plantation. Tears ran down my face as I thought about Pappy in these fields. I could only imagine the pain he must have endured when Tom was snatched away. Mammy and Pappy were humble people and counted their blessings every day despite their hardships. I was humble to God. But, 11 years later, I still could find no reason to be grateful to the Wilmingtons.

"Do these parts look familiar to you, Sarah?" Mr. Broughton asked, as he gathered the papers he had been reviewing and put them away.

"All too familiar." I looked straight ahead.

"I hope this all works out for you. I've heard about how you worked hard to get an education, and built a business making dresses. Just remember, whether or not you get your parents back to Boston with you, you should be proud of yourself. You're a dreamer, fortunate to have many of your dreams come true."

"Now, I am working on making my biggest dream come true. I want my family reunited, as free people." I was quiet again, because, for the first time in 11 years, I could see the big house. My heart dropped to my feet. I still hated the sight of it, but I had to come back to get a part of me, Mammy and Pappy.

Mr. Broughton helped me with the only piece of luggage I had. I stared at the cotton fields, but could not recognize the field hands. They were working as hard as ever. I walked behind Mr. Broughton, trying to look, and act, like a man. I was wearing pants, a jacket and a hat. I was also wearing a mustache that William had given me. I had had a taste of freedom, and did not want to be here. But, this was the plan. I had to do what was necessary to make it work. Mr. Broughton led the way to the front door of the big house. He waved for me to follow him. It was warm that August day. I prayed that Mammy would not answer the door. The sight of her face, along with the heat, would surely make me faint.

Mr. Broughton knocked at the front door several times before anyone answered. To my surprise, a woman I remembered opened the door. I thought her name might be Hattie. She had worked in the big house only if Mammy was sick. I stretched to look behind her, thinking that Mammy might show up, but she did not. I had to be careful not to ask about her.

"Hello, I'm Daniel Broughton. I'm here to see Frank Wilmington."

"Massa Wilmington ain't hure sir, but I specin him any minute now. He tell me dat ya wud be hure soon," she answered.

"Would you mind if I come in and wait for him? He and I have some business matters to discuss. This is Alfred. He's traveling with me, and needs a place to stay for tonight."

"Well, let me see if I kin fine him a place out back in our quatahs." This was what I wanted her to say. If she put me out back in the slave quarters, I could surely find my parents.

"Cum on in, Mastah Broughtin. An ya cum on wit me," she said, staring at me from head to toe. I was afraid she recognized me behind this disguise. "I go take ya out back an try to fine ya a place to res."

Her voice was kind when she spoke to Mr. Broughton, but changed when speaking to me alone. She was harsher. She was probably wondering what my relationship was to Mr. Broughton. She looked puzzled, as if she had lots of questions.

Perhaps she recognized me as an older Sarah. Maybe she saw the girl who once lived here, but ran away from her loving parents, to be free in the North. Maybe she hated me for what I had done. Or, perhaps, she hated me because I was free, traveling with Mr. Broughton.

"Ya live in de Norf, but ya jes a Negro lak me. Dont spec nuttin from us. Y'all from de Norf thank y'all is betta dan us down hure in de Souf, but ya ain't. Y'all ain't rilly free. I bet som of y'all wush ya was livin in de Souf. I been in de Souf aw my life an ain't neva been hongry. My massa see to it dat I gits my meals evry day."

So, this was it. She resented me because I was a free Negro who lived in the North. I felt relieved that she had not recognized me as Sarah. I prayed that none of the others would recognize me.

"So, kin ya talk, or is ya too good to spik to us slaves down hure?" she asked. She was looking directly at me, then turned and led me to the slave quarters in the back. I did not want to speak, for fear she might recognize my voice. Since I had to answer her, I tried to change my voice to sound like a man.

"I live in the North, but, like you, I am a Negro. You are my sister. There is no reason for you to talk to me like this. We must love each other. That is the only way we can help each other," I said.

"If ya luv us, den why dont ya git down hure an try to hep som of us git way?"

I had to be very careful with what I said. She would probably tell Mr. Wilmington everything.

"Do you like living here?" I asked. She was quiet, then answered.

"I lak it hure, but dere is times when I wush I cud git way an see som of dis wuld. De massa dont give me no free time."

"What is your master like?" I wanted to know if Mr. Wilmington had changed.

"He have good days an bad days. He loss one o his yung slave girls som years back. Dat made him rill mean."

"How did he lose her?" I stared at our cabin as I talked. Tears welled in my eyes.

"He took one o his yung slaves to Nu Yok wit him, an she jes run off in de night, fer no resin. He ain't been de sam since. Now he wont let his slaves outta his sight. Dat yung girl made thangs bad fer us back hure."

This woman was talking about me! It sounded as if Mr. Wilmington had gotten worse. I prayed that no one would recognize me. William was right. He would probably severely punish or even kill me!

"Dats why I dont lak y'all in de Norf. Evry time a slave run off, we catch it hure rill bad. Now when de massa an his famly go way, dey dont take no slaves wit dem. Dat girl dont know how mush trouba she caus us."

"Who was she?" I wanted to know if people were still talking about me, if the men were still looking for me.

"Ha name was Sally, or maybe Sarah, I bleev. She wuz Joshua girl, but ain't no need in talkin bout ha to ya caus ya dont know nuttin bout us slaves."

Joshua's girl, I thought. I wondered why she did not mention Mammy's name. Was she alive? My heart ached. All I could do was fight back the tears.

"Miz Martha, do ya know wher dis man kin stay tunite? He cum down wit a white man from de Norf, an need somwher to res."

"Let me see caus I ain't got nuff room fer us." Miss Martha was a kind woman. I hoped she did not recognize me, but I recognized her. She never worked in the big house, only in the fields. Hattie finally went back to the Wilmington house. I was glad to be rid of her.

"So, whuz ya name?" Miz Martha asked, as I entered her one room cabin. Hers was smaller than ours. I hurt for her and her family. Our people had endured poor living conditions for so many years. Aunt Clara and Miz Baker had made my life very comfortable. It was painful to come back to see my people living like this.

"My name is Alfred," I said.

"So ya is a free man," Miz Martha said. "God bless ya. Tell me, Mastah Alfred, what do it feel lak ta be free? I ain't neva lef dis place, an dont thank I eva will. I guess it jes wont de good Lord will fer me to leave hure." Miz Martha had to be close to 70 years old. I could see the pain in her eyes as she spoke.

"Miz Martha," I began, "I really do not think any of our people are truly free. Yes, I live in the North, and, no, I do not have a master. But, there are opportunities available to white people that are not, and may never be, available to me and other Negroes."

"God bless ya, caus ya kin trava an see dis wuld. Has ya eva been to Misippi befo?"

"Yes, Miz Martha."

"I bet ya ain't neva seen nuttin lak dis. Hure, tuch dis, an tell me whut ya thank. Ain't it sof? Dats whut ya close is made of, Mastah Alfred." She held two pieces of cotton in her hands, and smiled as she rubbed them against my skin.

"I done wuk wit dis stuff aw my lif, an som fokes dont know wher dey close com from," she said, laughing. If she had worked with cotton all of her life, then surely she knew Pappy, I thought. I had to be careful how I asked.

"Miz Martha, since you worked with cotton, could you tell me about some of the people you know who work in the cotton fields?"

"Oh, yes, I kin tell ya som tales bout dese fields, an de pepa who wuk in dem." She began telling me several stories about the long hours they worked, about how some slaves hated it, and some rarely complained. She even knew where the cotton was shipped. I had to ask more specific questions, without letting on that I knew Mammy and Pappy. She had been a slave all of her life, had never left this state, but Miz Martha was not ignorant by any means. I was very tired from the trip, but had to keep talking. I was here for one purpose. Nothing was going to get in my way.

"Who watches over you in the fields when the master ain't around?" Before I left, Mr. Wilmington had made Pappy a driver. He was under the white overseer.

"He done put sombody nu ova us. I dont cure mush fer dis nu fella. He ain't kine lak Mastah Joshua wuz." When she said "Joshua," my heart sank! She was talking about Pappy!

"What happened to Mr. Joshua? Why did your master replace him?" My heart was beating faster now. I was almost afraid to hear what she had to say. Surely she had noticed the concern in my voice. I looked down to avoid her eyes.

"Mastah Joshua," she began, then, a young boy came running into the cabin.

"Mammy Martha, Mammy Martha, we needs ya. Mammy dont feel too good an she say com quick!" Miz Martha stopped talking and jumped to her feet.

"I sorry, but I gotta go. Mus be time fer Lilly baby to com in dis wuld. We kin talk som mo when I finish." She was gone. I sat down, speechless; my heart pounding. I got up and decided there was only one way to find out how my parents were doing. I had to go to the cabin to see for myself. I walked toward our cabin.

I was amazed to see that everything looked almost as it did 11 years ago. The big house was as beautiful and well kept as ever. Based on the position of the sun, it was probably close to 8:00 that evening. I could see several men and women still working in the fields. I slowly walked toward our cabin, praying every step of the way, "Lord, please let them be alive." I wondered what Miz Martha was preparing to tell me about Pappy when the little boy ran in.

I looked hard to see if Pappy was in the fields, but could not see any of their faces. The fields were too far away. I moved along faster to avoid being noticed. I was a strange face here, and certainly did not want to attract any attention. I wondered if Mr. Wilmington had returned home. Had Mr. Broughton asked him for my parents?

As I approached our cabin, I heard voices coming from the direction of the big house. Apparently Mr. Wilmington had just arrived. I hid behind a large tree. I did not want to take any chances on getting caught. Being on Wilmington property frightened me. I was very anxious. Mr. Wilmington must have gone into the house. A few minutes later, he and Mr. Broughton came out of the house from the back door. They were pointing at the cotton fields.

I watched from behind the tree. After talking for about 10 minutes, they went back inside. I hurried toward our cabin and knocked at the door. Surely Mammy would be finished working at the big house by now. No one answered. I continued to knock, and looked around for fear that someone was watching me. I could remember some of our people running to tell Mr. Wilmington anything they thought he should know.

They might have seen me. Perhaps they would let him know there was a stranger walking around. No one answered. I opened the door and walked into our cabin. There was no one here! Where were Mammy and Pappy? I called their names, then sat down in a chair Pappy had made and cried. So they were gone! That was what Miz Martha was trying to tell me. I laid on their bed. Nothing had changed in this little cabin, except the papers plastered to the wall. I cried and cried. The two people I loved most in the world were gone. I wondered who might be living here now.

I was very tired and lonely, and soon fell asleep. I did not know how long I had slept when suddenly I felt a cool rag on my face. I could hear voices; one of them I recognized. It sounded like Miz Martha. She was telling someone that I had come from the North with a white man, and needed a place to spend the night. She went on to say how she had left me in her cabin to deliver Lilly's baby, and came back to find no one there.

The other person was quiet, and continued to stroke my face with the cool rag. I wondered if it was one of the Wilmingtons. Maybe they were trying to wake me up, to take me back to pay my debt. I was afraid to open my eyes. But, it could not have been any of them, because this person was very gentle. This person stroked my head as if they cared. For some reason, however, the person did not speak. I heard Miz Martha say she had to leave to get some work done. The other person still did not speak. Soon I realized that there were three people present, Miz Martha and two others.

"If y'all need me, ya knows wher to com an git me." Miz Martha said, then left.

"Thank you for every thang, Martha. We kin take cure of *him*." I began to cry. I could recognize that voice anywhere. It was Bertha Johnson's voice. It was Mammy who was stroking my head with such love and care. When Miz Martha left, I slowly opened my eyes.

29. Raini

CAREFULLY CHOSE WHAT I WOULD WEAR to dinner with Senator Christian that night. John and I pulled out our very best for the occasion. The thought of spending an evening with a presidential candidate was awesome!

We asked a close friend to take care of our babies; she was delighted to come over. John had known Evelyn Sanders for several years, and had the utmost respect for her. Haley hadn't been feeling well today – her breathing was labored, but Evelyn was a registered nurse. We felt comfortable leaving the children with her.

We were expected to meet Senator Christian at 8:00 at the Imperial Hotel. I hadn't been able to think clearly since the Senator called to extend the invitation. I suspect he wanted to discuss my work on the Committee To Help Hurting Children.

Although significant progress had been made toward finding an effective treatment, too many children still suffered from this dreadful disease. Congresswoman Anna Southerland was determined to get the country focused on this tragedy. I hadn't discussed it with John yet, but I'd been thinking about adopting one of these children. I was waiting for the *right* moment to approach him.

We saw limousines entering and leaving the hotel as we pulled up for valet parking. This place was first class; one of Rhode Island's finest in downtown Providence. I was nervous, but able to project a sense of calm. John's presence was very comforting.

"We're here to meet with the Senator Christian," John said to the hostess.

"Mr. and Senator Carrington, please come with me. She led us to the Senator's table. He stood as we entered the room. The Secret Service was close by. The Senator's campaign manager and publicist were seated with him.

"Mr. Carrington, Senator Carrington, I'm so happy you could join me this evening," he said in a friendly, but professional tone. I didn't know Senator Christian well, only that Senator Cole thought highly of him. Senator Christian was a democrat from Pennsylvania, serving his second term. I remember first speaking to him while working for Senator Cole, and had attended several events where he was present. Senator Cole had introduced us many years ago.

"It's so good to see you again, Senator," I said. "You're doing quite well in the polls. John and I are excited for you."

"Thank you," he said, with a bright smile. "I certainly appreciate your support. Senator Carrington, I want to congratulate you on your success with the Committee To Help Hurting Children. It's amazing what you and the other committee members have accomplished. Mr. Carrington, I understand that you care for your children during the day. I think that's just great." I wondered how he knew who cared for our children.

"Yes, I'm a stay-at-home dad, and love every second of it," John said, as he sipped his water. John then shared some fun stories about his adventures with Harry and Haley. The senator appeared to be genuinely amused. Senator Christian spoke fondly of his two grown sons and their families. I could see the pride in his eyes. He then apologized that his wife, Janna, couldn't join him because of illness. He talked about the good things he'd heard about me, prior to becoming a U.S. senator, and about our consulting business. We then ordered dinner.

"Senator Carrington," he began," I invited you and Mr. Carrington here tonight to discuss a very important matter." I was really feeling anxious now.

"As you know, I plan to be the next president of this country, and have given a lot of thought to possible cabinet choices, department heads and so forth. The party is preparing for our convention, so I must announce the selection of my running mate soon. Senator Carrington, I've heard great things about you from Senator Cole, Representative Southerland, Professor McWherter and others from Brown and Harvard. As chairperson of the Committee To Help Hurting Children, you have helped focus international attention on a major health crisis, because of your diligent, creative work.

"To get to the point, I need an energetic, focused, motivated and goal-oriented individual to run with me in November. I need someone who stands out from the crowd, is articulate and can get a point across quickly. I need someone who isn't afraid to challenge the status quo, someone who connects with youth in this country, someone who can get the job done. I like what I've heard about you. You're not afraid to be challenged or criticized. I'd like you and your husband to think about your joining the team as my choice for vice president."

I was speechless! John squeezed my hand and broke the silence.

"This is quite a surprise, and honor, I must say," he began. "Raini and I never expected anything like this." John gave me a most amazing glance that revealed his pride and support.

"I've been thinking about this for weeks, and have discussed it with my top advisors. We think this can be a winning team. It's now time to discuss it with you and your husband. I've read some of the work you've published and I'm very impressed. I think the two of us will make a great team," the Senator added, looking directly at me.

I snapped back to reality, and managed to say, "Senator, this is truly an honor, and a shock! Representative Southerland and Senator Cole are my mentors. I've learned so much from them. I'm humbled that they have spoken about me in such generous words.

I probably wasn't making any sense to him. For once in my life, I was at a loss for words. I was trying to make the point that these two individuals had far more to offer than I did. I respected Senator Christian, and wanted him to have the very best running mate. Unfortunately, I didn't feel I was that person.

John asked several questions about the process of choosing me and what would be expected of me as a running mate. The look in his eyes suggested that he was pleased with the Senator's answers. The question and answer period went on for at least three hours. We left the Senator that night not knowing what to think.

He understood that we needed time to weigh the offer before I responded. But the convention was only a few weeks away. An answer would be needed fairly quickly. Senator Christian had strong support from African-Americans, so I suspected he wanted me as a running mate for reasons other than the fact that I was African-American. I would soon be 39. My life was everything I had wanted and more. I was married to my best friend. We had two adorable children. I loved serving as a U.S. senator. I saw no reason to tamper with my life.

John and I had little to say on the way home. I didn't know if he was excited, or sad that his wife had been "scoped out" by a presidential candidate. He was basically a private person.

I suddenly felt guilty that I had gotten so involved with politics. Before we were married, I was politically active. John knew this. He had supported my decisions to run for City Council, state senator and the U.S. senate. I thought I'd accomplished all of my professional goals. Sometimes I felt guilty because John loved being at home with his family. He'd even moved his office here.

And now we learn that Senator Christian and his team have been checking us out. I decided to sleep on all of this, and call my parents in the morning. I would call when my head was clear. We had spent the last four hours with the presumptive Democratic presidential candidate, and he wanted me as his running mate. I was in shock, and emotionally exhausted!

30. Celia

THE INVESTIGATION GETS UGLIER each passing day, but David Turner isn't about to back off. He recently learned that two nurses at Willow Memorial Hospital, Jeanette Sparks and Toni Dalton, had been suspicious about some things that happened in the maternity unit back in the fall of 1977. They even approached the hospital administrator about their concerns. There was never an investigation.

Shortly after that, Ms. Sparks was moved to the geriatric unit at the hospital. Ms. Dalton moved to New Orleans, where she accepted a teaching position with Canterbury Medical Center. They both stand firm by their account of what happened that December 1977. But, they have moved on and are reluctant to get involved in the current investigation. David is determined to get answers through other means.

By the middle of July, Cynthia's condition had taken a turn for the worse. Shortly after our heated conversation, I had a long talk with my sister.

"Karen, I was trying to explain to Cynthia that Michaela was feeling rejected by her new family. They were constantly changing their minds about spending time with her. I couldn't take telling Michaela, again, that her biological parents didn't want her in Cleveland for the summer. So, I told Cynthia what I was feeling. And out of the blue sky, she exploded!

Karen was very blunt. "Celia, you are my big sister, and I love you dearly, however, you have a way of saying things to suggest that your way is the *only* way. Cynthia probably resented what she perceived as you telling her how to bond with Michaela. Celia, the woman has six children. You've said several times that she's done a good job with them. So, why do you think Cynthia needs *your* advice?"

"Karen, what would you have done if you were in my shoes? Would you have pretended that everything was fine, and just sat and watched your daughter's heart break? You tell her, once again, that the Williamses have other plans, so you can't come up. I'm sorry, Karen, but that's been difficult for Michaela, and for me."

"Celia, please, listen to me. Cynthia has been carrying a heavy load. Can you imagine having to deal with the knowledge that you have breast cancer, and then learn that the daughter you've raised and loved is not your biological daughter? You need to pick up the phone and call Cynthia to apologize. That's the decent, appropriate thing to do."

I continued to vent to my sister about my heated conversation with Cynthia. Deep down in my heart, I knew Karen was right. I felt terrible about Cynthia having cancer. I wished I had never confronted her about Michaela.

The next day I called Cynthia to apologize. She, too, had calmed down. "Cynthia, I want to apologize for what I said to you concerning your relationship with Michaela. I hope that you can forgive me for being insensitive to what you've been going through."

"I accept your apology, Celia. It's not in me to hold a grudge against anyone."

"Cynthia, I think Michaela needs to know that you have breast cancer. Do you want to tell her, or should I tell her." I asked, because I didn't want another confrontation with her.

"Go ahead and tell her, Celia. She needs to know."

I sat down with Michaela that afternoon and told her about Cynthia's health. Ten years had passed before she knew that Ralph and Cynthia were her parents. I wasn't about to keep anything else from her. I knew this news would hurt deeply, but she still had to know.

Michaela is now 11 and feeling that life is unfair. I tell her that life can sometimes seem to be unfair, but there is always a bright side. I try to teach each of my children to count their blessings daily, and never take anything or anyone for granted.

Although Cynthia had said she didn't think it was a good idea for Michaela to visit this summer, Michaela wants to spend time with her sick mother. I called Cynthia after my conversation with Michaela and asked if we could bring Michaela to see her. She said, "Yes." Michaela wanted to learn as much as possible about her natural mother.

Cole and I drove Michaela to Cleveland to let her spend a few days with the Williams family. We brought her back to the hotel each night. Miraculously, Cynthia started to feel better by the time we left. She was even comfortable with Sidney coming back to Nashville with us.

Her two older sons were home from school, so they could help her husband look after her. Allyson asked if she could come along with Sidney. I told Cynthia I didn't mind bringing her with us. Cynthia clearly didn't have the strength to care for a 6-year-old, and I thought Sidney and Allyson should be together during this difficult time.

Michaela, Sidney and Allyson shared a bedroom, which turned out to be an experience to remember. Michaela has twin beds in her room. Sidney and Allyson shared one of the beds the first night, then Michaela and Sidney, then Sidney and Allyson shared a bed. Apparently the three had a daily toss-up to determine who would get to sleep alone. Allyson, unlike

Sidney, is feisty. She is willing and quite capable of standing up to two 11-year-olds. Matthew would walk past the girls' room and shake his head.

"Mom, those girls are strange. One minute they're laughing, then they're crying."

"Who was crying, dear?"

"I think it was Allyson, because she wanted to sleep with Sidney. I knocked on the door to offer my advice, as someone older and more mature. All three came to the door and told me I was causing problems!"

"Son, it was kind of you to offer to help, but girls have a way of working things out."

"Good, because I don't plan to go back in there. By the way, how long are they going to stay with us?"

"Cynthia said they could stay for a week. We're taking them to Atlanta tomorrow to see the sites, and maybe shop. Would you like to come along? It's okay if you bring a friend."

"No thanks! Jason's dad is taking him fishing. He has invited me to come along. Is that okay with you?"

"I'd prefer that you come to Atlanta with us, but if it's okay with your dad then it's okay with me."

"Thanks, Mom. I'll talk to him. Poor McAlister; I feel sorry for him. He's going to be stuck in a car with three 'anxiety queens' for four hours!"

I called to check on Cynthia. Cade informed me that his mother was feeling better, and actually walking around. She has been bedridden a lot since her diagnosis. I spoke with her briefly, to tell her that we planned to take the girls to Atlanta. We would spend the night, then return on Wednesday. I was pleased to hear that her voice was stronger. Of course the girls were thrilled about going to Atlanta. They talked from the time we left Nashville to the time we arrived at the hotel.

Sidney and Allyson had never been to Atlanta, so were excited to see the sites. Fortunately, neither of them had developed an interest in shopping, yet. Michaela liked clothes, but shopping was not a priority. But they each wanted to learn more about Dr. Martin Luther King, Jr., so we spent most of our time visiting his church and the Non-violence Center.

Cole and I had planned to take Matthew, Michaela and McAlister to the Bahamas for our summer vacation. I mentioned this to Sidney and Allyson to see if they were interested in going.

"I would love to go, Ms. Celia, but Mom might need me to stay with her," Sidney said. Since I am her older daughter, she depends on me. I'll have to wait to see if she has improved. You know, I'm truly blessed to have two wonderful mothers. I love you both. Ms. Celia, if you were sick, I would also stay with you, until you were better."

I saw this as the perfect time to sit and have a heart-to-heart talk with my biological daughter. Sidney had asked me soon after we met how she should address me. I told her to address me in any manner that was comfortable to her. Well, she chose to call me "Ms. Celia" and Cole, "Mr. Bentley." We were both fine with this. We were determined not to force ourselves on this child. We wanted to give her the space she needed to become comfortable with us.

When we returned to Nashville, I asked Matthew and Michaela to stay with Allyson and McAlister. They understood that I wanted to spend time with Sidney, away from home. I decided to take her to lunch. I asked her about any preferences. She said she loved to watch the performances at some of the Japanese restaurants, so I took her to one that's popular with Michaela.

"Sidney, when I first learned that we had a biological daughter we'd never met, I was too shocked and hurt to realize that this was a blessing in disguise. For weeks I struggled with guilt, anger and lots of questions I was unable to answer.

"Then we finally got to see you in the hospital. You may have been unconscious, I don't know. But the moment I set my eyes on your lovely face, I knew you were our daughter. There are no words that can adequately explain what I felt at that moment. I spoke to you as if you were listening, because I had so much to say to you. I had 10 years of information to unload!" She smiled as if she'd actually heard me, but said nothing.

We both laughed. This was the beginning of what I knew would be a long, wonderful relationship. The waiter started the fire on the grill. Sidney was thoroughly enjoying his performance. I could feel her joy. Once we had our food, I continued to talk.

"I am thankful that you were raised by loving, caring people. Seeing what a good job Ralph and Cynthia have done with you, and all of their children, has brought a sense of peace to me. Seeing this helped me heal emotionally. Ralph and Cynthia are your parents; they are the people who have loved, fed and provided for you.

"Cole and I can never replace them. But you are our "natural" daughter, and we love you dearly. We always will. Sidney, you have a home in Nashville that you can come to whenever you want to. It will always be your home." I stopped talking so she could digest what I had said. She took her time.

"Ms. Celia, it's hard to explain what it's like to get sick, then slowly recover and learn that my parents are not my real, or rather, my biological parents. At first I was afraid. I was afraid that I would have to leave my family, and go to live with strangers. I started wishing that I would never recover. I wanted to stay sick, so that I wouldn't have to leave Mom and Daddy.

"Then, Michaela and I became friends, and I started to realize that you all were pretty nice people. You had to be good people to raise a daughter like Michaela. She called me everyday to see how I was doing. Sometimes we just cried together on the phone, and didn't say anything. She was just as hurt and confused as I was.

"We couldn't understand how something so horrible had happened to us. I mean, babies are born and they're supposed to go home with their natural mothers, not with strangers. We couldn't understand why our mothers didn't know any better. Now, after listening to my parents and other people, I understand that sometimes bad things happen in life, and innocent people, like Michaela and me, and our families, get hurt."

Sidney appeared to be enjoying every bite of her meal. I'd never seen her eat so much, or heard her talk so openly and with such maturity for her age.

"You are absolutely right," I said. "Sometimes bad things happen to nice people. We're gradually learning that the reason you went home with your parents, and Michaela came home with us, is because there were people doing some bad things at the hospital. We all, unfortunately, got caught up in it."

That was all I intended to tell her about the investigation at this point. She had the rest of her life to learn the truth. Learning the truth now couldn't undo what had already happened.

"What's important now, Sweetheart, is that your parents have met Michaela, and we have met you. Now we must figure out how to move forward with our lives. Cole and I aren't going to force you into our lives. But we want you to know that we love you, and that our hearts and our home are open to you, forever.

"We want to be actively involved in your life. If that means calling you daily, or having you spend time with us, then that's what we're open to doing." I had so much more to say to her. But she was only 11. I would in time bring everything out in the open.

"Thank you, Ms. Celia. You all have been so nice to me, and I like being here with you."

We finished our lunch. I offered to take her shopping; she accepted. Our first stop was in a shoe store. She chose a conservative pair of brown flats. I tried to talk her into getting a pair of sandals, but she decided they weren't for her. According to Sidney, sandals were for people with pretty feet. With shoes out of the way, we looked around in some of the teen shops. She didn't see anything she liked. She was so much like me. I didn't have a strong sense of fashion, so I bought classic clothing instead. I preferred outfits that I knew would be in style for years.

We stopped in a book store and she picked out several books relating to art. Then we headed home. Matthew had everything under control. As soon as I walked in, he grabbed his tennis racket and was off to the courts. Allyson was reading to McAlister. Michaela was on the phone with one of her friends. Sidney put her new purchases away, and began packing for the trip back to Cleveland. She and Allyson were leaving on Saturday. I was tempted to call Cynthia to ask if the girls could stay another week, but changed my mind. To my surprise I received a call from her.

"Celia, how is it going with the girls? I'm sure you're ready to ship Allyson back to Cleveland."

"Actually, I'd love to keep them here with us a little longer, but I know you miss them."

"Yes, I do. In fact, I'd love for Michaela to come and spend some time with us. Is that okay with you?"

"That's fine with us. You sound like you're feeling much better."

"I feel great. I've even made plans to take the girls to King's Island next week. Ralph will be on vacation, so we'll have a wonderful time."

Cynthia, like me, loved her children dearly. And, now she had another child to love. After we hung up I began helping the girls pack. Michaela was excited about spending time with the Williams family next week. She and Sidney began talking about all the things they wanted to do.

As I folded clothes and straightened Michaela's room, I wondered what I'd do with Michaela gone. I knew she had to spend time with Ralph and Cynthia, yet the thought of my child being away made me sad. Somehow, we all had to find a way to share our daughters' lives without causing each other pain.

Michaela and Sidney continued talking excitedly about their plans. I noticed that Allyson was just sitting and staring at them, so I took her and McAlister to the backyard to the swings. As I pushed McAlister, I talked to Allyson.

"Allyson, we have really enjoyed having you here with us this week. You are so sweet and well-behaved. I want you to know that you are welcome to come and visit with us again. Have you enjoyed yourself?"

"Yes, I have, Ms. Celia. You have been so nice to me. Sometimes Sidney and Michaela are not," she said, looking a little sad.

"What do you mean they haven't been nice to you?"

"Well, when Sidney is at home she talks and plays with me, but when she's with Michaela, she likes to talk and play with her. And, they don't like sleeping with me. They talk in bed at night. When I ask questions, they laugh and say, 'you wouldn't understand, Allyson, because you're too young.' That hurts my feelings, so I'm ready to go home."

"I don't think they intend to hurt your feelings, Sweetheart. They're four years older than you are, so their interests are not always the same as yours. Also, you probably wouldn't understand some of the things they talk about. Does this make sense?" I asked.

"Not really, but I guess I'll understand better when I'm older. That's what grown-ups always say."

"You will, Sweetheart. Tell me, would you like some ice cream?"

"Yes, I would. I love ice cream. Chocolate is my favorite."

"Well, I don't think I have chocolate. So how would you like to go with me to get a chocolate ice cream cone?" Her big, brown eyes looked like light bulbs. Suddenly she didn't look sad anymore.

"I want some, Mommy," McAlister said.

"Then let's just go and get some." We went into the house. I told Michaela and Sidney that we were going out for ice cream. They didn't want to join us. They were still in Michaela's room, laughing about something. We left them to finish whatever they were discussing. Allyson, McAlister and I went to a nearby ice cream store.

While we enjoyed our treats, Allyson talked about school. She said she was happy that her mother was getting better. She said her mother had told her that Michaela was also her sister, but she didn't understand how. I decided not to confuse her by trying to explain. She would understand in time. She told me that she really enjoyed the trip to Atlanta, and hoped that her Mommy and Daddy could take her again some day. We finished our ice cream and went home to get the girls ready to return to Cleveland.

Cynthia had two well-behaved daughters. We invited them to visit us again. The following week I missed having them. Fortunately, I had more than enough to do to keep busy. Matthew was packing to leave for tennis camp. Michaela was excited about attending camp at St. Ann's, after her visit with the Williams family. That left McAlister. I had decided to let him attend the preschool program at our church each day until noon, because he enjoyed it so much.

It was Thursday morning. I had just returned from dropping off McAlister when the phone rang.

"Hello, I would like to speak with Celia Bentley."

"This is Celia Bentley. How can I help you?"

"Ms. Bentley, I've wanted to talk to you for some time because there are some things you need to know."

"Who am I speaking to, and what things do I need to know?" The woman spoke in a very soft tone. I could hear traffic in the background.

"I can't give you my name, but please, hear me out. Do you have a few minutes to listen?"

I told her I didn't have a few minutes to listen to a stranger who wouldn't give her name.

"If I told you that I have information about your daughter, would you listen then?"

Now my heart was pumping faster. I immediately had a flashback to last July, when another stranger, Mary Noland, had called. What was I about to learn now?

"Who are you, and what do you know about my daughter?"

I was not in the mood for games. If she was calling to tell me that Michaela was not my natural daughter, then guess what, I already knew that.

"My name is not important, Ms. Bentley. What's important is that I know that your daughter was taken from you at Willow Memorial Hospital soon after she was born, and that you have raised someone else's daughter."

My heart was racing now, but I was telling myself to stay calm and not let this woman, or anything she had to say, upset me. Who was she, and what did she want?

"Were you a nurse at the hospital during the time my daughter was born?" I asked, hoping that she was one of the nurses David had not been able to contact. Maybe she could tell me what actually happened during that time. If only I could get Cole and David on the line to listen to her. I wanted to ask her to hold on, but was afraid she would hang up and never call back.

"No, I am not a nurse, but I did hold an administrative position at the hospital for several years. I am no longer employed there. Those babies were switched soon after they were born. It broke my heart to see the mothers go home with the wrong babies. The hospital ignored some of the information that was passed on to the administrator and his staff."

My heart was pounding now, but I had to appear strong and resilient as she talked. She said, *mothers*. I wondered how many victims there were.

"Well, if it broke your heart to see this, then can you imagine what I've gone through since learning the truth? Please, if you know what happened, let me call our attorney, or you call him. Tell him how we ended up bringing someone else's child home!"

I was desperate, and she probably heard it in my voice, but she continued to talk. She did not give her name, though.

"I have another administrative position with a hospital, so there's too much to lose if I give my name. Surely you can understand my not wanting to be dragged into the midst of an ugly investigation, where people could end up in jail."

I was silent. Yes, I could understand her not wanting to get involved in what could become an ugly mess. But couldn't she also understand what I was feeling as a mother?

"Ms. Bentley, I will call again, soon. Please continue to be strong. You've hired a good attorney. I believe he will get to the bottom of this."

She hung up. This stranger who had come into my life for a brief 10 minutes, had added salt to my wounds. Now she was gone. I stared through my kitchen window, wondering if I had dreamed this conversation. Then I heard my heart beating. I knew it had been real. I tried to reach Cole, but was told he was in a meeting. I called David. Thank God he was available.

"David, I just had the strangest call from a woman who says she has knowledge of what happened at the hospital back in December 1977."

"Who is she, and what did she say?"

"She wouldn't give me her name, but she knew that babies were switched, and that I did not bring my natural child home. She said she was an administrator at the hospital for several years and had valuable information. But she didn't want to get involved in the middle of what she said was an ugly investigation.

"She said she would call again, soon. I have no idea what *soon* means to her."

"Celia, if she calls again, ask her who her immediate supervisor was during that time. Ask her if she knows Carlton Jackson. Also, ask her if she would be willing to call me, or if I can call her. This woman could very well be able to provide the missing pieces to this puzzle."

David was excited about this new witness. He stressed the importance of staying calm while talking to her if she called again. He was convinced that there was an undercover drug operation at the hospital during that time, and that innocent babies got caught up in it.

I was reluctant to leave the house the next few days for fear I would miss her call. She didn't call. Hindsight is always so much clearer. I thought of a hundred questions I should've asked, but didn't. This was all becoming so complicated. I was tempted to tell David to drop the investigation, because what was done was done. I knew Cole would adamantly object. He was just as determined as David to solve this unfortunate mystery.

I was ready to move on with my life, and deal with what had happened. After all, we now know that Sidney, not Michaela, is our biological daughter. There was nothing we could do to change that. I knew I would always feel some pain, but the pain wasn't as sharp as it had been a year ago. Love can conquer anything. I have opened my heart to Sidney. She knows that we love and care about her, just as we do Michaela. They are both our daughters. There was nothing Cole and I wouldn't do for either of them. I was prepared to bury the past, to move forward.

The middle of June had arrived. It was time to start packing for our family vacation. This year we let the children decide where we would go. They chose the Bahamas. Sidney wanted to come with us, but she didn't feel comfortable leaving her mother for a week. I didn't push the issue. I wanted her to join us, because she had been through so much with her illness, and now Cynthia's. I knew I could alienate her if I tried to force her to come with us. I had to constantly remind myself that, although I gave birth to this child, someone else had fed and cared for her for the past 11 years. I had to respect that.

We went to the Bahamas without Sidney. Cole and the kids enjoyed the water while I relaxed on the beach and read. My interest in doing the things I enjoyed so much, such as playing in the symphony, reading and gardening, had resurfaced. So I knew the healing process was well underway. I would be just fine. I also knew that with lots of love and understanding, Michaela and Sidney would also be okay.

As I watched Michaela play in the water with Matthew and McAlister, I realized how blessed we were. I had learned so much about human nature by raising this child. Almost every month she went through a different stage of development. Although learning the truth about our daughters has been very painful, it was apparent that a lot of good would come out of this as well.

I was lying on the beach, baking in the sun. I refused to think about anything negative or stressful. I read, a second time, a letter I'd received from my cousin, Darlene, who said she'd combed through Dad's family roots, but there was no record or mention of a Sarah Johnson, or any Johnson. The old trunk belonged to Dad. Dad liked it because, like me, he collected antiques. Mother said it was in the attic when they bought the house. It was the same house I grew up in, very old. It had been vacant for two years when my parents bought it. Mother had no knowledge of any Johnsons in her family or Dad's family.

I wondered where a diary about a young slave girl had come from. Why was it tucked away in Dad's old trunk? Dad had never mentioned it to Mom. Dad couldn't have known this woman, because she was a slave. I had finished reading through the stack of old papers. I had gotten stronger since reading Sarah's story. I decided that Michaela and Sidney would also read it. Perhaps someday I would learn more about this strong, courageous woman. Darlene, a history professor, was driven to dig deeper into our family history. For now, I was grateful that I had found the papers.

My cell phone rang. It was Sidney. She was probably checking in to see what we were doing on the beach. I was thrilled that she felt comfortable enough to call me weekly just to talk. I wanted nothing more than to build a strong, healthy relationship with her.

"Ms. Celia, are you busy?" she asked, in a soft tone.

"No, Sweetheart, I'm not. What are you up to?"

"Mom is sick again. She's been throwing up blood since last night. Daddy's getting ready to take her back to the hospital. I'm just afraid that she's going to have to stay this time. Ms. Celia, do you think you could come up for a few days?"

I tried to absorb what my child had just said. Her mother's condition had apparently deteriorated. She was afraid, and wanted me to come back to help the family. I didn't have to think long. I'd always been there for Matthew, Michaela and McAlister. I would certainly be there for her.

"Why, sure, Sweetheart. Let me get things settled here. I'll be there sometime tomorrow. I want you to try to stay calm, okay? Are your brothers at home?"

"Yes, everyone is here. Grandma is coming over later."

"Good. Then I'll see you tomorrow. Love you."

"Thank you so much for coming. Bye."

I called for Cole to come out of the water so we could discuss the matter. We decided that he would stay here with the kids, and I would fly to Cleveland in the morning. I told the kids that Sidney needed my help, and that I would talk to them later with more details. I wanted them to continue to enjoy their vacation. Although I was thoroughly enjoying the beach, I had to leave. This call was no different than Matthew, Michaela or McAlister calling to ask for help.

I left early the next morning, tanned and feeling relaxed from the warmth of the sun and sand. I prayed that Cynthia would not have to stay in the hospital for long. If she did, I would ask Ralph if the girls could come to Nashville with us for a few days. I took a cab to the Williamses' home. Sidney and Allyson met me at the door with open arms. They had both been crying. I gave each of them a big hug.

The twins, Cade and Cary, were getting ready to leave for the hospital. Cynthia's mother had decided to go straight to the hospital instead of coming here first. I asked the girls if they wanted something to eat. Neither of them was hungry. They just wanted someone to hold on to, so I sat down, put my arms around them and let them cry and talk.

Sidney and Allyson had been so happy in Nashville with us, and so optimistic about their mother getting better. Sidney was only 11, and, as I stroked her head, my eyes filled with tears when I thought about the suffering she had endured at such a young age. First she's fighting for her life, now she's watching her mother fight for hers.

They both wanted to go to the hospital, so I told them to get dressed and I would call a cab to take us. This was their mother. They had every right to be close to her. Then I thought about Michaela. I suddenly realized that I should have told her that Cynthia was back in the hospital, but I didn't want to ruin her vacation. Still, she had a right to know. I called Cole.

"Hi, Sweetheart. I need to speak to Michaela to tell her that Cynthia is very ill. She needs to know that her mother is in critical condition. She may even want to come up."

"I agree. I've told her that Cynthia is back in the hospital, but not that her condition is critical. Hold on, let me get her," Cole said.

"Hi, Mom, is Ms. Cynthia okay?" Michaela asked, in a carefree voice.

"Actually, Honey, that's why I called. Cynthia is very ill. In fact, I just learned that her condition is critical. I need to know if you want to come to Cleveland."

"Yes, Mom, I want to come up."

"Then let me speak to your dad, so we can make some arrangements to get you here."

Michaela flew into Cleveland late that night. I met her at the airport in a cab, and we went straight to the hospital. Cynthia's eyes lit up when Michaela walked into the room. Her sons had already left to pick up their aunt. Ralph, Sidney and Allyson were sitting close to her bed. I left them alone. I decided to wait in the family room.

I prayed that Cynthia would soon be strong and healthy again. She had seven beautiful children to live for now. Once she was better, I planned to discuss with her, and our daughters, what was best for Michaela and Sidney. I had put this off because I didn't want to alienate either Cynthia or Sidney, by pushing to get Sidney into our lives more. Perhaps once Cynthia was stronger, she would also want to make plans for the girls.

I was dozing in the waiting room, trying to read, when my cell phone rang. It was Cole.

"How are you? Did Michaela get in okay?"

"Yes, she did. We're at the hospital now. I'm sitting in the family waiting room, almost asleep. Michaela is visiting with Cynthia. How are the boys?"

"They're just fine. Neither of them wants to leave in the morning. How is Cynthia?"

"She's still listed as critical. Ralph says her condition hasn't changed since this morning."

"Well I've got some great news. The mystery woman called David, and she is who he thought she was – Thelma Phillips. She worked as an administrative assistant to one of the VPs at the hospital. She left several years ago.

"I don't know how he did it, but David managed to get her to meet with him. She confirmed that there was an illicit drug operation among several employees at the hospital, around the time Michaela and Sidney were born. According to Ms. Phillips, Clarese Evers, the head nurse in the maternity unit at that time, and Raymond Hicks, who worked in the pharmacy, were the ringleaders. Apparently Ms. Evers later decided to clean up her life and wanted out. Well, Raymond wasn't about to let her off the hook, at least not without some consequences."

"What did he mean by that?" I asked.

"David doesn't have all of the facts yet, but according to Ms. Phillips, someone called Ms. Phillips to tell her that Ms. Evers was abusing drugs. This person said Ms. Evers wasn't fit to work at the hospital. This was an anonymous call. The man also said that if Ms. Evers didn't pay her debts, she would be destroyed. Ms. Phillips said "strange" things started happening in the maternity unit shortly after that call."

"What kinds of strange things?"

"Like staff not showing up for work, and babies getting sick."

"Cole, why didn't Ms. Phillips share this information with the administration?"

"She said she did, but was afraid to get more involved."

"So where are Ms. Evers and Mr. Hicks now?"

"Mr. Hicks is in Seattle. We think we can put our hands on him, but Ms. Evers' family has no idea where she is living. They haven't seen or heard from her in two years. They don't know if she ran off to hide, or if she's even alive. Apparently she wasn't close to her family."

"So who does Ms. Phillips think switched our babies?"

"She doesn't know for sure. But from what David has learned, Mr. Hicks was determined to destroy Ms. Evers' career as a nurse, so that no one else would hire her. He made comments about sabotaging the maternity unit."

"Does David have any idea how many children were caught up in this?"

"No, he doesn't, at least, not yet."

"So why has Ms. Phillips decided to come forth after so many years of silence?"

"According to David, she heard about the investigation. She decided she could no longer keep silent about information she had that could crack the case. Also, after Mr. Hicks, Ms. Evers and some of the others left the hospital, and seemingly disappeared, she isn't as afraid to speak out."

"Do you think Ms. Evers is alive?"

"There's no telling. According to her family, she got in with the wrong crowd, then realized that that lifestyle wasn't something she could walk away from overnight. David is pretty confident that Mr. Hicks has damaging information about Ms. Evers, and about how we left the hospital with Michaela, and not Sidney. Apparently Mr. Hicks and Ms. Evers were more than just co-workers."

"Are you saying they were lovers?"

"David seems to think so. But at some point Ms. Evers apparently wanted out of the relationship, and the "business.”

"This gets deeper and deeper. Keep me posted. The girls are here, so I need to go. Kiss the boys for me," I said.

"I doubt if Matthew will let me kiss him, but I'll tell him what you said. Take care."

Ralph came in with the girls. He looked exhausted. "Celia, if you don't mind, I'll take you and the girls home. It's pretty late and they're tired.”

"Why, of course I don't mind, Ralph. It's been a long day for everyone.”

We left the hospital. I stayed at the Williamses' home with the girls, while Ralph showered and went back to the hospital. The poor man looked distraught. I told him not to worry about the girls. I told him I would get them to bed, and stay with them until he returned. Perhaps one of the older boys could take me back to the hotel, I added.

After Ralph left, the girls showered and asked if we all could stay up and talk before going to bed. I said "yes," of course. The four of us sat on the sofa in the family room. This brought back warm memories of some of my all-night slumber parties with friends. Michaela and Sidney talked about entering middle school next fall, and wanted to know what to expect. I explained to them how middle school was different from elementary school.

Allyson joined in the conversation and talked about entering the second grade in the fall. I asked Michaela and Sidney to share their second grade experience with her. They were kind enough to tell her what to expect. Soon Sidney and Allyson fell asleep. Allyson was on my lap. Sidney and Michaela rested their heads on my shoulders.

As Sidney and Allyson slept, Michaela talked about Cynthia. She told me that when Ralph, Sidney and Allyson left the hospital room to get something to eat, Cynthia wanted her to stay. Apparently Cynthia wanted a few minutes alone with Michaela. Michaela said Cynthia told her how much she loved her, and how thankful she was to have found her.

"Ms. Cynthia thinks I'm pretty, and she said I am blessed to have parents like you and Dad. She also wants me to think about spending more time here with them. Mom, she's really a nice person. I'm beginning to feel close to her. I guess I could divide my time between the two of you. Would that bother you, Mom?”

"No, Sweetheart, that wouldn't bother me. I've come to terms with the fact that Ralph and Cynthia are your natural parents. They are going to want to spend time with you, just as your dad and I want to spend time with Sidney. It's taken me a long time to accept this, but I have. You have every right to spend time with them.”

Michaela continued to talk about her conversation with Cynthia. Soon, she, too, was asleep. I sat with three precious young lives leaning on me, asleep. I didn't move because I didn't want to awaken them. They wanted to be close to me, and I wanted them close. I thought about Cynthia's conversation with Michaela, and I was right. She was waiting for her health to improve, then she was going to discuss plans for Michaela to spend more time with them. She seemed to be a reasonable person. I hoped our discussions would go smoothly.

We had both inherited another daughter. Michaela and Sidney would be 12 in December, old enough to decide where to live. I couldn't imagine Michaela leaving us, nor could I imagine Sidney leaving Ralph and Cynthia. We had all been good parents. Surely our children wouldn't shut us out. I closed my eyes and tried to forget about all of this. Then, the phone rang.

"Hello."

"Hello, Celia, this is Ralph. Are the girls awake?"

"No, they're all asleep, right here in my arms on the sofa.".

"Well, don't wake them up now. Celia, Cynthia just passed away. The boys are here. I'll just have to tell the girls in the morning." Ralph was crying and hung up the phone.

Was I dreaming? Did Ralph actually call and say Cynthia was dead? This woman had seven beautiful children, and so much to live for, but she was gone.

I believed that every life has a purpose. Perhaps Cynthia had fulfilled her purpose here on earth. I didn't know her well, but Mother always said you should look at the fruit, because that tells you a lot about the tree. I found peace in knowing that Cynthia had accepted my apology. I hope she understood that I only wanted what was best for our children. Now, she had eternal peace.

I wanted this night to last forever. Tomorrow there would be so much to do. I wondered how Sarah Johnson would deal with this. I kissed Michaela, Sidney and Allyson, and held them close. I didn't want to ever let go.

31. Sarah

I COULD HEAR MAMMY'S VOICE. Was it real, or was I dreaming? I did not want to know. The trip from Boston had been long and tiring. The sight of this place sickened me. I left many years ago and never wanted to touch southern soil again. But, I had no choice, if I wanted to see my parents. Mammy and Pappy had always said it was too dangerous to runaway from the plantation. Pappy knew of slaves who had run away, then had been caught and whipped merciless. Thank God, I had the chance to run away and not get caught.

Some of the other slaves on the plantation had thought I was different. But, Mammy and Pappy loved me just the way I was. They are good, decent people, who taught me so much. I had seen my brother just before I ran away. He, too, is a good person. I longed to see Tom again, but had no idea where he was.

As I lay reflecting on my past, the cloth on my face got colder. I slowly opened my eyes. I could barely see the aged faces, nonetheless they still had warm, kind expressions. These were faces I could never forget. Sitting next to me were Bertha and Joshua Johnson!

"Thank God, thank God, itz my baby!" Mammy said over and over again. Tears streamed from her face to mine. "De Lord have brought my baby home! Look, Joshua, itz our baby!"

I still had my disguise on, but there was no hiding my identity from my loving parents. Mammy did not stop crying or saying those words. Pappy just stared in disbelief, without saying a word. I slowly got up and hugged Mammy as tightly as I could. Then Pappy reached over with tears in his eyes, and arms stretched open.

"Mammy, how did you know it was me? I spent hours dressing up to look like a man. Obviously I did a poor job," I said, trying to add humor to this tender moment.

"It dont matta whut you wearin, Baby, caus I know dose eyes anywhure," she said, as she wiped her own eyes. "I saw you when you walk up to de front door, an knew you was my baby. I wunted to scream an shout an praise de Lord, but did not wont nobody to reconize you. Yo Pappy look at me, an we jes smile an wipe away de tears. I got to git you outta dose clothes, an put a clean dress on you, Baby." She stood up, then fell into Pappy's arms.

They cried on each other's shoulders. I knew these were tears of joy. I fell on my knees and thanked God that they were alive and well. At that moment, I did not care if Mr. Wilmington had walked in and seen me. Mammy and Pappy were alive. That was all that mattered to me. I wanted to run through the cotton fields and shout for joy!

"Where were you, Mammy, when I came to the door? I did not see you."

"We was in Missus Wilmington room," Mammy said. She pulled away from Pappy. I could feel her hands shaking, because she and Pappy were holding me close.

"You ain't leavin us agin," Pappy whispered.

"Missus Wilmington is very ill. Yo Pappy an me been wit her almos evry hour. We betta git on back befo Mastah Wilmington come lookin for us," she said. She bowed her head.

"What is wrong with Mrs. Wilmington? Why do you and Pappy have to stay with her?" I did not want them to leave me.

"She got de fever. We ain't lookin for her to make it. Poor Mastah Wilmington is bout to lose his mine."

"Where are Melissa and Kate?" I asked. Mammy looked away.

"Missus Wilmington ain't seen her girls in years. Dey got angry ova some money deals an dont come round no more. It ain't Melissa an Kate fault, but dose greedy men dey married. Dey jes wants it all. Now, Baby, let me git you somethin to eat an a dress to put on. You cant be seen round hure. Mastah Wilmington ain't been de same since you lef. Ain't no tellin whut he might do if he fine out you back hure. I kin hide you for now, den we gotta decide whut we need to do."

Mammy brought me some fried pork and bread, and a dress to wear. I was relieved to get out of the men's clothing. Then Mammy and Pappy hurried back to the big house. As I ate, I thought about all that Mammy had said. So, Mrs. Wilmington was dying, and her angels, Kate and Melissa, had nothing to do with her. This did not surprise me. Those were two of the most selfish girls I had ever met. Mrs. Wilmington had lost her children, like Mammy had lost hers. The difference was that Tom had not chosen to go away. I should have been sad for the Wilmingtons, but was not. All I could think about was getting Mammy and Pappy out of here.

Mammy and Pappy did not come back to the cabin until the next morning. Mrs. Wilmington's sister had come to stay with her. Mr. Wilmington told Mammy and Pappy they could go home until his sister-in-law left. This gave me a chance to talk to my parents, finally. They had so many questions. I explained to them my plan to take them back with me.

"Chile, Mastah Wilmington wont let us leave hure! He need us to look afta his wif caus dere ain't nobody else he kin turn to," Pappy said.

I could see that Mammy agreed with him. I knew they would not simply jump up and come with me. I was determined to change their minds. This is one of the evil things about slavery. It caused some of us to believe that our own families were not as important as the master's family.

"If Mrs. Wilmington dies, will you come back with me then?"

"Chile, whut is you sayin? Lord, forgive ha. She did not mean a word of it!" Mammy stared at me as if I had lost my mind. I was not trying to be cruel, but they had said Mrs. Wilmington might not live. I was simply asking a question.

"Mammy, Pappy, please do not misunderstand what I said. I have been away for 11 years, have risked my life to come back for you. I am not going to let the Wilmingtons stand in my way. You have given them your lives! Now I want to take you back to Boston with me, to freedom! I was angry, and could not hide it.

"So, what do you think has happened to your son, and my brother?" Have the Wilmingtons bothered to find out?" Mammy began crying. I was sorry I had gotten angry with them.

"Last I heard, Baby, my Tom had ran away. I dont know if he made it to de Norf or not. Dere was days I cried caus Joshua an me had loss bof of our babies. But, you is hure now. I cant let you git away from me, agin, ever." Mammy continued to cry. Pappy tried to comfort her.

I was silent, out of respect for them. My mind was racing, though. I wondered if Tom could perhaps be in the North somewhere, maybe even looking for me. I would find out after I returned to Boston. I did not want to worry Mammy with that now.

"Mammy, has anyone from the Wilmington household asked about a stranger coming to town with Mr. Broughton?" I wondered what was going on between him and Mr. Wilmington. I wanted desperately to leave this cabin. However, I feared someone would recognize me, then run straight to Mr. Wilmington. Some of the slaves told him everything.

"Hattie ax som queshions, an, Lord, forgive me for lying, but I had to protec my baby. I told her dat you was sick from de long trip. I told her I wud take care of you til Mastah Broughton cud git you home. She believe me an ain't said anotha word."

Mammy had always said that telling lies is a sin. That was why most people believed whatever she said, even Hattie. Mammy explained that after Mrs. Wilmington's health began to fail, Mr. Wilmington decided to put Hattie over the household chores. He let Mammy take care of his wife.

Mammy had problems lifting Mrs. Wilmington because Mrs. Wilmington had gained weight over the years. Mammy asked if Pappy could come in from the fields to help her care for Mrs. Wilmington. Mr. Wilmington had reluctantly agreed. Joseph had replaced Pappy in the fields. Joseph had to be around 30 by now. He was born on the Wilmington plantation, was married and had two young children. Pappy told me that one of the happiest days of his life was when he passed his hat over to Joseph, and walked out of the fields!

Although Mammy would never complain about this, I knew it had to be a tough job caring for Mrs. Wilmington. She had always been a very demanding person. Her house, food and clothing had to be perfect. I had not forgotten what it was like working for her all those years, while Melissa and Kate pranced around in pretty dresses. Now, Mammy and Pappy were doing what her daughters should be doing, taking care of their mother.

I had been here for two days. I was resting when Mammy came into the cabin crying. I jumped up to see what was wrong. She had been so happy since I came home. Pappy was behind her trying to comfort her.

"Well, baby," she said to me, with tears and trembling hands, "Missus Wilmington is gone. De Lord done took her from us."

Charlotte Wilmington had passed. Death always made me sad; this one was no exception. However, I had a purpose in coming here. Nothing was going to get in my way. Mr. Wilmington would be busy with making the arrangements, and welcoming visitors. I had to take advantage of every moment.

"Mammy, I am truly sorry about Mrs. Wilmington, but could you please do me a favor? When you go back to the house, ask Mr. Broughton if he could meet me down by the large oak tree behind the cabins, just before dark. We have been here two days, and I know he has to get back to Boston."

"I will ax him, but dont you thank you bein careliss to leave hure, an go out whure evrybody kin see you, chile?"

"Mammy, everyone is grieving Mrs. Wilmington's death. They will not be thinking about me. You know how they all loved her."

"An I love her. You need to show her som respec. Now, you know Hattie Mae dont miss nuttin. If she see you she gonna tell!"

"Tell Mr. Broughton to meet me behind the big oak tree. It will be almost dark. No one will see us, not even Hattie Mae."

"I will do it, but dis plan worry me. It almos lak nuttin dont scare you no more, Sarah. Mastah Wilmington got a lot on him. De las thang he need is for somthin to upset him."

I let Mammy finish her speech. She was much too thoughtful of these people for me to ever understand. I certainly was not going to argue with her at a time like this. I just wanted her to deliver my message to Mr. Broughton.

Mammy and Pappy soon left to go back to the big house, as guests were starting to come. I began dressing to disguise my appearance again. I could not afford to look anything like Sarah. Someone could come over looking for Mammy or Pappy and recognize me. Even though I had been gone for years, someone might still recognize me, even with the disguise. I got away once, and would do it again. However, this time my parents would be with me!

It was almost dark. I stood by the big oak tree, waiting for Mr. Broughton to appear. As I waited, I thought about the days I had spent around this big oak tree. Sometimes the slave children played here. We had no idea then that the people in the big house would always own us. I wondered if Tom had played here before he was "hired out."

My thoughts turned to Charlotte Wilmington. She was dead. I had an eerie feeling as I stood by the tree waiting. It was getting darker. I was sure no one would recognize me now.

"Sarah, where have you been?"

I was afraid to look around when I heard my name. It was Mr. Broughton.

"I need to talk to you because I have to get back to Boston on some important matters. When I first mentioned buying your parents to Frank, he said he needed them to look after his wife. But, may God rest her soul, she's at peace now. Frank's been so upset that I've avoided discussing any further business with him, including buying your parents."

"Mr. Broughton, you can not just leave me here!" I was almost screaming, but had to calm down before Hattie or some of the others heard me. "Mammy and Pappy just have to get out of here! Mrs. Wilmington is dead. Mr. Wilmington does not need Mammy and Pappy anymore. They are too old to do any of the hard work around this place." This was not the time to get angry. I needed to stay calm, so that I could think and make rational decisions.

"The services are tomorrow. I'll talk to Frank afterward. But, Sarah, after that I must get back to Boston." Mr. Broughton squeezed my hand. He then left me standing behind the big oak tree, in the dark. I wondered what my next move would be if Mr. Broughton could not buy my parents.

Somehow, Mammy and Pappy were coming with me. I did not care what I had to do to accomplish this. As I slowly walked back to the cabin, an idea came to me. It was a chance I had to take.

32. Naini

WOULDN'T HAVE IMAGINED the opportunity presented to me. But, here I sit, sweating, with cameras in my face from every angle. I'm being interviewed on a news program by political analyst, Jack Singleton, about being Vice President of the United States. Mr. Singleton is the host of this weekly TV show. I am his only guest today.

"Senator Carrington, how do you plan to raise two children, twins at that, and take care of the business of this country?" Exactly four months have passed since Senator Christian asked me to be his running mate, as vice president. I knew my life would never be the same once I accepted. I was absolutely right.

"I have the support of a loving husband, who has been taking care of our children since their birth. I also have the support of both of our families. My children will not suffer from lack of attention, and neither will this country." This is the one question that is thrown at me several times a day. I understand why. I didn't make this decision without a lot of prayer and planning with my family. I am confident I made the right decision. At this point in the campaign, I don't know if mothers of young children support me or not. I can't worry about that now.

"If Senator Christian is elected, how do you think other countries will respond to a female African-American vice president?"

"Mr. Singleton, I am a U.S. senator, and a candidate for Vice President of the United States of America. I understand our relationship with other countries. How they respond to me is strictly their choice."

It is 7:00 on this brisk September morning in New York City. I've been up since 4:00, preparing for an interview with one of the country's top political analysts. John travels almost everywhere with me. Today, Mother and Dad also are here. I'm amazed at how much John has helped me prepare for the role of vice president. He fires questions at me daily; this keeps my mind sharp and alert. Just to see him, and hold the children after a long day on the campaign trail, is all I need to calm down and relax each night.

Although John is busy traveling with me, our consulting business continues to flourish. He asked a colleague to manage the daily operations of the company until November, or at least until the pressure of campaigning is over. I know my husband has to love me to put up with all of this.

The company he started has given us financial freedom at a young age. We could be living somewhere away from the spotlight, enjoying the fruit of our labor. Instead, John and our twins are flying around the country just to be close to me, as reporters and interviewers fire question after question.

My ability to think on my feet, deliver intelligent, but simple answers, and my family and faith are guiding me through this opportunity of a lifetime. It is 2016. A female African-American has never been tapped as a vice presidential candidate until now. Everyone has something to say about it. My family and friends don't miss a word of many of these exchanges.

There is criticism of my age, sex, race and level of experience. Then there is the fact that I am the mother of 3-year-old twins, with a stay-at-home husband caring for them. All of this makes me a hot topic of conversation in the papers, on network news and entertainment shows.

America still has a discrimination problem. I am a competent candidate, but still young, female and African-American as far as some people are concerned. However, I have an abundance of confidence in myself, and feel good about being me. Those who are trying to tear me down, for any reason, are in for a surprise. The tougher the questions, the tougher I get!

"What if something happens to Senator Christian, and you have to step in as President of the United States? Are you *really* prepared to handle this, Senator Carrington?"

"Mr. Singleton, if I'm not mistaken, you have publicly praised Senator Christian's judgment on several occasions. One could reasonably believe that you have supported decisions he has made. Isn't it only logical to think that if the Senator has a record of making wise choices, that he would not stray from that pattern when selecting his running mate? I happen to agree with you, Mr. Singleton; I think Senator Christian is a wise man, who makes wise decisions." Jack Singleton quickly changed the subject.

"If Senator Christian is elected, Senator Carrington, how supportive will you be of his agenda? Do the two of you agree on all of the issues?"

"Senator Christian has clearly outlined his agenda for the nation. I support his position on many issues. But it's certainly not unusual for a presidential and vice presidential candidate to have some differences of opinion. Choosing a running mate with diverse views shows character, a willingness to listen to other opinions. Senator Christian has been very supportive of my ideas and suggestions."

"And what's on your agenda, Senator?"

"First, I plan to work to ensure that DNA testing is used for appropriate reasons, such as helping to solve crimes by identifying perpetrators. But, I certainly do not want such testing to be used to deny anyone a job opportunity that he or she is qualified for. Secondly, I will work to see that all children are taught their language and Spanish, or another second language, upon entering elementary school. There are too many Americans who are crippled, educationally and culturally, because they cannot effectively communicate with other Americans."

"How exactly will DNA testing hold anyone back, Senator?"

"If an individual, for example, applies for a job or insurance and the recruiter has test results that indicate a high probability of the applicant succumbing to heart disease, cancer, diabetes, hypertension, sickle cell anemia, or some other disease or illness, then this is a form of discrimination. This cannot, and will not, be tolerated under the Christian-Carrington administration."

"And how do you propose to stop it, Senator?"

"By limiting the use of such results for appropriate reasons, such as the ones I discussed earlier."

"Do you think this can be accomplished, Senator?"

"It can, and will, be accomplished under this administration."

He then asked questions about teaching two languages to students in the early years. I gave thorough, detailed answers because this is a subject I had spent a great deal of time researching. After grilling me for two hours, Jack Singleton signed off from millions of viewers. I could feel my heart racing! I was anxious to spend time with my family to hear about my performance with Mr. Singleton.

John wants me to do more research on the dangers of DNA testing, because he feels it is a powerful tool that can be abused. Mother suggests that I talk about my children whenever possible, so the audience can see the "mother" in me. She wants them to know that I am a caring human being, who is also bright and capable of running this country. Dad wants me to stress teaching two languages in grade school, because he believes that public education should prepare people for dealing with the real world. And, of course, my dear friend Larkin thinks I'm too nice. She wants Jack Singleton and millions of viewers to see the "bitch" in me. They all have advice, because they all love me.

Many think Senator Christian and I are a great team. We complement each other. I'm stronger in some areas, such as reaching younger voters, and, of course, some minority groups. Janna Christian, Senator Christian's wife, and John spend long, tiring hours together on the campaign trail. But, neither shows signs of boredom or apathy.

John, against his will, is fast becoming a celebrity in his own right. Papers across the country run pictures of him with our children. If I'm criticized for not being at home with Harry and Haley, John, on the other hand, is praised for his devotion to his family.

He hates interviews but knows they are necessary, as part of the strategy, for the Senator and me to win in November. John is questioned primarily about his roles as stay-at-home dad and CEO of a successful company. He makes it quite clear that he decided to stay home with his children long before I was asked to run with Senator Christian. He adds that regardless of the outcome of the election, he will continue to care for our children. He praises me as a loving wife and mother, and as someone who is concerned about social issues and our country.

Although I didn't appear to be tired or exhausted, Senator Christian's fatigue was beginning to show. There were days when Janna Christian and I begged him to rest and let me travel for him. To our dismay, there was no way to stop him. The latest polls showed that we were ahead. We didn't intend to lose ground.

I'm especially comfortable on college campuses. There are days I miss the classroom, and the exchange of ideas with students. In a few months I'll be 39, but I can still relate to them. Today I am speaking to a group of students at Tulane University.

"Senator Carrington, I truly admire you for what you have accomplished. But, don't you feel that you've missed some of the most important days of your children's lives by campaigning, and being away so often?" a student asked.

"Yes, I do feel that I've missed some very special moments with my children. This is the most difficult aspect of campaigning. But once Senator Christian and I are elected, I will be there for my children, to be the very best mother I can be to them."

This is a good question, also a very painful one. This is the only answer I can give. My parents taught me years ago not to make excuses, or try to explain my way out of any situation. They told me to be truthful, to accept the challenge and consequences. The questions and comments from the students were as sharp as those from the professional journalists.

"If you're elected, how will you have any more time for your children than you do now? You'll be Vice President Raini Carrington. You'll have a country to help run."

"When Senator Christian and I are elected, yes, I will be Vice President Carrington. But, I am, and always will be, my children's mother. I'll go to the office as many mothers do each day, then return home to love, teach and enjoy both of them."

"Do you think you've cheated your husband out of having a wife and your children out of having a mother by accepting this challenge? Remember, Senator Christian's children are adults."

"No, I don't think I've cheated either my husband or my children."

"Senator Carrington, why don't you think an employer has the right to deny employment to an individual whose DNA tests show that he or she is predisposed to some illness? That illness could adversely affect that person's ability to be productive with the company in the long run. At the same time, why waste time and money when my test results, or yours, show that we will be healthy for many years and, therefore, a potential asset to the company?"

"Using test results could become a means of granting certain groups opportunities that will allow them to flourish in this country, while other groups could suffer severe hardships. I will do everything in my power to support laws that will not permit DNA test results to be used as a basis for employment in America," I responded.

"Senator Carrington, I don't think my tax dollars should be spent for children to learn two languages. Schools should teach the native language. If anyone wants their children to learn a second language, let them pay for it."

"That would be a perfect solution if we lived in a perfect world. Unfortunately, we don't. This country needs to prepare its youth to compete in a diverse, global society. This can only be done if they are properly educated. We have to spend more money educating our children about other cultures. If we don't, some will be prepared to compete, but too many will not."

I had learned to give short, but thorough answers, and not view the questions as personal attacks on my character. The citizens of this country had the right to vote for whomever they wanted to, and had the right to ask any questions on their minds. Even if I thought a question was intended to hurt or embarrass me, the person still had the right to ask.

In early October, Janna Christian, several advisors and I were finally able to convince Senator Christian to take a break from the campaign trail to rest. Although I was exhausted, I was more concerned about his health than my own. I truly admired and respected this man. He not only had the guts to choose a female African-American to be his running mate, but he also had been an effective and decent politician during the two terms he had served as a senator. It was truly an honor to have been asked to be his running mate. That was one of the reasons I accepted. Senator Christian could have asked any number of qualified, hardworking, experienced, well-known politicians. He had asked me.

I attended a Washington fund-raiser to speak on Senator Christian's behalf. This would be another opportunity to introduce Raini Hamilton-Carrington to the powerful, sometimes cruel world of politics.

I had never been overly concerned about fashion. I only wanted to look nice and professional. Even one's dress style was fodder for discussion. As long as John liked what I was wearing, it didn't really matter what others thought. However, Larkin, a fashion diva, insisted that I wear a two-piece suit that would cause everyone to stretch their necks when I approached the podium that night to speak. She explained that people voted for candidates for different reasons. Sometimes the important issues had nothing to do with one's choice. She encouraged me to dress to appeal to those women and men who were fashion hounds; the ones who would sit back to watch the evening news, just to see what Vice President Carrington was wearing today.

John thought she had a point, so I allowed her to select my outfit for the fund-raiser. And, oh, did she make a selection! I wasn't comfortable with the length of the suit Larkin chose. John and Mother, on the other hand, approved. The color was a deep orange mixed with fine gold threads.

I thought I heard gasps as I approached the podium. John, who was by my side, squeezed my hand to assure me that I would do just fine. I didn't really care why people had gasped. My mind was focused on what I had to say. These people had paid a small fortune to attend this event. I wanted my words, not my outfit, to grab and hold their attention.

"Good evening, and thank you for your support. I am Raini Hamilton-Carrington, the next Vice President of the United States. Senator Christian deeply regrets that he cannot be here with you on this lovely autumn evening. On his behalf, I want to thank each of you for your support. We assure you that your hard work and contributions will not be in vain.

"If only my great, great grandparents could be here tonight. Some of them worked in cotton fields, some were blacksmiths, others were house slaves. Their message, nonetheless, has traveled from generation to generation. It reached me: Their message was, 'Have faith in God, believe in and respect yourself, and nothing shall be impossible for you.' They would be proud tonight.

"Senator Christian invited my husband, John, and me to dinner four months ago. When he asked me to be his running mate, we were speechless. We didn't know what to think. I even gave him a list of people I thought would be great choices for the office of vice president. Senator Christian tuned me out. He asked me to think about it, and give him an answer later. He made it clear that I was his choice. I felt deeply honored. Having spent several weeks on the campaign trail, I want to publicly thank Senator Christian for ignoring that list. I believe we make a great team. Senator Christian and I share a vision for this country. Tonight, I want to tell you why we must win this election. I'm not going to waste your time tearing into our opponents. They will self-destruct. Tonight I want to focus your attention on four issues…" I went on to expound on those issues.

I spoke for the next 45 minutes. My words flowed smoothly. I sensed I had everyone's undivided attention. I wasn't quite sure if it was mostly because of my outfit, or my speech. But I had what I wanted, their attention. I intended to take advantage of it. After the speech, the guests stood as they applauded. That moment, second only to my wedding and birth of my children, was the proudest in my life. Senator Christian called me from his home shortly after I left the room to say, "Raini, I never even looked at the names on that list, and thank God I didn't." He had been listening by way of a telephone hook-up.

Mother and Dad, and John's parents, were great about caring for Harry and Haley when John was traveling with me. They assured me that I had nothing to worry about. I was anxious about getting home for the weekend. However, I didn't get home that weekend.

Senator Christian, still recovering from exhaustion and shortness of breath, asked me to speak for him in Los Angeles on Friday, then again on Saturday. Of course I agreed to do so, but was unhappy about not seeing my children for another weekend. More importantly, I worried that something was wrong with the Senator. It just wasn't like him to miss an important event, especially when the election was only weeks away.

I read over the material I had prepared to present to a group of mothers who wanted mandatory day care facilities in all work places. This was close to my heart. I didn't know if I could have survived as a working mother, and certainly as a vice presidential candidate, if I had to worry about care for my children. I am fortunate that John is a house husband.

"Do you think something is wrong with Senator Christian, or is he just exhausted?" I asked John, as I studied the material.

"I'm not sure, but if there is something wrong, he will certainly tell you. Until then, sweetheart, simply do what you've got to do." I decided to take John's advice. I was busy with health care issues, and was scheduled to speak to a group of medical professionals in Cleveland in three days. Health care for the elderly and the young was always a hot topic. I had done my homework for this question-and-answer session. We had sharp medical advisors on our team, so I was prepared to be grilled by the professionals.

This was my third trip to Cleveland since the campaign began. According to the polls, we were doing well here, and pretty confident we would win Ohio. Medical professionals from all over the country attended the conference. I shared with them some of Senator Christian's ideas on how health care can be provided to all Americans, especially those in high-risk groups. The message was well received. Several of the doctors clearly approved of Senator Christian's goals. Two even suggested ways to improve his plan.

Later in the day, I had lunch with some of the doctors. I was especially interested in the research that one of them, a pediatrician, was conducting and discussing. Her specialty was respiratory disorders; she had my undivided attention. I wanted to meet with her after lunch to talk about Haley's condition. Perhaps she could tell me something that our pediatrician had overlooked. I listened intently as she spoke.

"Sometimes rapid, labored respirations develop with the infant soon after birth, and the newborn struggles to initiate breathing. This is more prevalent among pre-term newborns, who are at a greater risk of multiple organ failure, or neonatal death. They should be monitored closely because lung function changes…" I was captivated by what she had to say, because this was what Haley, who was pre-term, had experienced.

After lunch, I told her about Haley's condition. She gave me some information to read, and discuss with Dr. Ashley Curry, Haley's pediatrician. I found Dr. Bentley to be a most interesting person. She was from Nashville, and had come to Cleveland to discuss health care for children. She appeared to be around my age.

"Actually, I'm here for two reasons. I want to discuss research on children with lung disorders, and to show my support for the Christian-Carrington ticket," Dr. Bentley said. "I like your ideas. I think you are the best thing that's happened to America in years. Senator Carrington, you are an inspiration to women around the world. It is an honor to sit and talk with you."

"Thank you, Dr. Bentley. It's always good to meet people who support what you are trying to do. I'm sure you are aware that I've been under scrutiny because I assume multiple roles. But if I've been an inspiration to at least one person, then it's all worth it," I responded.

"Please call me Michaela. Believe me, Senator, you've touched many lives. I know women and men who've gone back to school, or started their own businesses because of you. They feel that if you can keep a husband and two babies happy, and campaign for vice president, then there's no limit to what they can accomplish."

The others left after lunch. Michaela and I continued our conversation. It had been a long day, so it was nice to sit and talk about something other than the election.

"Medicine has come a long way since my birth in 1977," Michaela continued.

"I was born in 1977, too, in December," I said.

"Why, what a coincidence. Now I know why you're such a dynamite person. December 1977 was definitely the time to be born," Michaela said.

"I agree wholeheartedly. December 10 is absolutely the best day of the year."

"This is too much!" Michaela shouted. "That's my birthday! Are you telling me that I share a birthday with the next Vice President of the United States?"

"You're absolutely right. What a coincidence!" I responded. "Now, if you say you were born and raised in Alexandria, Virginia, I might pass out."

"No, I was born right here in Cleveland, under some tragic circumstances." Michaela looked down. Her big smile disappeared. I wondered what she meant by "tragic circumstances," but didn't ask. This was clearly difficult for her to talk about, but she continued.

"Shortly after my birth, my family moved to Nashville. That's where I grew up. However, I made several trips back to Cleveland during my teen years." She suddenly looked uncomfortable, so I changed the conversation back to respiratory disorders and Haley's condition. We finished lunch. Before leaving, I asked Michaela if she could call Dr. Curry, to discuss the new developments in respiratory disorders. She said she would be happy to call her. We exchanged telephone numbers, then I was out of there, headed to the next campaign stop.

The following week, Dr. Curry told John that she had spoken with Dr. Bentley at my request. She said Dr. Bentley wanted to examine Haley, because Haley's condition was unique. I was home from the campaign trail for a brief period. Dr. Michaela Bentley came to our home the following week to examine our daughter. That was the beginning of a solid, life-time friendship between us, but what would later become a nightmare for me.

Dr. Curry and Dr. Bentley prepared a detailed treatment plan for Haley. John and I agreed to let Dr. Bentley use Haley's medical records for research purposes. Before long it was clear that Haley was improving. Although my schedule was tight, I found time to talk to Dr. Bentley, or Michaela, as she'd asked me to call her. Since her intervention, Haley's breathing had improved tremendously. She was a much happier child. And, I was a happier mother. Also, I felt a certain connection with Michaela, because we shared the same birth date.

One night she had dinner with John and me at our home to discuss Haley's progress. Michaela apparently was relaxed enough now to share with us the "tragic circumstances" she had learned about surrounding her birth.

"I was among several other babies switched by hospital staff, so my natural parents did not bring me home from the hospital," she began.

Instead, she was raised by parents she loves dearly, but who are not her biological parents. She went on to explain that there was an investigation much later. Unfortunately, all of the victims were not notified because some of them could not be found. I had heard of such horror stories, but had never met a victim. Michaela went on to explain that she had been able to handle the situation, because of the love and support of a strong, devoted family. She had found inner peace as a young teenager, and moved on with her life.

Michaela had learned to live with the pain of her past. During that time she decided she would spend her life working in a hospital setting, with children. She had decided to become a pediatrician because she believed she could help hurting children, and somehow prevent this tragedy from ever happening to another child, or family.

I told Mother what Michaela had shared with us, and what a remarkable person she is. Mother was more visibly shaken than I would have expected. Her face turned white as I explained how Michaela learned the truth about her natural family, but found the strength to get on with her life. Mother wanted to meet Michaela. I told her I would arrange a meeting.

The election was getting closer. It was the middle of October. Senator Christian appeared to have bounced back to his old self. We traveled non-stop, with John and Janna at our sides. John had a great sense of humor about jokes that he would have to entertain and host parties at the mansion. After all, I would be busy running the country, and wouldn't have time to play hostess.

"And, please, don't forget, in addition to entertaining, I have two children to care for," he said, jokingly, during a recent television interview. "A man's work is never done!" No one who knew John well could believe that he had adjusted so comfortably to living in the spotlight. Plus he handled it with charisma and a sense of humor. Still, he was as anxious as I was for the campaign to end.

We were all tired. It was difficult to smile continually and be gracious to our supporters because of fatigue and lack of sleep. But, Senator Christian and I did our best. I talked to my children daily, by telephone, since I didn't get to spend much time with them.

I had one final debate to prepare for against my Republican opponent. I was anxious, but alert. By this time, the polls showed that the candidates from the two parties were running neck and neck. Senator Christian and I decided not to dwell on the polls. Instead, we focused on getting our message across to every American, and helping them understand the importance of casting their vote.

Three weeks before the election, John told me that Mother had been hospitalized. My family had tried to keep this from me because of the stress of the campaign. Apparently Mother needed a blood transfusion. She had been diagnosed with iron deficiency anemia. Her doctor had contacted John about me being a donor. I would have given Mother an arm or leg if she needed one. I was puzzled about why Dad or my aunts hadn't contacted me about donating blood. But, of course, it made sense that they didn't want to add more stress to my life at this time. Everyone knew, especially my family, that the campaign had exhausted most of my energy. Still, Mother was ill. Her life was far more important to me than being elected Vice President of the United States.

I rearranged my tight schedule to be at Mother's side the day before her surgery. I was hurt and disappointed after being informed that my blood type wasn't compatible with hers. I knew I had blood type O negative, but didn't know Mother's blood type. I was her daughter, and couldn't help her when she needed me most. It was heartbreaking.

"There's nothing I wouldn't do for you," I said to her between sobs. "Why didn't you tell me you were sick? Yes, I want to be Vice President of the United

States. But, more importantly, I want you to be well and healthy and happy, just like you've always been. I've never told you, but you are my hero."

I never would have accepted Senator Christian's offer without Mother's approval and support. She was truly one of a kind. Perhaps I should've told her this before now. It's just that I never expected her to get sick. I had never heard Mother complain about any health problems, not even a headache. Now, she was lying in a hospital, thin and weak, waiting for blood. I knew little about iron deficiency anemia. The least I could do was give my blood. Unfortunately, it wasn't compatible with her type. I didn't understand, so I made an appointment to meet with her doctor later that day.

Mother's voice was weak, so she spoke softly. "Sweetheart, I know you would do anything for me, as I would for you. You've been a perfect daughter, with a fairy tale life. I never wanted to ruin that. There's so much I need to say to you. As soon as the surgery is over, we must talk. Please don't meet with Dr. Jackson until we talk." Dr. Calvin Jackson had been Mother's primary care physician for several years.

The nurse removed Mother from her room on a portable bed. I stood speechless, as I watched her disappear down the corridor. Somehow, I knew she would be fine. She was much too strong not to bounce back. But what on earth did she have to say to me? I left her room in a daze.

33. Sarah

EDWARD BROUGHTON GREW UP in northern Canada, an only child. His parents moved to Boston when he was 12. As an adult, he became wealthy through the railroad and cotton industries. His father, Peter Broughton, was a railroad engineer who worked hard to make sure his family had the finer things in life. Mr. Broughton inherited his father's desire and ability to make lots of money.

The Broughton family was wealthy and active in social and political causes. They did what they could to right what they believed were the wrongs of society. They took a public stand against slavery, but were still accepted in elite, white Boston society. People found them fascinating, and somewhat mysterious, because of their money, power and activism.

Aunt Clara had explained to me that the Broughtons, along with other prominent white people, helped organize the anti-slavery movement. Many of them were white liberals who saw the anti-slavery movement as an upper class intellectual social cause. Some were appalled by slavery, and thought this movement was needed to bring an end to this injustice against fellow humans.

Mr. Broughton traveled extensively to Europe and the South making business deals in the cotton industry. He purchased cotton in the South, and sold it in European countries. On one of his trips to Mississippi, he met Frank Wilmington. They began a business relationship that lasted several years. To my knowledge, they were never personal friends.

According to Aunt Clara, Mr. Broughton never bothered to discuss his position on slavery with slaveholders. His only interest in them was to buy their cotton, and sell it abroad, to make lots of money.

Needless to say, Mr. Broughton was a brilliant businessman. But, he also was devoted to his family and was socially conscious. After his father died 10 years ago, he took his mother into his home; he was devoted to her. He hired several nurses to care for her over the years, but none stayed very long. Mrs. Broughton was apparently kind, but also a demanding perfectionist. Her only son, Mr. Broughton, never married.

He read the telegram that a messenger brought with a look of disbelief on his face. The messenger said the message was urgent.

"What is it, Edward? Is there something I can do to help you?" Mr. Wilmington asked, his face was as pale as Mr. Broughton's. He had just buried his wife. He stared at Mr. Broughton with deep, sad eyes.

"Frank, I must leave immediately. It's Mother. I'll send you the papers soon, and this matter should be settled at that time."

"Tell me if there's anything I can do, Edward. You know I want to help you."

"If you could arrange for me to get to the train station, that would be a great help. I'll get my things now."

"Hattie, get Mr. Broughton's possessions together quickly, while I get someone to take him to the train station." Hattie rushed to the room where Mr. Broughton was staying to pack his clothes and other items. As Mr. Broughton was leaving the house, Hattie called out to him.

"Dont fergit dat man you brot hure. He cant stay round hure caus he from de Norf an not mush hep to us slaves. Jus anotha mouf to feed."

"I almost forgot about her, I mean, *him*," Mr. Broughton said. Where is *he*?" Hattie led Mr. Broughton to Joshua and Bertha's cabin.

"Miz Bertha, dat man gotta go on wit Mastah Broughtin. He leavin now. Wher is he? Tell him to git redy to leave wit Mastah Broughtin."

"Don't trouble yourself. I am ready to leave, now," I said, dressed in my disguise. "Thank you for your help." I wanted Hattie to go somewhere, anywhere. Four days of her was more than I could stand. Thank God she got the message and left. With her gone, I could speak freely with Mr. Broughton.

"Mr. Broughton, what is this all about?" And what about Mammy and Pappy?" Mammy and Pappy just stared at Mr. Broughton. He stood just inside the cabin.

"I just received a telegram saying that mother has taken a turn for the worse, so I must get back quickly. Frank said earlier that I couldn't take your parents with me, but I'll ask one last time. Then I'm leaving, Sarah." His tone had changed. I knew he was quite upset. I reminded him not to call me Sarah, but my words did not seem to register with him. Mr. Wilmington was approaching our cabin. I stood back, moving further into the cabin, trying to stay out of sight.

"Ask him," I whispered to Mr. Broughton.

"Frank, you asked if there is anything you can do for me. Well, there is. Mother has gotten worse, so I really could use some help with her, if it's not too late. Would you allow me to take Bertha and Joshua back with me, at least until I know if Mother will survive?" Mr. Wilmington looked down, then at Mammy and Pappy, then at Mr. Broughton. His eyes were sad. He looked confused, and somewhat disoriented. He was clearly grieving the loss of his wife. As far as Aunt Clara and Mrs. Baker knew, Mr. Wilmington had no knowledge of Mr. Broughton's position on slavery.

Finally, Mr. Wilmington spoke. "Edward, you can take Joshua and Bertha, but they can't stay very long. They can only stay long enough for your mother to get better. I told Charlotte I would never sell Bertha and

Joshua, or send them away. I plan to honor her wishes." I moved further back into the cabin, and began crying, very softly. Mammy and Pappy were actually coming back to Boston with me! That was all that mattered now. I could not think of anything other than the fact that they were actually leaving Holly Springs, Mississippi. They were coming home with me to Boston!

"Hurry, we've got a train to catch!" Mr. Broughton said anxiously. I helped Mammy and Pappy get the few things they owned, and we quickly put them into my bag. Mrs. Baker had given me this bag when I left New York City for Boston; it was perfect for the occasion.

Mammy cried as she passed the big house, headed for the train station. Pappy stared at the fields and rubbed his head, as tears filled his eyes. Mr. Wilmington waved from the yard to Mr. Broughton. Hattie Mae stared from the opened front door of the Wilmington house. Some of the field hands stopped working and waved, sadly, to Mammy and Pappy. Mammy and Pappy waved until they could no longer see anyone. I cried with them. The three of us hugged tightly, determined not to ever be separated again!

As the carriage left Holly Springs, Mammy and Pappy finally smiled. I was not sure, but I did not think Pappy had ever left Holly Springs before. Mammy had, when we went to Atlanta with the Wilmingtons many years ago. Unfortunately, after I ran away, they decided not to take any slaves with them on other trips. They feared other slaves would do what I had done in New York City – run!

I prayed on the train as we headed back to Boston. I asked God to help Mammy and Pappy make the trip without getting too tired or sick. They had spent all of their lives in slavery, working for white people. They had every right to see other places in this country. I had saved money and was buying a home. They would certainly have what they needed.

I cried again when I thought about William. Now I could introduce Mammy and Pappy to the man I planned to marry! No one was more proud of their parents than I was of Joshua and Bertha Johnson. They were the essence of dignity and character, perseverance and faith. I was now an educated woman. But no one had taught me, nor could anyone teach me, more than what Mammy and Pappy had taught me in the 13 years I lived with them.

There was so much I wanted them to see once we got to Boston. They were nervous, of course, but everything would work out. I knew people who could help them adjust, and learn to enjoy their new lives.

Mr. Broughton was quiet the entire trip. He had no idea what condition he would find his mother in after he returned home. She was all he had. He cherished her. The rest of his family was still in Canada. There was one thing Edward Broughton and Sarah Johnson had in common – we loved our parents. I was almost certain that was one of the reasons he risked his business relationship with Mr. Wilmington to help me get my parents. Surely he must have seen the pain in my eyes when I spoke of them.

As we traveled, I thought about what Mr. Wilmington had said about my parents not being able to stay for very long, and the promise he had made to his wife. Whether Mr. Broughton's mother recovered or not, my parents would never set foot on Mississippi soil again. I would rather see them dead! I had already begun mapping out a strategy to keep them in Boston with me. Sorry, Frank Wilmington, but my parents and I will never be separated again!

34. Naini

I HAVE TWO SICK CHILDREN TO CARE FOR on this cold, February morning, 2017. They have asthma. When they catch a cold, it is a difficult time for them, and for me. John is dressing Harry, while I attempt to comb Haley's hair, and dress her. She is quite uncooperative this morning. The children have had to adjust to my new schedule, now that the campaign is over. I'm not so sure they're enjoying it.

John says it's only my imagination; that I'm overly sensitive to this issue because I had to be away from them for so long. Plus, I had to answer so many questions about my commitment as a parent. Many people were concerned about my ability to be a "good" mother, and campaign for such a high office simultaneously. I understood the concern. What I didn't understand was why it was such a critical issue for me, since my husband stayed home and took great care of our children. I think John may have started a new trend in this country.

As we traveled to the doctor's office, I thought about all the papers on my desk that needed to be reviewed and signed. I planned to get to the office as soon as possible. But, first, I had to know that Harry and Haley were going to be okay.

Dr. Michaela Bentley came into my life for a purpose, although I didn't know that when I first met her. Seemingly I was destined to meet her. We're still very close, because she is an amazing person. She's done so much to help improve Haley's health. But, still, there's a part of me that wishes I had never met her. But, if I had never met her then I probably never would have learned the truth.

Mother was anxious to meet Michaela after I told her about how Michaela was switched at birth at the hospital in Cleveland. At first I couldn't understand why she was so interested in Michaela's birth. Then I learned that Michaela and I had far more in common than the same birthday.

Mother is recuperating from her surgery and doing well. Fortunately, she was able to get the blood she needed to save her life. And, we had "our talk." She had said she "didn't want to ruin my fairy tale life" before going into surgery. After the surgery and her recovery I asked her to explain that statement. There are times I wish I had never asked. But, I learned the truth about my "fairy tale life."

Mother told me that she and Rachel French were students at Hampton University in the early 1970s, and became very close friends. Rachel was from Cleveland. Mother didn't know a lot about her family, other than the fact that her relationship with her parents was strained. Apparently Rachel didn't think she measured up to her parents' expectations. Mother, being the outgoing, nurturing person she is, often invited her friend to her home for weekends and some holidays. Mother's family pretty much "adopted" Rachel.

Rachel got pregnant, but the father didn't want to get married. He was from New Jersey and had plans to get an MBA, not a wife. He wanted Rachel to have an abortion; she wouldn't go through with it. Mother went home with her to break the news to her family. They flipped out and told her she had brought shame to the family name. Rachel was devastated. She returned to Cleveland to have the baby in December 1977 at Willow Memorial Hospital. She gave birth to a beautiful daughter.

Rachel stayed with her family for three months, but her relationship with her parents continued to deteriorate. She moved in with Mother's family, in McLean, Virginia. She was depressed and desperately wanted to get away, to figure out what she needed to do for herself and her baby. My grandparents offered to take care of the baby. Rachel left for Portland. She had family there, and went to spend some time with them.

In the mean time, Mother finished Hampton and earned a Master's Degree in Education. She met Dad, and they married six months later. Rachel came back to visit her daughter, but she was trying to get her undergraduate degree in political science in Portland. She wasn't able to take her child back with her at that time because of financial reasons. Needless to say, Mother's family had become very attached to the child. My parents told Rachel to take her time, to do what she needed to do.

After Mother and Dad married, they took the little girl to live with them. Mother kept Rachel informed about her daughter. Then one day Rachel called Mother in a panic to tell her that she had heard about some babies being switched at Willow Memorial Hospital in December 1977. She didn't know if it was just a rumor or not. But, she rushed to McLean to get her daughter, then went to the hospital. Some tests were done. Fortunately, it was determined that this little girl was Rachel's biological daughter.

Rachel French returned to Portland. Six months later, she was involved in a fatal car crash. Mother and Dad went to her funeral in Cleveland, and visited with her parents. Rachel's parents thought it was in the best interest of the child that she remain with Mother and Dad, at least until they had a chance to grieve the loss of their daughter. My parents stayed in touch with the French family, since this child was their granddaughter. Rachel's mother, as it turns out, was not in the best of health. She didn't think she could raise a child. Rachel had been an only child, and only had a few relatives.

Mother and Dad later adopted the little girl when she was 10 months old, and provided a "fairy tale life" for her. She was loved, pampered and well-educated. She was taught to believe that she could accomplish any goal she set her mind to, even Vice President of the United States!

Needless to say, I now have unresolved issues with Mother and Dad. I believe I had a right to know my history, long before now. I don't know if I would ever have learned the truth if Dr. Michaela Bentley had not come into my life, or if Mother had never needed blood. According to my parents, the French family never wanted anyone to know about my background. Since my biological mother, Rachel French, was deceased, they saw no reason to disclose this chapter of my life to me or anyone else.

"Rachel was like a daughter to us," Grandmother tearfully explained. "We promised her that she would never have to worry about providing for you. We told her to go on and finish her education, and do whatever she had to do to get her life together, because you would be fine here with us. Rachel was a beautiful person, just like you, Raini. She would be so proud of you!"

There were photos of her in our home, but Mother had only said, "She was a very dear friend." I never asked more questions; she never offered more information. Now I know why. If only I had "studied" those photos. Maybe I would have noticed that Rachel French and I shared some of the same features. I inherited her pointed chin, high cheek bones, expressive, brown eyes, girlish grin, sandy hair with natural highlights and small body frame. My mother, Sharon Hamilton, and I didn't share any of those features. I didn't think anything of it, though. Heredity is strange. Sometimes those genes can go "way back," and you can come out of your mother's womb looking like a complete stranger.

John is helping me cope with all of this new information. He's made it quite clear that he loves me, and will be here for me no matter who my parents are, or my true history.

Larkin has been wonderful. She knew nothing about any of this. She said she loves me for who I am, not for my parents.

Michaela Bentley has become, to some extent, my personal therapist. I wish I'd learned the truth when I was a child, as she did. But, I didn't. Regardless, I must move forward. I have too much to live for, too much to do. Michaela shared something with me that strengthened her. It appears to be a diary written by a young slave girl named Sarah Johnson. I've read her story and it has strengthened me. I feel a connection to her.

When Celia Bentley, Michaela's mother, found the papers in an old trunk in her attic, she had no idea how the papers got there, or who the owners were. Mrs. Bentley believed that Sarah Johnson was an angel, sent to comfort and strengthen the family. At that time, Michaela's family had just learned about the baby mix-up at the hospital. They were devastated.

However, Mrs. Bentley's cousin, Darlene Campbell, a professor at Clemson University, who taught African-American history, was fascinated with Sarah's story. She had been determined to find out what connection she had with the Bentley family, if any.

After talking to members of the Charleston Historical Society, several historians and elderly relatives, Professor Campbell began digging through papers at a Charleston courthouse. Through her research, she learned that a slave named Tom Johnson helped build the house that Celia Bentley, Michaela's mother, grew up in as a child. The house was built in 1858. Sarah Johnson had spent most of her life wondering what had happened to her brother, Tom. As it turns out, he was "hired out" to another slaveholder when he was only 10 years old. His family had been owned by a slaveholder in Holly Springs, Mississippi. He became a skilled carpenter and bricklayer, and worked throughout Georgia. He did carpentry work and bricklaying in Atlanta, Charleston and other cities in the South. Both Sarah and Tom Johnson were talented and skilled in their professions. Sarah was an outstanding seamstress.

Through her research, Professor Campbell discovered that the original owners of the house, Phillip and Carolyn Washington, had about five slaves on their farm.

Apparently after the Civil War, around 1865, Tom was somewhere in the North. Sometime after that, Sarah and her beloved brother found each other; they were reunited. Sarah had escaped to freedom in New York City years earlier. She had even helped to free their parents from that Wilmington plantation in Holly Springs. Tom went back to Charleston to help some of his friends get to the North. That's when he learned that Phillip and Carolyn Washington had died. They had no children.

By this time Sarah and her husband, William Harper, were financially prosperous from their newspaper and dress businesses. Tom apparently told them about the house, and about purchasing some property in Charleston. Sarah and William bought the house sometime in 1866. They thought it was a great way to invest some of their money.

Celia Bentley's parents bought this same house in 1940, and the rest is history. After going back to search through the trunk and attic, Mrs. Bentley and her cousin found papers, books and other items with Tom and Sarah's names on them. Apparently Sarah, her husband and children, her parents and Tom lived together in this house for several years. Sarah Johnson, a young slave girl from Holly Springs, accomplished her lifetime goal. She became a free woman, and reunited with her family!

I feel a connection to Sarah Johnson. Like threads manufactured from the fiber of cotton plants, she was very strong, and so am I. Like her, I, too, am a tree planted by the rivers of water.

Mother is getting stronger each day. She is working again and becoming more active in the community, especially with the adoption project. Mother started a program at her church a few years ago that finds temporary homes for children whose parents have died from HIV/AIDS. The program has been a huge success. Several children have been permanently placed. I don't think she would survive if she had to retire and be confined to her home.

We talk often, but our relationship has become somewhat strained. I have so many questions. Time will be needed to get all of the answers. Mother sincerely regrets that she didn't tell me about my biological family. She said I am special, that this is the life Rachel French would have wanted for her daughter. I wish Rachel French was here to speak for herself. Still, Sharon Hamilton is my hero.

I managed to get some rest after the election in November. John and I went to Aruba for a few days. We left the children with his parents. This was the first time we had taken a vacation since the birth of our children. Mother had often told me it was necessary to spend time alone with your spouse, to have a healthy and strong marriage. This had worked for her and Dad and for John's parents. John and I had always been too busy to even think about a vacation. Now, however, with the campaign behind us, we were free to get away.

The warm sun helped me relax. I tried not to think about the stress and headaches of the campaign, or my family history.

I discovered that Rachel's parents, my grandparents, were still alive. They had moved to Florida, to a retirement community. I plan to visit them, but not just yet. I have too much to sort out before meeting them. I am anxious to know what they have to say about Rachel, and my biological father. Mother doesn't know what happened to him. The last time she saw him was at Rachel's funeral. Perhaps Rachel's parents can answer some of the questions that are tearing at me. I believe Mother and Dad when they say they have told me all they know about the French family.

As I lay on the beach, soaking up the sun, I thought about the people who raised me. I thought about the "fairy tale life" they provided for me. No, they weren't perfect, but they didn't have to be perfect. They had taught me so much – how to set goals and reach them, how to sow seeds and expect a harvest, how to focus on the important things in life, how to give, how to share, and, most importantly, how to love someone unconditionally. This is what "parenting" means to me. In spite of my pain, I love Mother and Dad dearly.

Then I reached over and grabbed the hand of the man I love, unconditionally. I knew that only death could separate us.

I am relieved to hear Dr. Curry say that Harry and Haley only have the common cold; they will be fine. I could now return to my office, the Oval Office.

Sitting in the Oval Office is truly an honor. On my first day here, I sat, and cried for a few minutes, staring at the faces of all the presidents from the past. I thought about the conversations that could have taken place here. I am the first female African-American to occupy this office. I am still in shock!

President Steven Christian should be sitting here. However, he is still recovering from a heart attack he suffered two weeks after the election. He is 58. He and I talk daily. I'm praying that he will return to great health soon. I campaigned hard to be his partner, not to replace him. My agenda is full this afternoon, but I will make time for my daily visit with him. I love and respect President Christian. I promised him I would follow his agenda until he returned.

Unfortunately, the doctors don't know when he will return. Still, I am confident that I can run this country.

Although I was elected Vice President of the United States of America, I am now called President Carrington, because the elected President is incapacitated. Constitutionally, there has to be an exchange of authority until the elected President can resume his duties. I experience joy, pain, happiness, disappointment and every other emotion known to mankind these days. This comes with being human. I am no exception, just because of the office I hold.

I've spent years studying and teaching political science, practicing law, serving as a city council member, state senator, U.S. senator and working with politicians. Individuals in these positions of power make mistakes. I will too. But with God, and a loving family by my side, nothing is impossible.

This is a momentous period for me, my family and America!

35. Sarah

"Joshua, Tom was up til late las night. I know he must be tired.
Let him res today. When Sarah git home, we kin take him for a walk."

My "little" dress shop has grown into a prosperous operation. One
reason for the success is that I continue to give each of my customers
personal attention, just as I did when I first opened the shop. I am
recognized in the dressmaking business as someone who works hard to
please the customer.

Each customer is special. My designs flatter large and small figures.
My dream is to be the best in the business. Of course, it does not hurt to
know people like Aunt Clara and Mrs. Baker. They have helped me
through some of the most difficult times in my life. They are still very
much my family.

William continues to work at his family-owned newspaper. His father
and uncle have pretty much turned the daily operations over to him. He has
a gift for editing and selling newspapers. William and I were married just
over a year ago. We are very much partners, personally and professionally.

Mammy and Pappy have been in Boston for almost two years, and have
adjusted well. They are physically and mentally healthy. The joy of their
lives comes from caring for their only grandson, Tom. I named our son
after my brother.

We learned a few months ago that Tom came through the Underground
Railroad, however, no one knows for sure where he is living. I have several
people looking for him. I know it is just a matter of time before he shows
up at my door. We will soon be the happy family I have dreamed about for
so many years.

Frank Wilmington wrote several letters to Mr. Broughton asking him to
return Mammy and Pappy to the plantation. I guess he never found out that
Mr. Broughton returned to Canada after his mother passed away. He
decided to return to his roots, to rediscover his native land. I grew to love
Mr. Broughton for what he did for Mammy and Pappy. They did move in
with Mr. Broughton, soon after arriving in Boston, to care for his mother.
My parents are kind, loving people.

Frank Wilmington only allowed them to leave his plantation to care for
Mr. Broughton's mother, so, of course, Mammy and Pappy felt they were
obligated to do this. No one, not even me, could convince them to do

otherwise. They had worked for white people all their lives. Mammy said it was just her and Pappy's nature to make other people comfortable.

Now that they are no longer in Mississippi, and did not have the Wilmington family or Mrs. Broughton to look after, Mammy and Pappy have turned their attention to looking after their only grandchild. Mammy loves to hold him and tell him about his African ancestors. She says his skin is as soft as cotton.

Mr. Broughton's mother lived for 11 months after Mammy and Pappy came to care for her. She loved them, and made it quite clear that they would never leave her to return to cotton fields in the South. She said she was not the least bit concerned about Frank Wilmington, or any other slaveholder. Mrs. Broughton and her son taught me a powerful lesson – all white people are not cruel. Thank God the hate in my heart is gone. I can now turn that negative energy into something positive.

I finally confessed to Mr. Broughton that I was the one who had that telegram sent. He had received it at the Wilmington plantation that September afternoon in 1856, when we went to Holly Springs to try to get Mammy and Pappy. His mother had not taken a turn for the worse. I set this up, hoping that things would work out for my parents to come back to Boston with me. My plan worked.

I apologized for being dishonest, and for upsetting Mr. Broughton. I am also sorry that I took advantage of Frank Wilmington during his period of grief for his wife. But, I was so focused and determined to get Mammy and Pappy here that no one else's feelings mattered at that time. Mr. Broughton was angry with me for a while. But after his mother adjusted so well to Mammy and Pappy, he forgave me.

It is now 1860. There is a lot of tension between the North and South these days. William does not think slavery will survive much longer. He writes about this in the newspaper, and receives both hate mail and letters praising his courage. He has even been encouraging me to write for the newspaper. He believes others will be inspired and moved to action after reading about my family's story. I am still wary of slaveholders, but I like the idea of telling my family's story. Perhaps there are other ways to do it.

I am so thankful to God that Mammy and Pappy are here with me. I often say this special prayer:

"Lord, thank you for allowing Mammy and Pappy to live long enough to enjoy some freedom before You take them home. Now, if it is your will, please help me find my brother. Reveal to me his whereabouts. I believe some difficult times are ahead for us."

The End